This book to be returned on or before the last date below.

as
e
is

n
to
b

ll

d
en
he
ld
er.
at
at

D1347192

About the Author

Rafael Ábalos was born in Archidona, Málaga, in Spain and as a teenager became an avid reader of adventure stories. A lawyer for many years, Señor Ábalos discovered by accident that he loved to write these stories as well. *Grimpow: The Invisible Road* has been published in twenty-seven countries and is his first book for young readers. Rafael Ábalos lives and writes in southern Spain.

GRIMPOW

THE INVISIBLE ROAD

RAFAEL ÁBALOS

TRANSLATED FROM THE SPANISH BY NOËL BACA CASTEX

CORGI BOOKS

GRIMPOW: THE INVISIBLE ROAD
A CORGI BOOK 978 0 552 55461 9
First published in Great Britain by Corgi Books,
An imprint of Random House Children's Books
A Random House Group Company

This Corgi edition published 2008

1 3 5 7 9 10 8 6 4 2

Translation copyright © 2007 by Noël Baca Castex
Originally published in Spain under the title *Grimpow: El Camino Invisible*, by Montena
Illustrations copyright © 2005 by Fernando Gómez Labato
Extract from *A Brief History of Time* by Stephen Hawking, published by Bantam © 1988 by
Space Time Publications Ltd. Reprinted by permission of The Random House Group Ltd

The right of Rafael Ábalos to be identified as the author of this work has been asserted in
accordance with the Copyright, Designs and Patents Act 1988.

The Random House Group Limited support The Forest Stewardship Council (FSC), the leading
international forest certification organisation. All our titles that are printed on Greenpeace
approved FSC certified paper carry the FSC logo. Our paper procurement policy can be found at:
www.rbooks.co.uk/environment

Set in 12/16pt Goudy by
Falcon Oast Graphic Art Ltd.

Corgi Books are published by Random House Children's Books,
61–63 Uxbridge Road, London W5 5SA

www.**kids**at**randomhouse**.co.uk
www.rbooks.co.uk

Addresses for companies within The Random House Group Limited can be found at:
www.randomhouse.co.uk/offices.htm

THE RANDOM HOUSE GROUP Limited Reg. No. 954009

A CIP catalogue record for this book is available from the British Library.

Printed in the UK by CPI Bookmarque, Croydon, CR0 4TD

Acknowledgements

I'd like to express my gratitude to and affection for my good friends José Ángel Sanz Morales and Manoli Campoy Ramón, for the unforgettable nights Loli and I spent with them contemplating the sky in awe with their amazing telescope. The idea to write this novel was born in Stars Observatory, located in their fantastic terrace open to the universe.

I would also like to specially thank my friend Fernando Gómez Lobato, who shared his great skill as a painter with me to turn the cryptic map of the Invisible Road into a medieval work of art, as I had envisioned it so many times.

WHERE FACT MEETS FICTION AND
LEGEND MEETS TRUTH

In the dark winter of 1313, in a mountainous region of France, the story of *Grimpow: The Invisible Road* begins.

At the dawn of the fourteenth century, France had begun to pull itself out of the Dark Ages and toward the Age of Enlightenment. Such change came at a price. For King Philip IV (1285–1314), the rapid expansion of the empire led to drastic debt, owed to the Order of the Knights Templar.

Once a military group of monk-warriors, the Order of the Knights Templar was hired to protect pilgrims journeying to and from Jerusalem after the first Crusade, in 1095. By the twelfth century, the Knights Templar had become so wealthy and influential that, to those who were indebted to them, their power was an immense threat.

With Pope Clement V (1305–1314), King Philip conspired to eradicate his debt by eliminating the Knights Templar. And so in the year 1307 the Knights Templar were branded by the Pope as heretics. With no one to intervene on their behalf, they were searched out and burned at the stake.

Just months before the last Grand Master of the Order of the Knights Templar, Jacques de Molay, is burned on the pyre, a boy named Grimpow finds something in the snow.

These are two seemingly unrelated events, inextricably linked by a curse.

Grimpow's quest to find the Invisible Road is a tale of this curse, and of a journey, a magical stone, death, war, love and friendship.

So it begins . . .

WE LIVE IN A DISCONCERTING WORLD. TRYING TO COMPREHEND WHAT WE SEE AROUND US, WE ASK OURSELVES: WHAT IS THE UNIVERSE MADE OF? AND WHAT IS OUR PLACE IN IT? WHERE DOES THE UNIVERSE COME FROM? AND WHERE DO WE COME FROM?

—Stephen Hawking, *A Brief History of Time*

PART ONE

The Abbey of Brinkdum

A Body in the Snow

The fog hung low in the forest, obscuring Grimpow's way. The boy trudged through the deep snow, alert, despite the haze, but he didn't notice the body until he'd already tripped and fallen on top of it. He gazed into the face of the dead man; he appeared so peaceful, it almost seemed as if the man was just sleeping. Horrified, Grimpow jumped up and ran back to the cottage, panting like a deer being chased by hungry wolves. He raced up to the door and pounded on it with the full force of his body.

When the door cracked open, Grimpow almost fell into the modest home.

'Grimpow?' Durlib asked, surprised by the boy's sudden return.

But Grimpow could barely speak. 'A . . . a dead man,' he

stammered, pointing towards the forest of fir trees behind him.

Durlib turned pale. 'Are you sure, boy?'

Grimpow nodded, then dropped the rabbits he was clutching onto a nearby tree stump.

Durlib grabbed his fur cloak and paused at the door to take down a long sword he kept there; he attached it to his belt. 'Let's go. Show me where you found him.'

Grimpow walked fast, his bow in his left hand and a quiver full of arrows hanging from his back. He was determined to use them if even a shadow moved around him. His heart drummed in his chest as he retraced his steps; the snow was so deep that the footprints he had left were hard to miss.

'There it is!' he said, pointing at the dark lump half hidden in the snow.

The dead man lay on his side with his eyes facing the foggy sky, as if his last wish before dying had been to say goodbye to the stars. He looked to be around sixty years old and, judging from his clothes and the thick cloak on his back, there was no doubt he was of noble lineage. Durlib slowly walked closer to the figure and knelt by his side. He closed the gentleman's eyes. Small icicles hung from the man's long white hair, beard and eyebrows. His complexion had turned bluish and his dry lips seemed to be smiling.

'He is frozen,' Durlib called back to Grimpow, motioning for him to approach. 'I don't see any wounds – no rips in his clothes or signs of struggle. He was probably away from his horse and got lost in the dense fog last night. The cold must have penetrated his veins and frozen his blood. A peaceful end,' he concluded, 'though still an unfortunate death.'

As he stood surveying the body, Grimpow thought again that the man did seem to be sleeping. *Perhaps death is nothing but a calm and eternal dream*, he mused. Then he noticed something odd – the man's right fist was clenched, as if holding something so valuable he didn't want to part with it even in death. Grimpow pointed it out to Durlib, who took the man's stiff, frozen hand and wrenched apart each finger until the hand revealed a polished, rounded stone the size of an almond. Durlib plucked it from the gentleman's palm and held it up close to his face to study it. The colour seemed to change as he turned it in the light; Durlib was mesmerized.

'What is it?' asked Grimpow curiously.

'Just a stone,' Durlib answered. 'He might have used it as an amulet when it was time to entrust his soul to God.' He tossed it over to Grimpow. 'Keep it. From now on, this stone will be tied to your destiny.'

Grimpow held the stone and felt the mineral's warmth in spite of the cool mountain air. 'What do you mean, tied to my destiny?' he asked, confused. He'd never heard Durlib speak so enigmatically.

But his friend merely shrugged. 'If it is an amulet, it will protect you from evil spirits and bring you good luck.'

'But I already have an amulet,' said Grimpow. He opened his doublet and showed Durlib the linen pouch filled with rosemary sprigs that his mother had given him to wear around his neck when he was a child.

'Well, you have two now,' Durlib chuckled. 'There will be no evil eye, curse or poison that can harm you. Though, as you can see from this gentleman, you can't trust the cold . . . the amulet doesn't seem to have helped him much there.'

Grimpow stood in the snow, thinking of his mother and what she'd always told him. She'd said that he had been born with the fourteenth century and, according to the roundness of the moon on his birthday, the future would bring him all the luck and good things life had denied her. As he touched the polished stone's surface he sensed that his mother's predictions were beginning to come true. Yet at the same time something inside him was fearful . . .

'Look at these wonders!' Durlib exclaimed excitedly, breaking Grimpow's trance. He'd found a leather bag under the man's body.

The boy watched in surprise as his friend took off his fur cloak, laid it on the snow and poured onto it the contents: two daggers of different sizes, their handles studded with sapphires and rubies; silver coins and jewels; a letter sealed with wax; and a carved wooden box holding a heavy gold seal bearing the same image that was impressed into the wax.

Grimpow had never seen such a treasure. 'I hope you aren't thinking about keeping all this,' he said. Instead of feeling excited, he was disturbed. These were the most precious jewels he had ever laid eyes on – yet something felt very wrong.

Durlib looked at him incredulously. 'What are you saying, Grimpow? Have you forgotten who we are? We are tramps and thieves. This is the easiest fortune we've ever made!'

'But we're not corpse desecrators!' answered Grimpow with an authority that surprised even him.

The two friends faced each other in the quiet winter morning. Grimpow stood straight and looked into the older man's hard face until it softened.

'Come on, my friend!' said Durlib in a conciliatory tone. 'Never has Heaven, in my long and miserable life as an outlaw, put such a treasure at my fingertips. And it comes with no great risk to my life! Are you asking me to deny my nature? Have you gone mad?' he asked with exasperation.

Grimpow rolled the stone in his palm. 'First of all, we don't know who this person is, where he's come from, or even how he ended up in these mountains,' he said. 'He could have been travelling with someone who's looking for him at this very moment.'

'Don't worry about that. Didn't you notice? On our way here only your footprints could be seen. Last night's snowfall has erased any trace of those who passed in the night,' said Durlib soothingly. 'If someone's looking for him, they'll have a very hard time finding him. You know as well as I that this forest is a maze, and without footprints to track—'

'Well, what about his horse?' Grimpow interrupted.

'The wolves will take care of it – if he was even riding one.'

'The wolves won't be able to eat the saddle or the reins, and if anyone finds them, we'll be the first people they blame for this stranger's death,' argued Grimpow, amazed at his self-confidence. He'd never stood up for himself so strongly before.

Durlib paused, scratching his head. 'I hadn't thought of that,' he answered slowly. Then, as if he'd decided to stop humouring Grimpow, he added decisively, 'We'll hide the treasure near the cottage and come back at dusk to bury the body before nightfall – good Christians should never leave a corpse for animals to feast on. We'll pay ourselves for our good deed with these riches. His soul will be at peace and our sins forgiven.' With that, Durlib turned to make his way back to the cottage.

'We should let the abbot of Brinkdum know,' Grimpow said dryly.

Durlib stopped his retreat abruptly. He couldn't hide his surprise at the boy's suggestion. 'The abbot? He is the worst thief to inhabit these lands since . . . since the beginning of time! If he sees this treasure, he'll keep it for himself to pay for the many prayers and services his abbey will hold to save the dead gentleman's soul.'

'But,' argued Grimpow, 'he *will* be able to find out who this person was and give him a proper burial in the chapel, as a nobleman deserves.'

'I have no doubt that he will also pay himself generously for lodging a dead man such as this one,' Durlib remarked sharply.

'That's not our concern,' said Grimpow.

Durlib was suddenly quiet. After a few moments he murmured, 'I wonder who would ride across these mountains by himself, with a treasure like this in his bag.'

Grimpow didn't know if Durlib was talking to him or thinking aloud. He replied with a question of his own. 'What do you think?'

'He might have been a Crusader,' Durlib mused, 'returning from the Holy Land carrying treasures from the infidels. Or a pilgrim on his way to make amends for his wrongdoings at some saint's shrine. Maybe he was an overthrown king who left his kingdom with what fit into his bag. Or,' he added, looking slyly at his friend, 'he might have been a thief like us, dressed as a gentleman to conceal his identity. At any rate, I don't think he was from around here. I've never seen daggers like these – made of the best of steel, with ivory handles full of beautiful, flawless jewels.'

But there was still one thing that didn't fit. 'It looks like he was carrying a message,' Grimpow said, pointing at the letter with its wax seal.

Durlib picked it up and looked at it carefully. Then he took the gold seal out of its box and scrutinized the strange image: a snake biting its tail, forming a circle with its body, around which were a series of illegible signs.

'If we break the wax seal,' he told Grimpow, 'we might

be able to find out more about the dead man.' He clearly hoped that his young friend would also want to know the contents of the letter, despite the fact that neither of them could read.

Suddenly Grimpow's doubts were overwhelmed by a strong feeling that he should indeed open the letter. 'Open it,' he said, determined.

Durlib used the smaller dagger to remove the wax carefully, then he unfolded the parchment and scanned it. 'I wonder what these symbols mean,' he whispered.

Grimpow took the parchment from his friend. As he laid eyes on it, a chain of words formed in his mind, as if the meaning of the strange signs was no secret to him. He sucked in his breath sharply.

‘"There are darkness and light in the sky, Aidor Bilbicum, Strasbourg,"' he read, unable to understand how he could translate the message.

Durlib observed him with a mix of confusion and distrust. 'How can you know that is what it says?'

'I'm not sure,' Grimpow said in disbelief. 'It's as if I could read it without knowing the language, the same way I can say "bird" without knowing how to spell it. I wonder . . . I think it might be this strange stone,' he said, lifting his palm and gazing at the stone. He didn't know why that answer felt so right – but it did. And then suddenly he felt a warm sensation from the stone in his hand, and a strange feeling overcame him – almost as if something had passed into him. The feeling was so inexplicable that for a second he feared that the gentleman's soul had possessed him.

Suddenly the ice on the dead man's hair and eyebrows began to melt into droplets of water. His face turned pink. Then, slowly, his whole body began to dissolve on the snow like a wax doll exposed to a fire – until it vanished completely . . .

'By the scars of a beaten thief!' Durlib yelled. 'If this is not the Devil's work, I should be hanged from Ullpens' hanging tree!' The body had completely disappeared into the earth.

Strangely, however, Grimpow was not surprised at all. 'I think that the man has returned to where he came from,' he said contemplatively, still aware of the stone in his hand and not completely sure if it was he himself speaking.

Durlib looked at him, astonished. 'And where is this extraordinary place?' he asked. 'The man just vanished into thin air!'

'I don't know exactly,' said Grimpow, 'but I feel sure of it. Since I picked up this stone, something is making me see things that you could never imagine.' His mind was still filled with incredible and confusing images.

His friend crossed himself again in false devotion. 'The body was here a moment ago, right under our noses, and now it's gone! This has to be the spell of a necromancer dealing with the Devil.'

'Neither God nor Satan has anything to do with this, trust me,' answered Grimpow. And though he didn't know why, he felt sure that what he said was true.

'Well, I'm not staying in this haunted forest to find out.' Durlib quickly gathered the treasure from the fur cloak, put it in the dead man's bag and prepared to leave.

Grimpow stopped his friend. 'Durlib, I have a feeling that this mysterious man had a mission – an important task to carry out – and he hasn't been able to fulfil it. We must do it *for* him in exchange for keeping his treasure.'

'So he chose these godforsaken mountains to meet death, leave us his treasure and disappear, just like that?' Durlib asked sarcastically.

'He was on his way somewhere – Strasbourg, probably – to carry this message to "Aidor Bilbicum", whoever that is,' Grimpow reasoned aloud.

Durlib took a deep breath and glared at Grimpow.

'You may think what you wish, but only the Devil and his entourage of sorcerers and necromancers can do the things we have witnessed. Let's go to the abbey of Brinkdum before the night covers these woods with darkness. We'll attend the last service of the day and purify our bodies and souls with holy water. It's our only chance to avoid the curse that this dead gentleman – wizard, sorcerer, or whatever he was – has most definitely cast upon us.'

'Durlib,' Grimpow said, laughing, 'I realize that you're as superstitious as you are gluttonous, but I don't think the dead gentleman, who so generously let us discover his treasure, would want to take revenge on us as well. Besides, what have *we* done to him?'

Durlib frowned. 'I hope that this fortune-telling gift the stone seems to have given you is as accurate as your bow's arrows. If you are wrong, I am afraid a curse will follow us like the Devil's shadow follows a possessed mortal's flesh.'

'Don't fret, Durlib!' Grimpow answered. 'I don't know where our discovery of this man or the stone will take us. But I believe this same stone will help us solve this mystery. Something inside me is sure of it!'

Durlib looked at his friend with a weary smile and sighed. 'I'm satisfied with the riches Fortune has presented us with, even though she's used a dead man with the frightening power of invisibility, but if you wish to find out his mission in this world, then I will accompany you. Adventure is calling us!'

Flanked by the thorny skeletons of leafless bushes on both sides, the two made their way down to the abbey at the edge of the forest. Under the rising sun, the snow was thinning, and walking down the narrow trail to the valley became easier and faster. Durlib's fears of the dead gentleman's revenge seemed to have vanished with the fog, and he walked beside Grimpow humming a tune he usually sang when he was cheerful.

Durlib could play the lute, recite ballads, perform magic tricks and juggle with the agility of the best jugglers and acrobats in the region. But above all, Durlib was a swindler and a thief, able to trick the belongings from peasants, travellers, pilgrims, merchants, monks and even knights, using his clever words, his agile hands, and his mastery of the sword.

Grimpow had met Durlib during the spring festival the previous year when Grimpow had been working in Rhiquelwir as a server at a dark and foul-smelling tavern owned by his uncle. Durlib would visit the tavern to entertain the drunken patrons. One night, Durlib was recognized by a wealthy livestock merchant whose earnings he'd stolen earlier that morning. In exchange for a few coins, the humiliated merchant asked Grimpow to keep an eye on the thief while he alerted the Lord of Rhiquelwir's henchmen so that they could arrest the robber and hang him in the town's square when the sun came up.

Concerned however about the cruel punishment awaiting someone who, to him, was nothing more than a fearless but kind scoundrel, Grimpow approached Durlib and told him about the imminent threat he would face if he didn't leave the tavern immediately. Durlib hurriedly poured the remaining contents of the wine pitcher down his throat and wiped his mouth with his doublet's sleeve.

'Terrible is the fate of an outlaw!' he said, and winked at

Grimpow. 'Is there another door through which I can sneak out before the Lord of Rhiquelwir's men slaughter me like a pig?'

Grimpow waited until his uncle was distracted and then signalled to Durlib. Together they crossed the dark wine cellar and Grimpow pushed open a small door usually used for carts during harvest season. He instructed Durlib to wait outside where he could keep a sharp eye on the road while Grimpow sneaked into the stables. Inside he bridled his uncle's old dray horse, placed a shabby blanket across its back as a saddle and tugged the lazy animal toward the door.

'How can I pay you for your generosity?' asked Durlib, pretending to rummage for coins in the bag he kept under his doublet.

'Take me with you,' said Grimpow abruptly. 'When that merchant and my uncle find out I deceived them, they will beat me until they break my back.'

The thief pondered what to do. Finally, he said with a smile, 'Jump onto the horse and let's get out of here before that pack of hounds chasing me can track us. If we are captured, they'll be hanging two people in the morning instead of one!'

Thus did Grimpow climb onto the horse and they embarked on their journey. As they rode amid the receding storm, flashes of lightning illuminating the horizon, Durlib wanted to know more about his new companion.

'It seems that you don't enjoy your uncle's company so much?' he queried.

'He is married to one of my mother's sisters and is the only wealthy person in our family,' Grimpow replied. 'After my father died two years ago, my mother sent me to work with him so that I could learn the trade of tavern keeper. My aunt is a good woman, but my uncle is *not* a good man . . .'

'And what will you do now?'

'I can be your page if you'd like.'

'Vagrants like me don't have pages,' Durlib responded with a chuckle. 'Besides, I like to be on my own, and my life as an outlaw is no better than the life you had at your uncle's tavern.'

'But you are free to go wherever you wish!' said Grimpow adamantly.

'And that very freedom will end up getting me hanged in some godforsaken village. I can't allow you to come with me.'

'Let me follow you for a while at least, until I find my own way in life,' begged Grimpow.

Durlib turned slowly in the saddle to face Grimpow. He looked him in the eye and said, 'You should aim higher than to be a thief like me.'

'I've always wanted to be a squire and learn how to use weapons and fight in battle.'

'Men kill each other pointlessly at war; you should find a better thing to do.'

Silence enveloped them for some time until Durlib, evidently feeling he owed the boy for saving his life, said begrudgingly, 'Fine, you can stay with me. But only for a while.'

And so began Grimpow's new life with Durlib. A life full of thievery, begging, juggling and reciting. A life of wandering from village to village, castle to farm, and finally, forest to forest during the winter months to hunt. From Durlib he learned how to use a bow and arrow; how to track rabbits, deer, lynx, bears and foxes; how to live in poverty and to be a good friend; and how to gaze at the stars on moonless nights.

Now they walked in the snow to the abbey of Brinkdum, carrying the dead gentleman's treasure – unaware that soon they would part ways for ever . . .

Unexpected Visitors

Through the dim light of dusk, the abbey of Brinkdum appeared before them, a mass of reddish stone covered with snow-dusted tiles. Tucked in a lush valley surrounded by forests, winding rivers and steep mountains, the old abbey had been built by monks three centuries before Grimpow's time, yet it stood as strong and majestic as the day it was built. The high bell tower rose above the rest of the buildings grandly and could be seen from afar, both to guide lost pilgrims home and to ward off hungry demons.

This was not Grimpow and Durlib's first visit to the abbey. For with the abbot Grimpow and Durlib had a sort of agreement. In exchange for letting them hunt in the mountains and live in the cottage during the long winter months, the abbot demanded part of their stolen loot. In the end, the holy man's love for jewels was stronger than his vow of poverty.

'We'd better hide our treasure before we reach the abbey. The abbot is sure to be curious about the contents of the bag,' said Durlib as they drew nearer the abbey.

Grimpow looked around at the landscape. Tall fir trees dotted the land, and the wind had revealed masses of grey rock by pulling away their thick blankets of snow. They were approaching a little stream which they would cross at a ford; nearby a small stone cross stood on a rock pedestal, signalling the road to the abbey. He pondered for a moment, then pointed toward it.

'The treasure will be well hidden under that cross,' he said. Durlib nodded and walked toward the spot, opened the bag and pulled out the two daggers covered in gems. He handed the smaller one to Grimpow and kept the other one for himself.

'Hide it between your doublet and hose,' he said.

'But the monks in the abbey aren't dangerous,' replied Grimpow, confused.

'After what I've seen today, I'd rather not take anything for granted,' answered Durlib with a fleeting smile.

Durlib hid his dagger, then unsheathed his sword and dug a hole behind the pedestal supporting the cross. Before placing the bag in the hole, he opened it and took out some of the silver coins.

'We'll give them to the abbot of Brinkdum in exchange for two of the fine horses he breeds in the abbey's stables. I am not certain where Strasbourg is or how long it will take us to get there, but I am sure that we'll be better off riding than walking.'

After covering the hole with mud and snow, they resumed the last leg of their journey to the abbey. Grimpow couldn't stop thinking about how the dead gentleman had mysteriously disappeared in the snow. He thought about the amulet, its potential powers and its connection to the dead man. He could feel its presence even now, hidden as it was in the small linen pouch that dangled from his neck. Although he couldn't feel the heat emanating from the stone as he had when he held it in his hand, he could still feel its proximity . . . its pull.

He knew that it was more than a simple amulet, and felt nearly overcome with an unidentifiable desire to figure out exactly what the little stone was and what powers were contained inside it. The only clues he had, however, were in the letter and the gold seal the dead gentleman had carried, and his thoughts kept returning to them.

As they climbed the winding slope, Grimpow read the letter out loud again. 'There are darkness and light in the sky,' he repeated.

'I've already told you – those words sound like a magician's spell. It would be better if you didn't recite them so close to a church.' Durlib leaned over the parchment and pretended to read from it. 'A ray of lightning from Heaven could strike us and send us to the darkness of Hell.' Durlib chuckled, amused by his own translation of the obscure message.

'I believe that those symbols mean much more than that,

Durlib,' Grimpow answered seriously. 'This looks like a coded message, and this Aidor Bilbicum from Strasbourg could know its meaning.'

'Wizards and magicians are the only ones who know the meaning of the magical words they use in their rituals and spells. I once saw an old witch exorcize a woman whose body kept jumping and shaking on the ground. The words the witch spoke as she danced around her sounded like those of a diabolical monster.'

'You're talking about beliefs and superstitions, spells and incantations – I think this is about much more than that,' replied Grimpow, surprised once again by his own words. 'I think that the phrase means in Heaven there is both ignorance, or darkness, *and* light, meaning knowledge and wisdom. Those superstitions and spells you mentioned come from ignorance. Gods and demons don't exist, Durlib – they are a creation of humans to explain the world.'

'Are you sure it is you talking and not the dead man's spirit?' asked Durlib, looking at the boy curiously.

'Does it matter?' asked Grimpow, not sure how to answer his question.

'Yes, it matters, and very much. If the abbot of Brinkdum heard you, he would think you are possessed and have you burned at the stake as punishment for heresy.'

'Funny you say that, because somehow I sense that the stake is precisely what the dead gentleman was trying to escape from,' Grimpow said confidently.

'Another reason to consider him a wizard, sorcerer, or

Devil worshipper,' Durlib concluded as they arrived at the abbey's doors.

The night covered the valley with a thick veil of semi-darkness. The abbey's doors were opened to the travellers by the monks' servant, Kense. The tall, hunched man stared at Grimpow and Durlib without saying a word, as though the wind had knocked on the abbey's doors with its invisible hands and no one stood in front of him at all.

'My friend Kense,' asked Durlib with an unfinished bow, 'will you let in these two poor travellers with no fire to keep them warm nor bed to rest their tired bodies?'

The servant closed the door without uttering a word and Grimpow and Durlib could hear him scuffing across the stone floor as he trudged back through the abbey. Durlib knocked again, harder this time.

'Coming! Coming!' they heard a flutelike voice shout from inside.

It was Brother Brasgdo, a cheerful monk Grimpow always saw in the kitchen. Round like a wine barrel, he was usually busy over the stove with his pots, cuts of meat and bunches of vegetables. When he unlocked the door and saw them standing in front of him, numb with cold, Brother Brasgdo smiled in surprise. 'Come in,' he said, 'before the cold takes your breath away and freezes your bones.' As he closed the heavy door behind them he enquired, 'May I ask what we owe this unexpected visit to?'

Durlib entered the abbey determinedly, but answered the

monk's question vaguely. 'We've decided to leave the mountains and the cottage and never return to its Hell of ice again.'

'The only Hell you should be afraid of is the one made of fire, not ice,' said the monk with a chuckle, locking the door behind Grimpow.

'The reason why we've come to this holy house,' Durlib continued, in fake piety, 'is to replenish our souls in the abbey's chapel and join you in your prayers before embarking on a long journey to faraway lands.'

'And I assume that you'll want to fill your stomachs and sleep in our warm house as well?' asked the monk, a twinkle in his eye.

'Tonight, at least,' answered Durlib, ignoring Brother Brasgdo's jibe as he shook the snow from his fur cloak. 'A straw mattress and a blanket in the pilgrims' hall would be enough. And we'd be grateful for a piece of bread, a big slice of cheese and a pitcher of that wine you secretly keep in your cellar,' he added with a wink.

'This year's harvest has been terrible,' said Brother Brasgdo, laughing as he walked toward the kitchen, signalling for them to follow. 'So you're about to embark on a long journey?' he continued as he lumbered through the abbey, his big belly swaying from side to side underneath the brown habit of his religious order.

'Indeed,' Durlib answered. 'We're leaving tomorrow after sunrise.'

'And have you decided your destination?'

'We'll search for the end of the world!' Durlib mocked.

'From what I've heard, the *finis mundi* is quite far from here, beyond the deep western oceans, and only horrible monsters and demons live there,' whispered the monk with a grimace.

'Yes, but it is also said that there lie the invisible doors to Paradise and that the lands are full of gold and precious stones, as well as the most beautiful women anyone has ever seen. Food and drink are always at your fingertips, and life is eternal,' said Durlib with a wink.

Brother Brasgdo glared at him reproachfully as he opened the kitchen door.

'The doors to Paradise are in this valley, created by God for our eyes' delight,' he said abruptly, changing the tone of their banter. 'Nobody has ever seen that place you talk about – it exists only in some perverse and delusional minds that have succumbed to the Devil's temptation. I wonder if you might be one of those . . . ?'

'I am merely an ignorant man who fears God's power and prays every day to reach his divine kingdom,' answered Durlib flatteringly, to appease the monk's doubts.

'Aha,' said Brother Brasgdo, his smile returning, 'I see that you're a better comedian than scoundrel.'

The trio walked into the kitchen, where a few logs burned in a great fireplace, and Brother Brasgdo asked them to take a seat at a large table. The heat was suffocating, and Grimpow and Durlib both removed their fur cloaks. In one of the room's corners a small door led to the dining hall, and while they sat, a few servants walked back and forth with clay baking dishes. From his place at the table, Grimpow could see that the monks had just begun their evening meal. They were silent, their heads bent facing the food, deep in thought, with only the dim light of a few oil lamps on the tables. But Grimpow could hear a hollow whispering – the voice of the monk in charge of reading the Psalms.

Brother Brasgdo soon returned with a round loaf of bread, bowls of hot soup, some roasted pork, cheese and bacon and the pitcher of wine Durlib had requested.

'If the abbot asks what you're drinking, tell him it's just water,' joked the monk as he placed the pitcher on the table. Then he sat down with them quietly and started cracking some walnuts with his hands.

'Does the abbot know we're here?' asked Durlib, slurping his soup loudly.

The monk shook his head. 'I will let him know once they finish dinner, before the last worship of the day. It's our Christian duty to offer shelter to travellers and pilgrims, so be assured he'll make no objection to your staying here tonight.'

'I must speak with him before he goes to his quarters,' explained Durlib after a long sip of wine.

'Anything I can help you with?' asked the monk, without hiding his curiosity.

'I'd like to discuss with him the possibility of trading horses for silver.'

Brother Brasgdo raised his eyebrows in interest. 'I see

that you don't lack wealth at the moment. Who, may I ask, has been your prey this time?' he added suspiciously.

'Please, good brother. Who could I rob in these deserted mountains in the middle of winter, when not even crows fly over the woods?' parried Durlib.

'Perhaps a ghost . . .' whispered the monk, putting a walnut in his mouth and crushing it with his wall of yellow teeth.

Durlib glanced at Grimpow urgently but said calmly, 'They are merely a few coins I've saved for an occasion such as this.'

Grimpow watched the conversation expectantly, as silent as Kense, until the monk looked at him and asked him directly, 'Why don't you stay in the abbey as a novice and dedicate your life to serving God, instead of travelling the world with a thief like Durlib?'

'I'd like to find my own way in life,' Grimpow said shyly.

'Well, you won't find a more virtuous way than the one of work and prayer. These days, the countryside and forests are full of thieves, rebel friars and beggars,' the monk continued, looking at Grimpow intently, 'and there is no better place to avoid sin's temptation than God's house. Here you could learn how to read and write in Greek and Latin, take care of the farm, cultivate the land, collect flowers and medicinal plants, heal the ill, and copy, illuminate or translate manuscripts. You could even be the cook's apprentice and take my job when I die, which I hope will happen long after I reach old age,' he said, raising his eyes to the ceiling.

'I don't like the silence,' said Grimpow, animated by the monk's chattering.

Brother Brasgdo found this funny and burst out laughing. 'But, you see, the cook is exempted from this strict rule. It would be impossible for me to communicate with the servants if I had to gesture with my hands instead of talking,' he explained.

'And you would probably burst if you had to remain silent for a whole day,' added Durlib, the wine beginning to slightly slur his speech.

Brother Brasgdo took Durlib's comment as a joke – he knew him well enough to know he meant no harm – and they all laughed quietly, so as not to disturb the silence of the other monks.

It wasn't long before the sound of benches sliding on the floor indicated that the monks had finished dinner and were leaving the dining hall.

'You will excuse me for a moment now,' the monk told the visitors. 'I will let the abbot know of your arrival.'

As soon as Brother Brasgdo had left the kitchen, Durlib asked Grimpow quietly, 'Did you hear what he said?'

Grimpow nodded, not saying a word.

'When he spoke of a ghost, there's no doubt he was referring to the owner of the silver coins,' said Durlib hurriedly. 'What if the dead gentleman came here before we found him?'

But before Grimpow could answer, Brother Brasgdo entered the kitchen again, followed by the abbot of Brinkdum.

'Not a great time for these foxes to leave their lair in the mountains,' said the abbot, smiling, as he entered.

Durlib stood up and rushed to kiss the ring on the abbot's hand, which he was extending for that purpose. Grimpow followed suit and, as if he had kissed a piece of ice, felt the coldness of the ring on his lips. Not only was the abbot the highest authority in the abbey, but his power extended to the whole region of Ullpens and even farther, into parts of neighbouring regions. It was rumoured that he had been a brave knight who'd left the army at the age of thirty to become a monk and live the rest of his life secluded from the world like a hermit. However, according to what Brother Brasgdo had told Durlib long ago, the real reason for the abbot's religious devotion was a beautiful damsel who had denied him her love, and whom the abbot continued to visit as a confessor in a nearby castle. It was rumoured that he still showered her with all kinds of gifts. Grimpow pictured the lady wearing jewels he had stolen on the roads. The abbot collected them for a reason, after all. He liked gems as much as his monks' hymns or more.

After kindly greeting the visitors, the abbot asked Brother Brasgdo to take them to the pilgrims' hall until the last worship, when they should then go directly to the abbot's quarters next to the main hall. He then excused himself politely and headed for the cloisters.

The cook monk, Durlib and Grimpow left the kitchen through a side door, where a spiral staircase led them to the pilgrims' hall. They climbed the stairs in silence, with only a small lamp carried by Brother Brasgdo for light. The hall was dark, and only the flickering light allowed them to see the straw mattresses aligned on the stone floor. It was a big, rectangular room with a vaulted ceiling and small arched windows on one of the side walls. Located above the kitchen, it had a round pipe in its centre, through which travelled the smoke from the fireplace in the room below, keeping the hall warm during the cold winters in the mountains.

'At least you won't have to put up with other guests' snores and stench tonight,' said Brother Brasgdo as he pulled out a couple of thick wool blankets from an old chest.

'So no one's slept here in a while?' Durlib asked.

'Since the first snowfalls at the beginning of winter, probably. We've had no visitors since then.'

Grimpow could read Durlib's thoughts as his friend's expression relaxed. If Brother Brasgdo wasn't hiding something, there was no way that the dead gentleman had stopped by the abbey before going into the mountains.

'However,' continued the monk, lowering his voice in secrecy, 'yesterday I went outside the abbey to stretch my legs and collect some nuts, and I think I saw a lone horseman in the fog heading toward the mountains. I reasoned he was lost and, because of the fog, couldn't find his way to the abbey. I shouted to call his attention, but he turned his head, looked at me with empty eyes like those of a skull, and kept going into the forest.'

Brother Brasgdo's words left Durlib and Grimpow speechless and sent chills up their spines.

'You wouldn't happen to have seen the horseman in the mountains, would you?' the monk asked his guests, raising the lamp to better see their eyes.

Grimpow was about to shake his head when Durlib cleared his throat and said, 'Have you mentioned this to the abbot, Brother Brasgdo?'

'Had I done so, the abbot would have thought I was drunk – that it was the wine's vapours that made me see such an eerie image prowling around the abbey,' said the monk disdainfully.

'And were you?'

'I swear on Saint Dustan's remains in the chapel's crypt that I didn't drink anything but water yesterday.'

'Then you can believe your eyes, because we too saw that mysterious horseman riding like a spectre in the forest near the abbey,' said Durlib.

His words left Grimpow as cold as the body they had found in the snow that morning. For a moment, he thought that his good friend was going to tell the truth to Brother Brasgdo about what they'd witnessed that morning; about finding the stone, the sealed letter and the dead gentleman's treasure.

'It's true,' he blurted out instead to embellish the lie.

'When I saw the man near the cottage, I walked closer to greet him and stroke his horse's mane, but they both vanished into thin air as if they were a dream.'

'An unbelievable and horrible nightmare, I would say!' added Brother Brasgdo.

'We were so frightened after what happened that we left the cottage immediately and ran here to seek shelter. Neither ghosts nor demons can hide in an abbey,' said Durlib, crossing himself just as he had after the dead gentleman's disappearance in the snow.

The monk made the sign of the cross as well and whispered, 'I've heard several pagan legends about spirits, water and forest demons, giants, nymphs, witches, wizards and elves. But I've never seen an apparition as real as that of the dead man you are talking about, whose face seemed more like that of a demonic spectre than a man. One of those sinister invisible beings who roam the earth alone, paying their dues and righting the wrongs they committed during their sinful lives.'

Grimpow was sure Durlib had succeeded in deceiving Brother Brasgdo. In fact, he now thought Durlib himself believed they'd really seen a ghost.

'Have you talked to any of the other monks about this delicate matter?' Durlib enquired.

'Do you think I've lost my mind?' asked Brother Brasgdo, frowning. 'If such terrible and incredible stories reach the abbot, the friars or the people in Ullpens, they will consider this valley and its mountains haunted, and no monk, pilgrim or believer will set foot in the abbey for fear of running into the ghost of that stranger and suffering his anger and resentment.'

'Perhaps the gentleman has resumed his journey and by tonight is very far from here, on the other side of the mountains,' said Grimpow, trying to assuage Brother Brasgdo's fears.

'Let's trust that it is so,' replied the monk.

'So that his impure spirit will not inhabit our souls, let's go to the chapel and pray to God for our eternal salvation, which was our reason for coming to the abbey in the first place,' said Durlib.

They entered the abbey's chapel through a big open courtyard. It was extremely cold outside, and small snowflakes fell before them, dotting the night's darkness with white. They dashed across the open space to a studded door and pulled it open. Inside the chapel, thick candles on the central nave's corners barely illuminated the immense pillars that rose to form impossible braids that reached the dark, vaulted ceiling.

Durlib walked to a holy water font across from the door, wet his hand in it and crossed himself three times to avoid the evil curses the dead gentleman might have cast upon him. Grimpow even saw him take out the silver coins from the hidden pocket in his hose and dunk them discreetly, to rid them of any curse or spell.

After that he walked to the pews and sat next to Grimpow. Taking advantage of the fact that Brother

Brasgdo was kneeling with his hands covering his face in meditation and repentance, he whispered in his ear, 'You should dip the amulet in the font.'

Grimpow ignored his words and watched the monks' entrance to the choir for the last worship of the day, which the tower bells had just announced. Hoods covered the monks' bowed heads as they paraded with their hands together, single file, and stood in front of their respective pews. Grimpow counted thirty monks of different age and appearance, all in the same brown habit of the order. One of them, with the voice of a young boy, began singing so beautifully that Grimpow was lulled to sleep.

When the worship came to an end, Grimpow felt Durlib's elbow poke his ribs, letting him know that the abbot was approaching.

'It must be a miracle that a pair of thieves shows such devotion for the abbey's religious services,' said the abbot in a low voice, narrowing his small eyes even more.

They both stood up respectfully and Brother Brasgdo answered for them. 'They've decided to leave the cottage in the mountains and seek a new life someplace far away from sin. They'd like to leave with your blessing at dawn.'

'Is that right?' asked the abbot, peering at Durlib.

'We'll go to Strasbourg. Before winter began, I heard they were building a new cathedral there and we might be able to find work as stonemasons. We were hoping that you would recommend us to the bishop,' answered Durlib easily.

'I'm sure that with your help we won't have any difficulty finding honourable work so that Grimpow can begin a life away from sin.'

The abbot sighed and looked at each of them in turn. 'This boy's biggest sin has been to follow you all these years. God is kind and undoubtedly will understand that it wasn't the boy's fault, but instead the fault of the person who's been like a father to him.'

'Durlib has been the best father I could ever have imagined, and I will never leave his side,' blurted out Grimpow in defence of his friend, all the while biting his tongue to avoid telling the abbot what he really thought about the abbot's own sins.

There was an abrupt tug on his sleeve. It was Brother Brasgdo, scolding Grimpow for addressing the abbot so disrespectfully.

'We'd better go to my quarters, as I believe that you wanted to speak with me in private,' said the abbot, indifferent to the boy's words. He turned to leave; Durlib and Grimpow followed.

They returned to the main building through a small door in one of the courtyard's corners and walked down a short and narrow corridor illuminated by the dim light of a small oil lamp on the wall. Soon they reached the cloisters' galleries, brightly lit by torches. They were amazed to see a forest of beautiful columns and arches. Grimpow stopped to look at a small column on which was carved a small human figure surrounded by beasts. Below it was an inscription in Latin, and strangely, Grimpow had no trouble understanding what it said:

DANIELEM CUM LEONIS

The abbot, surprised by Grimpow's curiosity, stopped by his side and asked, 'Do you know what that image means?'

'It's an illustration of the prophet Daniel, whose enemies threw him into a lion's den because of his loyalty to God,' replied Grimpow in one breath.

Durlib looked as shocked as the abbot.

'And do you know if the lions attacked Daniel?' asked the abbot in a fatherly tone, staring at the boy with his sharp eyes.

'They did not,' said Grimpow. 'An angel sent by God closed the lions' mouths so they couldn't harm him.'

'Who told you that story?' asked the abbot.

Grimpow knew he couldn't speak of the stone he carried, but quickly realized he could use this opportunity to his advantage. If he said it was Durlib who told him of Daniel, the abbot's impression of his friend would change and he would be more generous when trading their silver coins for horses. So, trying to sound naive, he answered simply, 'Durlib's told me many stories about God.'

Durlib blushed and resorted to his imagination, as he did every time he was in trouble, adding, 'Well, I've only repeated the stories Brother Brasgdo has told me in the abbey's kitchen.'

The abbot looked at him suspiciously. 'At least I'm glad that God's name has not been taken in vain in that cottage where you spend the winters,' he said, and continued to his quarters.

They walked under the cloisters' vaulted arches until they left the main hall and entered a cold, square room where the walls smelled of dampness and burned wax. The abbot lit the candles in a candleholder sitting on a table next to a Bible, a Book of Hours and some rolls of parchment. He gestured to two chairs across from a sofa with a high engraved back and asked them to take a seat. When the abbot settled himself on the grand sofa he looked at the visitors with a patriarch's solemnity.

'So you plan to leave these lands at dawn?' he repeated.

'That's right,' answered Durlib. 'I've been thinking that the cottage in the mountains is not a good place for a boy like Grimpow, and I don't want him to spend his life running from one village to another the way I have.'

'And you want to go to Strasbourg in the middle of winter?'

'Strasbourg is a rich and prosperous city where we'll be able to find a place to live with dignity. And I know a way to cross the mountains safely.'

While Durlib and the abbot talked, Grimpow pretended to be listening, all the while peeking at the covers of the manuscripts on the table. To his surprise, he realized he could read their titles without difficulty.

'You know that if the boy wanted, he could take our

order's habit, become a novice, and stay in the monastery. Many young boys from noble but humble families have done so since this abbey was founded more than three centuries ago.'

'I've suggested that to him myself several times, and today Brother Brasgdo also recommended it, but Grimpow is too fond of his freedom to subject himself to the strict rules of your order.'

'In this world there are noblemen, clergymen and servants,' said the abbot, addressing Grimpow. 'The first serve the army, and the last serve the first; only the clergy has the privilege of serving God. You are but a servant, and that freedom Durlib speaks of is nothing but an illusion.'

'You might be right, but Grimpow refuses to leave my side, and I don't wish to leave him either,' said Durlib, clearly expressing both of their feelings.

'And you have nothing to say about this?' the abbot asked Grimpow.

'I don't think I could ever be a good monk,' the boy answered.

'Well, if that's what you prefer . . . I realize that you're as stubborn as your master. And now, tell me what you wanted to discuss in private,' said the abbot, reclining on the sofa and interlacing his fingers on his lap.

Durlib cleared his throat. 'We need two of the best horses from your stables.'

'You know well that the horses from the abbey's stables are not for sale,' the abbot said, his gaze steady.

As if practising a magic trick, Durlib's hand swiftly reached into the hidden pocket in his hose, removed the dead gentleman's coins and placed them on the table.

When the abbot saw the glittering silver under the dim candlelight he sat up, eyes widening. 'Where did you find these?'

'I stole them from a Venetian silk merchant near the city of Molwiler a long time ago,' answered Durlib confidently.

The abbot took one of the coins and studied it carefully. 'There's no doubt they are real silver, but I've never seen anything like these strange symbols,' he murmured.

'So we can have the horses?' asked Durlib.

'I'll speak with the churchwarden tonight. We'll ready the horses and prepare some supplies for the road tomorrow.'

'Will you give us your blessing and a letter of recommendation for the Bishop of Strasbourg?' asked Durlib, taking advantage of the abbot's sudden generosity.

'Your wishes will be fulfilled in the morning.'

As they were preparing to leave the abbot's quarters a loud bang sounded from the front of the abbey. The knocker on the front door boomed like thunder in the middle of the night, surprising all three of them.

'Who on earth, besides a pair of scoundrels like you two, would be roaming the mountains on a winter's night?' asked the abbot.

At a loss for words, Durlib and Grimpow exchanged looks.

'Let's go and find out,' said Durlib.

As they entered the cloisters, they saw the rounded shadow of Brother Brasgdo running toward them, followed by a small group of panicked servants.

'What's happening? Why this uproar? And why is no one answering the door?' the abbot asked the cook.

'No one dares do it. The clamour of horses and armour from behind that door sounds like the Four Horsemen of the Apocalypse have come to the abbey!' exclaimed Brother Brasgdo, shaking and short of breath from running.

Grimpow had no doubt that Brother Brasgdo thought the ghost of the man he'd seen riding around the abbey the day before had summoned the Holy Company, a fabled procession of tormented souls, to join him in taking the abbey by storm. Durlib must have thought something similar, judging from the frightened expression on his face. Grimpow, however, had a horrible feeling that the horsemen outside the abbey could be far more sinister than all the ghosts one could imagine.

A large group of monks had filed down from upstairs and gathered in the entrance hall. As they waited expectantly they lined themselves along the sides of the gallery, forming a narrow corridor. Some of the monks carried lit candles, while others folded their arms under their scapularies.

'Open the doors!' the abbot ordered.

Grimpow held his breath as the locks clicked open, one by one, and the door swung wide, revealing the outline of six hooded horsemen wearing long black cloaks as dark as the night around them.

'Which one of you is the abbot?' bellowed a deep voice.

The abbot walked forward and stood under the open door's frame.

'I am the abbot of Brinkdum,' he said. 'But it is you who should announce yourself and your company before entering the abbey.'

One of the horses neighed, rearing and pawing at the air fiercely with its legs.

'My name is Bulvar of Goztell, of the Holy Dominican Order, Inquisitor of Lyon and Pope Clement the Fifth's legate,' the horseman announced. 'In his name I request lodging for myself and the soldiers of the King of France who escort me.' As he spoke he unbuttoned his hood and revealed his heavily scarred face, partially hidden under a short white beard.

Grimpow heard Brother Brasgdo let out a deep breath – the monk was clearly relieved by the Dominican friar's credentials. But the monk's plump face darkened again as the visitors filed into the abbey, and he whispered in horror to Grimpow, 'There, behind the last soldier – I recognize that horse. It is the very one I saw ridden by the ghost – only now it has no rider!'

A Story and a Legend

While the commotion settled, Brother Brasgdo escorted the king's soldiers to the kitchen for some food and drink. The abbot invited Bulvar, the inquisitor, to his quarters, where he could enjoy a plentiful dinner while he talked about the reason for his visit. And Durlib and Grimpow went back to the pilgrims' hall for some rest. Slowly silence settled once again in every corner of the abbey.

As they lay on their straw mattresses with only a small oil lamp on the floor, Durlib shared his concerns with Grimpow.

'Are you thinking what I am thinking?' he asked.

'I believe so.'

'The riderless white horse could be the dead man's,' said Durlib.

'Brother Brasgdo is surely convinced of it. I saw the

horrified look on his face, when the horse walked before him,' said Grimpow.

'Perhaps the animal ran away from the forest and they found it in the lower part of the valley,' Durlib offered.

'I noticed the horse was limping. It looked like its leg was injured. There was blood and a wound – like a wolf's bite,' Grimpow said.

Durlib turned on his mattress. 'I'm worried about the Dominican friar questioning Brother Brasgdo. He won't be able to keep his mouth shut, especially if he's had a few pitchers of wine,' he said.

'I doubt Brother Brasgdo will dare tell an inquisitor that he's seen a ghost entering the mountains,' said Grimpow, trying to calm Durlib down. 'He'd be too frightened of being accused of heresy.'

'Well, what about the abbot? He was curious about the strange markings on the silver coins.'

'The abbot wouldn't talk to the Pope's legate about the money,' Grimpow pointed out.

'Perhaps the Dominican friar and his soldiers were simply on their way to Ullpens and happened to come across the horse in the valley,' thought Durlib aloud.

'No,' said Grimpow determinedly. 'I have no doubt that the inquisitor was following the dead gentleman to burn him at the stake. But I don't know why – although I have a feeling that it has something to do with the sealed letter and the stone he carried.' He closed his eyes and focused on the blurry images that appeared in his mind.

'I'll see to it that our horses are ready by dawn,' the older man told his young friend, 'and I'll try to find out more about the Dominican friar and his reasons for being here.'

'I'm scared,' admitted Grimpow, curling himself up under the blanket.

'I'm sure that stone hanging from your neck will protect you,' answered Durlib. 'Now, get some sleep. Tomorrow we'll be gone.' He stood up, took the oil lamp, and left the room through the narrow staircase that led to the abbey's kitchen.

Neither he nor Grimpow could imagine how wrong he was.

In the darkness, Grimpow took the dead gentleman's amulet from his linen pouch. Clutching it tightly in his palm, he noticed it had a pale glow to it, like an ember burning between his fingers. He opened his hand and the stone shone – red and alive – like a shooting star just fallen from the sky. Its light grew until the pilgrims' hall was lit with the colours of fire, illuminating everything around him. At that moment, he knew that nothing would ever be the same. He realized he was leaving his childhood behind for ever, scattered in his memory like pieces of fog dragged by the wind, and he suddenly feared he would be unable to face the dangerous challenges the stone's light was announcing.

Grimpow awoke not knowing how long he'd slept. He only knew that his dreams had been full of confusing images

– some of the past and others of the future – all interspersed nonsensically with strange faces, speaking strange languages. He had seen a sort of blue explosion that had multiplied the stars in the sky by millions, planetary cataclysms that turned continents and oceans into beautiful timeless landscapes, eternal ice that covered the world under skies darkened by impenetrable ashes, epidemics that covered the earth, enormous and unforgiving machines that threw balls of fire, causing horrific explosions, and wars that killed millions of men, women and children.

Then abruptly he was awake again. And lit by the dim light of an oil lamp, the grim, wrinkled face of a monk he did not know hovered above him.

'Come on! Get up!' urged the monk in a low voice.

'What's happening?' asked a startled Grimpow, half asleep still.

'There's no time to explain now. You must leave this room as soon as possible,' the monk said, dragging him out of bed.

'Where's Durlib?' asked Grimpow as soon as he realized that the straw mattress next to him was empty.

'We'll deal with him later. We must go now.'

The old monk blew out the candle he was carrying and grabbed Grimpow by the arm. They walked swiftly in the darkness toward the stairs leading to the chapel's courtyard. Frightened, Grimpow followed as quietly and closely as if he was the monk's shadow. At the end of the courtyard, the monk pushed a door with one shoulder and took him through a long corridor. In the deepest darkness, Grimpow could only hear his steps on the tiled floor. Next he was led down a spiral staircase where they stopped briefly at a landing and the old monk lit the candle again with his slightly shaky, bony hands. In a terrified moment Grimpow realized that countless skulls were piled one atop another all around him, their invisible eyes staring at him from the niches in the stone walls.

Seemingly indifferent to the boy's fear, the monk took a few steps forward and rotated one of the skulls, as if trying to break an imaginary neck. And before Grimpow's eyes, part of the wall in front of them slid away, revealing a cavernous hole. Grimpow thought for a moment that he was standing before the very door to Hell, and all of Durlib's warnings about the dead man's curse came back to him.

'Where are you taking me?' he asked frantically. 'Why won't you tell me where my friend Durlib is?'

'I'm only taking you to a safe place,' answered the monk. 'Now follow me – I'll explain everything downstairs.'

Then the old monk looked at Grimpow with such kindness that Grimpow's fears abated. Up close, he estimated that the man must be older than eighty, and still he moved and spoke as swiftly as a novice.

Grimpow knew he had no real choice, so he stepped into the tight space and noticed a staircase as narrow and crooked as the ones leading to churches' bell towers or castles' turrets, except this one spiralled downward.

Without pausing, the monk began his descent, agile despite his age.

Grimpow trod cautiously behind him until they reached a small square room, its walls covered from floor to ceiling with shelves stuffed full of manuscripts and parchment scrolls. There were no windows or doors other than the one they'd come through at the foot of the winding stairs.

'Where are we?' asked Grimpow, admiring the hundreds of books around him. He felt as if he could read them all without needing to open them, like he already knew every word in their pages.

'In a secret room in the abbey's library.'

The monk laid the candle on a wooden table in the centre of the room, took a loose wick, and lit it with the candle's flame. He proceeded to light all of the lamps hanging from chains attached to the ceiling until the room was flooded with a warm orange light. Grimpow could now see that the tips of the old monk's fingers were stained black by the ink he'd used to copy dozens of manuscripts.

'Fire is the only enemy you'll find here. You must be very careful when lighting and putting out the lamps, especially when you're alone,' he warned Grimpow.

'Are you leaving me locked in here?' asked Grimpow, shocked by the thought.

'You'll be better off here than in a rat-and-roach-infested dungeon. And I don't know a more comfortable place where you won't be found by the hounds that arrived at the abbey tonight,' said the monk.

'What about Durlib? What's happened to him?' asked Grimpow.

The old monk lowered his head, and by the sad look in his eyes, Grimpow knew that he didn't have good news.

'I don't know exactly, but it is possible that by now your friend is already locked in a dungeon and being interrogated by Bulvar of Goztell.'

Grimpow felt a pang of pain, as if he had been stabbed by the dead gentleman's dagger he had tucked in his waist. 'What do you think will happen to him?' he asked.

'Only God knows that.'

'Who are you, and why do you think the inquisitor would be interested in a penniless thief like Durlib and a poor village boy like me?' asked Grimpow incredulously.

The old monk sighed heavily and looked solemnly at the boy before him. 'My name is Rinaldo of Metz, and I was born on September tenth of 1228. I've been the librarian of this abbey for more than forty years,' he said.

Grimpow, who had never studied anything about mathematics, knew immediately that the old man talking to him had just turned eighty-five years old. The numbers had appeared in his mind just as the words had earlier.

'But what could the Inquisition want from us?' pressed Grimpow.

'What they want, my son, is information about a certain Knight Templar whom Bulvar of Goztell has been chasing, and who apparently came to these mountains running away from his pursuers. The inquisitor and the soldiers escorting him found the knight's horse at the valley's entrance, its legs injured by a beast – a wolf or lynx, who knows. The horse had one of those strange symbols of the Knights Templar branded with fire under the saddle.'

It was the first time Grimpow had heard about the Knights Templar, yet he had an odd sensation that he knew that story well.

'Did you say Knight Templar?' he asked.

'That's right. You are too young to have heard about them, but there was a time not long ago when the deeds by the Knights of the Temple of Solomon were known in all Christianity's kingdoms.'

'Neither Durlib nor I know anything about a Knight Templar, nor have we seen anyone in the mountains this winter,' Grimpow lied.

'Boy,' the monk sighed, 'you needn't lie to me. I am just trying to help you escape the claws of this evil friar. The inquisitor already knows that Durlib gave the abbot some coins with the Temple symbols on them in exchange for a pair of horses.'

'How do you know that?'

'Few things happen in the abbey that I don't hear about,' said the old monk.

'So it was the abbot who shared this information?' Grimpow pressed.

'Yes,' replied Brother Rinaldo briefly, 'but the abbot only talked to the Dominican friar about Durlib, not you.'

'Why?'

'For fear of being branded with the Inquisition's burning iron.'

Grimpow remembered a hot summer day in the village of Ullpens when they had seen a man on a cart wearing bloody rags. His hands had been tied and he held a wooden cross between his fingers. A big gash in his head was so deep it revealed his brains. His broken legs hung awkwardly from the bench he was tied to. A pair of drums preceded the group of soldiers leading him to a mound of firewood in the town's square, where he was burned alive amid his screams of horror and the cheers of those who had gathered to watch. Durlib had explained to him that the Church persecuted witches, wizards, sages, wise men and any mendicant friars and monks who didn't accept its wealth, teachings and beliefs.

'Take me before the inquisitor and I'll tell him the truth about that Knight Templar he's looking for,' said Grimpow, terrified by the thought of his friend ending up like that unfortunate man.

Brother Rinaldo looked at him with compassion. 'And you think that will stop him from killing you both after you've told him what he wants to know?' he asked, staring intently at the boy.

'I don't know, but at least I'll prevent Durlib from being tortured. I couldn't bear to know he was hurt because of me.'

'You should stop thinking about what is out of your control. Durlib knows how to take care of himself. Now, tell me something,' said the monk, pausing for a second as if he didn't quite know how to pose the question. 'Did you rob the Knight Templar in the mountains and take his silver coins?'

For a moment, Grimpow thought about lying and telling the monk that the knight had offered them the coins in exchange for help finding his way out of the mountains, but something inside him urged him to tell Brother Rinaldo the truth.

'No, I found him dead on the snow near our cottage, on my way back from hunting rabbits by the valley's waterfall. Durlib thought that perhaps the man had been unable to find his horse and got lost because of the fog. And that he died of cold in the night.'

'Did you bury him?'

Grimpow shook his head and added, 'This sounds hard to believe, but it wasn't necessary. We thought of coming to the abbey to tell the abbot about our find, and let him bury the knight in the chapel, but the man's body disappeared in the snow before our eyes as if it had never been there at all.'

Brother Rinaldo's eyes shone. 'So it's true!' he exclaimed in awe.

'What do you mean?' asked Grimpow.

'That there is a secret.'

'I don't understand,' the boy replied, frustrated.

'Listen very carefully to what I'm about to tell you, my boy. There exists an ancient legend that tells of a powerful secret – one the Knights Templar have protected for a very long time,' said the old man. 'That secret is what Bulvar of Goztell wants to uncover, which is why he was chasing the knight you found through the mountains. But before I recount the legend, you must tell me if you found anything else on the knight's body besides the coins.'

Again Grimpow hesitated, not knowing what to tell Brother Rinaldo, but once more he opted for the truth, sensing it was the better option.

'There was a bag next to the body with several silver coins, some jewels, two daggers, a sealed letter and a gold seal,' he said in one breath. He did not mention the stone.

'A valuable treasure, no doubt, which I assume you've hidden in a safe place,' said the monk dryly. 'But that's not what I am interested in – I gave up on the world's riches long ago. Tell me about the letter. Did you break the seal on it?'

'Durlib did, using this dagger,' explained Grimpow as he pulled out the jewel-studded dagger from under his doublet. 'It has symbols on it which we can't understand. Neither one of us knows how to read or write,' he explained – not lying completely, but not telling the monk about being able to read the letter with the help of the stone.

The old monk's eyes widened when he saw the dagger, as if he had waited decades to hear what Grimpow was saying.

'That dagger belongs to a Knight Templar,' he said in awe. 'Do you have the letter with you too?' he asked expectantly.

'We left it in the bag, along with the seal.'

'It doesn't matter. It doesn't matter. It all fits together perfectly,' he said to himself.

Grimpow was surprised that the monk didn't ask where Durlib had hidden the treasure. It confirmed that the man wasn't interested in the coins or the jewels. But Grimpow still had questions of his own. 'What about the old legend you were about to tell me?' he asked, attempting to stir the old man from his reverie.

Brother Rinaldo sat with his eyes closed for a while, as if he was about to enter the deep abyss of his memory. Then he slowly opened his eyes, looked seriously at the boy who sat before him, and began.

'About two centuries ago, in the year eleven eighteen to be precise, nine French and Flemish knights, tired of their lives as knights, decided to take the habit and travelled to Jerusalem. There they visited King Baldwin the Second with the purpose of becoming protectors of the Christian pilgrims who, ever since the First Crusade, had travelled in large groups to the Holy Land to worship Christ's Sepulchre. They stayed for a long time in the ancient Temple of Solomon, where they devoted themselves to prayer and meditation. But the legend says their real mission was to find something in the ruins of the temple – a secret described in very old manuscripts found by Crusaders after conquering Jerusalem. Whoever found this secret object was supposed to be granted immortality and the power to rule the world. Nine years after the knights' arrival at the Temple, seven of them returned to France with an enormous cart, which made many believe that they had accomplished their mission—'

'Did they discover the secret they were searching for?' Grimpow asked, interrupting Brother Rinaldo's retelling.

The monk shook his head. 'Nobody ever knew for sure, but many said that the Knights of the Temple of Solomon had returned to France carrying the Ark of the Covenant, which the Bible claims has supernatural powers – and that, once there, they hid it in an unknown place. Others, however, claim that what the nine knights really found in the Temple of Solomon was the Holy Grail.'

'The Holy Grail?' Grimpow repeated.

'Yes. It is said to be the chalice from which our Lord drank during the Last Supper,' Brother Rinaldo explained. 'It is said that the chalice has wonderful and unimaginable powers.'

'And does it really?'

'I don't know,' the monk confessed. 'All I know is that, soon after, the Templar Order spread rapidly to all the European kingdoms, establishing numerous commanderies, castles and chapels everywhere. The Knights Templar obtained so much wealth and power that even kings believed that they had actually discovered the treasure.'

'So why are they being persecuted now?'

'Some monks who came to the abbey from Paris told me that six years ago, the King of France, Philip the Fourth, blinded by his greed and cruelty, ordered his soldiers to capture all the Knights Templar in his kingdom, with the dishonourable intention of seizing their castles and treasures and, most importantly, discovering their secrets. Hundreds of Knights Templar were imprisoned, humiliated, and tortured to death. Under ruthless torture, numerous Templars pleaded guilty before the Inquisition and were burned mercilessly at the stake. Even Pope Clement the Fifth, afraid of the King of France's fury, asked all Christian kings to persecute any Templars who could be found hiding in their realms.'

'Is that why Bulvar of Goztell was after the knight in the mountains?' Grimpow asked.

'Partly, yes,' the monk said, shifting in his seat. 'But tonight I heard the Dominican friar tell the abbot that the last Templar Grand Master, Jacques de Molay – who's still imprisoned in Paris – confessed to his inquisitors that what the nine knights discovered two hundred years ago in the Temple of Solomon was known only by a group of sages, whom nobody, including himself, had ever seen.'

'And do you think that the knight the Dominican friar was chasing had something to do with that secret?' asked Grimpow.

'Bulvar of Goztell is convinced of it,' answered Brother Rinaldo. 'And judging from the coded message and the gold seal that you and Durlib found in the knight's bag, I have no doubt of it either.'

Grimpow suddenly thought of something. 'You were a

Knight Templar before shutting yourself in this abbey,' he stated simply.

The old monk winced in surprise and narrowed his eyes as he looked around at the manuscripts piled on the shelves around him.

'There was a time when I was one,' he whispered finally. 'But that was so long ago that my clumsy memory refuses to recall why that life came to an end.'

'Perhaps it is that you don't like remembering what you did then?' said Grimpow.

'It's possible,' admitted the monk, now staring at Grimpow as if he were in the presence of a prophet. And after a few seconds of deep silence, the old man began his story.

When he was a boy, not much older than Grimpow, he had followed the advice of his uncle and joined the Knights Templar commandery in his hometown of Metz, a small village in the northeast of France. Brother Rinaldo told Grimpow that he had lived in the Holy Land since he'd turned sixteen, defending the Templar fortresses of Safed, Tripoli, Damascus, Gaza, Galilee, Damietta and Acre against the infidels. He then joined the Seventh and Eighth Crusades with Louis IX, the King of France.

'That same year, sick of seeing so many dead and maimed bodies, so much blood spilled pointlessly in the name of God, I decided to run away from the world, its cruelty and misery, and I took refuge in the isolated abbey of Brinkdum, with the sole purpose of spending the rest of my days studying the valuable manuscripts housed in its enormous library. Look around you – these books have all been banned by the Church and have been kept here for centuries, preserved from ordinary monks' curious glances,' he finished, sighing.

'Have you read all of them?' asked Grimpow, looking around him in awe.

'All of them, without exception,' the monk said proudly, 'and they hold enough knowledge that I myself have doubted the existence of God many times.'

'I don't understand,' whispered Grimpow.

'The idea of God helps us explain everything around us,' the monk began. 'Many of these books refute or challenge the existence of God by explaining Heaven and earth and the universe scientifically. Because of this, the Inquisition has banned them. Even knowing all that I know' – the old monk motioned toward the bookcases – 'I still believe in God. But I do not believe in using my God as an excuse to wage war or use violence or as a reason to seek riches. Many evil things are done in the name of God, and sometimes things that begin with truly good intentions turn bad. The original Knights Templar were pure and good, but time and greed corrupted many in their order. Only a few remained faithful to their values, and those few – the Chosen Ones – are said to be the only heirs to the secret of the original nine Knights Templar.'

'The Chosen Ones?'

'A Chosen One can reveal the world's truth and channel

wisdom that will lead him to discover the secret of the wise. That wonderful treasure is accessible only to those who search for it following the proper signs and paths.'

'So do you believe that the Knight Templar who died in the mountains was a Chosen One?'

'I have no doubt about it. And fate has chosen you as well,' the monk said. 'If you found his body in the snow, along with the seal and letter he carried, it must be *you* who resumes the mission he could not finish.'

Upon hearing this, Grimpow's own thoughts were confirmed – the strange feeling that had surged through him when he felt the warm touch of the stone between his fingers in the mountains was what he had suspected. He knew he had to continue the knight's mission, but he didn't know how. The only clue he had was a man's name, Aidor Bilbicum – the intended recipient of the sealed letter in the faraway city of Strasbourg.

'And what can I do to discover that secret?' he asked.

'First you'll have to decode the letter's message. The Templars used the Kabbalah and many different hieroglyphic or coded languages. In spite of having been a Templar for many years, I am not sure I could help you even if I had the letter in front of me.'

Grimpow didn't doubt Brother Rinaldo's sincerity and decided to reciprocate by divulging the message he'd interpreted in the sealed letter. He thought that perhaps the monk could help him decipher the real meaning of that enigmatic text.

'And what if I told you that I understood the message in the sealed letter when I saw it?'

The old monk looked at him in disbelief. But when Grimpow remained silent, Brother Rinaldo asked in a low voice, 'Have you had a supernatural vision?'

'I am not sure what that is,' Grimpow answered. 'But when I looked at the strange symbols in the parchment, I could understand them as if a voice inside me was magically telling me their real meaning.'

'A miracle!' exclaimed Brother Rinaldo, bringing his hand to his forehead as if to wipe away sweat, even though the room was frigid.

'The sealed letter said, "There are darkness and light in the sky, Aidor Bilbicum, Strasbourg."'

The old monk's features settled into a satisfied expression when he heard Grimpow's words. 'A code, a person and a city,' he whispered meditatively. 'It all fits, it all fits.' He then repeated in a loud and melodic voice, '"There are darkness and light in the sky, Aidor Bilbicum, Strasbourg."'

'What do you think it means?' asked Grimpow.

'There are darkness and light, night and day, obscurity and clarity, ignorance and wisdom in the sky,' he said. 'I think it is a code. Upon receiving this message, this Aidor Bilbicum will know what to do. But what I can't understand is how you, a boy who doesn't know how to read and write, have been able to decipher this riddle.'

The monk got up from his seat, walked over to a shelf

behind him and took down a thick illuminated manuscript. He laid it open on the table and placed a candle near it, casting a golden light across the pages.

'Come closer,' he whispered to Grimpow.

Grimpow sat by Brother Rinaldo's side. In the thick book's open pages, a text written in two columns framed four equal circles; in each one of them, painted in vivid red and blue colours, were scenes of angels and monks next to a walled city framed in gold leaf.

'Can you understand what it says here?' the old monk asked, pointing to the beautiful Latin characters at the beginning of the text.

'"The wall was made of jasper, and the city was pure gold, as clear as glass. The wall of the city was adorned with all manner of precious stones,"' Grimpow started reading, as if Latin was his mother tongue.

'Enough, enough,' whispered the monk, his eyes sparkling brightly. 'Extraordinary and strange things are what you are telling me, and if I hadn't seen you translate that text in Latin with my own eyes . . . It's clear that, be it a miracle or a spell, something unexplainable has happened to you since you found that mysterious knight dead in the mountains.'

Grimpow only had to tell Brother Rinaldo about the amulet he had found in the Knight Templar's hand for the monk to know every detail of what had happened, and to confirm that it was the unusual stone that gave Grimpow's mind those powers. But before he had a chance, the abbey's tower bells chimed, announcing the morning worship.

'I must leave now,' the old monk said hurriedly, and stood. 'Neither the abbot nor the inquisitor Bulvar of Goztell must miss me at the morning's prayer.'

He left the table, and Grimpow watched him rummage through first one shelf and then another, until suddenly one of the bookshelves rotated on the floor and left a hole in front of him as dark as night.

Just before the old monk stepped into the passageway, Grimpow whispered urgently, 'Will you be back soon?'

'I will see you again at dawn, after prime,' the monk replied, stopping under the frame formed by the highest shelves. 'I'll try to bring you some food and news of your friend Durlib.'

'You are forgetting the lamp,' Grimpow warned him before he left.

But the old monk turned around, stepped into the darkness, and said, 'My eyes are used to the shadows.'

And when the bookshelf swung back, Grimpow was left completely alone.

A Square Peg in a Round Hole

When he opened his eyes the next day, all Grimpow wanted was to hear about Durlib. He had been awake nearly all night in that room full of books and shadows, shivering from cold on the uncomfortable makeshift mattress he had prepared on a table. After the monk left the night before, he'd blown out all the lamps, leaving only a tiny flame burning in a corner so he wouldn't be in complete darkness. Then he sat, the small flickering light beside him, and thought about what Brother Rinaldo had told him about the Knights Templar and their secret. And all night long he worried that Durlib would be tortured.

Gradually, as the night wore on, he began to doze in and out of sleep. Long after the tower bells had chimed and the monks had attended the first worship of the day, he heard the sound of the stone wall rotating above him, and knew that someone was entering through the trapdoor surrounded by skulls. He took his dagger from his waistband and held his breath while he listened to slow footsteps descend the spiral staircase, then exhaled, relieved, when he saw that the one who entered was Kense, the abbey's quiet servant. From a sack he held tightly, Kense took out a wineskin with water, a piece of bread, some pork sausage and a couple of sweet apples, which he placed on the floor. Without uttering a word, he disappeared back up the stairs as slowly as he had arrived.

Grimpow quenched his thirst with the water in the wineskin. Then he brought the food to the table he'd used as a bed during the night and devoured the bread, sausage and apples as if they were the best food he'd ever tasted.

He relit the lamps hanging from the ceiling, then busied himself studying the titles of the manuscripts around him. As he took each one off the shelf, he realized he could read all of them without difficulty, whether they were written in Latin, Greek, Hebrew or Arabic. But he was no longer shocked by his miraculous power. What had once been impossible for him to do was now so natural. Several books contained only text written in delicate, beautiful calligraphy, but others were illuminated with miniatures decorated with motifs in bright colours and plenty of gold leaf. There were manuscripts on philosophy, astronomy and astrology; anatomy and medicine; healing herbs, poisons, potions and incantations; magic, spells and sorcery; beasts, monsters, demons, fantastic animals, and exotic and faraway places; geometry, arithmetic and mineralogy; physics and alchemy. Grimpow was fascinated when he realized that these wondrous books had been written hundreds of years before and came from all over the world.

He was enjoying contemplating a sheet with the circular forms of the planets' orbits in the blue skies, drawn almost a thousand years before, when he heard a noise coming from the other side of the bookshelves. In came the old monk, Brother Rinaldo. Grimpow closed the manuscript and asked immediately for news about Durlib.

Brother Rinaldo smiled. 'That friend of yours is smarter than a cornered fox,' he said.

'Has he escaped?' asked Grimpow anxiously.

'Not yet, but I'm sure he will soon. Last night the king's soldiers captured him in the abbey's stable. He acted so docile and helpful that Bulvar of Goztell was convinced he had found the best ally to help find the Knight Templar he's been chasing.'

'So they haven't tortured him?' asked Grimpow, sighing with relief.

'For now, he's astutely escaped torture. Durlib told the inquisitor that yesterday morning near the cottage he ran into a horseless knight who seemed to be lost in the mountains. He described the unknown man's features and attire and explained that he had spoken to the knight about the purpose of his journey, and the knight had said he was travelling north to attend to an urgent matter. Durlib assured the inquisitor that he told the knight about the abbey of Brinkdum. Then he said that the knight gave him some silver coins and asked if he could go to the abbey and acquire a pair of horses for him to continue his trip.'

'So Durlib convinced the inquisitor that the Knight Templar is still alive?'

'He assured the inquisitor that he would find the knight in Durlib's cottage, awaiting his return. And he then offered to show the Dominican friar and the soldiers the way to the mountains.'

'And have they already left?'

'They did a moment ago; I saw them leave from the stables, with Durlib heading the escort with the arrogance of a drunk,' the monk said, laughing.

'I'm sure that Durlib will get rid of them somewhere along the tortuous trail leading to the mountains,' said Grimpow, convinced of Durlib's ability to escape the soldiers' watch. Durlib knew that hostile, snow-covered region like the back of his hand.

'Bulvar might have been naive to believe the story your friend made up, but he is not stupid. He tied Durlib's hands behind his back with leather straps before their departure.'

Grimpow still had no doubt that Durlib would take advantage of the first opportunity to escape, and most likely he'd succeed. 'Do you think the inquisitor will look for me too?' he asked.

'He doesn't even know you're here. The abbot only spoke to him about Durlib, and from what I know, your friend hasn't mentioned your presence in the abbey to the friar either,' explained Brother Rinaldo.

'So what will happen when the inquisitor finds out that Durlib fooled him?'

'If Durlib is still in the inquisitor's custody when the truth is uncovered, I'm afraid your friend will meet a gruesome end. I can only hope he manages to escape before he is forced to tell the inquisitor the truth. Bulvar would surely think Durlib was mocking him if he told of the knight's body disappearing in the snow.'

'But that's what really happened!' insisted Grimpow.

'I believe you, but Bulvar of Goztell wouldn't believe in the disappearance of a dead body if he saw it happen with his own eyes. This morning during breakfast in the dining hall, Brother Asben told me he met him years ago in the city of Vienne, near Lyon. The inquisitor had been a spy for the King of France, who placed him among the Knights Templar in the Holy Land to find out their initiation rites and secrets. Apparently Bulvar was one of the closest aides to the last Grand Master, Jacques de Molay, whom he ended up betraying upon his return to Paris, accusing him of heresy. Bulvar then entered the Dominican Order as an inquisitor and devoted his body and soul to persecuting the Templars who managed to escape the King of France's grip. Many of whom fled north to Germany, where they sought refuge in the Circle of Stone under the protection of Gulf, Duke of Ostemberg, and his loyal knights.'

This new twist in Brother Rinaldo's story sparked Grimpow's interest.

'What is the Circle of Stone?' he asked.

'I've never seen it with my own eyes, but from what stories say, the Circle of Stone is formed by eight small castles, built in a perfect circle deep in the rocky heights of mountains virtually inaccessible to man. And at the very centre, located on a high rocky peak, is a ninth castle – the Duke of Ostemberg's fortress.'

Brother Rinaldo explained that the circular formation of the defences allowed the castles to quickly help each other in times of war, and made sieges nearly impossible. As well, there were hundreds of secret passages in the rocks and an intricate labyrinth of underground tunnels and galleries that connected the castles with one another, allowing the inhabitants to avoid their attackers like a rabbit escaping a fox.

The circular design of the castles' location had been suggested to the Duke of Ostemberg's ancestor by a great sage. Since then, all the Dukes of Ostemberg have been trained by the wise Knights Templar, who have been their best advisers and allies. It is said that the current duke had an ancestor so wise that even as a child he could do complex mathematical calculations, prove difficult geometric theorems, and accurately locate the constellations in the sky. At twenty years of age, he built an observatory in his father's castle, where he and his teacher spent long nights observing the stars and planets in awe.

'Was that duke a Chosen One as well?' asked Grimpow,

remembering what Brother Rinaldo had told him the night before about the sages who knew the Templar secret.

'Nobody knows, but all his vassals considered him a great sage. And even if he never belonged to the Templar Order, at least officially, he must have been closely linked to it because his tutor was a Knight Templar.'

'How are the Circle of Stone's castles and the Knights Templar related?' asked Grimpow.

'Ah, my smart boy, this I will show you.'

The old monk walked to a small desk in the corner and sat down. He grabbed a quill, dipped it in an inkwell, and with the side of his hand flattened a piece of unused parchment that was lying on the desk. Grimpow walked closer to Brother Rinaldo and watched curiously as he drew on the parchment a perfect circle.

'The circle,' said the monk solemnly, 'is one of the most mysterious geometric forms. The continuity of its infinite line, without beginning or end, represents perfection and eternity. This eternity can only be found in the sky. The full moon and the sun have a circular shape, as do all the stars in the universe.'

Then the monk paused and drew a square of the same size under the circle.

'And if the sky is the circle—'

'The earth is the square,' interrupted Grimpow, without knowing why he made that statement.

'Indeed,' said Brother Rinaldo. 'If the infinite sky is represented by the circle, the earth's finiteness is symbolized in the square, which is the opposite geometric form and is limited. It's not coincidental that the four sides of the square correspond to the four cardinal points: north, south, east and west; the year's four seasons: spring, summer, autumn and winter; and nature's four essential elements: water, earth, air and fire. Besides, the square, which is the earth, can also be contained inside the circle, which is the sky, and both share the same cosmic centre.'

As he said this, he drew a second circle with precision and, inside it, a second square so that the centre of the circle was also the centre of the square.

'The sky and the earth form a dual whole whose ultimate fusion is as impossible as fitting a square peg into a round hole. Everyone who's attempted to convert the square and the circle into only one geometric form has failed, because that would be like uniting the earth with the sky and man with God,' said Brother Rinaldo.

'I don't understand why you say that fitting a square peg in a round hole is impossible. You've drawn a picture yourself,' Grimpow said, pointing to the square within the circle.

'That's right, Grimpow. But look at this now,' said the old monk, and started drawing yet another circle with a square inside it. This drawing, however, contained another figure – an octagon, situated between the lines of the circle and the square.

'As you can see for yourself, if we try to square the circle by approximating its shape to the square, what we'll get is a new geometric form: the octagon. The octagon touches the circle at eight points. Like the eight castles of the Circle of Stone, it represents the perfect harmony between the sky and the earth, the balanced union of the divine and the human, the equilibrium between the soul and the body and the invisible and the visible.'

'Between darkness and light!' said Grimpow suddenly, remembering the message on the letter.

'Aha! You've worked out why I have no doubt of the letter's Templar origin,' said Brother Rinaldo.

'And how did you manage to decipher the meaning of the octagon and the eight castles in the Circle of Stone?' Grimpow asked without looking away from the geometric figure.

'I discovered it in this very chamber. I had always been curious about the shape of many towers and chapels of the Templar Order because they were all octagonal. I wanted to know why the knights would use that specific shape in their buildings. After researching many manuscripts and reading as much as I could here, I was able to draw my own conclusions about the eight castles forming the Circle of Stone.'

'You were a Knight Templar – you didn't know?'

'A Knight Templar like me, devoted by oath to war and prayer, only had to follow orders and not question them. Until I came to this abbey, I didn't worry about acquiring any knowledge that didn't deal with the use of the lance, the bow or the sword.'

Sitting with the old monk, Grimpow couldn't stop thinking that the answer to the mystery was probably in the stone he carried.

'And why is the word *stone* linked to the name of the Circle's castles?' he asked, trying to get at least one clue about his stone.

'Because the walls and towers of the castles are made of stone, I suspect,' the old monk answered. Then he paused and looked intently at Grimpow, as if trying to divine the younger man's thoughts. 'But if you wish to know for sure, Grimpow, you'll have to search for the answer to that question, if there is one, among the forbidden parchments and manuscripts in this room. You may have to remain locked in here for some time, so I recommend you take advantage of it. On those shelves behind you,' he said, standing up with difficulty and pointing with his index finger, 'you'll find multiple books on mineralogy and alchemy, and some others that deal with the philosopher's stone. Perhaps you'll find a reasonable explanation to your question in them.'

'The philosopher's stone?' Grimpow was puzzled.

'A stone that could supposedly turn lead into precious metals and bring perfect knowledge – both goals of the art of alchemy for many centuries. Numerous Templars were great alchemists, having learned the difficult discipline from the Arabs after living near them for several years in the Holy Land. Some even say that the Knights of the Templar Order acquired their riches and treasures through the transmutation of base metals into silver and gold.'

'And if that was their secret?' asked Grimpow.

'You shouldn't make the effort to discover it. Gold's temptation is much more evil than the Devil's,' the monk added as he eyed the boy seriously. 'Now I must leave – it will be noon soon, and I can't miss the midday worship. I'll be back when the inquisitor has returned from his expedition to the mountains, to tell you what happened to your friend Durlib.'

'Do you promise not to hide the truth, as hard as it is?' begged Grimpow.

'I would never lie to you,' the monk answered matter-of-factly. 'Though I am sure that you haven't yet told me the whole truth about what you know.'

Grimpow blushed and looked at the floor to avoid the old monk's gaze. 'I'm afraid Brother Brasgdo might get drunk and tell the Dominican friar about my presence in the abbey. He also saw the Knight Templar entering the mountains.'

'Brother Brasgdo knows how to hold his tongue when he is afraid it will be cut off for using it,' said the old monk. And with that he turned and left the room without looking back.

Kense returned at lunchtime with a straw mattress, some blankets and plenty of food. But, as usual, he left everything by the trapdoor without saying a word. Grimpow yearned to leave that enclosed chamber and wait for Bulvar of Goztell's return by the abbey's doors. Then, if necessary, he would tell him everything he knew about the knight in the mountains and offer him the magical stone he had in exchange for Durlib's freedom. He looked in vain among the shelves for the hidden levers that controlled the invisible door to the library's adjoining rooms. But there were only dusty manuscripts on the shelves and some spiderwebs that stuck to his fingers.

As he was moving the books he was struck by the title of an old manuscript, written in Latin: *lapis philosophorum*.

'The philosopher's stone!' he exclaimed. He pulled the

manuscript off the shelf, laid it on the table in the centre of the room, and began flipping through the pages, excited by what he had discovered. Perhaps in its thick parchment pages he would find answers.

As he read, images of a story as old as time began to form in his mind. The main characters were sages from faraway countries, whose main task was to find the philosopher's stone. From what Grimpow gathered, the manuscript dealt with the sacred art of the transmutation of metals into gold, called alchemy, and it explained the endless and confusing methods used by those sages to succeed in creating the coveted *lapis philosophorum* in their labs. The stone was not only supposed to have the ability to turn base metals into pure gold, but it also was said to impart absolute wisdom and immortality to whoever kept it. But the risk of the philosopher's stone falling into the wrong hands – those of people who would use its prodigious power to become rich and rule the world – was too great. So the knowledge became guarded.

As Grimpow read, he slowly began to wonder if perhaps the stone he had was the philosopher's stone the book talked about. Could this be the secret the mysterious Knights Templar kept? That they created the philosopher's stone in a secret laboratory based on one of the manuscripts they found in the Temple of Solomon? The Pope and the King of France coveted it because they wanted to fill their empty chests with gold. The stone could have been responsible for the Templar Order's wealth. Could the knight Grimpow had found been on a journey to hide it in a safe place?

Sometime after the abbey's tower bells chimed to announce the evening prayers, Brother Rinaldo visited Grimpow in his hidden chamber. Grimpow, judging from the monk's expression, speculated that he didn't have good news.

Brother Rinaldo sat on a stool at the table, rested his elbows on it, and cleared his throat sombrely. 'Durlib has not returned to the abbey with Bulvar of Goztell and the king's soldiers,' he said. 'According to what the Dominican friar told the abbot, Durlib tried to escape. He jumped from a cliff and died when he landed on the rocks below.'

'He's dead?' asked Grimpow, holding back his tears.

'The inquisitor's rage would appear to confirm it. It seems as if he would have liked to take revenge on your friend by killing him slowly and with his own hands.'

Despite the monk's certainty, Grimpow refused to accept Durlib's death. Durlib's finest talent was deception, and he knew every corner of the trail, every narrow path, every cliff and every dangerous crevasse hidden under the snow. If he had decided to launch himself from the side of a mountain, he would have planned his jump accurately to land on a ledge hidden from sight.

'Durlib might have escaped by faking his own death in front of the inquisitor,' Grimpow argued, trying to convince himself, for in the back of his mind he remembered that his friend's hands had been tied behind his back, which would have made it difficult, if not impossible, to survive, regardless of his state after the fall.

The old monk sighed. 'Let's hope it's as you say, Grimpow, and that he doesn't have any injuries that he can't recover from. If he is alive, he will soon come for you, and if that doesn't happen, we'll look for his body when the snow begins to melt and bury him properly in the abbey's cemetery. All we can do now is wait – and hope that the inquisitor leaves the walls of this holy house as soon as possible. Since he and his henchmen arrived, it seems to tremble as if the end of the world is approaching.'

'Do you think he will leave soon?'

'He hasn't mentioned anything to the abbot since his return, but I don't think that staying will be of use to him – especially if he still believes that the Knight Templar is alive. If I were in his shoes, I would think that the fugitive is headed for the castles of the Circle of Stone, to seek shelter with his exiled brothers in the Duke of Ostemberg's fortress.'

Brother Rinaldo's last words comforted Grimpow, for he was eager to leave his captivity, and even more eager to discover if Durlib was still alive.

'I see that you've been busy,' said the old monk, pointing at the manuscript sitting open on the table. 'Have you been able to find out more about what you wanted to know?'

Grimpow tried his best to hide his excitement about his new discovery. 'Not exactly. It's a very complex and confusing text – though I have learned the principles of creating the philosopher's stone in a laboratory.'

'Are you sure of that? Alchemy is a hermetic art in which nothing is as it seems.'

'I think that the veil of mystery surrounding alchemists is nothing more than rumour,' said Grimpow shamelessly.

The monk grinned at the boy's new boldness. 'It is true that fake alchemists abounded throughout history – charlatans, deceivers and swindlers offering recipes to create gold, many of who ended up at the gallows because of it. There are real alchemists, though – ones who seek the philosopher's stone as the ideal of absolute wisdom.'

'Do you think that the philosopher's stone actually exists?' Grimpow asked.

'Several ancient texts speak of the so-called *lapis philosophorum* as a mysterious force that can transform a base metal into a noble one, but I am inclined to think that such a transmutation is only an allegory, a symbol to hide its real meaning – which is nothing more than the search for absolute wisdom.'

'Are you saying you think the real philosopher's stone isn't a stone at all?'

'Who knows?' said the old monk, raising his eyes to the wooden ceiling as if trying to find that answer beyond the abbey's roof in the infinite night sky. 'The only thing that's certain is that no sage, alchemist or not, has ever described its exact nature, although some experts on the art of transmutation claim that the philosopher's stone is as red as a fire's embers and shines in the darkness like a star.'

Grimpow had seen his stone turn red. He couldn't resist asking the monk, 'Have you ever tried to create the philosopher's stone following the process described in this manuscript?'

'In spite of my interest in astrology – for which patience is as necessary as time – I wouldn't have enough patience to endure such a long and uncertain wait,' Brother Rinaldo said with a smile. 'But Brother Asben, the abbey's herbalist, has been attempting the recipes for years in his small laboratory, using all the formulas and tricks he's found in these forbidden books. And since I've known him he hasn't been able to obtain more than a few gold inks.'

'May I speak with Brother Asben when I leave this room?' Grimpow asked eagerly.

'I'm sure that he'll be delighted to share his experiments with such a young and passionate disciple.' And without another word the old monk activated the mechanism that opened the revolving shelf and left the hidden room like a ghost who could walk through walls.

A Cry in the Night

When the tower bells announced the early morning prayer, the monks gathered in the chapel's choir and sleepily awaited the arrival of the abbot. As the minutes ticked by the novices began exchanging curious and anxious glances. Brother Rinaldo straightened up in his pew to try to silence the increasing whispers. Then a heart-wrenching scream from the servant Kense shattered the abbey's silence.

Amid a commotion the monks abandoned their seats in the chapel's choir and ran to the cloisters. In front of the abbot's quarters they found Kense lying on the floor, unable to speak. A brave monk entered the abbot's study and came out immediately, his face contorted with fear.

'The abbot has been murdered!' he shouted, crossing himself as if he'd seen the very Devil.

Brother Asben entered the abbot's quarters followed by

Brother Brasgdo while the rest of the monks swarmed around the door, whispering anxiously and straining their necks to better see the macabre scene. The abbot sat lifeless at his desk, his head unnaturally bent against his right shoulder, a grimace of horror on his face. A clean cut had split his throat in two, the gash unleashing a torrent of blood that had soaked his habit and collected in a dark puddle on the floor.

After tending to poor Kense, Brother Rinaldo made his way through the sea of monks to see Brother Asben close the abbot's eyes, making the sign of the cross with his thumb on each of the abbot's eyelids. Someone wanted to keep the abbot quiet for ever, he thought. And he was fairly sure he knew who it was.

Since the arrival of the inquisitor and his soldiers, Brother Rinaldo had been eavesdropping on their private conversations with the abbot. He suspected that the inquisitor of Lyon's visit was not coincidental. At first he even feared that the evil inquisitor was looking for him. But he realized now that the abbot's throat had been slit because he knew of the plans by the Pope and the King of France to steal the Templars' secret.

In the distance came the sound of footsteps under the dark arches of the cloisters – a funereal song for the murdered abbot's soul. The monks parted to reveal the inquisitor, followed by the king's soldiers.

The inquisitor's cold, indifferent voice broke the strained silence, 'Whoever did this must be a master of the Arabic dagger.' He looked around as if trying to find the murderer among the monks present.

'How can you be sure that it was an Arabic dagger and not a Christian knife that cut the abbot's throat?' asked Brother Rinaldo.

'If you had ever fought in the Holy Land, as I have, you'd know as well as I do how the infidels cut Christians' throats.'

The old monk knew all too well the violence both Christians and Muslims were guilty of, all in the name of God, but he kept his tragic experiences from the Crusades to himself.

'Are you suggesting that the abbot was slain by a monk using an infidel's dagger?' he asked.

'Many Crusaders, including the Knights Templar, have learned how to slit throats like the fearful Muslim warriors.'

'Then don't look for the murderer among us, but instead among the armed ones,' Brother Rinaldo countered. 'Why would we kill our best brother?'

'The same reason Cain killed Abel,' replied the inquisitor. 'But do not fret – the abbot told me he'd seen the same fugitive Knight Templar we've been chasing roaming the abbey's surroundings. I suspect the knight had something to do with this murder.'

'No one entered this abbey after you and the soldiers did last night,' said the old monk boldly.

'I suppose you are aware that the Templars have been declared heretics and outlaws by Pope Clement himself,' the inquisitor said with a raised brow. 'Their alliance with the Devil allows them to use sorcerers' and necromancers' spells to appear and disappear as they please.'

'So how then are you planning to capture that fugitive Templar? You speak of him as if he were Satan himself.'

'Unfortunately for them, their black magic is as fleeting as the glow of the stars, and for that reason, they can't run or hide for ever. I assure you that I will find that murderer even if I have to move earth and sky to do it. Now, as the abbot's closest brother, you should make sure that his corpse is taken to the chapel and the monks pray all night for his soul, before he is properly buried tomorrow. I will leave at sunset following the outlaw's footprints and won't stop until I've found him,' Bulvar said.

The monks returned to the chapel with their heads bent, softly chanting a prayer for the dead. And with the help of two servants and a stretcher, Brother Brasgdo and Brother Asben took the abbot's body to the infirmary to shroud him for burial.

It was shortly after sunrise when Brother Rinaldo visited Grimpow and told him what had happened during the night.

'You'll be able to leave this hideout,' the old monk said.

'Have the inquisitor Bulvar of Goztell and the king's soldiers left already?' Grimpow asked.

'They were in the stables preparing their saddles before sunrise, and ventured toward Ullpens with the day's first light. The inquisitor didn't even want to wait for the abbot's burial.'

The first thing he would do with his newly recovered freedom, Grimpow decided, was to find out if Durlib was still alive. He thought that if Durlib had been fortunate enough to survive his plunge into the void, he would have probably returned to the cross where they buried the dead knight's bag. So he planned to walk down to the cross on the road and check if Durlib had recovered the bag with his small treasure: the letter and gold seal.

The old monk led Grimpow through a series of library rooms lined with books, then down a wide and luminous corridor with big, open arches overlooking the cloisters. It wasn't snowing, but the intense cold woke Grimpow up as if he had washed his face in an icy pond. They descended to the cloisters and walked toward the chapel. Grimpow imagined for a moment the abbot's blood splattered on the walls and floor of his study and shuddered. He even wondered again if the dead knight's magical stone wasn't the *lapis philosophorum* but instead a demonic amulet, as Durlib had thought initially.

Down in the chapel everything was ready for the abbot's funeral. The monks' hymns resonated in the nave like the melancholy whispering of a choir of angels, and a soft light filtered through the stained glass, causing the face of the dead abbot to shine dimly. His body lay on a wooden catafalque, with his hands folded together. His eyes were closed, but Grimpow could see the abbot's mouth twisted into a grimace on one side in a strange expression that could almost have been mistaken for mockery. Four big candles burned in tall copper candleholders in the four corners of the chapel, and a strong scent of incense floated under the ceiling like an invisible but perfumed fog.

Grimpow sat next to the abbey's servants and listened with sincere devotion to the requiem mass for the murdered abbot's soul. As the ceremony went on, Grimpow dedicated his own thoughts and prayers to his dear friend Durlib. If he had jumped to his death, as the inquisitor claimed, his soul could now rest, Grimpow thought. And if he was still alive, there was no harm done by dedicating the sweet and beautiful songs the monks chanted to his friend.

'*Requiem aeternam dona eis, Domine,*' said Brother Rinaldo, and closed the ceremony.

Then the funeral procession began. Four robust servants hoisted the catafalque to their shoulders and, followed by two lines of hooded monks carrying thick candles, began marching toward the abbey's graveyard. Two servants awaited the procession next to a hole in the ground. The servants carrying the catafalque laid it down. They placed the abbot's body in the tomb and covered it with soil until they had formed a small mound, on which they placed an iron cross.

A few snowflakes slowly fell from the darkening sky, announcing that a strong tempest of wind and snow was approaching the mountains.

* * *

Most of the monks returned to their duties once the burial was finished, but Brother Rinaldo and the herbalist monk, Brother Asben, stayed, strolling among the tall cypress trees around the tombs. Grimpow waited close by, listening carefully to what they said.

The herbalist, a thin priest with pale skin and a sharp nose, spoke excitedly. 'I didn't know that a knight of the Templar Order was here in the valley on his way to the mountains.'

'No monk knew about it. And I am certain that not even the abbot was aware of it,' Brother Rinaldo replied.

'But Bulvar of Goztell assured us yesterday that the abbot had seen the fugitive Templar wandering the abbey's surroundings.'

'Do you truly believe all of the inquisitor's lies?' Brother Rinaldo remarked acidly.

'And who else could have killed the abbot last night?' retorted Brother Asben.

'I believe a better question to ask yourself is what the abbot could possibly have *known* to get himself killed.'

'I don't understand,' Brother Asben said, coming to an abrupt halt.

'The inquisitor spoke privately with the abbot the night he arrived at the abbey. In that meeting he explained why he was tirelessly chasing the Templar renegade. Stealing his secrets and treasures,' whispered Brother Rinaldo, looking discreetly around him.

Brother Asben snorted. 'The King of France long ago

seized the coffers full of silver and gold that the Knights Templar kept in their tower in Paris. It was the first thing he did after ordering the capture of all the *frères*.'

'I was referring to the legend's mystery,' clarified the old monk.

'The secret the nine knights discovered two centuries ago?' asked Brother Asben, sounding surprised.

'That's right. Bulvar told the abbot that Jacques de Molay confessed under torture that the secret was known only by a group of sages and that even he himself didn't know.'

'So the legend is true!' cried Brother Asben, wiping away a snowflake that had landed on his nose.

'So true that the same inquisitor of Lyon followed the fugitive Knight Templar into these mountains,' added the old monk.

'Do they think he has the clues to uncover the secret?'

'From what I've heard, he was carrying a message.'

Grimpow thought in a panic that Brother Rinaldo was about to tell Brother Asben everything he had divulged in their clandestine meetings in the secret library room but, to his surprise, the librarian didn't utter a word about that.

'I'm shocked that you're still alive, knowing as much as you do about this matter,' said the herbalist, sighing.

An ice-cold wind began to blow strongly over the abbey, bending the cypresses' treetops in the graveyard.

* * *

In the kitchen, an enormous pot simmered in the centre of the fireplace, releasing thick clouds of steam. It was lunchtime, and Grimpow's mouth watered at the mere thought of tasting the delicious stew.

'Hunger has always been a good bait to capture scoundrels!' exclaimed Brother Brasgdo when he saw Grimpow enter the kitchen. The cook smiled, his cheeks flushed by the heat. He motioned for Grimpow to sit at the table, and brought a steaming clay bowl brimming with the thick stew, a piece of bread and a pitcher of water.

'I'm sorry about Durlib,' he said, sitting by the young man's side. 'The soldiers have told me he jumped into an abyss in the mountains.'

'Yes, that's what Brother Rinaldo told me,' said Grimpow, saddened again.

Brother Brasgdo came closer so that nobody could hear him and whispered in Grimpow's ear, 'It's clear that the knight's ghost is up to his tricks: a fatal accident and a horrible crime.'

'Do you believe that both tragedies have been the work of the mysterious ghost?' Grimpow asked.

'As sure as death,' whispered the cook, kissing a cross hanging from his neck. 'I knew that that ghost would bring tragedy to the abbey, but I didn't want to believe it. Some of the brothers here claim that they've heard strange hissing sounds at night, like drowned whispers, and others say they've seen sinister shadows sliding down the roofs of the abbey. The calamities have only begun,' he continued in a low voice, 'like when at the close of the last millennium people feared the end of the world and ran terrified to escape the prophecy that predicted Satan's arrival, while plague, hunger and war took half of humanity's lives.'

When Grimpow remained silent, Brother Brasgdo continued, 'The inquisitor Bulvar of Goztell said yesterday that the abbot, may he rest in peace' – he crossed himself – 'was killed by the Knight Templar wandering around the abbey. But he is wrong if he thinks it is a being of flesh and blood like us. That errant spirit has come to settle a debt from his past and will not leave this haunted valley until he's done it. May God protect us from his killer dagger!' he exclaimed.

With this he took out a rabbit's foot and a head of garlic from his tunic's pocket and touched both of them to his forehead. Grimpow stifled his laughter and asked, 'Are you sure that a rabbit's foot and garlic will protect you from the ghost's sharp dagger?'

'I don't know a more effective remedy against the threats of evil spirits, but don't tell Brother Rinaldo any of this or he'll make me remain silent for more than a year as punishment for my sin,' confessed Brother Brasgdo.

'Don't fret; I'll be as discreet and mute as poor Kense. Do you know if he's recovered yet from his shock?' asked Grimpow.

'I brought him food in the infirmary some time ago and found him sleeping like a log on his cot. I think Brother Asben gave him a cup of linden tea last night mixed with a potion from his laboratory that's left him more dead than alive,' said the monk, chuckling.

Grimpow saw Kense again that very afternoon in the infirmary, when the tempest of wind and snow hit the abbey's rooftops with an apocalyptic noise. Brother Rinaldo had told him that since he had to stay with the monks until his future was decided in Durlib's absence, he could spend the afternoons helping Brother Asben in the infirmary and the mornings studying the subjects in the *trivium* and *quadrivium* in the library. The old monk told Grimpow that, if he didn't object, he would be his teacher, and Grimpow was delighted to accept. *Trivium* was the name the erudites gave to the three arts of eloquence – grammar, rhetoric and dialectic. The *quadrivium* dealt with the four mathematical arts – arithmetic, music, geometry and astronomy. And even though he was soon to learn the secrets of language and science from Brother Rinaldo, nothing would fascinate him more than the mysteries of alchemy Grimpow was to discover during his afternoon studies with Brother Asben.

The infirmary was located in the abbey's southeast wing, and it faced south so it could receive the warm rays of the sun on clear winter mornings. Brother Asben would say that there was no medicine as miraculous as the sun's light and warmth.

Next to the infirmary was the novices' hall, where the novices spent part of the afternoon praying in a small chapel. When they saw Grimpow walk by, some of the youngest monks looked at him with curiosity, and he could see in their clear eyes hints of envy for his freedom. They knew that Grimpow wasn't required to attend the religious services during every liturgical hour of the day, or remain in complete silence, or perform the abbey's manual labour, as they had to every morning after prime. They must have wondered what Grimpow was doing at the abbey. No doubt most of them yearned to live a life as free as his – for many of them had taken the habit following their parents' whims and not because of real religious vocation or divine calling.

Kense was lying on a straw mattress in the infirmary's entrance hall, under a wide window sealed with wooden shutters, behind which the wind roared like ghosts shrieking frenetically. The servant seemed to be sleeping, but he was startled upon hearing Grimpow's footsteps and stared at him terrified. Grimpow smiled at him, and to his surprise, his smile was returned with a gloomy but kind smile on Kense's face.

Brother Asben came to meet them from an adjoining room. There were several beds aligned under the infirmary's three windows, but only two were occupied by sick people. A young monk, who Grimpow later found out had broken his ankle when he fell from a ladder he had climbed to fix a leak in the abbey's roof, dozed in one of them. On the other bed Grimpow saw a mass covered by blankets. On it lay the motionless body of an aged, bearded monk who, from the way he looked at the vaulted ceiling, with his eyes staring at an invisible point, Grimpow assumed was blind. Brother Asben saw Grimpow's interest in the old monk and explained that he was the oldest brother in the abbey, nearly a hundred years of age. His name was Uberto of Alessandria.

The herbalist added that it was this ancient monk who had taught him everything he knew, yet the man had spent the last twenty years without moving or seeing beyond his thoughts.

Beyond the Stars

An ethereal smell of tin and burned sulphur enveloped Brother Asben's laboratory, which was located in a small courtyard next to the infirmary. The long, narrow room was lit with the day's light that squeezed itself through two small round openings in the wall. A pair of fat columns, blackened by the ovens' smoke, supported the low ceiling. The room was brimming with a multitude of transparent jars full of liquids of all colours. A variety of bottles, alembics, test tubes, crucibles, vials, trays, clay bowls and copper cauldrons were stuffed on shelves, piled on worktables, and stacked in every nook and cranny. A few manuscripts and parchment scrolls rested on a large, stained table in the middle of the room. Next to the parchment was a candleholder with five bent arms and several quill pens and inkwells. Everything in the room seemed to be covered with a patina of mystery as old as time.

Brother Asben didn't hide his enthusiasm for having Grimpow as his disciple. As soon as the boy entered his laboratory, he explained to him how the old monk had taught him about the illnesses of the body and soul, and about the herbs, plants, ointments, potions and brews that could heal them – even some poisons, in tiny doses, could have a salubrious effect. And like a scholar overwhelmed by the uncontrollable desire to show his medical knowledge to someone new, he talked to Grimpow extensively about death's most terrible weapons – tuberculosis, gangrene, tumours, smallpox, plague and leprosy.

Later, as the herbalist monk prepared a honey and mint syrup to clear the mucus in the lungs of the centenarian monk, he confessed his true passion to Grimpow: the mysterious art of alchemy. He had studied its secrets following Brother Uberto's teachings, until the explosion of an alembic sent shards of broken glass into the ancient monk's eyes, leaving him blind for ever.

'He lost his sight while he was looking for the philosopher's stone in this same laboratory?' asked Grimpow, interested in the story of the mysterious blind monk.

'Brother Uberto lost a lot more than that,' the herbalist replied sadly. 'Ever since the light disappeared from his eyes, so has his desire to live. He's lain in his bed night and day like a cataleptic, refusing to get up even when the abbot ordered him to. And despite threats as serious as excommunication, he has never since set foot on the ground – not even to go to the infirmary's privy.'

'And he doesn't talk either?' asked Grimpow.

'Only when he desires, and that rarely happens,' the monk answered. 'From what I remember, last time I heard him utter a word he cursed, and that was last winter. I think he is the only monk in the abbey who strictly follows our vow of silence.'

Grimpow accompanied Brother Asben to the room for the ill and watched him give the blind Brother Uberto of Alessandria a yellow liquid with a metal spoon. Grimpow observed the blind monk's white face, which despite being more than a hundred years old still preserved the features of a wise and noble man.

'You are surprised he doesn't look so old, aren't you?' Brother Asben asked Grimpow on their way back to the laboratory.

Grimpow nodded without saying a word, and the herbalist monk continued, 'Right before he had the accident that deprived him of the most beautiful of senses, Brother Uberto told me that he thought he had succeeded in creating the elixir of life, and – defying the Church's principles, and without fear of God's punishment – had drunk it, tempted by the idea of becoming immortal. When he was blinded the monks all believed that God had made the alembic explode because Brother Uberto had dared to challenge God's merciful power.'

'But it was only an accident! How could God be so cruel?' wondered Grimpow.

'Brother Rinaldo and I thought the same thing.'

'And did Brother Uberto ever reveal the formula he used to create the elixir?' asked Grimpow, burning with desire to know the answer.

Brother Asben shook his head. 'No, he never did, and if he had, it wouldn't have been of any use to me, for what matters to true alchemists is not the final result but what they learn on their quest. That's why every alchemist must find his own way in his effort to discover that brilliant and wise being that lives inside of him.'

'Brother Rinaldo told me that you spent many long nights in this laboratory trying to find the philosopher's stone. So you're not trying to transform crude metals into pure gold?' enquired Grimpow.

'Yes and no,' the monk said. 'It's true that I experiment with metals to try to make them as pure as gold, but it is not ambition that motivates me, nor riches that I desire. The extraordinary philosopher's stone that all alchemists long to find produces not gold, as many charlatans wrongly assume, but something intangible – like wisdom. The image of gold is merely a symbol, an allegory that represents the perfection of the soul – something true alchemists try to achieve through the knowledge that the alchemical process gives them. It's this knowledge that reveals nature's secrets. Alchemy's goal is to dominate matter, to transform and create it as God did when creating the world. This is what makes every time different from the one before and the one that will follow, and allows our lives and humanity's future to be so uncertain and fascinating.' Brother Asben cleared his throat and continued, 'Our only worry should be whether what is discovered serves the development of human beings and not their destruction. That's why our knowledge, research and discoveries are kept in absolute secrecy and can only be accessed by the initiated.'

'Is that why the Church considers alchemists heretics?'

'The Church and monarchs are only worried that someone will be able to create pure gold and become more powerful than the Pope. That is why they accused the Templar Order of heresy. The power and wealth that the order amassed threatened them.'

With the mention of the Knights Templar, Grimpow couldn't help thinking of the dead knight's magic stone again. Could the stone he possessed have been the beginning of all the legends formed throughout the years around the mythical philosopher's stone – the *lapis philosophorum*?

The tempest of wind and snow delayed for a few days his plan of going down to the cross in the valley where his and Durlib's treasure was located. But it didn't take Grimpow long to discover that the abbey's walls contained as many secrets as souls that inhabited it.

One morning close to midday, Grimpow was alone in the library, studying a treatise on astronomy by an Egyptian called Ptolemy, when he saw Kense's face peeking from behind a column. The servant motioned for him to follow.

Unable to restrain his curiosity, Grimpow left the manuscript he was reading and followed Kense.

They descended to the cloisters, passed the main hall and the abbot's quarters and headed for the noblemen's lodgings, where Kense opened a door that led to the servants' house, the vegetable garden and the farm. A strong wind lashed the trees and swirled the snowflakes over their heads, forcing them to squint.

'Where are we going?' called Grimpow, but obtained no reply.

He followed until Kense entered the stables, where, oblivious to the storm, at least a dozen purebred horses chewed happily on hay overflowing their troughs. They were all jet black, except for a single white one – the horse of the knight who had died in the mountains. Grimpow stepped closer to the white horse and, from its friendly look, realized that the animal was glad to see him – almost as if it already knew him. Grimpow patted the horse and then saw the scar on its back. The horse was branded with a sign Grimpow had seen before: just like the figure on the dead knight's letter and gold seal, the horse bore the mark of a snake biting its tail, forming a circle with its body.

'I thought the inquisitor took this horse with him,' said Grimpow, hoping that Kense would finally talk to him.

But Kense only pointed to the animal's hind legs, at the bandages covering them, and Grimpow realized that the wounds inflicted by the fangs of the beasts that attacked it in the valley hadn't healed and that Bulvar of Goztell must have been forced to leave the horse in the abbey's stables. Grimpow decided to ask Brother Rinaldo if he could take the animal for a walk as soon as the tempest of wind and snow ended, and thanked Kense for taking him there to see the horse. Upon hearing Grimpow's words, a satisfied smile appeared on Kense's lips, and the servant pulled Grimpow's sleeve, insisting that he follow him again. It wasn't the injured horse that Kense wanted to show him.

Kense walked to the end of the stables, where the top of a hay mound touched the thick ceiling's beams. He moved the hay aside and opened a trapdoor, revealing a hole as black and deep as a dry well. He easily slid in. Grimpow knew there was nothing to fear, so he followed him without hesitation in spite of the deep darkness they were entering. The trapdoor closed itself over their heads and, unable to see anything, they descended down an iron ladder attached to the hole's walls. Once downstairs, Kense lit a torch that allowed them to see in the shadows the narrow tunnel they were in. At the end of the long subterranean passage was a spacious cavern through which ran a dark stream. Pointy stalactites glimmered over them like transparent molluscs under the moonlight.

Kense walked toward what looked like an ancient wooden chest and motioned for Grimpow to come closer. He handed him the torch and removed the lid that covered the chest. Grimpow brought the torch's light to the open chest and was amazed to see a magnificent sword resting on the neatly folded attire of a knight: most likely the clothes

Brother Rinaldo had worn when he had arrived at the abbey of Brinkdum years ago to seek refuge in the mountain's solitude. The sword's handle was golden and covered with precious stones, similar to the ones in the daggers the dead knight had carried in his bag. A circle was engraved in its handle, with a red eight-pointed cross inside, and where the handle joined the iron blade was a small medallion of a galloping horseman raising a lance in the air.

Grimpow returned the torch to Kense and took the heavy sword in his hands. As soon as the handle touched his fingers, he clearly saw a series of images of Brother Rinaldo of Metz. His face hidden underneath a helmet with a visor, he was wearing chain mail and a white tunic with a great red cross embroidered on the chest – the same cross that was sewn on the shoulder of his white cloak, blazoned his large shield and crowned his sword's handle. He was riding a spirited black steed among a multitude of fleeing children and women, who shouted as they ran, enveloped by flames, and whom the monk mercilessly beheaded with his sword, intoxicated with blood, hatred and fury. Unable to bear that horrible vision of blood and death, Grimpow closed his eyes and threw the sword to the floor, frightening Kense. The servant looked at Grimpow confused and scared, as if he too had witnessed that gruesome massacre.

In spite of the cold, the snowstorm was followed by a clear and bright day. The mountain peaks pierced the northern horizon like sharp fangs wanting to devour the sky with a snap of their jaws, and the sun unhurriedly roamed the highest sky in its eternal journey from east to west. The snow weighed down the fir trees, making their branches hang low; to the south, by the waterfalls, a flock of vultures drew whimsical spirals over the valley, anticipating a succulent feast of carrion.

Grimpow told Brother Rinaldo that he was going to the stables to tend to the Knight Templar's wounded horse, and left the abbey as soon as the monks entered the dining hall. The main door was closed, but Kense had showed him how to reach the vegetable garden and the farm, and from there he only needed to jump over a small fence to be outside the abbey. He brought with him the dead knight's small dagger under his fur cloak and a strong desire to find out if Durlib had returned to the cross on the road.

He only had to climb down the snow-covered slope to find the winding road that led to the cross. Then it didn't take him long to spot it in a clearing among the fir trees. As he descended, driving his legs into the snow up to his knees, he noticed a number of zigzagging wolf tracks. Packs of hungry wolves climbed down from the mountains in winter in search of prey among the herds of sheep in the valley's villages, especially after hard snowfalls like the recent one. He hadn't remembered to take his bow and quiver from the pilgrims' hall when he left the abbey, and he regretted not having them.

The pedestal on which the cross stood was covered with

snow. Grimpow swept aside as much as he could until his hands went numb from the intense cold, then he took out the dagger and dug in the ground to reach the bag. It wasn't hard to find, but when he saw it lying there, in the same place Durlib had left it, he felt his heart turn to ice. If the bag was still there, it was clear that Durlib had not returned to take it, and that had to mean that he had indeed jumped to his death.

There in the snow Grimpow broke down and cried. Like an overflowing stream, all the tears he had suppressed in the hope of finding his friend alive poured from him freely. He remembered the day he'd met him at his uncle's tavern and had decided to leave with him to see the world, and how slowly, with time, Durlib became the father he had always wanted but never had.

But when Grimpow took the bag from the hole and opened it, surprise stopped his tears. Neither the remainder of the silver coins nor the dead knight's jewels were in it. He rummaged with his frozen hands in the leather bag to make sure that his eyes weren't betraying him, and discovered that next to the parchment and gold seal was a sprig of rosemary that hadn't been there before. A cry of happiness escaped his throat, and he listened as it echoed off the mountains. Then he shouted again – so loudly that if Durlib was still hiding in the nearby forests, he probably would have heard him – because Grimpow had no doubt now that his friend was alive. The rosemary he found in the bag proved it so. Durlib must have remembered that that was the amulet Grimpow's mother hung around his neck when he was a child. The rosemary sprig was a message. Only he could have put the rosemary sprig in the bag and taken the jewels and silver coins. Grimpow took the letter and gold seal and placed the empty bag in the hole again. He was sure his friend would come back to find out if he had received his secret message, and to rule out any doubts that it had been he who'd opened the bag, he picked up a small stone from the hole, similar in size to the dead knight's one, and placed it in the leather bag. He was sure Durlib would also understand his message and wouldn't take long in coming back to the abbey for their reunion.

Such was Grimpow's happiness that when he returned to the abbey, he ran straight to the kitchen to tell Brother Brasgdo the good news. But, to his surprise, the cook monk already knew about it.

'How could you know that?' asked Grimpow, confused.

The cook monk held a ladle full of soup to his lips, sipped with pleasure, and put the ladle back in the pot simmering on the stove.

'Durlib was here after midmorning prayers, when the monks were busy with their duties and you were studying with Brother Rinaldo in the library,' he said, as if he found it hard to talk about it. Brother Brasgdo was looking at the kitchen's floor, trying to avoid Grimpow's eyes.

'And why didn't you tell me? You knew very well how eager I've been to see him again!' reproached Grimpow, furious.

'Durlib begged me not to tell you he had been here,' he said with distress. 'He thought it would be better for you not to see him.'

'How is it possible that Durlib didn't want to see me? He knew that I was expecting his return! We have to continue our journey to the end of the world! He said it himself the night we reached the abbey, don't you remember?' shouted Grimpow, full of anger and sadness.

Brother Brasgdo walked closer to Grimpow and put his warm hand on the boy's shoulder.

'Grimpow, Grimpow, boy,' he said hesitatingly. 'Your friend Durlib didn't want you to keep leading the life he was burdened with – the life of a vagrant and outlaw. He told me that during the days he spent in the solitude of the mountains after having almost died in the hands of the inquisitor Bulvar of Goztell, he thought about your future and arrived at the conclusion that if you stayed by his side, you would never be rid of poverty and ignorance and would end up one day hanged in the square of some godforsaken village.'

Grimpow remembered then that when he first touched the stone of the dead knight, he foresaw some fascinating and tragic changes in his life, and at that moment a strong curiosity for knowledge about everything around him had been born inside him. He was glad he'd come to the abbey of Brinkdum and met Brother Rinaldo of Metz, the librarian who could teach him so much about nature and the cosmos; but deep inside, he was still the same cheerful and rebellious rascal who freely wandered villages and roads, with no more worries about the future but the hope of being alive with every new sunrise. Had he been able to choose, he never would have traded life by Durlib's side, despite its miseries, for all the wealth and knowledge in the world.

'But I never wanted to leave him! Durlib is my only real friend!' he said, crying again.

'Durlib decided it was better for you to part ways now that you had grown used to living without him. He is convinced that in this abbey you'll learn everything he would never be able to teach you, and you'll be able to find your own way in life. He asked me to tell you never to stop searching for that magical road you dreamed of one day, and if you ever found it, to think of him as if he were by your side.'

Grimpow thought that was Durlib's way of telling him to not stop trying if he decided to continue the mission of the knight who died in the mountains – that's why he hadn't taken the letter or the gold seal. The silver coins and jewels would be enough for Durlib to begin a new life away from poverty.

'But why didn't *he* tell me all of that? At least I could have said goodbye,' he complained.

'He feared that if he saw you again he wouldn't have the courage to abandon you here,' said Brother Brasgdo, somewhat more cheerful.

Grimpow resignedly accepted that Durlib had decided

they shouldn't see each other again and wanted to avoid showing the sadness that he knew would linger in his heart for many days.

'And Durlib didn't tell you where he was thinking of going or what he'd decided to do from now on?' he asked.

'He only said that he wanted to see the ocean, to prove if sirens really exist.'

The next morning, Grimpow asked Brother Rinaldo if he had ever seen the ocean. Melancholy flooded the old monk's eyes, and he explained that the ocean was like an enormous lake without shores, that it was sometimes green like emeralds and at other times bluer than the sky. He told him that the ocean could look asleep when it was calm or be as terrible as Hell when its gigantic waves curled, mercilessly wolfing down any ships that dared challenge them.

'And did you ever see a siren in the ocean?' asked Grimpow, recalling what Durlib had announced to Brother Brasgdo.

'Ah, a creature with the body of a woman and the tail of a fish . . . No, in my voyages at sea I was never fortunate enough to come across one of those beings of which sailors tell fabulous legends.' The old monk walked toward the secret chamber of forbidden books and returned with a thick manuscript titled *Liber Monstrorum* that he placed on the desk. He opened it and flipped through its pages until he found a wondrous illustration of a young lady of unusual beauty, whose golden mane of hair fell on her shoulders like a waterfall of gold filaments. Under her navel, the woman's body turned into the shimmering silver tail of a fish, resting placidly on the rocks of a cliff. Next to the image, a column of text in Latin read: *The sirens are sea maidens who seduce sailors with their striking figures and sweet singing. From head to navel, they have a female body and are identical to human beings; but they have the scaly tails of fish, with which they swim to the depths of the ocean.*

Grimpow stared at the half-fish, half-human creature as Brother Rinaldo told him a story he'd heard on one of his journeys. The story claimed that an expedition of Christian Crusaders who were headed by sea to the Holy Land were dragged to an unknown island by a powerful tempest. On the island the stranded voyagers clearly heard the whispering, singing and giggles of sirens. Seduced by their sweet voices, the Crusaders surrendered to the temptation of loving them, and they were never heard of again until years later a ship of Venetian merchants arrived at the mysterious island and found the knights' skeletons, dressed in their best attire, scattered around the rocks.

Grimpow was disturbed by this legend, for if Durlib's goal was to find the sirens, he feared his friend would encounter in the ocean the death he had escaped in the mountains. But the old monk calmed him down, telling him that beautiful sirens such as the ones illustrated in the book before their eyes were surely nothing but an illusion, symbolizing the dangers of lust and the flesh, which had brought so many misfortunes to men since Adam was tempted by Eve.

Grimpow spent the morning browsing the many images in that bestiary. He discovered such fantastical creatures as the unicorn, the centaur, the dragon and the basilisk, a mythical animal that could kill a person with a mere glance. But Brother Rinaldo assured Grimpow that, as with the siren, all those beings and legends were nothing but fantasies created by humans from the beginnings of time to represent all the magic and mystery in the universe.

Grimpow spent the following days studying old manuscripts in the abbey's library and found that indeed, earlier inhabitants of the earth had used those myths of divine and fantastical beings to explain the wonders around them, establishing the sky as the home of gods, the earth as the home of animals and humans, and its dark depths as the home of monsters and demons. For them, everything that happened in each of those worlds was chaotic and random, and only the gods could bring order to the uncertain outcome of those events. However, he also found out that, with the invention of writing, which made it possible to preserve and share ideas across time and great distances, some sages had changed their perception of nature and the universe, arriving at the conclusion that the phenomena around them weren't a product of the gods' whims but followed constant laws contained in things themselves, the ultimate essence of which humans could discover.

But nothing surprised Grimpow more than studying the

mathematical theories of a Greek sage named Pythagoras. Pythagoras had founded a school for young sages in Crotone. These students were called Pythagoreans, and their knowledge and teachings were kept in the utmost secrecy. Without knowing why, Grimpow had the feeling that the dead knight's stone he now carried had a lot to do with those mysterious sages of olden days.

One snowy afternoon Grimpow went to see Brother Asben in the infirmary. Tranquillity had finally returned to the abbey after the uproar and fear the brutal murder of the abbot had caused among the monks. Everyone had gone back to their tasks and prayers, evidently including the young monk who had broken his ankle, for when Grimpow walked by his cot, he wasn't in the infirmary any more.

He was walking past Brother Uberto's cot on his way to Brother Asben's laboratory when he heard a voice behind him that paralyzed him like a snake's bite.

'That stone could end up killing you!'

Grimpow turned his head and realized that the only people in the infirmary were Brother Uberto and himself. Even though the blankets shielding the elderly monk from the cold prevented Grimpow from seeing his face, the boy assumed it was he who had spoken.

'What do you mean?' answered Grimpow, walking over to the monk's cot. 'I don't understand.'

'You can't fool me,' Brother Uberto said. 'Since I first heard your footsteps in this room, where even the putrefaction of illness is invisible to me, I knew you had the stone with you. In the darkness of my blind eyes I felt its light – like a star's brightness in the middle of the night. I've been waiting since then for the privacy to speak with you.'

'I don't know what you are talking about. I think you're confused,' Grimpow hedged, unable to believe that the blind monk could have deduced that he carried the stone in the linen pouch hanging around his neck.

'I am talking about the wise men's stone – the *lapis philosophorum*, if you'd rather call it that,' said the monk dryly.

'I don't have any stones, and least of all the alchemists' philosopher's stone,' Grimpow insisted as he sat on the cot next him, to better see the blind monk's inexpressive face, almost hidden under his long white beard.

'I can feel it closer now; denying it is useless,' the old man said, sounding pleased.

'I think you are delusional. I'd better tell Brother Asben so he can give you your medicine,' said Grimpow, to avoid the old monk's accusations.

'My only delusion was to desire that stone so much that I went mad because of it,' he replied emphatically.

'I see that you really have lost your mind. You speak of the philosopher's stone as if it were a beautiful lady to whom you gave your love.'

'I wouldn't have desired it so much if it had been a woman,' said the monk. 'I always followed my vow of

108

chastity and have never been tempted by the pleasures of the flesh.'

'However, you have looked for the philosopher's stone until you lost your sight and mind because of it, so you didn't follow your vow of poverty. What were you planning to do with the gold you obtained in your laboratory?' asked Grimpow, trying to extract more information from him. He reasoned that if the monk could deduce he had the wise men's stone, he must also know a lot about it.

'Gold is nothing compared to God's power!' Brother Uberto said emphatically, moving his body under the blankets for the first time. 'There was a time in which I had the *lapis philosophorum* and I had the pure heart of an exceptional disciple. There was no question I couldn't answer or secret I couldn't uncover in my mind. It was like climbing up to the confines of Heaven and sitting next to God to enjoy contemplating a universe without mysteries, where everything was explainable and comprehensible, as it was in the beginning for the Creator.'

Grimpow himself had felt the magical power of the stone, which hinted at all the knowledge in the world – what was already known and what would be discovered in the future. There was no doubt that Brother Uberto of Alessandria knew very well what he was talking about.

'So did you achieve absolute wisdom?' he asked.

'Not completely, but enough to not want anything else in my life. While I used the stone with the goal of achieving wisdom, I wrote tirelessly about all the branches of knowledge – astronomy, arithmetic, geometry, alchemy, medicine, botany, mineralogy and harmony . . . The most accurate arguments and the most complex theses were at the reach of my quill, as close as the fruits of a tree were to my fingertips. And I owed everything to the philosopher's stone. It was my drive and inspiration.'

'I've seen numerous books written by you in the library,' said Grimpow.

'But despite my access to knowledge, I made a mistake typical of the worst of the ignorant.'

'You made a mistake?'

'I became greedy and tried to use the stone to create gold and reach immortality. I betrayed all my values and beliefs. Carried away by my greed and arrogance, I shut myself in the abbey's laboratory and spent sleepless days and nights until one morning, anxious to move the transmutation forward, I heated an alembic so much that it exploded before my eyes and I lost the gift of sight for ever.'

'Brother Asben told me what happened to you, but I believe it was only an accident, one that could have happened to any alchemist,' Grimpow said to console him.

'It's possible,' admitted the blind monk, 'but the only truth is that my eyes dried up and with them all my ambitions. I've been lying on this bed for more than twenty years without being able to see any light other than that of my mind, and without any company other than my memories. Throughout these years I haven't thought of anything besides the mystery of the philosopher's stone.

And I know now that it is impossible to create it in any laboratory other than the soul. If you forget this, the stone will finish you, just as it has finished me and so many others who've coveted it, for as in everything else in life, in it exists both good and evil.'

'Why do you say that it is impossible to create the stone in a laboratory?' asked Grimpow.

The blind monk seemed to hesitate, but after an instant of deep silence said, 'The only philosopher's stone that exists now and has always existed is the one that two thousand years ago was in the hands of the magi in Babylon, Egypt, Greece . . . It's the stone possessed by ancient sages such as Thales of Miletus, Pythagoras, Homer, Parmenides, Ptolemy, Socrates, Plato and Aristotle, as well as all their disciples who followed them in their schools and secret societies. Never since then have human beings made such a great effort to explain the world. Our time, however, is dark and rotten, and dominated by fear and superstition, hunger and poverty, disease and death.' He sighed like a dejected prophet.

Hearing the names of the Greek sages whose manuscripts Grimpow had studied in the abbey's library made him ecstatic. It confirmed that the stone he possessed had much to do with them, as he had assumed days before. So he asked, 'And how did that stone reach the hands of those sages?'

'If anyone knew that, there would be no secret to uncover. That mystery's solution is beyond the stars,' concluded Brother Uberto of Alessandria, and with that, the conversation was over. The blind monk refused to speak another word, and Grimpow never heard his voice again.

The Alchemists' Gold

Days went by, and slowly winter left and spring arrived. Soon there were no traces of snow left near the abbey, and grass began to sprout in the nearby meadows, painting the mountains' slopes a deep green.

With the arrival of spring Grimpow's daily duties in the abbey changed. Every morning, from six o'clock to nine o'clock, he studied with Brother Rinaldo in the library. Then he ran to the stables and saddled the Knight Templar's horse, which he had named Star, and rode to the valley's waterfalls, or climbed up the frozen glaciers to gaze at the horizon. He missed Durlib, and he hadn't given up hope of finding him. Since they'd parted ways, there hadn't been a single day when Grimpow didn't think of him.

After the abbot's murder, the monks had gathered in the main hall to appoint his successor and discuss other matters of the abbey, among which was Grimpow's future as a novice. Several monks suggested that he take the brown habit and observe the rule of silence and liturgical hours like any other young monk in the abbey. But Brother Rinaldo deemed it more appropriate that, for several months at least, Grimpow devote his time to studying in the library and helping Brother Asben in the infirmary. If it was then his desire to join the brotherhood, he could take the habit as a novice. Brother Rinaldo's suggestion was accepted unanimously and ratified by the new abbot – a serene-looking monk, with grey eyes and a pale complexion, who was well respected in the abbey for his good sense and kindness.

Even though Grimpow wasn't present during the monks' discussions, he could hear them from the adjoining room. Brother Rinaldo had revealed to him a section in the stone wall where he only had to place his ear to be able to hear everything that was being said in the main hall. Soon Grimpow discovered that there was a similar secret point in every room in the abbey, including the abbot's quarters. The old monk confessed that this was how he had been able to discover the inquisitor Bulvar of Goztell's schemes and his confession to the now-dead abbot about the Knight Templar and the secret of the wise. Brother Rinaldo had known of this unusual acoustic resource since it was revealed to him by his predecessor in the library, who in turn had learned about it from his predecessor, and he from his own predecessor, and on and on, back to the very creation of the abbey. Grimpow had no doubt that this was how the secret of the wise had been passed down as well from generation to generation, and he wondered if the knight who died in the mountains might have been the last of them, leaving Grimpow the only person left aware of the existence of the stone.

As soon as the weather was warm enough, Brother Rinaldo began to leave the abbey after the final service on clear nights to continue his astronomical observations from a hill nearby. For years, he had been writing a voluminous treatise on astronomy called *Theorica Planetarum*, which he told Grimpow he wanted to finish before God decided to bring the monk to his side. Grimpow accompanied him every night and helped him carry the astrolabe – a curious brass instrument that allowed them to observe and record the stars' different positions in the sky.

Each night, when he'd finished his observations, Brother Rinaldo would draw charts of what he'd observed that evening. He'd record a star's position and the time, and then would copy them the next day in Latin into the manuscript he was writing. It wasn't long until Grimpow learned how to use the device on his own.

One moonless night, while Grimpow contemplated some shooting stars crossing the sky, Brother Rinaldo unrolled a scroll of parchment he carried in his hand. It was a beautiful circular planisphere in which was painted the sky's dome.

'All the stars above us now are gathered here. Sit down and see for yourself. Look at the sky and at the map.'

Grimpow followed Brother Rinaldo's suggestion, and once seated on the hill's damp pastures, he raised the planisphere with one arm until he could see both the real starry night sky and the parchment the monk had given him, full of phosphorescent dots as if he had the whole sky trapped in his hands. Each dot was connected by a straight line to the other stars in its constellation, and next to each, written in luminescent ink, was its name. It didn't take Grimpow long to locate the strong light of Venus in both skies. Then he spotted Saturn and Jupiter, and the stars Betelgeuse and Bellatrix in the Orion constellation. He could find the Castor star to the east and Rigel to the west. And as he gazed at the real sky and at the fake one, his eyes began to cross – flashing dozens of sparks around the sky like disoriented fireflies.

'Isn't it marvellous?' asked Brother Rinaldo, sitting by his side.

For weeks Grimpow had been contemplating the starry sky and he'd succumbed to its haunting beauty. He had spent his days in the library reading everything he could find about the earth, the sun, the planets, their moons and the stars, and all the mysteries surrounding the universe's darkness. There was much still unknown – but he knew deep in his soul that humans would one day understand it in its entirety, even if thousands of years had to go by first.

'Someday men will travel around the heavenly bodies as naturally as they ride their horses today,' he said without taking his eyes off the starry night sky.

'What you've said is a sacrilege,' said Brother Rinaldo, looking at Grimpow from the corner of his eye as if he were a possessed person. 'Only God can inhabit the ethereal cosmos.' But the monk fell silent, perhaps pondering what the boy had said. Finally he added hesitantly, 'Perhaps you're right. There are eyes that can see beyond our time, entering the far future like the prophets, and yours seem to have some sort of extraordinary nature since you found the dead knight's body in the mountains. I don't know why I'm surprised by what you say.'

'It has nothing to do with prophecy and everything to do with science,' said Grimpow. 'About a month ago, before the end of winter, I spoke with Brother Uberto of Alessandria at the infirmary, and he said something that helped me understand it.'

'You talked to Brother Uberto? He hasn't spoken to any-one for years – not since he went blind. What did he say?' asked Brother Rinaldo, sounding eager to hear anything the ancient monk had uttered.

'He talked of the philosopher's stone and the sages, and he assured me that the mysterious origin of the so-called *lapis philosophorum* is beyond the stars.'

'Brother Uberto is insane. Only God is beyond the stars!' exclaimed the monk, his expression troubled.

'You told me yourself that it was hard to believe in God when humans had started to explain themselves and every-thing around them,' Grimpow replied.

Brother Rinaldo looked anxious. 'The fact that it is

sometimes difficult for me to believe in God doesn't mean that I deny his existence. If I stopped believing in him, I wouldn't be able to continue living. A monk's life has no meaning if he doesn't pray every day to praise God's greatness.'

'Perhaps there's not much difference between what we're talking about. Perhaps what is God for you is the same as wisdom for me. After all, they both have the same meaning – they're just viewed from a different angle. You think that God created the world without having explained it, while I think that wisdom explains the world without having created it,' said Grimpow.

'I believe that during these past weeks you've learned more than is good for a boy your age. But don't forget that there will always be one question you will not be able to answer.'

Grimpow waited as Brother Rinaldo finished making annotations in the star charts. He wanted to hear *which* question had no answer. But the librarian monk remained silent and lost in his observations of the immense sky above them, as if Grimpow wasn't there.

'What's the question without an answer?' Grimpow finally asked, breaking the silence.

The monk stopped what he was doing and looked at the boy next to him. 'How did it all begin? And where did it all start? If you don't believe in God, you'll never be able to explain it,' he said.

'Nor does believing in God answer that question,'

Grimpow insisted. 'It only adds another question: who created God? And if we admit that humans created God to explain the world, it is then a contradiction to think that God also created humans,' he argued, delighted to be able to engage in a debate on such complex matters.

'Right, but at least God gives me comfort in my ignorance.'

'Your ignorance doesn't let you appreciate the absurdity of your arguments,' said Grimpow, knowing that something beyond himself was speaking for him.

'You might be right,' said the librarian monk. 'Human beings' minds and imagination are mysterious and surprising. Without them, everything we have learned about ourselves and the universe wouldn't have been possible. Deprive people of their dreams and imagination and you will have the most primitive and dull-witted animals on earth.'

Grimpow couldn't fall asleep that night. When the inquisitor had left the abbey, the boy had been moved from the secret room to a straw mattress in the hall for the novice monks. That night when he lay down the novices were already asleep. The bells would be chiming again soon, announcing the early morning worship, and they needed their rest. Grimpow silently curled himself under his blankets and thought of all that had happened since he found the dead knight in the mountains. He knew a lot more now than he had then, not only about nature and the universe but also about the mysterious stone he carried around his neck.

He had arrived at the conclusion that the miraculous stone was older than anyone could imagine, and that it had been passed down throughout the centuries in utmost secrecy until it had reached the hands of the knight whose body he had found. Grimpow even doubted that the knight was actually a Templar – he was convinced that the man had been a sage, beyond weapons, wars and religions – though he still believed the legend of the Temple of Solomon's nine knights and the valuable object they'd discovered and later hidden. And it seemed obvious that the Pope and the King of France coveted the stone at any price – even murder.

Grimpow had also decided that the philosopher's stone the alchemists were trying to create in their laboratories was not the one he carried. He had no proof his stone could transform a metal as poor as lead into gold.

Until one afternoon when Grimpow made an interesting discovery. He had spent the day with Brother Asben studying, and in the afternoon the herbalist monk started to prepare for an experiment.

'Let's imagine we are in ancient Greece and have stepped into the laboratory of one of the first known alchemists,' said Brother Asben as he prepared the burner and the flask. The brother had spent the morning teaching Grimpow about one of the many methods of the alchemical process in an old manuscript titled *Physika kai*

Mystica, and decided it was time to attempt transmutation.

He took four glass canisters from a shelf and extracted from each of them a small amount of lead, tin, copper and iron.

'These are the four minerals left after subtracting from the seven known minerals the two noble minerals, gold and silver, and what is known as the transition metal – mercury.'

He placed the metals in the flask, and as they heated up they began to melt, slowly forming a pungent-smelling black paste.

'This is called original matter. It's what we get once we've combined the metals – a thick paste as dark as the night from which the day is born.'

'Or like the sky's darkness from which light arises,' said Grimpow, remembering the message carried by the dead knight in the mountains.

'That's right. I'm glad to see you understand,' said the herbalist monk, not knowing that Grimpow was referring to other matters completely. Then he added, 'But we will go even further and add silver to our poor blend of metals.'

As he said this, he took another jar and with a small metal spoon scooped out some silver dust, then added it to the flask, stirring the mixture slowly.

'Now let's wait until this silver takes effect and blossoms – and what's hidden will reveal itself,' he said mysteriously. 'And while we wait, let's also look at some of this unusual metal that's neither liquid nor solid.'

'Mercury!' said Grimpow.

'Indeed, Grimpow,' the herbalist monk admitted, wrinkling his kind face while he submerged the flask's paste in mercury.

Grimpow watched as the dark paste slowly turned into a piece of silver – beautiful and perfect – and began to swell before his eyes.

'Though it contains trace amounts of the metal and shares its noble appearance, this silver is as false as Judas was,' the herbalist monk said with a smile, clearly proud of the fast transmutation he'd obtained. 'And it's capable of fooling even the Pope's very treasurer in his Avignon fortress.'

He took the silver piece out of the flask with a pair of thin, long pliers and dropped it in a washbowl with cold water, producing a spurt of steam that rapidly subsided with a weak hissing sound. He wrapped the cooled piece with a cotton cloth and rubbed it until it was completely dry.

'Now we must try to conclude our great work successfully,' he said, sighing, 'adding a bit of gold dust and introducing this silver piece to the *theion hydor* or holy water, called by many alchemists "the gods' water".'

He inserted the fake piece in the flask once more and returned it to the heat, waiting until it melted again. He then added a small amount of gold dust to a separate flask of holy water and looked at his student. 'Until now I haven't obtained more than a yellowish dye, which even the most naive of men wouldn't believe is gold,' he admitted.

While they waited for the divine water to acquire the necessary qualities to perform the miracle of the transmutation of silver into gold, Brother Asben told Grimpow that an ancient master alchemist, Zosimus, had discovered the miraculous water through the distillation of hens' eggs in the flask. 'I am sure that the eggs Zosimus mentions in his work are nothing more than symbols,' he added.

But that was something that Grimpow already knew, for in the manuscripts he had read in the library, there were plenty of references to symbolic figures that represented the alchemical process – sun, moon, planets, lovers, dragons, serpents. Even the alchemists' symbol – the ouroboros – was a serpent swallowing its tail, forming a circle. That was the sign on the gold seal the Templar had carried, and the sign branded on the back of his horse.

When the heavenly water was free from impurities, the small herbalist monk poured the flask's liquid into a pot and performed a quiet ritual, then added the piece of silver. Gradually the piece of fake silver began to acquire a yellowish colour.

'Is this the alchemical gold?' whispered Grimpow in disbelief.

The herbalist monk sighed, disappointed. 'Giving that name to this fake yellowish silver would be granting it a virtue it unfortunately does not possess.'

It was at that moment that the abbey's tower bells chimed, announcing the evening prayer. Brother Asben excused himself and left for the chapel, leaving the piece of silver in the container and Grimpow alone in the laboratory with the instruction to clean up their disappointing experiment. As he worked by himself, putting away the canisters and instruments that were scattered around the work surfaces and table, he decided to do a little experiment of his own. He took the stone from the linen pouch around his neck and put it in the gods' water the herbalist monk had meticulously prepared.

Grimpow watched as the stone burned like molten rock from an active volcano, and the heavenly water began to boil again like water in a haunted cauldron. Gradually the piece of yellowish silver Brother Asben had left in the flask acquired a beautiful, bright golden colour, stronger than the colour of the sun shining in the skies . . .

It Was the Sun's Wish to
Win the Moon's Heart

Gradually a pressure was growing inside Grimpow. A voice stronger than the force of reason was urging him to abandon the abbey to try to uncover the secret of the wise himself as soon as possible.

Grimpow knew that very soon he, like his friend Durlib, would leave.

The first pilgrims from the north arrived at the abbey at the beginning of April and with them came the news that the Templar Order's Grand Master had been burned alive at the stake, along with other Knights Templar. Before dying, Jacques de Molay had cursed both the Pope and the King of France, proclaiming that they too would die within a year.

One dark day, the skies crackling with the luminous claws of lightning, Grimpow watched from the library's window as a group of noblemen dressed in colourful attire arrived, followed by an entourage of pages and servants. Attracted by the hustle and bustle, he went down to the cloisters and walked from there to the lodgings to help Kense and the other servants. Under Brother Brasgdo's relentless and intimidating orders they were already helping the newly arrived pilgrims settle into their quarters. The cook monk's belly swayed from side to side as he bowed and greeted the ladies and damsels getting off the carriages. Grimpow was about to ask him what he could do to help in that jumble of coffers and chests when he saw, alighting from a carriage, a young lady adorned with wreaths of flowers, her eyes as clear and transparent as two drops of water. The young lady noticed the boy who stood staring at her, and smiled, sending Grimpow's thoughts scattering like a flock of birds taken by surprise, and turning his cheeks red. Brother Brasgdo caught their exchange of glances and ordered Grimpow to return to the library to continue studying before the Devil crossed his path and tempted him with impure and sinful feelings. Grimpow grudgingly obeyed and returned to the library, though he spent the afternoon daydreaming, staring off into space, and prowling around the noblemen's lodgings, searching for a glimpse of the girl again. But just as the body of the mysterious knight in the mountains had vanished into thin air, so had she.

The pilgrims had crossed the Alps from the northeast to the south, following the route that united the region of Ullpens with the road leading to the faraway French abbey of Vezelay. There they joined other pilgrims from Germany or Paris and made their way to the lands of Spain to do penance and purify their sins at the tomb of Saint James of Compostela.

Pilgrims from nearby regions came as well, lured to the abbey by the miraculous reputation of the skull and bones of Saint Dustan. Saint Dustan had been the first hermit monk to arrive in the valley of Brinkdum, when only wolves and bears inhabited the forests. He built a small wooden hermitage in which he would live in seclusion, away from all human contact. Legends said that his real name was Dustan of Guillol, and that he had been a pilgrim himself in the time of the First Crusade. Along with Peter the Hermit and his army of impoverished adventurers, fugitives and paupers, he had travelled to Jerusalem in hopes of finding the end to their miseries and the salvation of their souls in the Holy Land. Unfortunately, they found only the face of death hidden behind the sinister veils of epidemics, famine and the Muslims' sharp swords.

Dustan of Guillol was one of the few survivors who came back from that Hell to recount the mishaps. He travelled through towns and villages on a donkey, haggard-faced and barefoot, preaching holy war against the infidel, inspiring anyone who heard him. One day, though, Dustan of Guillol disappeared from the roads, and nobody heard from him again. Years went by until a group of monks crossing the mountains found his dirty hermitage in the middle of the forest and, inside, his naked bones piled up on his bed.

Mesmerized by the beauty of the mountains, those monks decided to stay in the valley of Brinkdum and build an abbey. There they would guard the hermit's skeleton in the crypt. Soon the abbey became known as miraculous throughout the Ullpens region thanks to the relics of the saintly preacher of the Crusades buried in it.

Grimpow was surprised that the Church would canonize those who made such an effort to kill their fellow men. The next morning, as he watched out the window for the girl amid the pilgrims rushing to get ready to resume their journey to Compostela, he asked Brother Rinaldo, 'If God proclaims in the Bible that human beings should love each other, why did the Church preach the Crusades to conquer the Holy Land and kill the infidels?'

The old monk said nothing, evidently caught off guard by his disciple's question and frustrated at having to answer something so difficult.

Grimpow went on, 'Brother Brasgdo told me that Saint Dustan spent half of his life riding a donkey through towns and villages, proclaiming that God had spoken to him and told them to urge all Christians on earth to liberate the Holy Land of Jerusalem, killing any infidels who got in their way or were opposed to their purpose.'

'Brother Brasgdo is unable to keep his mouth shut unless there's a chance it will be sewn up for what he's said,' grumbled the old monk angrily.

'Is it true, then?' insisted Grimpow. He was upset about the church's contradiction, but also sad. As he watched out the window he realized that the caravan of pilgrims was moving away and he hadn't ever seen the girl again.

Brother Rinaldo thought for a moment, then answered, 'Three hundred years ago, Christianity fell into an unjustifiable religious fanaticism. They decided then to recover the Holy Sepulchre from the Muslims, who they felt were not treating it with any respect, and that God wanted it that way.'

'And did God tell them to sacrifice so many lives?' asked Grimpow, knowing that he was putting Brother Rinaldo on the spot again.

But the monk answered immediately. 'God spoke to Christians through Pope Urban the Second, who was his visible head on earth then. After the first millennium, everyone wanted to go to Jerusalem because they thought that the Kingdom of Heaven was there. But when pilgrims journeyed to these holy lands they were attacked by the Muslims. The Pope urged all noblemen and knights to take up their swords in defence of the pilgrims. In the year 1095 the Pope proclaimed the First Crusade in the Council of Claremont. He shouted to them, "Go, brothers of Christ, go and attack the enemies of God who have usurped our Lord's Holy Sepulchre!"' As the old monk recited the Pope's words he seemed to recover the vitality and strength of his days as a Knight Templar.

'You told me you participated in the Eighth Crusade. How many were there?' asked Grimpow.

'The Muslims never stopped lashing our fortresses in the

Holy Land, and it was necessary to recover them time after time. It was almost two centuries of bloody and never-ending battles,' said Brother Rinaldo with grief.

'Is that why you killed those women and children, beheading them with your sword?' said Grimpow, needing to know if what he had seen in the cavern was truth.

Brother Rinaldo staggered back a step when he heard Grimpow's statement, and looked at him in utter disbelief.

'How can you know that?' he whispered, trembling.

'Kense showed me your sword and the robes you wore as a Knight Templar. When I picked up the sword, I saw the massacre in my mind as clearly as I can see you now.'

The old monk sat down heavily and let out a resounding sigh. 'I will answer your question – but only if you promise to be as honest when I ask you one.'

'Sounds fair,' said Grimpow.

There was a brief silence that seemed an eternity to both.

'At the time,' the monk began, 'I was convinced I would reach Heaven by killing those helpless people. I believed it was God's will to eradicate the infidels, even if they were only women and children.' He was clearly troubled by his memories.

'Were you that blind to believe so many lies?' asked Grimpow reproachfully.

'Faith can blur the judgment of the most sensible of men, but believe me, I've paid for my faults,' concluded the monk sadly.

Grimpow didn't agree with his answer about faith, but the monk's explanations had told him what he wanted to know, so he said: 'Now, you can ask me your question.'

Brother Rinaldo cleared his throat and asked, 'Did you help Brother Asben in his transmutation of base metals into pure gold in his laboratory?' He looked deep into Grimpow's eyes, as if expecting them to prove the sincerity of the young man's answer.

'Yes,' said Grimpow simply, hoping that a brief affirmation would be enough for the librarian monk.

'Well, you've almost driven Brother Asben mad. When he saw the piece of gold in his flask he thought he'd found the ultimate formula for alchemical transmutation. He's been desperately trying to reproduce it in his laboratory day and night but has had no success. How did you do it?'

Grimpow thought about lying to the old monk, but he had made a promise and knew he had to fulfil it. He took the stone from the linen pouch around his neck and held it out to Brother Rinaldo. The monk looked into the boy's palm and stared at the stone, as fascinated as if Grimpow had shown him a relic of the cross on which Jesus was crucified.

'I put this stone in the gods' water Brother Asben prepared in the flask.'

'May I examine it?' the monk asked, extending his hand.

Grimpow offered him the stone, and the librarian monk brought it closer to his eyes to see it better. He whispered: 'So it is only this.'

'What do you mean?'

'This insignificant mineral is without a doubt the legendary philosopher's stone – the stone capable of turning lead into gold and men into sages,' said the monk. 'Where did you find it? Did the Knight Templar have it?' he asked, giving the stone back to Grimpow.

'Yes. He had it in his hand when Durlib and I found him on the snow,' the boy confessed. 'Durlib thought it was only a simple amulet and gave it to me. He told me that this stone would be tied to my destiny.'

'And he was right. Durlib realized that your destiny was very different from his, and that's why he left you in the abbey. You've learned everything I can teach you here, and I have no doubt that you are already wiser than many sages I've known throughout my long life. But perhaps it is time now for you to begin your own journey to the city of Strasbourg and look for Aidor Bilbicum. Perhaps he can help you discover the secret of the wise, to which this mysterious stone you have seems to be related.'

'Sometimes I feel as if this mysterious stone is urging me to leave the abbey,' admitted Grimpow.

'If you leave the abbey and follow your heart, the obstacles you'll find on the way will only encourage you to keep going. But if you ignore your desires and stay with us, the smallest obstacle you face will mean your failure. The choice should be yours only. I will accept whatever you decide.'

* * *

After long and tedious days of spring rains and storms, the morning finally dawned clear and bright, and Grimpow left early to hunt rabbits with his bow. Not far from the abbey he spied a lone horseman mounted on a beautiful black horse. Unhurried and clumsy, a mule walked next to him carrying large saddlebags and sacks, on which were fastened the pieces of an old suit of armour. Unlike most of the pilgrims arriving from the north, the horseman came from the south.

Grimpow ran to meet him without hesitation. The knight was a young, strong man with soft features and a kind face. His outfit was worn, but something in him suggested the daring of a knight without lands or possessions. A long sword with a golden handle hung from his belt and, on the mule, Grimpow could see his shield, which was curiously adorned with signs suggesting a relationship with alchemy – a sun over a blue field and a full moon over a black field. They immediately reminded him of a poem Brother Asben had recited to him while they had been working on the transmutation of lead into gold:

It was the Sun's wish to win the Moon's heart
And it followed its trail through the infinite sky.
'Come closer, beautiful lady, and admire my courage;
don't avoid me or ignore my voice.
I am the king of the day,' said the Sun,
'and light and warmth are my best gifts.'
'The moon and queen of the night I am,

and silence and darkness I offer for love.'
'So love me, cherished Moon,
sweet syrup to my bitter suffering.'
'I will love you, oh, fortunate Sun!
Ideal comfort to my eternal wandering.'

When he reached Grimpow, the rider stopped his horse and, looking at the bow in Grimpow's hand, asked: 'Have you caught anything, boy?'

'No, the rabbits must have all drowned with the last rainfalls,' answered Grimpow.

'Are you sure you know how to use that bow?' asked the knight, letting a smile pull at his lips.

Grimpow didn't respond. He just took an arrow from the quiver hanging from his back, placed it in the bow and aimed at a purple flower swaying in the breeze about sixty steps away. When he released the string, the arrow whistled in the air and cut the flower's stem as if a being as invisible as the wind had severed it with a sharp knife.

'Not bad,' said the horseman, still smiling. 'Do you know the abbey of Brinkdum? Do you perchance live there?'

'Only since a few months ago. I arrived here at the beginning of last winter.'

'What's your name?'

'My name is Grimpow, from the village of Obernalt. And who are you, if I may ask?'

'My name is Salietti. Salietti of Estaglia.'

'Are you Italian?'

'Yes.'

'In the abbey lives a blind, ancient monk who was born in Alessandria, in the Italian county of Piedmont. His name is Uberto,' said Grimpow.

'I've heard of him and his alchemy theories,' said the horseman, holding the reins of his restless horse tightly.

'Are you an alchemist?' asked Grimpow curiously.

'No,' the knight answered, 'but my father was one, and he sometimes spoke to me about certain monks who were also in search of the great secret of the philosopher's stone. Uberto of Alessandria was well known among the alchemists of his time.'

Hearing those words from the mouth of a stranger made Grimpow's stomach flutter.

'And where are you going?' he asked, to change the subject.

'I am heading north, on my way to Strasbourg,' the knight answered. 'I intend to participate in the spring tournaments in the castles of Alsace, which Baron Figueltach of Vokko will hold in his fortress.'

'You'll be fighting in the jousts?' exclaimed Grimpow, thrilled. The idea of leaving the abbey with this man suddenly crossed his mind. If he did, he'd be able to reach Strasbourg and look for Aidor Bilbicum.

'That's my wish,' the traveller answered. 'And I hope to defeat all the knights who confront me in a fair fight. I've heard the heralds of Figueltach of Vokko announce that the winner will choose the queen of the tournaments among the ladies who attend the jousts, and I hope to find the princess of my dreams there.'

'So you'll need a squire to loyally serve you and help carry your weapons at the tournaments,' thought Grimpow out loud, hoping Salietti could see the desire in his own eyes.

The knight gave him a knowing smile. 'Would you like to come with me?'

'There's nothing I would like more than to be your squire,' was Grimpow's heartfelt answer.

The knight told him that if that was truly his wish, he could consider himself appointed to his new role. And having said that, he unbuckled the leather belt that bound his sword to his waist, unsheathed the sword, and tapped Grimpow's shoulder with it lightly, saying solemnly: 'With this touch of my sword, the symbol of noble obedience to the laws of knighthood, I name you my squire.'

He then handed Grimpow the heavy sword so he could begin his duty of carrying the knight's weapons. And when he touched it, Grimpow felt a new world filled with fascinating mysteries was opening up before his eyes.

PART TWO

The Circle's Castles

The Hanging Tree

The time to leave came and the abbey's monks said good-bye to Grimpow and the knight Salietti of Estaglia. Grimpow was sad to leave the stone walls that had given him shelter during the past months, but he knew that he needed to continue the unfinished mission of the knight who had died in the mountains, and Salietti's presence gave him a unique opportunity to reach the city of Strasbourg that he couldn't miss. Brother Rinaldo not only did not raise any objections to his leaving with the Italian knight but seemed pleased when Grimpow told him that he had already been appointed the knight's squire in a brief but solemn ceremony.

On the afternoon of Grimpow's departure the old monk called him to the library to tell him that, hearing the news of Grimpow's plans, Brother Uberto – miraculously – had spoken again, informing him that he knew of someone in the city of Strasbourg who might be able to help Grimpow find Aidor Bilbicum – an innkeeper by the name of Junn the Cripple.

'His inn is called the Green Dragon's Eye and is very close to Strasbourg's old square, where they are now building a new cathedral,' Brother Rinaldo told Grimpow. 'You should tell him Brother Uberto of Alessandria sent you.'

The monk then took his former disciple to the stables. Grimpow's melancholy was growing as they entered the stables, and as Brother Rinaldo walked straight to the dead knight's white horse, he felt it would burst. The thought of leaving Star was almost too much to bear.

Brother Rinaldo stroked the horse's face and turned to Grimpow.

'The new abbot has allowed me to give this mount to you as a gift,' said the old monk. 'It is only fitting that if you are going to fulfil his former master's unaccomplished mission, this horse should go with you.'

Grimpow could not have wished for a more generous gift. He thanked Brother Rinaldo, then put the saddle and bridle on Star before the monk could change his mind.

With a smile that made his eyes sparkle, the old monk gave Grimpow one last piece of advice. 'Never forget that the search for wisdom is a long and tortuous road. I hope you find it someday and that you are able to finally discover the secret of the wise. By then, I will probably be on the other side enjoying the eternal peace of Heaven, or perhaps burning for ever and ever in the depths of Hell, but my thoughts will be with you wherever I am.'

Salietti was waiting for Grimpow by the abbey's doors. His mule was loaded with his armour and the supplies Brother Brasgdo had given them for their long journey. When he saw his squire appear holding Star's reins, he exclaimed, laughing, 'It is the squire who is supposed to wait for his knight!'

'On this occasion you must forgive him, Sir Salietti. You can consider me responsible for the delay,' said Brother Rinaldo with a chuckle.

'We may begin our journey when you so desire, Master Salietti,' Grimpow announced with pride as he climbed onto Star's back.

As they turned their horses to leave, a silent choir of monks bid them farewell, waving their arms in the air. They had just started walking away when Grimpow heard the voice of the small herbalist monk call out.

'Wait!' the monk shouted as he ran toward them. When Brother Asben reached Grimpow he passed him a small leather bag and told him, 'This may be of use to you. After much thinking, I've reached the conclusion that perhaps the piece of gold I found in my laboratory is more yours than mine. I have melted it again and turned it into small gold nuggets that you might need on your trip.'

'You are very generous,' said Grimpow, touched by the kindness of his friend.

'Not more than you've been with me,' replied the

herbalist monk. And then he stood watching as the two horsemen rode away from the abbey and disappeared from view.

They began to climb the mountains to cross the Alps in the west, and a blanket of clouds covered the sun, darkening the still-snowy peaks until they were enveloped in a dark shroud of shadows. Grimpow looked behind him for the last time and knew that he was leaving his past within the abbey's stone walls. There he had seen his dear friend Durlib for the last time; he had hidden in its safety from the evil inquisitor Bulvar of Goztell; and there he'd learned everything he now knew. Now he had to look forward to his journey. He had to find out who Aidor Bilbicum was, what the text in the sealed message meant, what exactly was the philosopher's stone that he carried around his neck, and what its connection was to the secret of the wise that the Pope and the King of France so much desired to own.

All these questions raced through Grimpow's mind until Salietti's voice broke into his thoughts.

'Are you concerned about something, Grimpow?'

'No,' the boy answered, trying to shake the questions from his mind. 'I was just thinking about how I will never see this valley again.'

'Oh, come now – don't say that! The future is uncertain and capricious, like a summer storm. You might come back to the abbey someday,' said Salietti.

But Grimpow knew deep within his heart that he would never return.

'You haven't asked what the herbalist monk told me while saying goodbye,' said Grimpow, changing the subject.

'I don't like to meddle in my squire's business,' said Salietti, grinning at his new friend.

Grimpow handed the leather pouch to the knight. 'I think it will be better if you keep this,' he said.

Salietti held it gingerly, looking at it with curiousity. 'What is it?' he asked.

'See for yourself.'

The knight dropped his horse's reins and undid the knot securing the pouch. He rummaged in it until he took out a handful of gold nuggets, as small and round as toasted corn kernels.

'By the smoke-filled beard of an alchemist!' he shouted, and then let out a whistle that resonated through the mountains. 'There's a small fortune here!' he added happily.

'You can consider it yours. After all, you are the knight and I am merely your squire. It wouldn't be right that I carry your riches,' explained Grimpow ironically.

'A good knight would never deprive his squire of his possessions,' Salietti said, looking at Grimpow intently. 'But if you'd rather I look after this bag of gold, you'd never find a better guardian for such a noble mission. I swear by my honour and the jaws of the mythical Cerberus that I will defend your gold with my sword, and, if necessary, with my own knightly dignity.' And the knight tucked the pouch under his doublet.

'What do you think about using some of the gold to buy

new armour and clothes that are more appropriate for your lineage?' Grimpow asked. 'The armour you own isn't worthy of a knight such as you. It's more dented and rusted than Brother Brasgdo's pots – and doesn't deserve the care of a rich squire such as yours,' he added, laughing.

'I would be happy to accept,' Salietti answered, 'as long as you don't ask me to exchange my sword for a nobler one as well. This one is the best sword a good knight-errant could ever dream of. I call it Athena because of the numerous times it's saved my life,' said Salietti proudly.

Upon hearing the name of the goddess, Grimpow enquired, 'Do you know much about Greek mythology? Athena was a fearless warrior, wasn't she?'

'But she was also considered the goddess of wisdom,' Salietti countered. 'And she controlled the arts.'

His answer left Grimpow with no doubt that, even though he was as poor as a beggar, his new friend and master was wiser than he let on.

The two travellers continued climbing and crossed a series of green meadows where, during the summer, migrating shepherds lit fires to protect their herds from wolves. They passed high waterfalls that dropped like long horses' tails over an abyss of rocks and white foam, circled frozen glaciers with enormous crevasses and unfathomable depths, and led their horses on foot through narrow and seemingly never-ending passes, until they finally crossed the mountains' pointy peaks. Then suddenly, on the other side of a deep gorge, emerged the city of

Ullpens, surrounded by walls that rose over a large plain.

The sun hadn't yet set when they reached the gates of the city. Grimpow and Salietti watched as men with carts full of hay crossed the bridge without being stopped, so they followed suit. Before they had left, the abbot of Brinkdum had given them a safe-conduct letter, but it looked as if it wouldn't be needed.

The streets of Ullpens were deserted at that time of the afternoon. All that could be heard was an uproar near the square, which Salietti attributed to merchants loudly announcing the qualities of their trinkets from their ramshackle stands.

Grimpow didn't think twice about the noise until they entered the square. But there, to his horror, he saw Durlib hanging like a scarecrow from Ullpens' hanging tree! His half-naked, bloodied body swayed in small circles like a pendulum. His eyes, still open, were bulging out, and his tongue hung from his gaping mouth as if he were mocking his executioners. The crowd around him was laughing and shouting, captivated by the excitement and madness of witnessing a public execution. Attempting to contain his horror, Grimpow closed his eyes and clenched his fists until his nails pierced the palms of his hands.

Salietti immediately noticed his squire's reaction. 'Did you know that unlucky soul?'

Grimpow could barely manage to speak, but he told his new friend how the poor man hanging from the tree was his old friend, Durlib, the closest thing he had known to a father before his time in the abbey.

'Let's get out of here,' said Salietti. 'There's nothing we can do to help him now.'

But Grimpow was frozen. Even if he took Salietti's sword and spurred his horse to attack that crowd, they still wouldn't stop shouting and laughing at his friend's lifeless body.

'Let's go, Grimpow,' Salietti urged again. The knight leaned over and pulled Star's reins.

They left the square through a low, arched alley and passed by the ruins of an old church. Further on, in a narrow street flanked by small broken-down houses, they found an open tavern, inside which a thin woman whose face had been devoured by the pox was cleaning some earthen pitchers on a filthy counter. Salietti and Grimpow dismounted, and tied up their horses and the mule.

The woman eyed the newcomers with distrust. She wiped her hands with a rag and asked them why they weren't in the square enjoying the hanging.

'The whole town is there, fluttering around the corpse like crows looking for carrion,' she said. 'They find watching others die amusing and forget that the time will come for them to report to Heaven too.'

Salietti motioned for Grimpow to sit at a table and ordered some brandy. Then he asked casually, 'What did that man do to have been executed?'

'From what I know, he'd been drunk for several nights.

Each night he got drunker and drunker, boasting of having found treasure on a dead knight in the mountains. Some say that he was nothing more than a thief, a swindler who arrived months ago and has been wasting silver coins ever since. When the count's soldiers tried to apprehend him, he unsheathed his sword and cut two soldiers, then killed another one,' the woman told them. She pointed at Grimpow: 'What's wrong with the boy?'

'He is not well. Though I suspect this will help him recover quickly,' answered Salietti as he offered some brandy to his squire.

Grimpow drank the liquor halfheartedly. He couldn't stop thinking about Durlib and his fate at Ullpens' hanging tree – the same tree he'd always joked would be the end of him. Like a never-ending nightmare, the image of his friend's body hanging from the tree kept replaying itself in Grimpow's mind. And he couldn't understand what had happened after Durlib had left the abbey with the treasure.

Grimpow's thoughts were disturbed by Salietti asking the woman if she knew of a place where he and his squire could spend the night and feed their horses.

'The horses and mule can stay in the stables,' she said, 'and, if you'd like, you can stay in a room in the attic. I could also offer you something for supper and make the boy a good soup – it seems that the brandy hasn't had much of an effect.'

Salietti nodded. Grimpow just hoped he would soon be left alone to fall asleep so he could forget about the day.

*   *   *

The tavern's attic room was a dirty hole with a low ceiling made of wooden beams that were covered with mould from leaks. The only furniture it held was a stool and a pair of cots as hard as the floor. After the tavern keeper brought him some warm garlic-and-bread soup and two scorched eggs, Grimpow drifted easily off to sleep. He didn't even hear Salietti leave the room.

The following morning, while Grimpow was still in bed, his face hidden under the blankets, Salietti told him he had left the night before to make sure someone buried Durlib's body properly. He hadn't wanted Grimpow's friend to be left hanging in the square for days, rotten from exposure and nibbled at by vultures. Convincing the gravedigger had cost him two gold nuggets and a sleepless night, for he had waited until the square was deserted to cut the rope, then carried Durlib's lifeless body in a wheelbarrow to the graveyard.

From what the knight was able to gather, it was true that Durlib had spent a few months coming and going in the city of Ullpens dressed as a nobleman. He would get drunk in taverns and brothels, and spent his fortune playing dice and card games. Eventually his story about the knight he'd found dead in the mountains had reached the bishop's ears. Alerted by the inquisitor about the escape of a Knight Templar, the bishop had sent the Count of Ullpens' soldiers to arrest him. After Durlib killed one of them, and seriously injured two others, the count ordered that he be whipped a hundred times in the square and then hanged in the gallows tree.

Grimpow couldn't help feeling guilty about his friend's death. If he hadn't found the dead knight in the mountains, maybe none of this would have happened and Durlib might still be alive. He wished he could get rid of the dead knight's stone hanging around his neck. Was it a curse? It had already seemed to lead to the deaths of the knight in the mountains, the abbot of Brinkdum, and now his good friend Durlib. He couldn't stop thinking, either, that if he and Salietti had arrived at Ullpens sooner, they might have been able to help Durlib. But when he spoke to Salietti of the bad luck that seemed to follow him, Salietti answered with the wisdom of the librarian monk Rinaldo.

'Chance is as mysterious as the dice games that fascinated your friend Durlib. We begin playing when we are born and repeat the game with every breath, without knowing if luck will favour our wishes, our illusions or our dreams. And in that deceitful and fantastic game we make progress every day, despite the fact that all efforts to avoid fate's tricks are as futile as crying over death.'

'At least crying is a comfort,' Grimpow answered.

'So do it, then. Cry for the death of your friend until there are no tears left in your eyes. But when you are finished, remember that you will continue to live, and you can be happy when you realize that. And your friend Durlib will continue to live too – in your memories.'

Grimpow recognized the wisdom in the knight's advice,

and like a new person, he jumped out of bed, ready to go down to the stables and prepare his horse to leave for the city of Strasbourg immediately.

'I will saddle the horses,' he announced.

'Hold on.' Salietti stopped him by raising his arm. 'If we are to continue our trip together, we should first have an honest conversation. Forget that I am a knight and you are my squire. From now on, there should be no differences between us besides the ones necessary to keep up appearances.' He raised his eyebrows, waiting for Grimpow to agree.

'That's fine,' answered Grimpow, and sat down on the bed again.

Salietti looked Grimpow in the eye. 'Who was your friend Durlib, really?' he asked. 'And what was the story he told about the dead knight in the mountains?'

So Grimpow described how he and Durlib had met, and how they spent the winters in the mountains surrounding the abbey. Then he told him about the body they found in the snow and the small treasure in his bag: the silver coins, the jewels, the daggers with rubies and sapphires, the letter and the gold seal. He also told him how the body of the dead knight had disappeared in the snow before their eyes. Then he explained that he had managed to decipher the strange signs in the message, and about his and Durlib's goal to find Aidor Bilbicum in the city of Strasbourg. He outlined everything that had occurred after the inquisitor had arrived in the abbey with the king's soldiers – Durlib's escape, the abbot's murder, Grimpow's education in the library and his conversation with Brother Uberto.

'And what happened to the stone?' asked Salietti.

'What stone?' answered Grimpow, pretending not to know what he was talking about.

'We have sworn to be honest . . .' said Salietti, frowning.

Grimpow sighed and took the stone from the small linen pouch around his neck. 'I am not sure this is exactly a stone,' he said, offering it to the knight.

Salietti took the stone in his hands, and Grimpow noticed how it didn't change colour or acquire the shimmering tones he'd seen when he had touched it for the first time.

'Brother Uberto of Alessandria told me you had found the *lapis philosophorum*,' said Salietti.

'Brother Uberto?' Grimpow was unable to hide his surprise. But then he recalled that Salietti had told him he knew the blind monk, and that the sun and the moon emblazoned in his shield were clear alchemical signs. 'Did Brother Uberto call on you?' he asked curiously.

'No, my friend,' the knight answered, sincerity filling his warm eyes. 'It was Brother Rinaldo of Metz. He sent a message asking me to come to the abbey of Brinkdum so I could travel to Strasbourg with you. When I found you on my way to the abbey, I knew you were the young boy he had spoken about – though I hadn't imagined that you would make it so easy, telling me your desire to become my squire.'

'Why did they choose you?' asked Grimpow, still confused.

'As I told you when we met, my father was a good friend of Brother Uberto's. They shared many years of discoveries and alchemical experiments, as my father was his disciple at the University of Padua. Brother Uberto and Brother Rinaldo both know me well, and the monks decided that I would be the best person to escort and protect you on your journey.'

'So I assume that you know about the secret of the wise?' said Grimpow.

Salietti stood up and looked out at Ullpens' blue sky through the small window, turning the mysterious stone in his fingers.

'Not a lot more than you do. Do you have the message?' he asked, changing the subject.

Grimpow opened the pocket hidden between the seams of his doublet, took out the dead knight's folded message, and offered it to him. Salietti looked at it carefully, then waved the stone over it as if he was expecting it to somehow help him to understand the strange signs it was written in.

'I can't believe that you've interpreted this language by yourself,' he whispered, lost in thought.

Grimpow shrugged. 'The stone allowed me to decipher it, I'm sure of that, but why, I don't know.'

'And are you sure of what it says here?' insisted Salietti.

'"There are darkness and light in the sky, Aidor Bilbicum, Strasbourg." It's carved in my memory,' Grimpow answered. 'I assume Brother Rinaldo has told you that ever since I found this stone, I can somehow understand any language I read.'

'He mentioned something about it, but it's hard to believe that such an insignificant mineral could cause such wonders in you,' said Salietti, handing back the stone and the message.

'Brother Rinaldo is convinced that the knight who died in the mountains was a Templar, and that this stone is part of the secret the nine Knights Templar discovered in the Temple of Solomon.'

'Well,' said Salietti without much conviction, 'we must find out for sure.'

That morning, the two travellers agreed that it was time they trade their poor attire for some more suited to the lineage of the Duke of Estaglia and his squire. The woman from the tavern directed them to a clothing merchant, and Salietti paid for the lodgings and the woman's kindness with a gold nugget – she kissed Salietti's hand as if it were the relic of a miraculous saint! Later, decked out in elegant boots, belts, shirts, hose and doublets, Grimpow and the knight entered Ullpens' most renowned armourer's shop.

'Welcome, sir!' said Master Ailgrup, the armourer, bending in a deep bow with some difficulty; he was a chubby man, whose face was as shiny and greasy as his bald head. 'Tell me what you desire and I'll do all I can to help you.'

Salietti returned the master armourer's courtesy by nodding slightly. 'I need good armour to fight in the jousts,' he said, gazing at a group of beautiful suits of armour, the smooth, polished plates of which hung from large red velvet panels attached to the wall. Grimpow stood at his side, entranced by a large collection of swords.

Master Ailgrup bowed again. 'Be sure that you have come to the best armoury in Ullpens. Our steel armour plates are not only valued for guaranteeing the safety of the knight wearing them, but they are also admired as real works of art.'

Salietti pointed at a suit of armour made with light steel plates that glimmered like the rays of a silver moon. The accompanying helmet was crowned by a sun from which hung a yellow crest like a torrent of light; it had a curved visor with large airholes.

'I'd like to try that one over there, Master Ailgrup,' he said, looking as though his mind was already made up.

'You know what you are looking for, of that I have no doubt, Sir . . . ?' said the master armourer.

'Salietti,' the knight answered. 'Duke of Estaglia,' he added without arrogance.

'If you wish to participate in the jousts at the castles of Alsace, Sir Salietti, the armour you have chosen is perfect. You will be admired by the ladies and envied by the bravest knights,' said the armourer in an obvious attempt to flatter the knight. 'I can assure you that you won't be able to find such original armour anywhere else in the city – it's as light as a feather and strong as a diamond.' He grabbed a long stick crowned by a hook and lowered one of the plates of the armour selected by Salietti.

As the shopkeeper placed the plates on a large table, he described in detail the virtues of each piece: the helmet that protected the head, the visor that covered the face, the beaver that covered the chin and the mouth, the gorget that shielded the throat down to the breastplate, the brassards, the gauntlets and the boots. Grimpow knew that he had to make sense of the jumble of pieces, straps and fittings. As a squire, it would be his job to outfit Salietti in armour to participate in the tournaments.

Master Ailgrup slowly and patiently fitted each piece of the armour to Salietti's body. He worked in quiet concentration, then asked casually, 'Will you join Figueltach of Vokko's army?'

'Figueltach of Vokko's army?' Salietti was confused.

'I see that the rumours of war haven't reached Italy yet,' replied Master Ailgrup. He lowered his voice. 'My lord, you'd better be warned. This year, the jousts are nothing more than an excuse to gather as many knights as possible in the fortress of the greedy Baron Figueltach of Vokko and ask them to join the new Crusade.'

He spoke so quietly that Grimpow could barely hear his voice, but the word Crusade echoed in his mind and made his ears perk up.

'Does Figueltach plan to command a new army to reconquer the Holy Land?' asked Salietti disbelievingly.

A chuckle escaped Master Ailgrup's lips. 'Oh, no, Sir Salietti!' he said. 'This Crusade isn't against the infidels, but against the heretics of the castles in the Circle of

Stone.' He paused to adjust a plate over Salietti's right shoulder, then whispered, 'According to my sources – all noblemen, as you can imagine from the nature of my job – the King of France will attend the tournaments, and there he will announce a Holy Crusade against the outlawed Knights Templar.'

Grimpow's thoughts snapped back to his conversation with Brother Rinaldo. Everything the old monk had told him about the castles of the Circle of Stone and Duke Gulf of Ostemberg and his loyal knights rushed into his mind, and he had to bite his tongue, for his humble position as squire required that he remain silent. Grimpow trusted, however, that Salietti wouldn't miss this opportunity to extract as much information as he could from Ailgrup.

'Are the rebellious Templars also involved in this? I thought King Philip the Fair had finished with them and their diabolical heresies after raiding Paris six years ago,' said Salietti, subtly goading Master Ailgrup to tell them everything he knew.

'The news from Paris,' said the armourer, in a voice so low Grimpow had to sidle even closer to be able to hear, 'is that the great Templar master was burned at the stake in front of Notre Dame. Apparently, before dying he invoked a terrible curse against the Pope and the King of France, promising that both would die within a year. Now people say that King Philip is looking for the secret the nine knights of the Temple of Solomon found in Jerusalem two centuries ago. Only that secret can ward off the curse.'

'And what do the castles of the Circle of Stone have to do with the secret of the Templars?' enquired Salietti, pretending ignorance as he readjusted the armour on his arms and legs.

Master Ailgrup picked up the helmet and lifted the visor. 'Some believe that the nine knights hid the treasure in the fortress at the centre of the circle formed by the castles,' he said.

'I understand. What better place than the castles of the Circle of Stone to guard such a valuable and coveted secret?' answered Salietti.

The master armourer placed the helmet on Salietti's head. The knight, now decked out in the shining armour, looked positively majestic. Then Master Ailgrup added: 'Now, Sir Salietti, you are ready to decide on which side you will be fighting with your new and spotless armour!'

The Curse of the Hermit

As they continued on their journey Salietti visibly burned with his desire to fight in the spring jousts. Every once in a while he gazed at his armour on the back of the mule, as if he sensed that those polished metal plates glimmering under the sun like the alchemists' gold would save his life.

Master Ailgrup's news of a new Crusade distressed him, he told Grimpow, especially since the secret of the wise he and Grimpow were searching for could be hidden somewhere within the Circle of Stone. What Master Ailgrup had said also made sense – that the King of France would lead a Crusade against the castles, even though legend deemed them unassailable.

The plains of Ullpens were covered by vast vineyards and wheat fields, and small villages dotted the landscape, flanking a broad river that zigzagged through thick poplar forests like a long water serpent. On both sides of the horizon the terrain undulated into low hills, on top of which rose small castles of red stone that, from afar, looked like sleepy road watchmen. Several lords of Ullpens would participate in the spring tournaments in the castles of Alsace, as they did every year. And some were already on their way to Figueltach of Vokko's fortress, accompanied by their ladies, squires and pages, and carrying their flags, weapons and banners.

Grimpow and Salietti stopped when they reached a crossroads where there was a hermitage which served as a site for prayer for travellers and pilgrims. It was a tiny but long church with an arched porch supported by two thick columns. Next to it were a well, and a trough for the horses.

Sitting beside it on a stone bench, basking in the sun, was an old hermit. He was barefoot and wore a long, ragged sackcloth held tightly around his waist by a cord of esparto grass. He had only one hand – in it he held a long cane that curved at the end like a pastoral staff – and seemed to be crazy. When he saw them, he grinned, revealing the only tooth that hung from his gums.

'Run away! Run away, now that you still have time to avoid God's wrath, damned sons of the Devil, or enter this holy hermitage to kneel down before the cross of martyrdom and beg God's divine clemency for your sins!' he shouted as Grimpow and Salietti walked towards the trough to water their horses.

Then he stood up, raised his staff to the heavens, and continued shouting his litany.

'The trumpets of the Apocalypse resonate in the sky, and on earth worms writhe under the tombs to hide from the light that sees it all! The eternal fire is ready to ignite your souls! You will burn in Hell! Traitors of faith! Slaves of lust! Servants of gluttony and greed! Listen to the announcement of the end! Death's scythe will make your arrogance of gods roll in the mud, and your heads will be crushed mercilessly by your horses' hoofs! Your lances and swords will be good for nothing! The prophecies will come true! Repent your sins and pray with me!' he concluded, and knelt before them, seemingly in a state of ecstasy, while he mumbled an incomprehensible prayer.

Salietti looked at the old monk with compassion and spoke to Grimpow quietly. 'He's a fake – he's doing it to receive generous alms,' he said.

Grimpow knew that poverty and hunger made many rogues and rascals wander roads and villages hungry, and they didn't hesitate to resort to any schemes to bring a piece of bread to their mouth. But in that hermit's faraway look, Grimpow had seen a sadness that made all his other miseries seem small.

'It wasn't us he was talking to,' he said with sudden awareness.

Salietti looked around. 'Who else, then? There's no one else here besides the mule and the horses.'

'He was talking to the Knights Templar. Perhaps he has

mistaken us for them in his delusion.'

'And what makes you think that?' asked Salietti, intrigued.

'The words he's spoken.'

'I don't know what you mean. What he's said is nothing more than what any apocalyptic prophet would say.'

'What he's said is what the Knights Templar were accused of before being condemned as heretics,' said Grimpow. 'That's why he urged us to run when he saw us – we could still avoid being persecuted. And that's why he spoke of the damned sons of the Devil; of the worms that hide from the light that sees it all; of the fire of Hell where their souls will burn; of the traitors of faith, the slaves of lust, and the servers of gluttony and greed; of death, which will roll its godly arrogance in the mud; and of their heads, which will be crushed by their own horses while their lances and swords will be useless,' he explained.

Salietti was shocked by what Grimpow had just said.

'You're right, Grimpow. The Knights Templar were accused of worshipping the Devil; of hiding under the ground like worms to celebrate their rites hidden from the eyes of God, who is all-seeing; of betraying faith; of having perpetrated the sin of lust and committed obscenities with each other; of eating meat during Lent and of having accumulated wealth until they thought themselves gods.'

'And it is true that they've been crushed by the Pope and the very king who, like their horses, paid homage to them

161

before,' added Grimpow. 'And their lances and swords didn't save them from being burned at the stake.'

Grimpow left his horse drinking from the trough. He stepped closer to the old man, who was still on his knees before them, and helped him back onto the stone bench.

'What's your name?' he asked.

'What does my name matter?' the hermit said dully.

Grimpow had noticed under the nape of his neck the brand of an eight-pointed cross, like the one he'd seen on Brother Rinaldo's white cloak and sword in the abbey's subterranean cavern.

'Are you a Knight Templar?' he asked.

'Does the Order of the Temple still exist?' replied the old man, staring into space.

Grimpow sat by his side and studied the stump of his right hand, a mixture of wrinkled and rotten skin.

'How did you lose your hand?' asked Grimpow.

'They cut it off so that I couldn't hold a sword any more,' answered the old man.

'Who are "they"?'

'The King of France's executioners,' said the old man.

'Did they torture you?'

The old hermit nodded, humiliated.

'We didn't have a chance to defend ourselves. They entered the Temple's tower in Paris at dawn, like foxes in a pen, and captured us all. They took our documents and treasures – there's nothing left now but the burned bodies of hundreds of Templars who were killed at the stake and left unburied.' The old hermit spoke to himself, carried away by the tide of his sad memories, and Grimpow let him continue. 'They separated me from the rest and put me in a dungeon full of water and infested with rats, where I stayed imprisoned and tortured and unable to see the light for years. They said I knew things they wanted to know, and they were willing to pull them out of me with the Inquisition's claws.'

'And how did you manage to escape your captivity?'

'They thought I had gone mad and nobody would believe me, so the inquisitor Bulvar of Goztell let me go after I had given them what they wanted. Then I wandered aimlessly until I found shelter in this abandoned hermitage. I will await the end of my days here,' he said weakly. 'The worst things imaginable were said against us, and our brothers were killed just because they wanted to know our secret.'

Salietti, who had stayed silent, was startled but stayed calm. 'What secret are you talking about?' he asked.

'The one the legend says the nine knights found in Jerusalem, before they founded the Order of the Temple.'

'I imagine you knew that secret?' Grimpow prompted.

'No,' he said.

'Are you saying that there *was* no secret?' Salietti blurted out.

'I am saying that the nine Templars didn't discover any secrets; they merely transported something from Jerusalem to Paris at the request of a secret society of sages, in

163

exchange for vast amounts of gold. Their only mission was to protect the contents of a mysterious carriage from the attacks of the Muslims and ensure its arrival in France. They never knew what was in it.'

What he said confirmed Grimpow's suspicions that the knight he had found dead in the mountains was not a fugitive Templar but a persecuted sage.

'How do you know that?'

'In the Temple's fortress in Paris were some old parchments that confirmed it: letters, agreements and receipts, that I was in charge of guarding. When they tortured me, I told them where they were hidden.'

'Was the name of that secret society of sages in those parchments?' asked Salietti.

'Ouroboros,' he said, pronouncing the word with pleasure.

Yes! thought Grimpow.

'Are you talking about the snake swallowing its tail?' he asked.

The old man nodded.

'And did you ever meet any of the sages of that secret society?' he asked.

'Did those documents mention where the secret of the wise is hidden?' asked Salietti.

'No, those parchments only talk about a simple agreement among the nine knights and Ouroboros. There are many stories surrounding that secret, but nobody has been able to find it or discover what it is about or where it is hidden.'

'So why is the King of France searching for it?' asked Grimpow.

'He believes that if he finds that secret, there will be no power on earth like his, and that he will even become immortal, exorcising the curse the Templar Grand Master, Jacques de Molay, cast upon him before dying at the stake. I know that you are looking for that secret too – I can read it in your thoughts. Many have been looking for it for centuries, and many have lost their lives trying to uncover it. But they have all forgotten about the old curse. It is there, though, lurking in the shadows like a beast ready to devour anyone who dares disturb its eternal sleep.'

'The curse? Do you mean the curse of the Templar Grand Master?' asked Salietti.

The old hermit opened his eyes and rolled them until the whites were all that showed.

'No, the curse I'm talking about is as old as time. *Damned are those who dare penetrate the essence of the secret, for the doors they manage to open will be closed behind them for ever!*' he shouted, staring into space. 'If you want to reach it, you'll have to learn to interpret the language of the stone,' he added in a mutter.

'The stone? Are you referring to the *lapis philosophorum?*' asked Grimpow.

But the old hermit had narrowed his eyes and began mumbling a stream of meaningless words, as if he had entered a trance. Then he stood up and walked toward the church, leaning on his staff, shouting once again at them.

'Run away! Run away, now that you still have time to avoid God's wrath, damned sons of the Devil, or enter this holy hermitage to kneel down before the cross of martyrdom and beg God's divine clemency for your sins!'

Cornill in Flames

At dusk they camped in an empty plain. All around them was the long, straight line of the horizon, where the blackness of the sky met the earth. Above, the infinite heavens shone full of stars. There was no moon and, around them, the world was swallowed by darkness. The travellers ate in the dark – dry pork sausage, bread, cheese and some grapes they had gathered in the vast vineyards they had crossed in the day.

The constellations glowed above them like swarms of fireflies frozen in place.

'Brother Uberto of Alessandria told me that the answers to all the questions about the secret of the wise are beyond the stars,' murmured Grimpow without taking his eyes off the immense night sky.

'Well, that's just a metaphor, a way to refer to the

mystery that surrounds everything that's unknown to us,' Salietti replied. 'Brother Uberto had a passion for deciphering the mysteries of the cosmos. It's logical that he believes the answers to the questions we humans consider unreachable are beyond the sky. When I was a boy like you, my father used to tell me that there is nothing more mysterious than the universe, and I gazed, fascinated, at the sky every night. I learned to find Mercury, Venus, Jupiter and Saturn in the constellations of the zodiac. I imagined that one day I would be able to touch the stars with my hands,' he added, pointing at Venus with Athena as if the star sparkling above was the shimmering tip of his sword.

'When . . .' Grimpow faltered, unsure, 'when I spoke with Brother Uberto, I had the impression that he knew a lot about the philosopher's stone.' He took out the stone and stared at it as if it was the first time he had seen it. 'He knew I had this stone without being able to see it. He *felt* it.'

'Perhaps it was just a hunch,' Salietti offered. 'An ability he acquired in the deep darkness of his thoughts. Some blind men have developed such an acute sense of hearing that they can detect the most silent cat approaching.'

'No, I think it was more than that. I could almost swear that Brother Uberto was one of the sages who guarded the secret of the *lapis philosophorum*.'

'What makes you think that?' asked Salietti, looking with interest at the reddish glow the stone in Grimpow's hands was beginning to emit under the infinite night sky.

'When I spoke to him, he said things which surely only a sage of that secret society, Ouroboros, could know. Something tells me that that group of sages still exists somewhere, and that Brother Uberto of Alessandria had a lot to do with it at one time.'

'My father talked about him often when I was a child,' said Salietti quietly. 'They met at the University of Padua, where Brother Uberto taught philosophy and astronomy. He'd developed revolutionary theories about the universe that contradicted both Aristotle and Ptolemy. My father called him "the monk of Alessandria", and told me that he believed that the planets rotated around the sun. That earned him many enemies within the Church, as they were convinced that the earth was the centre of the universe and that the celestial bodies rotated around it. For years the monk travelled; through Spain, to Paris, where he was a professor at the university; to London, where he wrote more than fifty books; even to Asia and Africa. Everyone considered him a great sage until, at seventy years of age, he was accused of heresy by the Holy Office, brought to Rome and subjected to trial. If he hadn't recanted his ideas, he surely would have been burned there at the stake. Humiliated and tired, he sought refuge in the abbey of Brinkdum, and his name has been completely forgotten by the world since then,' finished Salietti, letting out a sigh.

Grimpow suddenly sat up. 'Of course!' he cried out, and Salietti looked at him, surprised. 'I see it now. Can't you? Brother Uberto had this same stone. He was in charge of keeping it along with the gold seal with the Ouroboros symbol, and when the time came to give it to the secret's new guardian, he must have refused to part with it. He told me himself in the abbey's infirmary that he was tempted by immortality and wealth, and he betrayed the principles and beliefs he had respected for so long. Then he regretted it and returned the stone to its secret source, only to try in vain to create an identical one in his laboratory. That's why he told me that this stone could end up killing me, just as it had clouded *his* reason and sight.'

'Perhaps Brother Uberto was referring to the same curse the old hermit mentioned this morning?' said Salietti.

'I've thought of that, too. But since I've found this stone, I've heard of nothing but tragedy occurring around it – Brother Uberto's blindness, the death of the knight who carried it, the abbot of Brinkdum's assassination, my separation from Durlib, his execution on the gallows, and the approaching war against the castles of the Circle of Stone,' said Grimpow, saddened by so much misfortune.

'If you look at it that way, you'll have to blame it for all the tragedies humanity has suffered since inhabiting this planet,' said Salietti, smiling gently. 'The knight in the mountains died from cold; the abbot of Brinkdum was assassinated so that he couldn't tell anyone about the Pope and the King of France's intentions to uncover the secret of the wise; your friend Durlib was hanged because that's the most likely ending for thieves who kill noblemen's soldiers; and the war announced is a mere consequence of the excessive greed of such powerful men as the king and Baron Figueltach of Vokko. As for Brother Uberto's blindness, it was just an accident, and it was the shards of glass of his alembic, not your stone, that left him blind. There is no curse – those things would have happened even if you hadn't found the stone.'

'You might be right – but I think there's truth in the old hermit's words. I don't think he was lying to us,' said Grimpow. 'The ouroboros is the symbol in the gold seal and in the letter's wax seal. And the old hermit had the Templar's cross branded on the nape of his neck, I am sure of that.'

Salietti rose on one elbow to look at Grimpow. 'Why didn't you tell me that?'

'I thought you had seen it too. So now we know that the Templars had nothing to do with the secret of the wise – except for carrying it from Jerusalem to Paris to protect it from the Muslims' attacks.'

'If that's true, it seems clear that it was the members of the secret society of sages who found it in Jerusalem,' remarked Salietti.

'And only they knew where they hid it in France,' added Grimpow.

'But, according to your theory, at least one of them kept the stone you have now, and passed it on to his disciple before dying, and that one to his disciple, and so on until it reached Brother Uberto of Alessandria's hands.'

'Right. And the knight who died in the mountains must have been the last holder of the stone,' said Grimpow.

* * *

The stars still dotted the night sky before dawn, and as the sun rose in the west, a pale blue light slowly erased them from the sky. By the time the travellers began moving again, its golden rays reigned over the enormous plain that spread before them like an ocean of brown soil. They rode north.

By midmorning, the landscape had begun to change before them. High hills and deep forests were visible in the distance, and it didn't take them long to reach them. They avoided trails and roads, not wanting to run into the caravans of pilgrims going south and the groups of knights en route to the spring jousts, and rode through the forest, not leaving until nearly nightfall.

They rode single file and in silence, and as they moved forward, the landscape changed, turning from the colours of earth and crops to woods and scrublands and then to swamps and barren plains. As they travelled Grimpow wondered what they would find upon reaching Baron Figueltach of Vokko's fortress, and if they would ever succeed in entering the city of Strasbourg's gates.

He wondered, too, if Brother Uberto's friend there – Junn the Cripple – would be able to help them. From what he knew, Brother Uberto hadn't left the abbey in two decades; his friend might well not live in the city any more, or even still be alive. If Junn the Cripple could help them find Aidor Bilbicum in Strasbourg, perhaps the mystery would finally be revealed.

He felt that he'd know what to do with the stone just as the sages who had had it before him and the knight who carried it in the mountains must have known. Since the day he found it, Grimpow had known there was something magical in it, something that was not of this world, something mysterious and so miraculous it was capable of turning a boy like him into a sage. But sometimes he doubted that there really was a secret to uncover beyond that of the stone itself. Wasn't the stone itself a mystery? Who had originally found it? Where, how and when? Was it really the philosopher's stone? The *lapis philosophorum* of the legends and treatises on alchemy? Who was the dead knight? Was he a member of the secret society of sages? Why did the Pope and the King of France want the stone? Why did they want to attack the castles of the Circle? Who was Aidor Bilbicum? And what did the message in the letter mean?

All these questions were spinning through Grimpow's mind as they approached a hill – a lookout point from which they could see the road north zigzagging among vineyards and small hills.

A dense cloud of smoke rose in the distance and blended with the grey clouds layered along the horizon. The wind blew powerfully from the west, imitating the murmur of agitated voices, and the sky had the metallic glow of a pale and cold sunset. Alarmed, Salietti rose in his saddle and scanned the distance in search of a clue about what was happening.

'There is fire in the village of Cornill, and I think the wind is dragging the screams of battle and death. Let's go and see what's happening,' he said, sitting back and spurring his horse to gallop downhill.

Grimpow imitated him, spurring Star and pulling the mule's reins to force it to follow. His heart beat fast in his chest and his ears perked up, alert to the sounds ahead of him. He was able to pick out the tower bells of a church ringing in alarm in the distance.

'Giddyap, giddyap! Giddyap, mule!'

As they got closer, they could see that several houses and stables in the village of Cornill were ablaze. Sharp tongues of fire danced over the straw roofs like ghosts in a macabre dance from Hell. Some men and women fruitlessly tried to put out the devastating fire, hurling buckets of water at the flames. Salietti brought his horse close to a strong-looking man wearing a blacksmith's apron, whose skin glistened with sweat under a sky of black smoke, and yelled to catch the man's attention amid the chaos.

'What happened?' he asked.

'A group of Baron Figueltach's soldiers entered the village before sunset looking for the inn where a man named Gurielf Labox was staying – a visitor who arrived in Cornill a few days ago with his daughter. They dragged them out of the house, beat them, handcuffed them and then took them away in a carriage. As they left they set everything they passed on fire.'

'Do you know why they captured them?' Salietti asked.

The man wiped the sweat dripping down his forehead with his naked arm. 'The soldier's captain said they were burning our houses for giving shelter to a sorcerer – one of those worshippers of the stars,' he answered.

'Is there anyone here who knew the man?' asked Salietti as his horse shied, frightened by the fire.

'You can ask the parish priest. He might be able to help you.'

Houses blazed on both sides of the street, and the horses refused to move forward between the walls of fire around them. The flames crackled in the air, igniting the nightfall with the colours of a sinister sunset. Sadly, Grimpow watched the men, women and children desperately trying to prevent the fires from destroying everything they owned.

'Why do you want to know who the soldiers took from the village?' he asked Salietti on their way to the church.

'If, as the blacksmith says, they captured him for worshipping the stars, he must be a sage astronomer. So it wouldn't hurt us to find out as much as we can about this Gurielf Labox. If they have taken him to the baron's fortress, we might be able to speak to him and get information about Ouroboros,' he said.

And without knowing why, Grimpow suddenly suspected that Salietti hadn't been entirely honest with him.

In the church's square a priest was desperately shouting to a group of peasants, ordering them to move aside some beams that had fallen off a burning house and now blazed beside a wall of the old wood-and-stone building. He was a thin, pale man in a long black habit with a white cincture knotted around the waist; there were dark circles under his eyes.

Salietti jumped off his horse, walked towards the parish priest and made a slight bow. 'I know you wish to tend to your parishioners at such a difficult time, but I must speak to you about an urgent matter,' he said.

The priest raised his head and looked at Salietti. 'What do you wish to speak to me about?' he asked.

'The sage Gurielf Labox.'

'The Baron of Alsace's soldiers have just taken him and his daughter.'

'I know,' announced Salietti with an air of self-confidence. 'I've come to Cornill precisely to warn him that the inquisitor Bulvar of Goztell has ordered his arrest.'

Grimpow was astonished by Salietti's words – he didn't know if he was lying or telling the truth.

'As you can see for yourself from this spectacle of fire and misfortune, you are too late. But pray tell me, who sent you?' asked the priest.

'I am afraid I can't tell you. That's part of the secret.'

'The secret?' asked the priest, frowning.

Salietti nodded.

'I understand,' said the priest pensively. He looked Salietti in the eye for a while, then finally asked, 'Are you a friend of Gurielf Labox?'

'Let's say that I want to help him, but for that I need to

176

know if he found what he was looking for in this village.'

The priest looked at the mule and the coat of arms on Salietti's shield tied to the animal's back; he studied the painting on it – the sun over a blue sky and the full moon over a black sky.

'Your shield is a riddle,' he whispered.

'Not for those who understand,' said Salietti vaguely.

And with that the priest's doubts seemed to evaporate.

'Leave your horses here and come inside with me. We'll talk in the sacristy.'

They tied the horses and mule up by the church's door and entered the damp darkness of the sacred space of Cornill. In the dim light Grimpow could see that it was an old, medium-sized church with a central nave and two smaller aisles on each side, separated by thick columns and wide arches, and full of small niches housing statues of the Virgin and saints. Several thick candles burned on the altar; their light fractured the darkness and illuminated the body of a crucified Jesus that seemed to have magically emerged from the shadows.

Grimpow realized that the church was full of symbols and mysteries, just like the alchemists' manuscripts. Every image, every square, every sculpture and every column's capital had a meaning most people ignored. But the priest, like any good scholar, probably knew their unusual language well.

Once in the chapel, a vaulted room with low ceilings and small closed windows on one of its stone walls, the priest lit the candles in a four-armed candelabra sitting on a table. On one side hung the sacred vestments adorned with trimmings embroidered with gold, worn by the cleric during Mass, and on a carved wooden cupboard sat a tray with a copper jug. The priest took out three copper tumblers and poured the jug's liquid in them.

'It is a plum liquor made by me, very soft and healthy during times like these, when the shadows take over the world and our fears lie in wait for us at night,' he said, offering the tumblers to his unexpected guests.

Salietti gulped down his glass while Grimpow and the priest sipped theirs slowly, enjoying the sweet taste of the plums.

'Dark are the hours awaiting us indeed,' said Salietti. He licked his lips. 'I assume you are aware of Baron Figueltach's intention to attack the Circle's castles.'

The priest clucked his tongue and nodded. 'That's all people are talking about in the whole of Alsace. The baron's heralds are going from village to village and city to city recruiting soldiers for his army in exchange for good profits and special favours. I don't believe there has been such a large army since the Crusades.'

'Yes, the King of France has formed an alliance with the baron because he thinks that the Templars' secret is hidden in the castles of the Circle,' confided Salietti to win the priest's trust.

'I thought it was because the duke had sheltered the Knights Templar in his castles,' said the priest.

'A small group of fugitive Templars doesn't justify a war. It's just an excuse for the King of France to enter Duke Gulf of Ostemberg's castle and search for the secret he covets,' answered Salietti. 'And that's why they've arrested Gurielf Labox. They think that sages such as he know where the secret is hidden.'

'Do you promise to be discreet about what I am going to say?' asked the priest.

'You wouldn't find among Cornill's tombs a corpse less talkative than myself, I swear on my knightly honour,' answered Salietti, bringing his index finger and thumb to his mouth in the form of a cross and kissing them as if they were a crucifix.

'What about your squire?' asked the priest, looking at Grimpow uneasily.

'You can trust Grimpow as you can trust me, for there are no secrets between us,' said Salietti solemnly.

The priest refilled the copper tumblers with liquor and they drank again, enjoying its exquisite flavour.

'A few weeks ago,' he explained, 'an elderly man I didn't know came to see me from Paris with his daughter, carrying a letter with the wax seal of the Holy See in Avignon and addressed to the humble parish priest of the village of Cornill – me. You can imagine my astonishment and happiness. The letter confirmed the visit of the carrier of the letter, the knight Gurielf Labox, and ordered me to give him access to the church's archives, where he was to be able to move around freely. I was only to help him when he asked. I was to keep my knowledge of the letter and its contents in utmost secrecy. I assume you know what this is about and what the man was sent to look for in the church's archives,' concluded the priest.

Salietti took another sip of his drink and cleared his throat.

'As I'm sure you'll understand considering the secret nature of my mission, I can't tell you much. But given that Gurielf Labox has been taken and we don't know if he found what he was searching for, you should show me the archived documents he was studying. I will send message to the Pope before I leave tomorrow to rescue the old sage from Baron Figueltach's fortress.'

'If you wish, I can put them at your disposal right now and you can study them while I go back to the square to help the villagers who have lost their houses in the fire,' offered the priest. Saying this, he took the candelabra and beckoned them to follow him to a chamber adjacent to the sacristy, the entrance to which was a small arch without a door.

The archive of Cornill's church was just a small, square room with a plain desk in the centre – heaped with parchments – and a shelf that reached the ceiling on one of the walls.

'Here are all the documents this church has generated since it was built in the times of the Visigoths,' said the priest, placing the candelabra on the table. 'There are books full of certificates of baptism, marriage, death, receipts of purchases, donations, renovation expenses, records of noblemen's and kings' visits, and appointment of priests and burials. As you can see, the stay of men in this world is short, and if it wasn't for the eternal redemption awaiting us in Heaven, our life here would be nothing more than a pile of documents that someone will burn someday. You can look at them as long as you wish. I will return later.'

As soon as the priest had left the archive, Grimpow had to ask Salietti the questions that had been burning in his mind.

'Did you know that Gurielf Labox was coming to this village as the Pope's legate, and was going to be detained?'

'I had no idea,' admitted Salietti, absorbed in a thick book he had just taken off the shelf. From over his shoulder Grimpow could see that it held the names of all the parish priests for more than three centuries.

'So how did you persuade the priest to believe that you were also a legate from His Holiness?'

'I reasoned that if I mentioned the secret, I would avoid having to explain anything to him, and the priest wouldn't doubt that we had something to do with the same mission that brought Gurielf Labox here. After all,' Salietti continued, 'I'm sure that the old man was searching for the same thing we are. The Pope's spies probably found out that there's something valuable hidden in this church, then sent one of their experts in solving riddles to look for it.'

'Gurielf Labox?'

'The same.'

'Could he have found the secret?' asked Grimpow in disbelief.

'That's what I'm trying to find out, if you'd stop pestering me with your questions for a moment. Take one of those records of the visits of noblemen and kings and check if any of the names stand out to you,' directed Salietti. Grimpow had never seen him so annoyed and tense before.

'That sage might not have even looked at these documents,' said Grimpow, discouraged as they began to examine the documents in the archive.

'Maybe not. But it's clear that he was looking for something here – why would he come to this village with a letter addressed to the parish priest otherwise?'

'What if what he was looking for is *inside* the church?' suggested Grimpow.

'Hmm . . .' Salietti thought for a second, then admitted, 'You could be right.' Just then he noticed the tip of a small piece of parchment sticking out from beneath the pile of manuscripts on the desk. 'What's this?' he asked out loud, inspecting the parchment closely. A message was scrawled across it in perfect calligraphy.

> If you pass the misty Vale of Scirum in Sciripto,
> The crypt without a corpse will open;
> There History sleeps.
> Go to the city in the message
> And there ask for he who does not exist,
> And you will hear the voice of the shadows.

'It mentions a crypt – that must be in this church,' said Grimpow. 'Perhaps this is what Gurielf Labox was looking for. Let's look for the church's crypt. I suspect that if we can find the mysterious Vale of Scirum, we will learn much more. Then we'll go to the city of Strasbourg, which is the city mentioned in the dead knight's message. There we will ask for he who does not exist and perhaps we'll hear the voice of the shadows. Everything fits.'

They walked through the sacristy in silence. The light from their candelabra flashed on the images of the Virgin and saints, resting pale and motionless as wax in the vaulted niches, and the two felt the icy weight of their spectral stares. They walked down each aisle of the church, studying every tile, every nook, every crack in the floor. They checked the graves of the noblemen flanking the presbytery, the holy water fonts, the baptismal chapel and the pulpits and altars. They found nothing that demanded their attention until – behind the main altar – they discovered a narrow stairwell leading down to the crypt.

'All the parish's priests must be buried there,' said Salietti, frowning.

'We'd better go down,' Grimpow said unenthusiastically. He wasn't excited about entering such an eerie place with only a few candles to light their way – but after the skulls piled up at the secret entrance to the abbey of Brinkdum's library, there were few things that truly scared him.

Salietti held the candelabra over the narrow entrance; its dim light illuminated the vault and the steps spiralling down to a pit of darkness. 'I'll go first,' he said, ducking his head to avoid hitting the low ceiling.

As they reached the end of the stairs and entered the crypt, the candles' flames shook as if a ghost had blown on them, and Grimpow and Salietti's shadows danced on the damp stone walls. The vaulted ceiling was still low, but they could now stand straight. Consecutive arches supported by columns opened to their right, and in each arch they could see an ivory sarcophagus. Salietti walked around the circle and passed the candlelight over each of the sarcophagi. There were eight in total, and on top of each one was the image of a man in a long tunic. They all had long hair and beards, and their arms were folded on their chests as if they slept peacefully. There were no inscriptions on them, no names or dates.

'These are tombs that are centuries old,' said Salietti.

As they stood there an idea was slowly forming in Grimpow's mind. 'The crypt's base is an octagon!' he exclaimed, remembering Brother Rinaldo and his drawing of the square peg in a round hole.

He explained the meaning of the octagon and the Circle's castles to Salietti, telling him how many of the Knights Templars' fortresses and chapels had an octagonal shape to represent the fusion of Heaven and earth.

'But this was never a Templar church,' said Salietti.

'That's why it might have something to do with the secret of the wise. And that's exactly what Gurielf Labox must have been investigating,' said Grimpow, instinctively passing through one of the arches and walking to the circular centre of the crypt. When he saw the inscription carved in the central circle there, he nearly burst with happiness. The eight graves surrounded the centre as if they were eight knights protecting it. 'Here it is!' he shouted.

They stared at the symbols engraved inside a circle on the stone floor: the same symbols as in the sealed message Grimpow had found on the dead knight.

ᛏᛁᛏᛁ ᚲᛖ ᚦᛁᛏᛏᛏ ᛉᛉ ᛏᛄᛏ
ᛃᛏᛏᛉᛄᛃᛚᛄᛄᛏ

'What does it mean?' asked Salietti impatiently.

Grimpow had a piece of parchment and a charcoal pencil he had taken from the church's archive. He stood under the candlelight and wrote:

Pass the misty Vale of Scirum in Sciripto

'It must be the same Vale of Scirum mentioned in Gurielf Labox's note,' he said. Lost in thought, Salietti stared at the inscription in the rock. Then he said: 'What if it's not old parish priests who are buried here, but the eight sages who protected the secret? That would explain why the graves are so old and have no names or dates.'

'Do you think the secret of the wise could be under this rock?' asked Grimpow in disbelief.

'It's just a guess,' answered Salietti.

'Perhaps the Vale of Scirum is a place. Maybe it's where the secret of the wise is hidden, and the secret can only be found by walking through it,' suggested Grimpow.

'Perhaps,' admitted the Italian, 'but I've never heard of it, nor of any place called Sciripto.'

'In any case, it's clear that this is a new riddle to add to our collection. I wonder if Gurielf Labox was able to solve it before he was apprehended.'

'We'll never know that unless we speak to him,' said Grimpow.

Salietti sighed. 'I hope the Inquisition's executioners can't make him confess what he knows. If he's tortured and tells them what he was looking for in the church, it won't take long for the baron and the King of France's henchmen to return.'

They remained absorbed in their thoughts and fears, trying to find a reasonable solution to the inscription.

'And if it was a cryptogram?' Salietti conjectured suddenly, interrupting Grimpow's thoughts.

Grimpow remembered that in the abbey Brother Rinaldo of Metz had talked to him extensively about the coded messages used in the past to conceal mysteries.

'Do you mean a coded language?'

'Exactly.'

'But the inscription is already written in a strange language,' pointed out Grimpow.

'Yes, but sometimes hidden messages are protected by

186

several layers of code,' Salietti explained. 'This could be one of those cases. In order to reach the riddle's final solution, we might have to solve all the cryptograms protecting it.'

At that moment, they heard a commotion that sounded like a mob of people entering the church.

'The villagers are coming in,' Salietti murmured. 'Many of them will probably spend the night here as their houses were destroyed by the fire. Let's leave before we arouse any suspicions.'

'But what about the inscription?' Grimpow asked.

'We'll continue studying it upstairs in the sacristy. Now let's go, quickly.'

As the two climbed up the narrow staircase and hurried to the sacristy a group of people surrounded the parish priest in the back of the church by the entrance door. The priest was giving instructions for the pews to be placed in the central nave as makeshift cots, separating the women and children from the men. They all looked overwhelmed by sadness and exhaustion.

In the sacristy, Salietti helped himself to another tumbler of liquor while Grimpow leafed through a book. His attention wasn't on the words in it, though – both he and Salietti were consumed with trying to solve the enigma of the crypt. The words *Vale of Scirum* and *Sciripto* ran through Grimpow's mind over and over – something told him they were not mere place names. What did they signify?

When the priest entered the sacristy Grimpow broke from his reverie. The priest asked if they had found anything interesting in the archive, and Salietti shook his head.

'There's nothing more than names and the church's bills in those documents. It would be easier to find a needle in a haystack,' he said.

'That's what I said to Labox when I showed him the archive, but he still examined every document as if he was trying to solve the mystery of the Holy Grail,' said the priest, smiling.

'Does the *Vale of Scirum* or *Sciripto* mean anything to you?' interrupted Grimpow, disregarding the silence required of his position as a squire.

The priest repeated the words aloud and frowned at their oddness.

'Are they Greek, perhaps?' he asked thoughtfully. 'No, I've never heard either, and I don't believe I've ever seen those words or places written anywhere – certainly not on any documents stored in the archive.'

'Who's buried in the eight sarcophagi around the central circle in the crypt?' asked Salietti nonchalantly.

The priest looked at the ground, grabbed his habit's cincture and played with its knots. 'This church is no different from any other,' he said. 'In all churches, sanctuaries, chapels, hermitages and cathedrals, you'll find something nobody can explain – the real origin and meaning of which is only known by those who built it. The church's crypt was here long before this place of worship was built over it, and those tombs are at least three centuries old.'

'There are no names on the headstones and, judging from the sculptures on them, it doesn't look like its residents were of noble origin. They look like scholars in a sweet sleep,' said Salietti.

'None of the archive's documents mention the name of those corpses. I searched it myself when I was put in charge of the parish five years ago,' admitted the priest.

'And what about the inscription on the central circle of the crypt?' asked Grimpow.

'Gurielf Labox spent hours in the crypt trying to decipher that inscription. As far as I know, nobody has succeeded. They are strange, old symbols that can mean anything – they could even just be marks from the stone-masons who built this church. Stonemasons have been known to sign their work with the symbols of their lodges.'

'No, these signs hide a mystery, I am sure of that, and Gurielf Labox's mission was to decipher it,' Salietti assured him.

'Perhaps by praying and resting you'll be able to shed light on those doubts that trouble you so much,' answered the priest.

He apologized to Salietti for not being able to offer appropriate accommodation for a knight to lodge with dignity, but was able to offer them the church's granary for shelter. Behind the sacristy, it hadn't been affected by the flames.

* * *

The next morning Grimpow was awakened by a rooster announcing dawn. Almost immediately a new word echoed in his mind as if he had been thinking of it all night: *inscriptio*. He jumped out of bed and shook Salietti to wake him from his sleep.

'*Inscriptio!*' shouted Grimpow, excited.

'Yes, yes, I know . . . we have to figure out the meaning of that inscription. I haven't stopped thinking about it either, and I've barely been able to sleep all night,' Salietti grumbled, still drowsy.

'Don't you understand? *Inscriptio* is an anagram of in *Sciripto*.'

Salietti sat up as abruptly as if he'd been sloshed by a bucket of cold water. 'You've deciphered the cryptogram?' he said incredulously, opening his eyes wide.

'I think so,' said Grimpow. He grabbed the piece of parchment on which he had taken notes the night before and showed Salietti the text of the inscription again.

Pass the misty Vale of Scirum in Sciripto

'If we replace in *Sciripto* with *inscriptio*—' he began.

'We still have another riddle to solve: ' "*Pass the misty Vale of Scirum,*"' Salietti interrupted.

'But at least we know that we are looking for an inscription of some kind in the Vale of Scirum. Now we just

190

have to find out where that place is and we'll find the secret of the wise we're searching for.'

'If Gurielf Labox didn't find it first and tell the baron and the King of France. We must leave for the baron's fortress now, before it's too late,' said Salietti, grabbing his sword from the ground and attaching it to his belt.

They were about to leave the church's granary when an idea entered Grimpow's mind.

'Wait a second,' he said. 'The Vale of Scirum doesn't exist!'

Salietti stopped abruptly and turned to his friend. 'How can you be sure of that?'

'If *in Sciripto* was an anagram, maybe the first part of that phrase is one, too,' Grimpow pointed out.

'But you've already solved the cryptogram – there's an inscription somewhere in the Vale of Scirum. That's where we need to go. Perhaps Aidor Bilbicum of Strasbourg can tell us something about it – if we are able to speak with him.'

But Grimpow wasn't paying attention to Salietti. 'There must be something else hidden among the letters. The symbols protect the riddle, which in turn hides a complicated message that has to be deciphered completely in order to be able to understand its real meaning,' he said aloud. Then Grimpow thought of the other message, 'There are darkness and light in the sky,' and a spark of brightness went off in his mind.

'I have it! I have it!' he shouted.

'There's *more?*' asked Salietti, looking at his clever friend, perplexed.

'Yes, there is something more. The mystery lies in "Pass the misty Vale of Scirum".'

'You've already said that!' complained Salietti. 'I'm afraid that this riddle is driving you a bit mad. Let's drop it now and get out of this granary.'

Grimpow's eyes were glued to the text of the cryptogram he had copied on the piece of parchment.

'I mean that the words *misty Vale of Scirum* are also anagrams and don't mean what we think.'

Salietti took up a piece of parchment and tried to change the order of the letters in the words to find others with a different meaning, but Grimpow beat him in the riddle's solution.

'It's an anagram of *clavis mysterium* – roughly, "the key to the mystery".'

'That's fantastic!' said Salietti, amazed by Grimpow's new discovery.

Below his annotation of the original cryptogram – 'Pass the misty Vale of Scirum' – he wrote:

Pass the key to the mystery

'And where is the key to the mystery and what do we have to pass it through?' asked Salietti, clearly discouraged again by what he thought was another difficult and confusing riddle.

'It's our stone!' said Grimpow without hesitation.

'The stone?' repeated Salietti.

'Yes, the philosopher's stone. The sages' *lapis philosophorum* is the key to all the mysteries of nature and the cosmos, as well as to the mystery we are trying to solve with our journey. We must pass our stone, the key to the mystery, over the inscription on the crypt.'

'Grimpow, you are a genius!' Salietti exclaimed.

'It's not me, it's the stone,' answered Grimpow humbly.

The Key to the Mystery

There was no one in the church. The pews in the central nave had been put back in their original positions and a strong scent of incense purified the air among the sparks of the candles alight on the altar. They looked for the priest in the sacristy but he wasn't there either, so they took the candelabra and lit its candles to illuminate their way to the dark depths of the crypt. Would they find the secret of the wise there?

Standing over the inscription in the central circle of the crypt, Grimpow pulled out the stone from the linen pouch around his neck and squatted down. He held it to the symbols on the circle and watched as the miraculous mineral began changing colours until it looked like a burning ember. Then the carved symbols in the circle began to glow red, as if they had been written with fire.

Yet nothing else occurred.

'What now?' asked Salietti impatiently. He clearly thought that something surprising and magical should have happened when they passed the stone over the inscription.

'I don't know. I don't know what else we can do,' said Grimpow, disappointed himself.

'Perhaps the philosopher's stone isn't the key to the mystery,' said Salietti regretfully.

'Or maybe this isn't the inscription where the stone should be passed!' answered Grimpow, as something suddenly dawned on him.

He instinctively raised his eyes to the vault a few inches over Salietti's head. There it was, in the centre, where the radial ribs of the vaulted ceiling converged.

'The ouroboros!'

The sign of the serpent swallowing its tail – the same sign on both the gold seal and the letter sealed with wax – was located precisely over the crypt's inscription.

'Give me the stone. I can pass it over the ouroboros by just raising my arm,' urged Salietti. But when he passed the stone over the sign, still nothing happened.

'Let me try,' said Grimpow, taking the stone from Salietti's hand.

And as soon as he placed the stone over the ouroboros sign, a ray of light like heavenly fire emerged from the centre of the crypt's vault and cast itself on the inscription. They heard the creaking of a rock and, when they turned around, saw one of the sarcophagi rotating on its centre, as if the door to Hell was opening right in front of them.

'It's clear that that stone, or whatever it is, has *chosen* you,' said Salietti.

'What do you mean?' asked Grimpow.

'Only in your hands does it show its magic. Obviously, it chooses its owner and it needs you to show its essence,' said Salietti emphatically.

'And if someone else had found it?' asked Grimpow.

'I think that person would have found nothing more than a worthless stone.'

Grimpow remembered what Brother Rinaldo had told him in the library's secret chamber at the abbey of Brinkdum: 'A Chosen One can reveal the world's truth and channel wisdom that will lead him to discover the secret of the wise. That wonderful treasure is accessible only to those who search for it following the proper signs and paths.'

'Do you think . . . do you think that the secret of the wise can be there?' murmured Grimpow, overwhelmed by emotion, as he pointed to the sarcophagus.

'If we don't take a look inside, we'll never know,' answered Salietti. He brought the candleholder to the open grave and put his head inside the black, sinister hole.

'Can you see anything?' asked Grimpow.

'There's not even a bone in here,' said Salietti, feeling around.

'Wait – there does seem to be something here.'

'What is it?' Grimpow asked impatiently. 'Tell me!'

'Just an old manuscript,' muttered Salietti, the

disappointment clear in his voice. He stood and gave Grimpow an ancient book covered with dust.

Grimpow blew on the cover, raising a thick grey cloud. He wiped it with his sleeve, revealing a golden cover that shimmered with a magical intensity. It was an exceptionally beautiful book with a gold clasp and golden reinforcements in its binding. In the centre of the cover was the ouroboros sign, a serpent swallowing its tail, and above it was a title written in the same hieroglyphics Grimpow already knew.

'What does it say?' asked Salietti.

'*The Cosmic Essence of the Stone!*' exclaimed Grimpow, excited. It looked as though the old manuscript he held in his hands would finally reveal what exactly the stone was, and also might contain the clues they needed to find the secret of the wise, wherever it was hidden.

Salietti smiled happily as the meaning of the old manuscript's title clicked in his mind. 'Is the author's name on the cover?' he asked.

'Under the title is the name *Muciblib Rodia*, or at least

that's what I think it says,' answered Grimpow. 'It sounds like it could be a strange language, but considering what we've seen so far I'm sure that's not right.'

Salietti asked Grimpow for the piece of parchment and charcoal pencil and wrote down the name his friend had told him.

'I think that you've overlooked something important,' said Salietti, hiding a playful smile.

'What?' asked Grimpow. Not another riddle!

'You should have read it back to front.'

Grimpow did as Salietti said and let out a cry of happiness. 'Aidor Bilbicum! It was written by *Aidor Bilbicum*!'

'Correct,' said Salietti, pride dancing in his eyes. 'Now, let's take a look at it before the candles burn out and we're left in the dark.'

The manuscript wasn't thick – it contained only eight parchment pages – but with only a glance through, Grimpow knew that it was the most spectacular and mysterious of all the hermetic treatises written by the alchemists.

'Read some of those symbols out loud. What's the manuscript about?' asked Salietti.

Grimpow opened the book and began reading:

> *The first time I spoke with the mysterious sage I thought he was mad.*
> *I met him during one of those whims of the universe, on a trip to the other side of the ocean, sailing in a big galley that carried silks and spices from those*

exotic lands. A warm breeze blew that night and the calmness of the waves invited me to stay on the ship's deck, contemplating the starred heavens and their miraculous luminescence. The absence of a moon gave me the perfect occasion to enjoy contemplating the constellations of the zodiac, and I began to locate them, pointing at the sky with my staff. I had just found the sign of Aries in the western quadrant, for the spring equinox was drawing near, when I felt someone watching me from behind.

I turned my head to discover the face of my unusual companion. It looked as if the very moon was alight in his eyes. He was a man of medium height, with a shaggy beard and long hair, who looked at me expectantly, hoping perhaps that I would be polite and tell him about my observations in the majestic night sky.

I was about to introduce myself when he pronounced my name and told me that, if I desired, he could take me to a castle whose walls merged into the stars I was contemplating with such zeal.

I wasn't surprised by the fact that he knew my name, for, being a passenger like myself, he could have heard it from one of the sailors or from me when I introduced myself to the captain before setting sail. But on hearing his words, I thought the man was having delusions due to the many days roaming the oceans exposed to the merciless sun, the ship's swaying and the lashing of the winds.

I smiled to conceal my amazement at the absurdity of his offer, for not only did I think it was impolite to make it clear that what he'd said was irrational, but I was afraid that he could have a fit of fury in his madness and throw me overboard to feed the sharks that were so abundant in those deep waters. I opted for going along with his story and letting myself be dragged by the gentle tide of his fantasy.

I answered that I would have been pleased to accept such a novel and daring flight if I didn't have to reach shore to visit a good friend and expert in the heavens with whom I was planning to discuss the movement of the planets and their elliptical orbits around the sun. I thought that explanation would suffice and allow me to resume what I was doing, leaving for another time the visit to the stars he suggested.

But, contrary to my expectations, he seemed to understand my excuses and praised me for having such a sublime reason. His time, he told me, was dedicated to such matters as well, and he thought he could illustrate, if I so desired, the chemical composition of the heavenly bodies or the measurement of the distances between stars. Pleased, I accepted his offer, as it didn't require abandoning the galley or any mad flights through the night skies, and also seemed more suitable to the origin of our conversation.

My companion then began a rambling speech on the universe, grounded on such solid and original theories that I couldn't help but listen to him stupefied. And my surprise was such that I thought I myself had suddenly gone mad or fallen victim to a heartless hallucination. In no other part of the world, of the many places I had visited following my passion for astronomy, had I heard such advanced and accurate ideas about the science of the stars. So I surrendered to his brilliant erudition and begged him to let me enjoy his company during the length of our journey and even accompany him as his assistant anywhere he went.

The mysterious sage received my words with joy and we continued our pleasant conversation until well into the morning. He told me then that he too wanted to reach the shores we were headed to, for he was planning to explore on those lands an unknown paradise inhabited by extraordinary and magical beings. When I heard this I doubted his sanity again, but his previous exposition had been so pleasant and magnificent that I soon forgot my suspicions and continued listening to his story until I felt the sharp stinging of drowsiness in my eyes and the pleasant invitation of sleep.

We said goodbye, promising to continue our fascinating conversation the following day. Later, in the cabin on the stern, I surrendered to sleep's sweet embrace, letting my cosmic dreams fly high. And very near the stars, I still heard the rhythmic splashing of the waves caressing the galley among the whispering of algae, sirens and conchs.

'Up to here it sounds like a fantastical voyage,' said Salietti.

'I have a feeling this is only the beginning, and that this old manuscript tells the story of the stone as well as the secret of the wise and how to uncover it. I think that in order to do that we'll have to solve many riddles, but if we find Aidor Bilbicum, he might be able to help us get out of this maze.'

'So let's go back to the church – the candles are very nearly nubs, and we still have to try to close this sarcophagus. On our way to the baron's fortress you can tell me about the cosmic essence of the stone this manuscript talks about. I can't understand the hieroglyphics it's written in, but it seems you can read it as if it was the language you grew up with.'

As he had done to open the sarcophagus, Grimpow passed the stone over the ouroboros sign on the crypt's vault. The grave closed with a deafening sound, returning the now-empty tomb to darkness.

They found the priest in the sacristy again.

'Have your prayers helped? Have you found what you were looking for in the crypt?' he asked them as he put on his chasuble.

'There's nothing but bones in this church's crypt!' said Salietti harshly.

The priest laughed. 'If you were looking for gold, you should have looked in the Pope's coffers in Avignon!'

But his face changed as soon as he noticed the handful of gold nuggets that Salietti was offering him.

'Have you found treasure?' he asked, astounded.

'No. However, the Pope sends you this gold to thank you for your help and discretion. With it you can fix the church, help the villagers in need, and rebuild the houses destroyed by the fire.' The priest reached to take the gold nuggets from the knight's hand but Salietti suddenly snatched them back. 'First you must make an oath,' he said seriously.

'An oath?'

'You must swear by the cross on your chest that you will speak to no one of Gurielf Labox or us. Listen to me well – speak to no one, even if you think that person knows our secret.'

The priest clutched his crucifix, brought it to his lips, and kissed it with devotion. 'I swear!' he said swiftly.

'If you break your promise, God will fill your stomach with worms and they will devour your insides. But if you respect it, God will grant you a long, healthy, happy life,' said Salietti, and he gave the priest the gold nuggets.

'Go, and do not worry. I assure you that the worms won't devour my body until I have died, and I will never tell anyone that I have seen you anywhere – neither you nor your squire.'

Disturbing News

They left the village of Cornill and travelled north. The priest had given them provisions – wild boar, a large loaf of bread, and a wineskin full of his delicious plum liquor, which they ate as they rode when they became hungry. Around them was a landscape of small hills covered with evergreens and bushes, and the road flowed easily through the fresh shade of the trees flanking it.

As they travelled they went over the latest events of their journey, which had begun to bear the first fruits in their uncertain search. They now had in their power not only the philosopher's stone but also the mysterious manuscript, *The Cosmic Essence of the Stone*, which they hoped would help them solve the riddles they'd been unable to decipher until now. They also knew that the stone, the manuscript and the secret of the wise were coveted by both the Pope and the King of France – the two most powerful men on earth, who had sent out their best spies to search for the secret.

Grimpow supposed that was the reason why the Pope had sent Gurielf Labox to the village of Cornill, and why the king had ordered Baron Figueltach to detain him. The Pope and the King of France had no idea that Salietti and his young squire possessed the stone. And, from Aidor Bilbicum's manuscript on the cosmic essence of the stone, both Salietti and Grimpow knew that without the stone, it was impossible to reveal the secret of the wise, wherever it was hidden.

In the first part of the manuscript Grimpow had read to Salietti, Aidor Bilbicum narrated his encounter with a mysterious sage, whom he'd met in one of his journeys to the Middle East a few years before the first Crusade to the Holy Land. The nameless sage had revealed to him surprising mysteries about nature and the cosmos, and had given him a strange stone fallen from the stars that not only could turn base metal to gold, but also could allow the bearer to achieve ultimate wisdom and even immortality. He had also shown him an unusual object in an underground cavern of the Temple of Solomon in Jerusalem that, upon contact with the stone, could perform unimaginable miracles.

Shortly after, the mysterious sage disappeared, and Aidor Bilbicum never saw him again. Upon his return to France, he secretly founded a small school of sages, which he called

Ouroboros; he chose the sign of a serpent biting its tail as a symbol of infinity and fusion.

Time passed, and Aidor Bilbicum returned to Jerusalem with seven other sages from his school. The eight men planned to take the unusual object hidden in the Temple to France. At the time, nine French and Flemish knights were in Jerusalem, so Aidor Bilbicum and his disciples asked them to guard the magical object during its transfer to Paris in exchange for generous amounts of gold. Seven of the nine knights accepted, and the sages wrapped the object in sheepskins and the caravan left Jerusalem.

Once in Paris, surprised by the infinite power of the miraculous object, Aidor Bilbicum and his disciples decided to hide it in a safe place and keep its existence a secret.

Years passed, and the seven other sages of the Ouroboros society died and were buried in an old octagonal crypt in the village of Cornill, where Aidor Bilbicum was born.

'But his name didn't appear in the church's archive,' interrupted Salietti. 'I read the book of births and baptisms from front to back.'

'Perhaps Aidor Bilbicum wasn't his real name, but a pseudonym behind which to hide his true identity,' suggested Grimpow.

'That's possible,' said Salietti. 'But keep going, this is interesting.'

'He was the only one left alive,' continued Grimpow, 'for as the keeper of the strange stone, he had not only become a great sage but was immortal like a god. Yet Aidor

Bilbicum knew that he should pass down the stone to one of his disciples, as the old sage had advised him, for if he didn't, the stone would destroy him. So he looked for a suitable young man and taught him everything he knew. Eventually the time came to pass the stone on. Aidor Bilbicum gave the stone to his disciple and asked him to bury his body next to the manuscript in the sarcophagus in the crypt in Cornill where the bodies of the seven sages of the Ouroboros secret society rested. That's why the tombs in the crypt number eight and why the manuscript was in one of them. The sarcophagus we opened must have been Aidor Bilbicum's,' added Grimpow.

'So Aidor Bilbicum is dead?' Salietti was somewhat confused, for they had found no skeleton in the sarcophagus.

'That's what the manuscript says.'

'That means that we won't be able to find him in Strasbourg, and that the message you found on the knight makes no sense,' he reflected.

'Perhaps the text of the letter is another secret code, or a new cryptogram. I don't know,' admitted Grimpow. 'In any case, the manuscript explains where the secret of the wise is hidden, but the last page and a map seem to be missing. Aidor Bilbicum thought that a time might come when the miraculous object found in the Temple of Solomon should be discovered again by other sages, so he wrote down the way to find it, protecting the secret with the hieroglyphic writing of the Ouroboros society and a multitude of riddles. Everything is here, except for the map and that last page.'

'But what will we look for in Strasbourg if Aidor Bilbicum is not there?' asked Salietti.

'The real beginning of the end,' said Grimpow. 'Even though Aidor Bilbicum is dead, if we look for him we might be able to find clues in Strasbourg to solve the riddles contained in this manuscript. That's what the note Gurielf Labox left in the archive must mean. Only by going to the city mentioned in the letter and asking there for *he who doesn't exist* will we be able to hear *the voice from the shadows,*' he added.

'What can that voice tell us?' wondered Salietti.

'If I am not mistaken,' said Grimpow gravely, 'how to uncover the mystery of the stone's cosmic essence.'

On their way to the Baron Figueltach's fortress, they ran into several groups of knights also heading north to participate in the spring tournaments. Grimpow was fascinated by the colourful and majestic entourages and their caravans. The carriages transporting the ladies and their maids were decorated with flower wreaths and silk ribbons, the lances' tips shimmered under an intense sun, and a multitude of small flags and banners waved on the saddles of a large group of soldiers and knights.

A noble-looking man who rode alone at the head of an entourage, followed closely by his squire, saluted them politely when they were about to pass him. He wasn't old, but he wasn't young either. He had grey eyes over a straight nose, and his hair was a strange ash colour, as were his eyebrows and short beard. He was wearing a pointy hat with a pheasant feather and his clothes were elegant, though they were discoloured from the dust covering them. The handle of his sword was thick and golden at the bottom.

'Your shield's coat of arms looks familiar. Are you headed for Baron Figueltach of Vokko's fortress?' he asked Salietti.

Salietti pulled the reins to adjust the march of his horse to the knight's; Grimpow slowed down to ride beside the other squire, a dark-skinned young man who looked at him indifferently.

'That is in fact my destination, and I assume it's yours too, Sir . . . ?'

'Rhadoguil of Curnilldonn. And you? What's your name?' asked the knight.

'Salietti of Estaglia, grandson of Duke Iacopo of Estaglia.'

'You are a foreigner?'

'Yes, born in the Italian region of Piedmont.'

'And have you crossed the Alps to attend the tournaments?'

'For a knight hungry for adventures and feats, the alpine mountains are like giants to be defeated in hard battles,' answered Salietti.

The knight laughed kindly. 'You are right, my friend. Tell me, do you also intend to fight in Baron Figueltach and the king's new Crusade against the Circle's castles?'

'I didn't know of the approaching war when I left

Piedmont, and I've only vaguely heard about it on the way. I've heard that the baron has allied himself with the King of France to hunt down the Templars sheltered in the castle of the Duke of Ostemberg. Am I wrong?'

'Nonsense!' said the knight disdainfully. 'Everyone knows that the King wants to destroy the Circle's castles – as he did six years ago with the Temple tower in Paris – to loot them and look for the secret of the Templars.'

'But the secret of the Templars is surely only a legend,' said Salietti.

The knight moved in his saddle and readjusted his sword's sheath behind him. 'My friend,' he said, 'when a Templar Grand Master – accused of having dealt with the Devil and the arts of necromancy – in agony in the stake's flames, announces to the Pope and the King of France that they will die within a year, his threat is taken seriously.'

'And if the threat by the Temple's Grand Master has no power? In times like these, people are prone to invent stories of magic and spells, and they end up believing them as if they were true,' said Salietti.

'Take my word – you can be sure that the curse is as real as the fact that you are talking to me now. I witnessed his execution at the stake on the eighteenth day of last March, in front of Notre Dame on the Île de la Cité in Paris. I heard the Templar Grand Master proclaim his curse in a loud and strong voice. When Jacques de Molay was in the crackling flames, and everyone present thought he had already exhaled his last breath, he suddenly raised his voice and shouted: "I curse my killers! Within a year, you will report your crimes against the Templar Order to God's tribunal!" And his curse has already begun to come true.'

'What do you mean?' enquired Salietti.

'A messenger told the knights riding behind you that Pope Clement the Fifth died a few days ago in the castle of Roquemaure, near Avignon.'

'What?' Salietti was alarmed.

'It seems he felt slightly ill, then began suffering from severe pains, and ended up vomiting blood as if his insides had exploded.'

'So the curse has been loyally fulfilled,' said Salietti, disconcerted.

'Did you have any doubts?' asked the knight mysteriously.

'Well, I don't really believe in curses, charms or spells,' admitted Salietti pensively.

The knight laughed again. 'Neither do I, my friend, neither do I. What's killed the Pope is not a spell but poison,' he murmured without losing his composure.

Salietti didn't know if the knight was saying that because he had accurate information or because he had made an assumption. 'How can you be so sure of that?' he queried.

'Because only a poisoned potion could cause such a horrible, gory death, and because it is clear as water that this was revenge.'

'Revenge? From whom?' Salietti demanded. 'Six years ago, the Templars who had escaped the dungeons and the stake left France and fled to Spain and Portugal, to the castles of the Circle of Stone, and to Germany.'

'There are still Knights Templar in France willing to reclaim their order's honour,' the knight answered. 'King Philip knows it, and now, after Pope Clement's death, he is more terrified than a pig during slaughtering season. He's realized the same fate awaits him, and knows that if he doesn't find the secret of the Templars in time – the legendary elixir of life – he will probably be dead by next spring.'

'Why are you telling me all of this?' Salietti dared ask. 'If things are the way you say, you're risking your life.' Salietti wondered if Rhadoguil of Curnilldonn could be a Templar in a nobleman's disguise.

'Don't worry. I've already told you – your shield's coat of arms is familiar to me.'

And as they rode in silence, the wind blew and night began to fall. The sky was still clear, though clouds, swollen and soft, peeked from among the crests of the nearby mountains.

Magic in the Stars

Baron Figueltach of Vokko's fortress sat on a hill rising from the Alsatian plain. It was a magnificent and gigantic castle, full of inaccessible watchtowers, posterns, barbicans, machicolations and high crenellated turrets, many of which were round and topped with roofs that looked like black cowls. The main gate was flanked by two thick towers and protected by a large portcullis and a drawbridge that crossed the ditch. As the entourages of knights arrived, a pair of the baron's heralds, surrounded by banners and a band of musicians, greeted them and assigned each group a pair of servants – one would escort the noblemen and ladies to their quarters, and the other would guide the carriages and horses to the stables.

Inside the castle, the pace was even more intense. Hundreds of knights and soldiers in shimmering coats of mail and helmets moved to and fro between the high walls and towers, and in every corner burned torches whose tongues of fire seemed to want to fly away with the wind. Grimpow couldn't stop looking around, fascinated by the hustle and bustle, while a servant walked them through a wide esplanade to their quarters and another one took their horses and mule to the stables.

Grimpow suddenly had to jump back to avoid being crushed under the hoofs of a rearing horse

'Who's that knight?' Salietti asked the page accompanying them.

'Every year a handful of adventurous but penniless noblemen come here and call attention to themselves by doing strange things like that,' the page complained. 'But I'm sure you're not like them – one has only to see you to know you aspire to win in the jousts. You might even be the one to choose the queen of the tournament.'

'And what's your name?' Salietti asked the page, a boy a little older than Grimpow, with big ears and teeth like a mouse.

'You can call me Guishval, sir.'

'Guishval,' repeated Salietti slowly. 'Not a bad name for a boy as sharp as you.'

From Salietti's flattering tone, Grimpow realized that they might have just found the perfect informant within the walls of the fortress.

'If you need anything, you only have to ask,' said Guishval. Suddenly he shouted: 'Look! There's my master, the baron!'

Next to the pit, a richly dressed nobleman was giving orders to his knights. He was younger than Grimpow had imagined, had no beard and his long black hair swayed slightly in the wind. His eyes had a merciless radiance and his voice and gestures were as harsh as his look. A long black velvet cloak with gold trim hung from his shoulders, and on the front of his white blouse was embroidered a large black bear. Attached to his waist was a long sword whose handle glistened as if a handful of precious stones had blended with the steel.

They bowed upon reaching him and then continued crossing the courtyard. They passed the sheds and the kitchens, and entered a tower guarded by two soldiers wearing coats of mail and helmets, who raised their lances to let them in. On their shields was painted the same bear that waved in the wind on all the castle's banners. After climbing a set of narrow stairs to the first floor of the tower, they finally reached a room with thick walls and low ceilings in which was a line of about twenty comfortable cots with straw mattresses on the floor next to them. The room was as noisy as the courtyard, for many of the joust's participants had already reached the castle and were placing their possessions by the cots they had been assigned.

'These are your quarters – the cot is for you and the straw mattress for your squire,' explained Guishval unnecessarily, for it was obvious to Grimpow that he would have to sleep on the floor. 'You can leave your bags on that bench, and there is a pail with water there; the privies are at the end of

215

the courtyard. My master the baron wishes you a pleasant stay at the fortress. Dinner will be served in two hours, in the great armoury. The heralds will announce the pairs of contenders at dawn and the jousts will be celebrated afterward.'

'Thank you, Guishval. You are very kind,' Salietti flattered him again.

The page bowed to leave, but Salietti stopped him.

'Just a moment,' he said, lowering his voice to avoid being heard by the other knights shuffling about around them. 'Tell me, Guishval, have you ever seen the shine of a gold nugget?'

Perplexed, Guishval looked at Salietti and then turned to Grimpow, as if to enquire about the sanity of the knight he served.

'No, sir,' he said shyly. 'The only gold I've ever seen in my life is the one my master's seal is made of, and that of the jewels and bracelets worn by the ladies of the castle.'

'Perhaps I could give you a gold nugget in exchange for your services,' Salietti whispered into Guishval's ear.

The page started as if he had been stabbed in the back with a knife.

'What do I need to do?' he asked, his eyes wide.

'For now, only tell me if two prisoners, an old man and his daughter, were brought to the castle a few days ago,' replied Salietti without hesitation.

Guishval checked the room to make sure no one was watching them before answering.

'I am not sure if I should talk about it. If my master the baron finds out that I've been loose-tongued, he'll have no problem cutting it out and throwing it to his dogs,' he said, scared.

'You can be sure that he will never know. I swear by my knightly honour,' Salietti reassured him.

'The old man and his daughter arrived at the fortress two days ago, escorted by the baron's soldiers. My eyes have never seen such a beautiful young lady,' said Guishval.

'Are they locked in the castle's dungeons?' pressed Salietti.

'No, sir,' replied the page. 'The old man was very ill when he got here. They put him in a dingy room in the watchtower and he died last night. His shroud was brought down to the ossuary by the dungeons this morning, without a Mass or ceremony, and they left his body there as if he'd been an outlaw. The soldiers say that he was a sorcerer or a necromancer.'

Salietti's face looked as if he'd just been pierced by an invisible dagger. And though the Italian tried to conceal the sorrow that filled his soul, Grimpow knew from his watery eyes that old Gurielf Labox wasn't a simple stranger to him. As he had suspected when they had arrived at the village of Cornill, Salietti was hiding something.

'Does his daughter know that the old man has died?'

'I believe so. Since her father died last night, she hasn't stopped crying. Her name is Weienell.'

'Where is the lady now?'

217

'Locked in a chamber in the keep. My master, the Baron of Alsace, was mesmerized by her, and I suspect he is trying to win her love despite having made her his prisoner.'

Grimpow noticed that a grimace crossed Salietti's face again.

'Who keeps the key to that room?' he asked, anguished.

'My master the baron keeps it in a small chest in his study.'

Salietti took out two gold nuggets from the pouch hidden under his belt and gave them to the servant discreetly.

'Thank you for your help, Guishval. Make sure nobody finds these on you, for they will think you've stolen them. I will still need other favours from you . . .'

'If you need me, just send a message to the stables with your squire and I will be ready to serve you, sir,' replied the page cheerfully, and he bowed several times as he backed away.

When they were left alone, Grimpow and Salietti tidied up their bags and washed their hands and faces in the pail of water. Salietti took off his dust-covered clothes, shook them out, and then laid them on the bed. He grabbed from his bag a new pair of hose, a shirt and a doublet they had bought in the city of Ullpens, and he dressed as if he were attending the investiture ceremony of a knight.

'We swore not to keep secrets from each other,' said Grimpow crossly.

Salietti turned, evidently taken aback by the words of his friend.

'I don't know what you're talking about, Grimpow,' replied Salietti in a low voice as he slid his sword into his belt. 'You know as much about me as I know about you.'

'I'm talking about Gurielf Labox and his daughter. You knew them. And our arrival at the village of Cornill was not coincidental. You knew they were there, though it didn't occur to you that they would be taken by the baron's soldiers, right?' pressed Grimpow.

'We can't talk about it now, Grimpow – but I promise it's not what you think,' Sallieti replied.

Grimpow couldn't stop the tears from streaming down his cheeks. The exhaustion from the journey, the influence of the magical stone he possessed, his fear of the uncertainties awaiting them in the baron's fortress, plus the feeling of being betrayed by someone he thought was his best friend . . .

'Oh, come on, Grimpow! I didn't mean to hurt you. I just can't speak of that right now. It's a long and complicated story, but I swear I'll tell you everything later. We have more important things to worry about at the moment.'

Salietti's words made Grimpow feel better. He apologized, and Salietti accepted with a smile and winked at him.

'Don't worry about it. Finish washing up – we're going to take a walk around the fortress before dinner, where I hope we'll be eating something warm and tasty.'

'Do you have any plans for finding Gurielf Labox's

daughter?' asked Grimpow, knowing that it was now the only thing on Salietti's mind.

'Not yet. I first need to meet with Baron Figueltach of Vokko. While I speak to him, I might be able to find the keys to the chamber – I'm sure he keeps them nearby at all times.'

'What?' exclaimed Grimpow. 'You're going to put yourself directly into the wolf's mouth?' He was worried about the idea he could see forming in Salietti's eyes.

'It's the only way I'll be able to find out how sharp its teeth are.'

Salietti walked toward the bench they had left their bags on and dug through them. He took out a thick deck of cards Grimpow had never seen before.

'Are you going to play cards with the baron?' Grimpow asked.

'No,' said Salietti, laughing. 'These are different cards. They're used in some Middle Eastern countries to foretell the future. Many noblemen and women are weak when it comes to the uncertainties of their destiny and want to know it in advance in hopes of avoiding anything unpleasant. Figueltach of Vokko is one of them – I've heard he has a passion for the divinatory arts. But I'm sure that he's never heard of fortune-telling through this simple game of cards. I'm going to give them to him as a gift to win his trust.'

'And what will I do in the meantime?'

'Do you still have the charcoal pencil and piece of parchment you took from the sacristy in Cornill's church?'

'Yes, they're in this bag.'

'Get them. I need to write something important.'

Grimpow grabbed the charcoal pencil and tore off a piece of parchment. Salietti asked him to turn around and bend over so he could use Grimpow's back as a desk, though Grimpow suspected he was also doing it so he wouldn't be able to see what his friend wrote.

'Don't worry, I'll let you look when I'm done,' Salietti told him, as if reading his mind.

He leaned on Grimpow's back and with a calligraphy more suited to a copyist monk than to a knight-errant, he wrote:

> There is magic in the stars
> And enchantment during full-moon nights
> Gaze at them and you will find your dreams

'Is it for her?' asked Grimpow after Salietti let him see the message.

'Yes.'

'Is this another message in code?'

'Not exactly, but she'll understand it.'

'Aren't you going to sign your name?'

'My name wouldn't mean anything to her,' said Salietti, seeming to grow tired of his friend's questions. 'And now, listen to me carefully. While I try to speak to the baron, you go to the stables as if you were only going to tend to our horses. When you've found Guishval, and nobody's watching you, give him another gold nugget. Tell him it's a gift from me and that I need him to promptly deliver this message to Gurielf Labox's daughter.'

Of all the riddles, mysteries, and secrets Grimpow had come across since finding the dead knight in the mountains, nothing intrigued him more than what Salietti had in mind now. And while they walked under the torchlight among the soldiers, knights, squires, pages, carriages and horses coming and going from the many parts in the fortress, Grimpow wondered who Gurielf Labox had really been, why he had been looking for the secret of the wise in Cornill's church, what his relationship to Salietti was, and what made his friend worry so much about the old man's captive daughter. He couldn't stop thinking either about the message Salietti had given him for Guishval to deliver to her. What could it mean?

Grimpow sighed. With a shrug, he set off to find the page.

The Death Card

After wandering around damp passages and narrow spiral staircases for some time, Salietti reached the castle's armoury. A large group of noblemen and ladies were forming a circle around Baron Figueltach, who was conversing with them animatedly. Everything was ready for dinner, and several knights sat at the long tables in the room, which was adorned with bright tapestries, ostentatious hunting trophies, long banners hanging from the ceiling, and a multitude of coats of arms crossed by lances and swords. The light from the oil lamps and burners looked like little suns, and in a great fireplace in one of the side walls roared a huge fire, over which was a whole deer rotating on a spit.

Salietti stepped up to a knight giving orders to a few heralds in full dress attire and asked him, 'Are you the mayor of the fortress?'

'Correct,' he said with a slight bow, which Salietti responded to by bowing as well. 'What can I do for you, gentleman?'

'My name is Salietti of Estaglia. I know that the baron is busy as the host of the tournaments, but could you be so kind as to tell him that I wish to speak with him in private?'

'I will relay your message to the baron, my master, as soon as we sit at the table,' the mayor answered. Bowing again, he stepped toward another group of heralds awaiting his orders.

Salietti was satisfied. He'd set out the bait – now he only had to wait for the baron to take it.

Shortly trumpets announced the beginning of dinner and a crowd of servants spilled out of the kitchens carrying trays full of roasted pheasant, lamb and venison. At the sight of all the delicacies Salietti's appetite came back with a vengeance. Paying no attention to the merriment around him, he surrendered wholeheartedly to devouring whatever food he could get his hands on.

Suddenly he felt eyes on him, and looked up to see that Baron Figueltach was staring at him, the fortress' mayor murmuring in his ear. In a hint of a greeting, Salietti gave a brief nod, which the baron returned, evidently intrigued. To the baron's left was a Dominican friar with a red beard and deep scars on his face; Salietti had no doubt that it was the evil inquisitor Bulvar of Goztell.

Before dinner was over, the baron addressed the crowd and, with grandiloquent gestures, gave an impassioned speech to his knights urging them to join the war against the castles of the Circle, telling them about the Templars' heretic acts and the need to burn them all at the stake. After that, a few acrobats entered the great armoury blowing long tongues of fire from their mouths while they did amazing jumps and tumbles to the music of trumpets and drums. The knights raised their pitchers and toasted as the ladies applauded, mesmerized by the spectacle.

Salietti noticed the baron get up from his table and walk toward his quarters. It didn't take long for the herald to approach his own table.

'Excuse me, sir,' he said in Salietti's ear. 'The baron wishes to see you in private. Please follow me.'

'Please, come in and be welcome!' said the baron when Salietti entered the large room. The baron was pacing restlessly in front of an ornate tapestry with an embroidered bear, to the sides of which were the mounted heads of two enormous stags.

Salietti crossed the threshold and smiled politely. Though he feigned respect and admiration for the man in front of him, inwardly he was overtaken by rage and disdain.

'The mayor has informed me that you wished to speak in private about something you deemed of interest to me.'

'Yes, sir,' the knight answered, bowing humbly. 'My name is Salietti, grandson of Duke Iacopo of Estaglia, from the Italian region of Piedmont.'

The baron nodded. 'What you wish to tell me must be

very important if you have taken such a long and arduous trip to do so.'

'Well, that is for you to decide. My main reason for coming to your fortress was to participate in the tournaments of the Alsatian castles, the fame and reputation of which, as you well know, reach the north of Italy every year.'

'Yes. There are more and more knights from Padua, Trieste and Bolsano who come to celebrate the spring jousts with us. We're very happy to be their host,' said the baron.

'I met some gentlemen during my journey who were also heading to your fortress. And they informed me of your plans to attack the castles of the Circle. They told me that you intend to capture the rebel Templars whom your eternal enemy, Duke Gulf of Ostemberg, has given shelter to, against the bulls of the sadly deceased Pope Clement the Fifth. I hope you will let me join your army.'

The baron stepped closer to Salietti and put his arm around his shoulder. 'Of course – you will be most welcome among my knights. And I can assure you that together we will attain a victory troubadours will sing about in their romances for centuries. But I still haven't heard anything from your lips that has piqued my interest as you've suggested,' said the baron.

Salietti took the hint.

'You are right,' he said, 'but I am sure that this will satisfy you immensely. I would like to give you a present.'

'A present?' asked Figueltach curiously.

'I know of your passion for the divinatory arts, and I thought you'd like these cards. Please keep them – they might help you avoid any unfavourable plans destiny might have in store for you,' said Salietti, pulling out the deck of cards from under his doublet.

Figueltach of Vokko was about to take the cards when Salietti pretended to drop them on the floor. He apologized profusely, and as the baron bent down to grab them, with one hand Salietti felt around on the desk and opened a small chest. He groped around for the keys to the room where Gurielf Labox's daughter was locked, but found nothing.

'Are you a fortune-teller?' the baron asked. He was admiring the beauty of the cards as he collected them.

'Telling the future is an ability I have worked to develop since childhood,' explained Salietti, enjoying his fib.

'Where did you get them?' the baron asked.

'I bought them from a peddler in the city of Venice. The same peddler explained their meaning to me and told me about their origin. Apparently he found the cards among ruins in a faraway country while ransacking tombs looking for jewels buried with the dead. He assured me that these cards have unexplainable powers, as if they had invisible eyes to see beyond time and reality. I can show you how to read them if you'd like.'

The baron's rough hands touched the cards one by one as if trying to get used to their feel. He remained silent for a while, attempting to hide his excitement at having the exotic cards in his possession.

'Are you sure that they really work to tell the future?'

'Not only the future, Baron, but the past as well,' explained Salietti confidently. 'Please have a seat and let me show you.'

Figueltach sat on the table where he dealt with the everyday matters of his vassals, and the torchlight cast furtive shadows over both men's heads.

Salietti placed the twenty-two cards face down on the table, creating four horizontal rows of five cards each. He placed a single card in the centre of the middle row before and after the formation. On the backs of the cards were two silver swords crossed over a sun setting against a clear blue sky.

'Pick a card,' Salietti invited courteously.

Figueltach glanced at the cards on the table as if trying to reveal a mystery hidden among those recurring images, still silent before his eyes.

His gaze finally landed on one card. He took it decisively and turned it face up.

'The lovers!' exclaimed Salietti when he saw the figures of a man and a woman holding hands underneath a bright sun. 'You couldn't have had a better beginning.'

'Will I be lucky in love?'

'There's no doubt about it. That card predicts happiness, well-being and passion. Even if your love is not requited now, as I can see in the disappointment in your eyes, this card foretells that those conflicts will vanish very soon, giving way to everlasting love. Soon you'll be extremely happy.'

Pleased, the baron picked another card. It had the beautifully painted image of a pyramid cracked at the apex by lightning, the sight of which seemed to submerge Salietti in a deep trance.

At Salietti's silence, the baron asked impatiently: 'What do you see?'

The knight took some time to answer. Finally he said: 'That the earth will tremble under the intense light of your sword, which will destroy inaccessible towers and high walls like lightning falling from the sky. I can see you arising triumphantly after cruel battles that will change the course of history. The past will be only a sad memory compared with the glory awaiting you. Now, choose another card that is at least two rows away from the first one, in any direction, and show it to me.'

The baron's face was bright with happiness as he chose and turned another card. On it was a carriage wheel with strange symbols circling it. Before the baron could ask, Salietti explained, 'This is the wheel of fortune. It seems that fortune is in your favour tonight.'

'And what does it mean?' Figueltach demanded.

'You are looking for something that is hiding from your eyes, something that was unjustly denied to you long ago. I cannot see what it is . . . perhaps a precious treasure? . . . No!' corrected Salietti, shaking his head. 'I think it's something more valuable.'

'More valuable than a treasure?' asked the baron, unable to conceal his anxiety.

'Yes, it's a polished and brilliant object many men wish to possess and are chasing desperately, but which only a few chosen ones will find.'

The baron glanced up uncomfortably. 'Did you say "a few chosen ones"?'

'Yes,' confirmed Salietti surely. 'I don't know who they are, but they're here, in the card, in one of these symbols. Perhaps you know better than I what I'm talking about. What you're looking for is . . . something perfect, something different from any other form imaginable. It's an object of a metal more precious than gold.'

'And will I find it?' asked the baron, holding his breath.

'Please choose another card, and we'll find out the answer to your question,' said Salietti, enjoying his new role as fortune-teller.

The baron hesitated over which card to pick, and his hand hovered over the table indecisively. He finally selected a card, turned it over, and saw a crossroads in a dense grove. He seemed fascinated by the beautiful picture.

'Let me see,' said Salietti, trying to build the tension of the moment. He held the card in his hands and continued, 'When you could have taken the right road to find it, you chose one that took you away from it.'

'But will I find that treasure?' insisted the baron.

'I'm afraid that you will not, for that treasure is not

where you believe it is, or in any other place where you can find it.'

'I will destroy their castles until I find the last hole in which those bloody Templars might have hidden it!' shouted the baron, swept up in his own desperation.

'I don't know what you're talking about,' Salietti said, feigning confusion. 'But please take another card if you'd like to know anything else about your future.'

Figueltach of Vokko's hand hesitated in the air and landed on the last card on the second row, as if he wanted to finally end the misfortune announced to him.

'Bad omens appear in your destiny now,' Salietti whispered with a mysterious air.

'What do you mean? Explain,' demanded the baron, frowning.

'This is a card of war and desolation. You should avoid exposing yourself to danger, for terrible battles approach that will fill the country with death. However, I also see that you have a great army.'

'More than fifteen thousand men,' said the baron arrogantly.

'But I don't see as many horsemen,' added Salietti to extract more information from him.

'Close to five thousand armed men on horses – and more than five hundred knights have already left for the north borders to wait for my army and begin fighting. Do you think that's not enough to attack the castles of the Circle?'

'I sense that you will need more than that to accomplish your goal.'

'We'll also have machinery that has never been seen in these lands before, and a group of incredibly strong mercenaries from the south.'

'You'd better pick another card – perhaps it will take you out of the darkness surrounding you. Choose the one you like the most,' urged Salietti.

The baron picked the lonely card on the last row and was horrified to discover what was painted on it – the figure of death.

Lances and Swords

Grimpow was happy to see Salietti in his cot when he woke up, for he hadn't seen him since he'd left to talk to the Baron the night before.

'Where were you last night? You weren't back when I went to sleep,' Grimpow asked as he stretched.

'It was a long and productive night,' said Salietti in a low voice. 'I ate abundantly and spent long hours with the baron, talking about his future and his plans to attack the castles of the Circle of Stone. A part of the army is already approaching the northern border and will wait there for the baron's arrival with his soldiers and knights soon after the end of the tournaments. I gained his trust quickly and he shared very valuable information with me, but I wasn't able to find the key to the room where Labox's daughter is locked. You should have seen his face when I spoke to him of his war plans and the precious object he's looking for and hasn't been able to find. He asked if he would find it soon.'

'And what did you say?'

'I told him the truth – that he'll never find it, for it's not where he thinks it is. But the best was when he picked the death card. His face turned as pale as wax.'

'The death card?' asked Grimpow, intrigued.

'Yes. It's a card that can mean different things, depending on the fortune-teller's so-called visions. I told him that in his case that card meant the shadow of uncertainty, for he might find death during the approaching battle. So I didn't lie.'

'I don't understand.'

'If he attacks the castles of the Circle of Stone soon, his death will be as certain as my word, and there will be no fortune-teller or hidden force that can prevent it.'

'I also found out some interesting things last night in the kitchen,' boasted Grimpow.

'I'm glad to know that you didn't waste your time while I risked my life deceiving the baron with my cards. Did you deliver my message to Guishval as I requested?' asked Salietti, putting on the clothes from the journey again and leaving his elegant attire for the evening celebrations.

'Let's have some breakfast and I'll tell you on the way. Unlike you, I didn't eat much last night.'

While they walked, Grimpow told Salietti what he had done the night before. He told him he had found Guishval in the stables with other young servants of the baron, who were secretly drinking beer while they took care of the horses.

'He was so happy to see me, it was as if he'd seen his guardian angel. I handed him the gold nugget, as you asked me to do, and explained what he needed to do with the message. Guishval pocketed the gold immediately but told me that he didn't know how to send the message to the lady. A soldier guards the room's door constantly and was warned by the baron that he would pay with his life if anyone got through. It occurred to me, however, that the baron must be feeding Labox's daughter, and someone in the kitchen must be in charge of taking food to her. Guishval told me that, if I dared, he could distract the servant while she prepared the basket, and I could hide the message in the food. So we did it. We talked for a while and Guishval told me that he was the baron's falconer's son and there was no secret in the art of falconry that he didn't know about. We talked about that as we wandered around the main kitchens, until the servant finally arrived and began preparing the food – fish, bread, some cheese and a pitcher of water. When she was about to leave, Guishval approached her, and whatever he said made her leave the basket unattended. Then I slipped over and hid the message.'

'And where did you hide it?' asked Salietti, clearly afraid that the letter hadn't reached its destination.

'I left it floating in the pitcher of water.'

'You threw it in the water?' asked Salietti, his voice rising. A few knights walking by turned to look.

'I couldn't think of a better place. Water won't erase charcoal pencil,' he explained.

'You could have hidden it inside a piece of bread,' whispered Salietti.

'I thought about that first, but then I realized that she might not even try the food. Her sadness over her father's death might have left her with no appetite.'

Salietti was lost in thought.

'Well, perhaps your idea wasn't so absurd. Thirst is harder to soothe than hunger. And if Weienell drank anything, I'm sure she found the letter,' admitted Salietti as they reached the stables' great courtyard.

Before he could say anything more, though, they were approached by a few servants offering a quick breakfast to knights and their squires. They grabbed some pieces of bread and cold roasted meat and sat down to eat.

'What else did you find out?' asked Salietti, tearing into a piece of meat with his teeth.

'The inquisitor Bulvar of Goztell is in the fortress,' said Grimpow.

'I know – I saw him yesterday in the armoury during dinner, sitting to the baron's right. I knew it was him from the description Brother Rinaldo of Metz gave me at the abbey.'

'I also learned that Gurielf Labox died when he was being interrogated by Bulvar of Goztell. He couldn't withstand the executioner's torturing,' added Grimpow, not enjoying the subject.

'Are you sure of that?' asked Salietti, a horrified expression on his face.

'Every servant in the castle knows about it. They say it is all they talk about in the soldiers' circles. Apparently, the old man's screams could be heard in the whole watchtower. Then silence reigned, and the next day his body was carried away and buried in the dungeons.'

'That Bulvar is a *murderer*!' hissed Salietti.

'Do you think that Gurielf Labox might have confessed what he was looking for in the village of Cornill?'

'I don't think so. Had he done so, the Dominican friar wouldn't be here now.'

'But Labox carried a letter with the Pope's seal. How could an inquisitor persecute him?' asked Grimpow, trying to make sense of everything.

'The letter was fake,' Salietti said simply, staring at the floor. 'Now let's get the horses and my armour.'

And before Grimpow could ask Salietti anything else, the trumpets blared in the towers and the drums announced the beginning of the jousts.

A translucent fog floated over the castle's high walls and the knights' banners loomed above the plain like big colourful mushrooms adorned with bright flags and coats of arms. Dozens of suits of armour glistened atop moving horses as both horses and riders anxiously awaited the beginning of the tournament. Baron Figueltach of Vokko and Bulvar of Goztell, sitting under a pavilion covered in luxurious purple velvet and accompanied by the most influential noblemen and the most distinguished ladies of Alsace, led the celebrations.

Gathered in small circles, everyone commented on the performance they had witnessed during the dinner the night before, and talk turned to rumours that the King of France had filled the baron's coffers with thousands of coins of pure gold, and how the baron had promised to divide his treasures among the knights who joined his army to conquer the castles of the Circle of Stone. Not many wanted to miss such a generous distribution, so the whole plain was filled with knights who were anxious to show their abilities with the lance and sword in the tournament and win a place of honour next to Baron Figueltach. Also at stake was the choice of the queen of the spring jousts of the Alsatian castles, and many young knights hoped for the privilege of crowning their beloved.

When they arrived at the jousting field, the tournament hadn't yet begun. The heralds were only beginning to call the first contenders by their name and title, and Salietti and his squire still had to wait for their turn in the palisades reserved for the knights. Salietti glowed in the armour sold to them by Master Ailgrup from Ullpens, whom Grimpow thought he recognized in the crowd of hundreds thronging the stands.

When the trumpets announced the first joust, the crowd burst out cheering. Two horsemen came out to the field, sporting their coat of arms on their shields and their horses' elegant uniforms. The visors of their helmets were raised and their blunt-tipped lances sat vertically on the saddles. They took their positions opposite each other, separated by a short wooden fence. They lowered their visors and lances and, among a roar of shouts, spurred their horses to a gallop until they clashed violently in the centre of the field. The impact was brutal, and one of the knights brought his opponent down, injuring him so badly that he had to be carried away by several squires. The winner went to the royal grandstand and raised his lance in a gesture of triumph amid the roaring of his followers. Then he slowly rode his horse off the field and headed toward his pavilion to wait for a second round of combat.

The knights continued fighting in pairs, rarely lasting more than a few confrontations with their opponents, and the ladies offered beautiful silk handkerchiefs to the winners of each round. The knights showed them off with pride, hanging them like precious relics from the tips of their lances.

Among the many screaming people on the sides, Grimpow spotted Guishval, to whom he had taken a special liking since they'd succeeded in delivering Salietti's message to Gurielf Labox's daughter. Guishval had found a privileged spot across from the baron's grandstand, at the centre of the field, so as not to miss the spectacular clash-ing of the lances, and cheered the winner of every round with enthusiasm. Grimpow waved to him to get his attention, and when he saw him, Guishval instantly abandoned his spot, as if he'd suddenly remembered that he had something to tell them.

He ducked under the palisade, and when he reached them, Guishval looked at Salietti with admiration and said, 'Have you seen her, sir?'

Salietti was startled.

'Who?'

'The captive damsel. She's there, next to the baron,' he said, pointing at the grandstand.

Salietti and Grimpow turned their heads at the same time. Between the baron and the mayor of the fortress sat a young lady with her black hair up, decorated with a tiara. Her sad gaze seemed to be lost in the void. The baron, however, looked delighted to have her by his side and chatted to her enthusiastically.

'Are you sure it's her?' asked Salietti disbelievingly.

Her face was so ethereal and delicate that Grimpow understood why every knight in the tournament had succumbed to her beauty.

'I told you that you would not find anyone else like her in all Alsace, or in the whole kingdom of France, for that matter,' said Guishval proudly. 'Do you know a more beautiful lady?'

Salietti looked mystified. 'If she is really Gurielf Labox's daughter, I'm sure she's read my letter. That's why she must have asked the baron to let her join him during the celebration of the tournaments. She knows that the message she found in the water pitcher could only have come from someone who wants to help her, and the sole way to leave the room was to acquiesce to the baron's wishes despite the pain of her father's death.'

'I'm glad I was able to help once more, sir,' said Guishval, smiling.

'Yes, Guishval, you can't imagine how much. We'll talk later, and please remind me that I owe you another gold nugget.'

Guishval took his leave of them, saying he wanted to go back to his spot before a new knight entered the field. But as he passed Salietti, he whispered, 'Beware of the sword of that rider entering the lists.'

Salietti and Grimpow scanned the entrance to the field and saw the imposing figure of a knight clad in black combat gear. On his shield was painted a tower crossed by the wing of a crow, and his helmet was crowned by the miniature head of a large bird. A long black skirt covered the horse up to its head, revealing only the animal's big dark eyes.

'Who is that knight?' asked Salietti, stopping the boy before he could leave.

'The fearful Valdigor of Rostvol. The stories about him would leave the most agile and daring knight terrified. He is the baron's right hand now, and a close friend of the inquisitor. Not only have they offered him great sums of money to join their war against the castles of the Circle, but they have promised him the very fortress of Duke Gulf as a reward.' With that the boy darted off.

Valdigor of Rostvol knocked down his opponent as easily as if he was a scarecrow, then paraded around the field showing off his victory and the emblems on his banner. Soldiers cheered, ladies smiled bashfully, and from the grandstand the baron beamed with satisfaction over the triumph of his ally.

Salietti moved restlessly under his armour. 'How many more jousts before our turn?' he asked Grimpow when the trumpets announced the next pair of contenders.

'Two more and you'll have a chance to fight. Your rival is the one who almost hit me with his horse yesterday.'

'So I will avenge that offence with the first blow of my lance,' laughed Salietti, without taking his eyes off the lady languishing sadly at the baron's side under the inquisitor's glare of hatred and distrust.

Salietti mounted his horse and put on his helmet – which was crowned by a sun and golden feathers. Grimpow was proud to be his squire. He passed Salietti his lance and emblazoned shield, then grabbed the horse's reins and guided it to the jousting field's entrance. The heralds pronounced the Duke of Estaglia's name, and Grimpow saw Salietti glance at the grandstand to see if Weienell showed any reaction to hearing it. But the young lady appeared indifferent to the bustle of the crowd and the heralds' voices.

The trumpets blasted, and Salietti and his opponent took their positions in front of each other. Both spurred their horses to a gallop and aimed their lances. The tips of their lances crashed against their shields and then flew, splintering in the air, but neither contender fell from his horse. A roar rose from the crowd, and the two knights returned to their original positions.

Grimpow handed Salietti a new lance and a moment later Salietti spurred his horse until it charged again, this time with less good fortune for the other knight, who was knocked to the ground violently. Grimpow jumped ecstatically, and Guishval shouted with glee from the side.

The victorious Salietti approached the grandstand, raised his visor, and asked Gurielf Labox's gorgeous daughter – Weienell – to cover the tip of his lance with her veil. As Weienell noticed the sun and the moon painted on his shield, her face changed colour. It was clear that she recognized their significance and saw in them the light of hope.

The Queen of the Tournament

That afternoon, after the jousts, there was a banquet in the fortress' great armoury. The baron didn't hide his satisfaction about having the beautiful young Weienell by his side, and he chatted animatedly with Valdigor of Rostvol and the inquisitor about the jousts and the war preparations. Salietti watched, and waited for the opportunity to be able to talk to Gurielf Labox's daughter himself.

Grimpow spent his time in the corrals where the baron's birds of prey slept with their heads covered in leather hoods. He was in awe of the majestic hawks and eagles Guishval's father trained. To his surprise, Guishval put a black leather glove on his left hand, took a beautiful peregrine falcon from its cage and removed its hood so that Grimpow could see its sparkling honey-coloured eyes.

'This one is my favourite,' he said, stroking the animal's soft feathers. 'When the tournament is over we'll let it fly from the tower.'

The falcon moved its neck inquisitively but let Grimpow touch its head and thick beak, powerful talons and long, pointy wings. Grimpow had always dreamed of one day having a bird of prey like this one and was happy to have met Guishval, whom he already considered a friend. For the first time in a long while he'd met a boy his age, someone like he used to be before finding the dead knight's stone – a boy who couldn't read or write, had never seen an illuminated manuscript or heard of the sages who had written them, but who was simply happy to be alive. And Grimpow thought that he should feel lucky as well, for his childhood dreams of becoming a squire had magically come true. He was now Sir Salietti of Estaglia's squire, and they were both participating in the spring jousts, determined to win them and elect the queen of the tournament. For a short time he forgot about the stone and the search for the secret of the wise.

Later, Grimpow spent time in the stable courtyard, winning archery bets against other young squires who watched, amazed, as Grimpow repeatedly hit the target – a plucked chicken hanging from a log.

'Where did you learn to use the bow like that?' he was asked by a freckled blond squire.

'I learned in the mountains, hunting rabbits,' answered Grimpow modestly.

'You would be a great archer. Have you ever thought of joining an army as a soldier?'

'The baron would probably accept you in his select group of archers,' said another one with dull eyes and an aquiline nose.

'I'm a squire. I wouldn't know how to do anything else,' said Grimpow, bringing the bow up. He drew the string as he stared at the target, released it, and sent the arrow flying, whistling like a whip until it pierced the chicken's breast.

'Well, if you mastered the lance and sword as you master the bow, it wouldn't take you long to become a knight. I hope to become one someday – with my master's consent, of course,' said the blond boy.

'I'll think about it,' murmured Grimpow as he collected the coins the other squires had bet, naively thinking that Grimpow wouldn't be able to hit the target from more than a hundred feet away.

'Have you heard of the approaching war?' the blond squire asked Grimpow.

'I suppose the same as you have,' said Grimpow.

'I don't buy that story about the Templars' legendary treasure,' broke in another squire, this one taller with reddish hair.

Grimpow perked up when he heard this. 'What story is that?' he asked, as if he had no idea what they were talking about. He returned the bow to one of the boys and sat down on some rocks next to them.

'It is said that some knights of the Templar Order found

a valuable treasure long ago in the Holy Land and hid it in Duke Gulf of Ostemberg's castle,' explained the blond boy, lowering his voice as if afraid that someone would hear them. 'Baron Figueltach wants to find that treasure, so he's going to attack the castles of the Circle of Stone as soon as the jousts are over. That's why we're all here and why the fearsome Valdigor has joined the baron. He's rumoured to have been a friend of the Templars.'

'How do you know that?' grumbled Guishval.

'I heard my master say so after the last round of jousts this afternoon,' the squire said. 'He also said that Valdigor has sworn by his honour to win the tournament and name that beautiful lady the baron is holding prisoner queen of the spring celebrations.'

'Valdigor of Rostvol will never defeat my master, Salietti of Estaglia!' blurted Grimpow.

'I bet you anything that Valdigor will knock your master down in the tournament's first duel,' said the blond squire arrogantly as he stood up, showing how much taller he was than Grimpow.

Just as Grimpow was about to respond to the challenge, the squire stepped closer and shoved him in the chest, making him fall on his back into a pile of manure.

'You might be brave with the bow, but with your fists you're only a coward,' said the squire, spitting in the dirt with disdain.

Grimpow clenched his fists and, infuriated, stood up and threw himself at the blond boy. As they grappled in a violent embrace, rolling across the floor, the other boys circled the contenders, laughing and shouting.

In the fortress's great armoury, meanwhile, a group of jugglers wearing hats with long feathers interpreted soft ballads with their lutes, cymbals and flutes, and the noblemen and ladies danced before them, to all the knights' delight.

Salietti hovered discreetly around the beautiful Weienell and Baron Figueltach all night until Gurielf Labox's daughter was left alone for a moment, when he seized the chance to address her.

'There's magic in the stars,' he said, extending his hand with a brief bow – a clear sign that she should dance the next piece with him.

'And enchantment during full-moon nights,' answered Weienell, blushing at the sudden appearance of the unknown knight.

The lady's hair was up and a few strands fell on her forehead. She had eyes as green as emeralds and her voice was warm as a summer's breeze. She stood with a pride that seemed as solid as a fortress.

'I will set you free tomorrow,' he whispered as they moved to the rhythm of the melody.

The young lady smiled as she tried to conceal her confusion. 'Who are you?'

'Consider me a good friend who has suffered the death of your father as much as you,' said Salietti.

'What's your name?' she asked.

'Salietti of Estaglia.'

The young lady's eyes moistened, glistening as if all the stars in the sky were inside them.

'Please hold your tears,' begged Salietti. 'Nobody must know I am trying to help you.'

'How will you do it? The baron never leaves my side during the day, and at night one of his soldiers watches the door to my room as if guarding a treasure.'

'You shouldn't be surprised about that. You are the most valuable jewel a knight could dream of,' said Salietti, smiling, unable to conceal that he was beginning to fall in love with her as well.

'I'd rather die a thousand times than remain imprisoned in this fortress,' mumbled Weienell, lowering her voice when she realized that they were being watched by the baron and the inquisitor.

'Just act as if you don't mind the baron's presence and beg him to let you accompany him to the jousts and celebrations tomorrow. I will take care of the rest,' concluded Salietti confidently.

And to that Weienell smiled and whispered in his ear, 'Don't worry. Whoever you are, I will do as you say.'

When the music ended, Weienell curtseyed and Salietti bowed. He turned to walk away, but before he had left Weienell's side, the baron and the inquisitor were already there.

'Let me introduce you to the Pope's legate and inquisitor

of Lyon, Bulvar of Goztell,' said Figueltach. 'He is honouring us with his presence during the tournaments.'

Salietti bowed in a gesture of respect, and the Dominican friar offered the sparkling ring on his hand for him to kiss.

'The baron has spoken wonders about you and has told me that you're planning to join our army in the Holy Crusade against the renegade Templars who are hiding like rats,' Bulvar said in a grave voice.

'I have also heard about your exploits as an inquisitor, and I'm glad to know that you remain implacable in the face of the heresy in the world,' Salietti lied shamelessly, feeling the weight of Weienell's stare. 'And now, if you'll excuse me, I'll retire to my quarters. I will be fighting hard tomorrow and don't want to miss the opportunity to elect the queen of the tournament,' he added.

As he walked away, he glanced out of the corner of his eye and saw Bulvar standing there, watching him with a thoughtful expression on his face.

The following morning, even more spectators came to the fortress eager to watch the tournaments. It was Sunday, and people from all the nearby villages had abandoned their duties and rushed to watch the spectacle, taking any free spots they could find where the jousting field was still visible. The stands and high walls were crowded with men, women, boys and old people, and – to the delight of both noblemen and peasants – among the crowd wandered a cohort of acrobats, puppeteers, comedians and jugglers. Most of the crowd ate and drank, laughed or sang, while some begged and were kicked out by the soldiers. In each fight, the victory of the strongest or most skilled knight was cheered and applauded, while the defeated one abandoned the field on foot or on a stretcher, amid insults, shouts and whistling. Salietti had gracefully won the preliminary rounds and gained the admiration of many of those in attendance for his ability with the horse and lance, but no one had provoked the crowd's frenzy like Valdigor of Rostvol.

The day was long and tiring, but finally it came to a close, and the heralds named the two best knights of the jousts – Salietti and Valdigor. There would be one more fight, and it would determine the tournament's winner.

Salietti's horse was exhausted from the previous jousts, so they decided at the last minute to replace it with Star. They were dressing Grimpow's horse up with the Duke of Estaglia's emblazoned skirts when Grimpow asked anxiously, 'Do you think that the inquisitor will recognize the horse he found in the mountains?'

'With the caparison covering it up to its head, even you won't recognize it,' answered Salietti, seemingly lost in thought. Grimpow knew his friend was thinking about more than just defeating Valdigor of Rostvol and winning the tournament. It was becoming clear that freeing Weienell was just as important.

'I want you to win the tournament,' Grimpow told his friend. 'Please try not to think about what will happen after.'

'I'll do my best, Grimpow. I will do it for you and Weienell. Now fulfil your duties as a squire and help me mount Star,' he ordered, ruffling the boy's hair with his steel-covered hand.

One of the baron's heralds announced the tournament's final joust. He called the last two contestants, pronouncing their names and noble titles, and Salietti and Valdigor entered the field amid the clamour of trumpets and beating drums. The crowd cheered excitedly, applauding to the beat of the horses' slow honour march around the jousting field so the knights could lower their lances before Baron Figueltach of Vokko.

As soon as the knights were lined up opposite each other, the racket ended. The silence was so profound that their rapid breathing could be heard amid the clanking of their armour. The animals snorted and danced around restlessly, sinking their hoofs in the ground under clouds of dust, while they waited for the signal to burst into full gallop against their opponent.

Salietti drew his horse's reins and spurred hard, and Star charged like a runaway horse toward his opponent. Everyone's eyes were on the centre of the field, waiting for the brutal impact of the knights' lances. Valdigor of Rostvol kept his lance firm in front of him, and when it banged against Salietti's shield, it broke in two with the roar of a tree struck by lightning. From their respective seats, Grimpow, Weienell and Guishval all closed their eyes, fearing that Salietti had been knocked off his horse. But he didn't seem affected by the blow; he was still sitting straight in his saddle, with his lance intact.

The two horses returned to opposite ends of the field and turned around immediately. Valdigor of Rostvol's squire handed him a new lance, and the knight lowered it to a horizontal position. He spurred his horse with rage. Again the knights collided brutally, but this time Salietti managed to topple Valdigor of Rostvol cleanly, and his fall from the horse sounded like a hundred pots shattering.

The crowd roared wildly and Grimpow shouted and jumped up and down, but then Valdigor, bruised and battered, sat up and unsheathed his sword. The expectant crowd hushed instantly. Salietti got off his horse, raised his sword and attacked Valdigor of Rostvol.

The fight on the field was long and bloody, and both knights were exhausted and injured from sword wounds. Still, each time one tried to strike a final blow, it would then be answered with unusual strength by the other one. Finally Salietti rotated his sword, Athena, in the air and lunged at Valdigor of Rostvol with such force that the latter's sword broke in two, and Valdigor collapsed to the ground like a marionette whose strings were cut.

The field was dead quiet. Nobody dared say a word but Grimpow, who jumped and shouted excitedly. He leaped over the wooden fence surrounding the field and ran to the spot where his horse quietly snorted and pawed the ground. He petted its neck and whispered something in its ear, then gave Salietti the reins. It was at that moment he saw the threads of blood running down the knight's hands.

'Are you hurt?' he asked, snapping back to his role of squire.

'It's nothing, boy, it's nothing,' said Salietti, sounding exhausted. He sheathed his sword and stepped toward the grandstand, presided over by Baron Figueltach of Vokko and the inquisitor Bulvar of Goztell.

Silence and expectation enveloped the jousting field again as they awaited the election of the queen of the spring tournaments. She would be treated as a real goddess during the several days of celebration.

'As a winner of the tournament, you, Knight Salietti of Estaglia, will have the honour of choosing the queen of the spring celebrations,' announced the baron solemnly.

Trumpets sounded and the crowd cheered, but when the drums blasted, silence fell again.

'Name the lady you've chosen and bring her to the grandstand, where she will be crowned!' shouted the baron, holding up a gold crown studded with precious stones.

'My lord, the lady I've chosen is none other than the woman whose beauty has captivated every knight present at this year's jousts, including yourself. I choose her for everyone present, and I hope that it will be a pleasure for you to hear her sweet name, which is none other than Weienell!' shouted Salietti, looking at the crowd around him, who, after hearing her name, began chanting it loudly, repeating it again and again.

Grimpow smiled to himself, recognizing Salietti's

abilities when it came to lying. He now looked like a peacock proudly showing its feathers. His friend's words sounded so sincere that Figueltach preened, evidently thinking that the Italian knight and fortune-teller had named his beloved the queen of the celebrations to encourage her to stay in the fortress. But the young Weienell seemed as bewildered as she was touched.

'So come up to the grandstand and put the royal crown on her head yourself!' said the baron, satisfied.

Salietti took off his helmet, gave Star's reins back to Grimpow, and walked to the grandstand, cheered by the crowd. But just as the baron was about to give him the crown, the inquisitor shouted out, 'Perhaps the knight Salietti of Estaglia should explain to us where he got his horse!'

The jousting field was silent again, and everyone stared at the horse the Dominican friar was pointing at. Grimpow stepped closer and petted Star to calm him down – it was as if the animal recognized the voice of the fearsome inquisitor.

'What do you mean?' asked the baron, not seeming to understand what the Dominican friar's point was.

'You'll see for yourself if any of your soldiers removes the dress on that horse,' said Bulvar arrogantly.

Despite Grimpow's objections, a soldier walked toward Star and tore off the emblazoned skirts covering the animal's body.

The crowd became restless once more, for nobody

understood what they were supposed to be looking at. The inquisitor shouted, 'There's the proof! The brand! Salietti of Estaglia is—'

But before the inquisitor could finish, an arrow shot from a hidden spot whistled by and pierced the baron's chest.

The crowd was paralyzed, as if the arrow that had hit the baron had struck them too. The knights took up their swords but did not know where to go, each one fearing he was the next target of the hidden archer.

Salietti too looked around wildly, not appearing to know where the arrow that had hit the baron had come from, but he recovered his wits more quickly than the others and seized the moment of confusion to take out the dagger he kept under his armour and with a swift move of his hand put the sharp blade under the neck of the inquisitor. He called his horse with a whistle and ordered one of the soldiers to bring the baron's horse to the grandstand.

'Can you ride?' he asked Weienell.

But instead of answering, the young lady ripped the skirt of her dress to give herself more freedom and jumped from the stands straight into the saddle.

It took Grimpow a moment to understand what was happening, but when he saw Weienell on the baron's horse he mounted Star and got ready to run when Salietti ordered him to.

With the inquisitor's body as a shield, Salietti climbed down out of the stands and ordered the friar to get on his horse. Then he warned the knights and the crowd that if anyone moved, they too would be hit by an arrow. He mounted the horse behind Bulvar, still holding his dagger to the inquisitor's flesh, grabbed the reins and shouted, 'If anyone follows us, I will cut this pig's throat!'

Finally, the Truth

They fled the jousting field at a full gallop, Grimpow, Salietti and Weienell all silently wondering who had shot the arrow that had struck the baron. They rode until they arrived at a river near the fortress. Salietti stopped his horse and brought it to the edge of a stone bridge. Grimpow and Weienell pulled their horses to a halt, correctly deducing their friend's intentions.

'What are you doing?' cried Bulvar of Goztell, trembling, his face contorted with fear.

'I hope you know how to swim!' answered Salietti, and he pushed the Dominican friar off the horse and into the water below.

All three watched for a moment as the Pope's legate struggled in the water, lashing out with his hands to avoid being swallowed by the current. Then Grimpow urged, 'Let's go before the baron's soldiers reach us!'

They turned around, spurred their horses and galloped along the riverbed to hide any trace of where they were headed.

By the time the three travellers reached the outskirts of Strasbourg, night had begun to fall. A twilight of red blazed in the horizon, and fog floated over the Rhine like steam from a thick broth. They stopped at a bend of the river and dismounted. Weienell sat on the shore's damp grass and, without uttering a word, she covered her face with both hands, and wept inconsolably. Grimpow realized that this must have been the first time since her father's death that she had truly had the opportunity to mourn.

Salietti walked to her side, helped her up and hugged her tenderly.

'Your father was a great friend of my father. Now they've both lost their lives searching for wisdom,' he told her. 'When you were just a child, I lived in your parents' house in Paris for a few years, and endured your mischief while I studied in the attic. I can still remember that house full of books, and the nights when your father and I stared at the starry sky of the calligraphers' quarter in Paris. You were too small to remember, but your father used to tell me then that there was magic in the stars and enchantment during the full-moon nights, and that if I gazed at them, I would find my dreams.'

Weienell wiped her eyes with her sleeve and looked at Salietti.

'He used to say that to me too, every night when I went to bed,' she said with a hint of a smile. 'That's why when I found the message in the water pitcher, I knew that someone very close to him wanted to help me. I even thought he might have written the message himself – that he was still alive. But I would have never imagined it was you, that young man whom I played with when I was a child – whose name I had completely forgotten,' she said through her tears, embracing Salietti again.

Grimpow felt a few tears roll down his cheeks too. 'Someone will have to explain all of this to me,' he said, letting out a laugh.

'I warned you that it was a long and complicated story, Grimpow,' replied Salietti kindly. 'And I assume that you and Weienell are dying to hear it.'

They sat on some moss-covered rocks on the riverbank under some high elm trees. As they waited for the dark veil of night to envelop them before they entered the city of Strasbourg, Salietti began his long story.

'My grandfather always wanted my father to be an intrepid knight,' he began. 'Someone who would inherit his ruined dukedom of Piedmont and bring back to it the splendour the Estaglias had known before. But my father's interest was always in study, not battle. As he grew up he excelled in all the areas of knowledge, from arithmetic and philosophy to physics and astronomy. When he turned fifteen he left for Padua, to attend the recently founded university there. Far from the Pope's influence, it enjoyed great academic freedom. There he met a monk, also born in the Piedmont region – Uberto of Alessandria,' he said, looking at Grimpow.

'He became the sage monk's disciple, and they travelled until my father settled down in Paris and met the woman who would become my mother. When I was born we moved to Lyon, where my father taught philosophy at the university. My father wanted to make a wise young man of me, and when I turned sixteen he sent me to Paris to study under an expert on the stars – Gurielf Labox,' said Salietti, smiling at Weienell. 'But when I was eighteen my father sent me to live with my grandfather so that he could train me as a knight while I continued my studies in the nearby university of Padua. And I lived there until my grandfather died. Because my father renounced the dukedom, I inherited it instead.'

At this point, Salietti paused and looked at the other two. 'I'm telling you all this because it's the only way you'll be able to understand the rest of my story. At the end of last winter, in Padua,' he continued, 'I received a strange message, without any signs or marks in the wax sealing it. To my astonishment, I found that it was a letter from the librarian at the abbey of Brinkdum – Brother Rinaldo of Metz. He said he was writing on behalf of Uberto of Alessandria. In his letter, Brother Rinaldo told me about the death of my father in the mountains surrounding the abbey—'

'Your father was the knight I found dead in the mountains?' interrupted Grimpow, amazed.

'Yes, Grimpow,' said Salietti apologetically. 'I'm sorry I didn't tell you before, but now you will understand why I was forced to lie to you.'

'So your father was the holder of the stone?' asked Grimpow, unable to control his excitement.

But Weienell looked confused, even though she had appeared to follow everything Salietti had said before.

'What stone are you talking about? And what does it have to do with my father and yours?' she asked.

'Let me finish, both of you – then you'll understand everything,' said Salietti.

'All right, go on.' Grimpow fished the stone from the linen pouch hanging from his neck and offered it to Weienell, who delicately took it in her hands as if holding a fine, precious jewel.

'As I was saying, in that letter Brother Rinaldo announced my father's death and urged me to come to the abbey of Brinkdum. He said he needed me to help take care of a very important matter. I knew that the tournaments of the Alsatian castles were celebrated in Baron Figueltach of Vokko's fortress in spring. And since I was heading north, I decided to take advantage of my trip to find fame and fortune in those lands. I loaded my armour onto a mule, saddled my horse and began my journey to the abbey. After a week in the sharp peaks of the Alps, I reached Brinkdum and found you, Grimpow, eager to become the squire of a knight-errant.

'When I entered the abbey and you brought me to see

the librarian monk, he took me to see Brother Uberto. The monk told me he was sorry about my father's death – he loved him as his own son – and that he needed to talk to me about a secret. That was when he told me that my father had been the holder of a miraculous stone – called, in legends, the philosopher's stone. He too had possessed it at one time, having received it from his master, and it was he who had given it to my father. The stone, he explained, allowed one to reach wisdom and even immortality, but no one was supposed to have it for an extended period of time. It was meant to be passed on, so that others could enjoy its miracles and slowly uncover the mysteries of nature and the cosmos. He went on to explain to me that throughout the years the holders of the stone, and the sages close to them, had been part of a secret society called Ouroboros, which was now at risk of disappearing, for the stone had fallen into the hands of a boy named Grimpow who lived in the abbey.'

Grimpow wanted to interrupt, but his friend's story was so fascinating that he decided to wait until he was finished.

'He told me then that you had found my father's body in the snow, and that a petty thief you lived with had given you the stone thinking that it was nothing more than a sentimental amulet. Then he told me that my father's body had vanished into thin air, for – according to legend – all those who've possessed the stone leave this world without a trace and live eternally in a castle whose high blue walls rise among the stars, where they will finally enjoy immortality.'

'That must be the same castle in the stars Aidor Bilbicum mentions in the manuscript!' exclaimed Grimpow.

'Brother Uberto told me that there is an object even more miraculous than the stone,' continued Salietti, ignoring Grimpow's outburst. 'It was found by a group of ancient sages of the Ouroboros society in the Temple of Solomon in Jerusalem. Apparently they hired a group of Knights Templar to bring it to France, where it was hidden so that no one outside of Ouroboros could ever find it. Throughout the last three centuries, only the sages of the Ouroboros society have known about this secret. But though their first masters hid it, they left clues in code so that it could be found again one day for the benefit of all humanity.

'Brother Uberto assured me then that the time had come, for ignorance and superstition had taken over the world. It was necessary to reveal the secret so that wisdom would end the Church's violence and greed. The Church had decided to take possession of the stone and the miraculous object he was telling me about; and they had captured and tortured a sage, who had given them the name of my father – the last holder of the stone.

'Apparently the person designated by the Pope to dis-cover the secret of the wise was the inquisitor of Lyon, Bulvar of Goztell – the same friar who had instilled in the King of France the idea that it was the Templars who were hiding the secret of the wise in the castles of the Circle. My father was able to flee Lyon in time and he headed toward the abbey of Brinkdum to take refuge there, but he got lost in the fog in the mountains and died of cold.

'Brother Uberto then told me that I should continue my father's mission and recover the stone, for without the *lapis philosophorum* it was impossible to discover the secret.'

As Salietti finished, Grimpow realized that his fears had been confirmed – all along, Salietti had intended to betray him.

'You were planning to take the stone from me? Was that your mission?' he asked Salietti, suddenly wild with anger.

Salietti lowered his head in shame, and Grimpow snatched the stone from Weienell's hands and thrust it brusquely into Salietti's.

'Keep it then! You can keep this damned stone for ever!' screamed Grimpow. 'You lied to me!'

'I had to do it,' replied Salietti softly.

'And now that you have the stone in your hands, what will you do? Are you going to kill me, as they killed the abbot of Brinkdum and Gurielf Labox? Will you hand me over to Bulvar of Goztell so that he can torture me and burn me alive at the stake? Is that what you were planning to do after taking the stone from me? I thought you were my friend,' he concluded despairingly.

Salietti moved to comfort Grimpow, but the boy jerked away.

'Grimpow, please forgive me – I am sorry. If I deceived you, it was for your own sake. How could I think of hurting you?' asked Salietti sadly. 'Yes, at first my mission was to take the stone and get rid of you, but when I got to know you and saw how much you knew about life's great mysteries, I decided to take care of you and help you find the secret. I realized that the stone was part of your soul. I don't know why, but I knew that Brother Uberto was wrong and that without you, the mission he had asked me to carry out would be impossible. I told you myself, don't you remember? In the church of Cornill's crypt I said that the stone had *chosen* you. It's *you*, not me, who is destined to continue the mission my father left unfinished.

'Brother Uberto had also told me that he had sent a message to a sage – whose name he didn't divulge – whom I should meet in the church of the village of Cornill, since the first clues they had gathered from the ancient manuscripts indicated that the search for the secret should begin there. When we got to the village and the man we ran into told me the name of the old man the baron's soldiers had captured, I realized that it was my father's old friend, whom I had lived with in Paris.'

Salietti's face seemed to age suddenly as he conveyed these last details.

'Now you know everything,' the knight said, looking as tired as when he'd finished the tournament's last joust.

Weienell approached Grimpow and took his hand. 'My father never told me about the stone, or that society called Ouroboros, or the secret of the wise. He was always very private about his studies and discoveries. But I did hear him say to my mother once that there was a time when he used to meet other sages in those castles of the Circle you have mentioned.'

'Do you know if your father found anything in Cornill's church?' asked Grimpow timidly, wiping away his tears with his doublet's sleeve.

'I don't know,' said Weienell. 'My father didn't want me to go to Paris with him, but he was very ill and I insisted on taking care of him. When he received the message you have talked about,' she said to Salietti, 'he suddenly seemed rejuvenated, and I remember he said, "Very soon, the light of knowledge will shine on humankind's universe again."'

'He knew that the manuscript by Aidor Bilbicum was hidden in the church of Cornill, that's for sure,' Salietti interjected. 'That's why he left the message in the parish's archive.'

'But without the stone it was impossible to open the sarcophagus. Weienell's father wouldn't have been able to find anything until you arrived at the village and gave it to him,' reasoned Grimpow.

'So the missing part of the manuscript by Aidor Bilbicum must be somewhere,' thought Salietti out loud. 'Let's go to Strasbourg – what we are looking for might be in that city,' he finished. He stood up decisively.

'Who is Aidor Bilbicum?' asked Weienell.

'Get on your horse and we'll explain it to you on the way,' said Salietti. The black cloak of night had descended as they spoke, and it was time for them to continue their journey.

Junn the Cripple's Inn

Junn the Cripple was sleeping when he heard the strong banging on the main door to his inn. He groped his way out of bed, lit a candle, put on the shoes that made his legs the same length, and went to see who it was interrupting his sleep. He opened a window on the front of his house, next to which hung a brass sign with the head of a green dragon painted on it, and squinted at the newly arrived with distrust. It was pitch dark on the street, and all he could see was the hazy image of three motionless riders.

'Who is it?' he called grumpily.

'You can't recognize friends any more, dear Junn?' came a voice Junn recognized.

'Salietti, is that you?' whispered Junn from above, not hiding his excitement.

'Who could disturb you at this time of night if not a

knight-errant who has no place to sleep or money to pay for a decent inn?' answered Salietti, laughing.

'Just a moment, my friend,' Junn called down. 'I'll open the wine cellar's gate so you can bring your horses in.'

Junn shut the window, hobbled down the inn's corridors and stairs, and reached the wine cellar's courtyard, which was crammed with a multitude of oak barrels containing what looked like enough wine to make it through several years. He opened both halves of the courtyard's gate and said: 'Come on, get in quickly before the neighbours wake up and start snooping from their houses, wondering about this racket.'

Salietti urged his horse into the courtyard behind his companions, then dismounted and ran to help Junn close the gate. The two men hugged, and Salietti said: 'Come, I'd like to introduce you to my friends.'

'Yes, I see that you are not alone,' said Junn, following Salietti's quick steps with difficulty.

Grimpow and Weienell got off their horses as Salietti introduced them. Junn greeted them cheerfully, pleased with the unexpected visit.

'Let's go into the tavern,' he told his visitors cordially. 'We'll have some wine while you tell me what I owe this nice surprise to. I'll make food, as I am sure you're hungry, and it's never in good taste to let someone go to sleep with their stomach growling.'

The tavern was in semi-darkness and emanated a bittersweet smell, a mix of wine and barley. Junn placed his candle on a table covered with a thick layer of dirt and invited his companions to sit down. Then he took some pitchers from the tabletop, filled them with wine and gave them to Salietti to pour. Junn disappeared into the kitchen and soon returned with a tray of cheese and rye bread.

'Now tell me, Salietti, what can I do for you?'

Salietti took a piece of cheese and bread and began to explain.

'First I'd like to say hello from someone you know – Brother Uberto of Alessandria,' he said.

'It was he who suggested we come to see you,' added Grimpow.

Junn smiled. 'Then old Uberto is still alive!' he said happily. 'I haven't seen him in more than twenty years. Where is he now?'

'In the abbey of Brinkdum,' explained Salietti, and though Junn sensed there was something Salietti was leaving out, he didn't press his old friend.

'And what about your father? How is the tireless Iacopo of Estaglia?' enquired Junn.

'He died last winter,' said Salietti. 'But if you don't mind, I'll tell you about that another time.'

'I'm very sorry,' said Junn, saddened. 'He was the first to give me a pair of boots like these,' he added, showing them his legs under the table, 'with a heel to help my limp. I've never met anyone as ingenious as your father. But tell me, what brings you to the city of Strasbourg?'

Grimpow and Weienell remained silent, devouring the cheese and bread in between sips of wine.

'We need lodging and your help finding a man named Aidor Bilbicum,' said Salietti, cutting straight to the point.

'Aidor Bilbicum?' repeated the innkeeper thoughtfully. 'I've never heard that name.'

'We think he was part of a secret society of sages called Ouroboros,' said Grimpow.

'That will make it a bit harder,' murmured Junn, scratching his head. 'There are many craftsmen's and merchants' guilds in Strasbourg who gather in secret lodges to discuss their issues – especially since they started building the new cathedral. There are also the jewellers, the metalworkers, the alchemists, the sorcerers and necromancers, and, until a few years ago, the Templars. But none of those groups wishes to reveal the names of those who belong to their societies. Many of their members' lives depend on that, and they use fake names to communicate their meetings and secrets.'

'Yes, we know finding him won't be easy. The other detail you should know about is that Aidor Bilbicum is dead. According to the information we have, he died almost two centuries ago,' said Salietti.

'So you should start looking in the graveyard!' exclaimed Junn, laughing at his own witticism.

'I should also warn you that we are being followed by Baron Figueltach of Vokko's soldiers,' Salietti cautioned. 'Our presence in the inn might cause you trouble.'

Junn stirred on his seat and widened his eyes, intrigued by Salietti's story.

'You know I would do anything for your father and for you,' he said, helping himself to more wine.

'I know, Junn, I know. The good thing is that at this point, anyway, our persecutors probably think that I am a Knight Templar and we've sought refuge in the castles of the Circle.'

'You – a Knight Templar?' asked the innkeeper in disbelief.

'At least that's what the inquisitor Bulvar of Goztell believes. He was at Figueltach's fortress during the spring tournaments,' explained Grimpow.

Salietti told Junn about their experiences since arriving at the baron's fortress, and the rescue of Weienell.

'The attack on the baron must have been plotted by the Templars in revenge for his plan to destroy the castles of the Circle,' murmured Junn after hearing Salietti's account.

'I have no doubt about that. The feathers on the arrow that killed him were black and white, the colours of the outlawed Templar Order's flag,' replied Salietti.

'All right,' concluded Junn. 'Let's leave this till tomorrow before it disturbs your sleep. It is late and you are probably tired from your adventures. Follow me, I'll take you to your quarters.'

Junn took the candle still burning on the table and guided them through a short corridor to the dark stairwell leading to the inn's rooms. With the same candle he carried in his hand, he lit the wicks in the lamps hanging from the ceiling, revealing a wide hallway with doors on both sides.

'I'll give you the same room your father stayed in when he came to Strasbourg,' Junn said. 'He liked it because you can see the river and the three bridge towers from the window.'

Junn showed each guest to his or her own room and provided a lit candle. He said goodnight, wishing them a pleasant stay at his house, and returned to his room, where he climbed into bed and fell fast asleep.

The new lodgers at the Green Dragon's Eye, however, found it hard to sleep. Grimpow blew out his candle, but his eyes stayed open in the darkness. He was now in Strasbourg, and the sand of a new period had begun to slip through the slow hourglass of his life. What he had left behind didn't matter now – the cottage in the mountains, his friend Durlib, the abbey of Brinkdum, the monks, long hours of study in the library, nights gazing at the sky with Brother Rinaldo, the meals from kind Brother Brasgdo, the alchemical experiments of Brother Asben, and the mysterious words of the blind centenarian monk, Uberto of Alessandria.

For an instant, he imagined what his life would have been like had he continued wandering with Durlib or had he decided to stay in the abbey of Brinkdum as a novice and taken the religious vows of the order. He was sure that he still had much to learn and many riddles to solve before finding and revealing the secret of the wise. From the very first time he had held it in his hands, the miraculous stone had helped him see things this way, and now he felt so close to it that it seemed to be part of his mind and body.

As Grimpow lay awake in his dark room, so did Salietti in his own comfortable room in Junn the Cripple's inn. His imagination wandered through inhospitable battlefields, humans' fears and love. He worried about the future awaiting them in the castles of the Circle of Stone, but also felt Weienell's presence a few steps away from him. He could almost hear her breathing.

Lying in bed with her eyes closed but her mind wide awake, Weienell thought about the events of the past weeks and of her father's suffering, and his sad death. But a feeling of hope danced in her chest also, triggered by her newfound freedom and meeting Salietti, whose love for her she sensed would be eternal.

The following morning, Junn the Cripple brought news as welcome as the trout and bread he served for breakfast. They were sitting in the tavern, still half asleep, when the innkeeper said: 'News travels as fast as the north wind in the city of Strasbourg.'

'What information do you bring us?' Salietti questioned, anxiously.

'Nobody across this city is talking about anything other than the arrow that hit the baron.'

'Is he still alive?' asked Weienell.

'Fortunately for him, the arrow pierced his left shoulder – nothing fatal. He's just badly hurt and furious at the Italian knight who won the tournament and took from him the woman of his dreams.' Junn winked at Salietti. 'I've even heard that some troubadours are already preparing their romances about these events, to recite them in villages, squares and markets.'

'Do they know who shot the arrow that wounded the baron?' asked Grimpow, for that question kept hovering around his mind like an annoying bumblebee.

'No, but nobody doubts that it was a Knight Templar disguised as a villager. It seems that he attacked one of the baron's archers, put on his soldier's uniform, and stationed himself in one of the towers' minarets, located across from the grandstand.'

'Have they arrested him?' enquired Grimpow.

Junn twisted his lips into a grimace. 'Not yet, and they probably won't until the King of France's and the baron's armies attack the castles of the Circle, where they assume he has run to.'

'I know who shot the arrow,' declared Salietti, making everyone stare at him.

'You saw someone draw the bow?' asked Junn.

'No, but I talked to him on our way to the baron's fortress, when we passed the entourages of noblemen.'

'Do you mean the knight Rhadoguil of Curnilldonn?' asked Grimpow.

'Yes. He told me about Pope Clement's death by poisoning. It can't be a coincidence that his squire carried a big bow across his back and, next to his saddle, a big quiver full of arrows with black and white feathers. They probably planned to assassinate King Philip during the tournament, but as he'd already returned to Paris, they decided to kill his ally, Baron Figueltach of Vokko, instead so that their trip wouldn't be in vain,' said Salietti.

'The rumours of that curse and the news of the Pope's death have also reached Strasbourg. I wouldn't be surprised if soon both become part of another tragic and mysterious legend,' added Junn.

'That knight said that the coat of arms on your shield was familiar to him, do you remember?' said Grimpow.

'That's true,' confirmed Salietti.

Junn scratched his chin.

'The Templars have always known about alchemy and the alchemists. If that knight you're talking about was a Templar, he knew that the sun in your coat of arms represents gold, and the moon silver. He might have even known your father or grandfather – the Templar Order had contacts and allies across the whole world.'

'And what is being said in the city about the war?' asked Weienell.

'The baron ordered Valdigor of Rostvol yesterday to lead his soldiers and knights. They will leave this morning for the north border, where a large regiment of the King of France is waiting for them. His plan is to begin the siege of the castles of the Circle tonight.'

'More than five thousand armed horsemen and hundreds of knights are as eager to attack the castles of the Circle as the King of France's forces are,' said Salietti.

They were silent for a moment, as if a shadow hovered above the tavern's smoke-darkened ceiling.

'So the war has already begun,' said Grimpow, downhearted.

'I'm afraid it has, boy, and there's not much we can do to avoid it,' said Junn.

Salietti stood up. 'Let's not forget about what we've come for. We still have to find "he who doesn't exist" and hear "the voice from the shadows",' he announced, using the words that Weienell's father had written in the archive of Cornill's church.

'I see that you use the same mysterious language as your late father,' said Junn as he stood as well. He told them he would do all he could to help them.

According to Junn, everyone in the city knew that it was three riders – a beautiful lady, an Italian knight and his young squire – who had fled Baron Figueltach of Vokko's fortress, so they decided to form two groups and divide the city into sections to avoid investigating in the same places. Salietti and Weienell would go to the craftsmen's and merchants' neighbourhood. Meanwhile, Grimpow and

Junn would cover the squares and the construction of the new cathedral, where they would speak with stonemasons and quarry workers, then visit a few alchemists Junn knew in the canal district. They would leave no corner of the city unexamined.

A Voice from the Shadows

Despite the lootings and fires that had ravaged it in the past, the original majesty and splendour of Strasbourg were preserved. The city seemed to rise from the thick fog that covered the Rhine – the river that ran through it. On the river's shores stood big houses with wooden structures and slate roofs that extended to the very walls of the city, where three colossal towers emerged like three sentinels. The canals were spanned by numerous bridges, over which marched horses and carriages coming from the farthest cities to sell goods in Strasbourg's fairs and markets.

For two days, Salietti and Weienell travelled around the city, from north to south and east to west, going deep into the quarters of tanners, goldsmiths and silversmiths, scribes, blacksmiths, weavers, carpenters, shoemakers and jewellers. They asked every man and woman they encountered if they knew Aidor Bilbicum, but received only negatives and looks of distrust. It was as if people were afraid to risk their lives by talking to strangers, or possibly afraid to hear that name. Junn and Grimpow weren't able to obtain any leads either, and were starting to worry they never would.

On the second afternoon Junn's frustration was beginning to show. 'If, as you and Salietti said, Aidor Bilbicum isn't alive, how can we expect to find him? What if nobody knows anything about him?' Junn said exhaustedly to Grimpow. They had just visited an apothecary who lived on a corner of the cathedral's square. His shop smelled of sulphur and burned tin, medicinal herbs, spices, ointments and syrups, like the laboratory where Brother Asben did his alchemical experiments; Grimpow had no doubt that the apothecary was an alchemist as well. The boy had hoped that perhaps he could give them some clues about Aidor Bilbicum, but not only did the name mean nothing to the apothecary, he even feared that Junn was a spy for the Inquisition and would barely speak to him, despite their having known each other for years.

'Well, if nobody knows anything about him, we'll never be able to find what we're looking for,' answered Grimpow.

'And what is it that you are looking for, besides a sage who doesn't exist?' asked Junn, frowning.

'Wisdom,' replied Grimpow, gazing in awe at Strasbourg's magnificent cathedral. He watched as hundreds of apprentices, skilled craftsmen and master builders worked, trying to finish the front's large rose window. Grimpow knew that in order to build that extra-ordinary church, it was necessary to apply complex theories of physics and astounding mathematical formulas, which the freemasons' lodges kept in the utmost secrecy and were only known by sage men they called architects. As he looked at the sculptures decorating the central portico, he couldn't help wondering if perhaps he might hear the voice from the shadows in the darkness of those prodigious stone walls.

In the square, they spoke to a few masons who were carving huge blocks of stone. None of them had ever heard the name Aidor Bilbicum, but Grimpow noticed that every stonemason carved different signs on the blocks, like personal insignias that allowed them to recognize their work. Those signs reminded him of the signs in the message carried by Salietti's father when he died in the mountains, and an idea began to form in his mind. The more he thought about it, the surer he was that the hieroglyphic language used by the sages of the Ouroboros secret society had been created by converting the alphabet into a series of different symbols copied from the stonemasons, each one of them corresponding to a different letter.

On their way back to meet Weienell and Salietti at the inn, night crept up on them. By a wide canal, they ran into a large funeral procession surrounded by torches. A group of men with masked faces carried a dilapidated wooden catafalque on which was a skeleton shrouded in black silk veils that revealed a horrible skull. A deafening roaring of drums accompanied the cortège, followed by a masked crowd that jumped and shouted, waving their torches in the air.

'They are celebrating the Night of the Spells. They bury the skeleton of winter a month after the equinox to honour the abundance of spring,' said Junn, stopping to gaze at the flurry of torches and masked faces dancing and jumping around him. Grimpow was watching acrobats performing, and swaying balls of fire hanging from long chains, and didn't notice that he had left Junn behind. When he finally realized they had been separated, Junn was nowhere to be found.

It was then that Grimpow noticed a young woman walking toward him. Her face was largely hidden underneath a veil, but he could see her wide black eyes. She had an intense and disturbing gaze.

'Come closer, boy,' the young woman said in a sweet, hypnotizing voice. 'Let me read your palm, for only I can see in it what fate has in store for you.'

Grimpow stepped closer and extended his hand. He didn't know why, but in that moment he felt lured by that voice, as if he'd heard the singing of the sirens Brother Rinaldo had told him about. He remembered how Salietti had laughed when describing Figueltach's stupid face when he 'foretold' the baron's future with the strange deck of cards, but Grimpow was now seduced by the thought of his future written invisibly on his hand. He tried to resist and run away from that bewitched place, but when he felt the delicate touch of the young woman's fingers on his skin, his body shivered, arousing in him fantasies he'd never felt before.

'You have the hands of a prince,' whispered the woman, 'but I don't see a noble origin in them.'

'I am part of a caravan of migrating shepherds,' lied Grimpow, seduced by the black eyes staring at him intently.

'You come from very far, and there are scents in you of grass and flowers that blend with the smell of smoke and the stake,' stated the young woman, taking a deep breath, as if by so doing she could deduce where Grimpow came from.

Grimpow remained silent, captivated by this woman, who seemed to see in his hand the indelible marks of his past.

'There is an old sadness inside of you as well – sorrow for the dead, and bitter tears that have been forgotten.'

The young woman slid her finger down Grimpow's palm softly.

'My mother died long ago,' lied Grimpow again, his hair standing on end.

'But you are not alone,' the woman continued. 'You are protected by those accompanying you, who are sliding throughout your history like a slipknot that moves along the rope of a fortunate existence.'

'I don't understand you,' said Grimpow.

'Those looking after you are many, though they won't

always be by your side to help you,' explained the woman. Then she fell silent for a while and closed her eyes as if trying to see beyond reality. 'You are hoping to find answers in the contemplation of the universe.' As she spoke, the woman's expression turned more serious and profound.

'Who are you? What do you want from me?' whispered Grimpow, perplexed.

Despite the roaring of the drums, the whole city had become silent to Grimpow's ears – the only thing he could hear was the mysterious woman's voice. Even the crowd of people with torches and masked faces seemed soundless, like a mirage. He could see their exaggerated gestures, their hurried running around and the frantic waving of their hands under the torchlight, but he couldn't hear anything other than the intoxicating whispers of the mysterious woman.

'Go to the cathedral and knock on the right-hand door, where you see the sculptures of three wise virgins,' said the young woman without releasing his hand. 'A person you've been looking for is searching for you. But go alone, for if anyone accompanies or follows you, you won't find him again.' Saying this, she slid her hand over Grimpow's once more, then lost herself in the crazed crowd dancing around him.

Grimpow could see Strasbourg's cathedral silhouetted against the dim moonlight. He tried once again to find Junn, to tell him where he was heading, but the crowd around him was an impenetrable mass of faceless bodies that seemed to have gone wild in the heat of a demonic ritual.

He pushed his way out of the crowd and entered a dark and isolated stairway, wondering if someone had set him up in order to take the stone from him. Asking for Aidor Bilbicum in the city had seemed to be the only way of finding someone who didn't exist, but it was also true that they were loudly announcing exactly what they were searching for: the secret of the wise. If, as Junn had assured them, there were more secret societies in Strasbourg than they could imagine, someone might well have worked out their plan and could now be trying to find the stone themselves. Scoundrels abounded everywhere, and all they had to do was to act as though they were interested in talking about Aidor Bilbicum to coax out of Grimpow everything he knew about the stone and the secret of the wise.

With these thoughts lurking in his mind, Grimpow reached the cathedral's portico, dimly lit by the torches on the square's corners. He looked to his right and saw the sculpted figures of three women, which he assumed were the three wise virgins the mysterious woman had mentioned. He stepped closer to the door and knocked hard three times, following the rhythm of his intense heartbeats. He didn't know what was in store for him inside, but there was no turning back now. If he left, he might not have the opportunity to hear the voice from the shadows, and his search for the secret of the wise would be over for ever.

The door opened with a rusty screech, but nobody came to meet him. Grimpow waited for some time, tilting his head to peer deeper into the darkness behind the door, but there were no signs of anyone waiting for him. Then he saw a spark of light begin to flicker inside, and despite the tremors that shook his legs, he walked toward it determinedly. He should have told Salietti, he thought, though the woman had been very clear – if anyone accompanied or followed him, he wouldn't be able to find this person again.

The dim flame of a candle lit the centre of the nave, surrounded by shadows. Grimpow stepped into the light so that his face became visible under the cathedral's vaulted ceiling. Suddenly, he heard a voice coming from the shadows.

'Who are you looking for?' asked the voice of a man echoing in the silence.

Grimpow, relieved and satisfied that someone was in fact there, glanced around him trying to figure out its origin, but to no avail.

'I'm looking for Aidor Bilbicum,' he said simply.

The voice sounded again, the echo prolonging its words.

'Aidor Bilbicum doesn't exist any more; he died centuries ago.'

'I know,' admitted Grimpow.

'I thought Iacopo of Estaglia would come here.'

'Iacopo of Estaglia died last winter in the mountains near the abbey of Brinkdum,' explained Grimpow calmly.

There was a moment of silence, which Grimpow took advantage of to ask a question.

'Who's the woman who urged me to come here?'

'A young woman wearing a witch's disguise to go unnoticed during the Night of the Spells,' replied the voice, and then asked, 'Why do you wish to see Aidor Bilbicum?'

'I have a message for him.'

'You can tell me,' said the voice, which Grimpow could tell belonged to an old man.

'There are darkness and light in the sky.'

'Did you pass the misty Vale of Scirum?'

'Yes, in the crypt of Cornill's church.'

'How did you do it?'

'I passed the key to the mysteries over the inscription and over the sign.'

'And what happened?'

'The crypt without a corpse, where history sleeps, opened.'

Grimpow knew that the voice belonged not to a ghost but to a human being who didn't want to reveal himself. Nevertheless, he wished he could get out of that empty cathedral as soon as possible.

'Do you have the stone with you?' asked the voice.

'Yes,' answered Grimpow without hesitating. 'Do you want it?'

'No, the stone has chosen you,' answered the voice.

'And what should I do?'

'Interpret the secret's signs as you have been doing.

Behind this candle you will find the complete text of the missing page in Aidor Bilbicum's manuscript.'

'Where was it hidden?'

'I found it long ago in a scribe's workshop in this city.'

'Gurielf Labox has also died,' said Grimpow.

'So only two of us are still alive,' said the voice from the shadows. 'That's why you need to find the secret of the wise. You must spread it so that the light of wisdom shines on humanity, and the obscurity of superstition and ignorance will not prevail.'

Grimpow walked toward the candleholder and, behind it, on the cathedral's floor, found a piece of parchment. He held it up to the flame and read the full text:

> Follow the path of the sign
> And look for the sealed chamber,
> Where time is life and is death.
> But only if you reach immortality
> Will you be able to see the Invisible Road.
> It will lead you to the island of Ipsar,
> Inhabited by monsters and fantastical beings;
> Confront the Devil,
> And at his feet you will find the last words.
> Then cross the gateway
> And enter the labyrinth.
> Plant the seed there
> And you'll see the flower grow.

'But this is another cryptogram!' exclaimed Grimpow, his mind spinning with questions. Would he *ever* reach the secret of the wise?

The voice from the shadows didn't respond.

Inside a Barrel

On his way back to Junn's inn through the narrow and dark streets around Strasbourg's cathedral, Grimpow ran into a few soldiers who seemed to be celebrating the Night of the Spells in their own way. One of them was singing a song Grimpow had heard his friend Durlib sing. Others swayed unsteadily, their helmets tilted on their heads and their swords grazing the ground.

In the tavern, located on the inn's ground floor, several groups of peasants, craftsmen and stonemasons drank wine from enormous pitchers. Grimpow silently climbed down the steps separating the tavern and the street and spotted Junn behind the counter, conversing with a rough and tattered-looking man. When he saw him, Junn left the man's side for a moment and walked over to Grimpow.

'I was afraid that something had happened to you,' he

murmured as he wiped his hands with a greasy cloth hanging from his hip.

'I've found he who doesn't exist!' whispered Grimpow, eager to share what had happened with someone.

'Aidor Bilbicum? By yourself?' asked Junn in disbelief.

But Grimpow was too excited to answer. 'Where are Weienell and Salietti? I need to see them as soon as possible,' he said urgently.

'When I returned to the tavern, I told them how we lost each other among the crowd in the neighbourhood by the canals. They went to look for you, but they shouldn't be gone much longer. You'd better wait for them in your room – there's a candle by the stairs,' said Junn, turning back to the man with whom he'd been talking.

Grimpow opened the rickety door by the counter, groped his way down the dark corridor and found the candle, which he lit. The candle created a halo of light around him, illuminating his face in the darkness; with only his own shadow on the walls for company, he walked up to his room.

Using the glowing candle he lit a second one on the floor, then he sat on the bench under the window and took out the parchment from the cathedral. He was just about to read the riddle again when he heard a few soft knocks on the door. His heart skipped a beat, but when he opened the door, he saw the angry faces of Salietti and Weienell.

'Can you tell us where on earth you've been? You've scared us to death,' said Salietti, visibly furious.

Grimpow ignored his friends' complaints. 'I've found he who doesn't exist and heard the voice from the shadows!' he blurted out.

'How?' asked Weienell.

'I'll tell you everything, but first look at this,' urged Grimpow, offering them the missing page from Aidor Bilbicum's manuscript.

Salietti grabbed the piece of parchment and brought it to the candlelight while Weienell looked curiously over his shoulder.

'So what does this mean? Everything seems to have been written in code,' the knight murmured.

'What did you expect? Aidor Bilbicum already warns about it in his manuscript, don't you remember? "He who searches for the secret of the wise must see through the shadows that reign over the chaos of the undecipherable riddles",' Grimpow recited.

'Grimpow is right,' said Weienell. 'Now at least you finally know what riddles you must face to find what you're looking for.'

Salietti looked Weienell in the eye. 'You mean what *we* are looking for. You're a part of this as well – we owe it to your father and mine,' he said earnestly.

'So let me look at the text carefully,' said Weienell. She studied the cryptogram for a while, then made an interesting observation. 'I think there are three parts in this – three different riddles. The first one is this.'

Follow the path of the sign
And look for the sealed chamber,
Where time is life and is death.
But only if you reach immortality
Will you be able to see the Invisible Road.

'The second one,' she continued, pointing, 'is here.'

It will lead you to the island of Ipsar,
Inhabited by monsters and fantastical beings;
Confront the Devil,
And at his feet you will find the last words.

'And the third and last one,' she said confidently, 'is this one.'

Then cross the gateway
And enter the labyrinth.
Plant the seed there
And you'll see the flower grow.

Salietti, who was unable to hide the fact that he was in love with Weienell, grinned with pride at her intelligence.

'All right,' he said. 'In front of us we have all the riddles we need to reveal the secret of the wise. But how do we interpret all this?' he asked.

'We begin at the beginning,' said Weienell simply. 'My father always said that was the best way to tackle a mystery.'

'So the first thing we need to find out is the location of the sealed chamber in which time is life and is death,' Salietti responded.

'And for that, we need to "follow the path of the sign",' added Weienell, now clearly fascinated by the text full of riddles.

'I think I know where the sealed chamber is, where time is life and is death,' said Grimpow. 'I've been thinking about it on my way here. The sign can't be any other than the ouroboros, the serpent swallowing its tail, and if we follow its path, what we find is . . .' He stopped, waiting to see if Salietti or Weienell could complete his reasoning.

They were both lost in thought for a moment, but it was Weienell who answered first.

'A circle! The ouroboros sign draws a circle from the head to the tail the serpent bites!' she exclaimed.

'The sealed chamber is in the castles of the Circle!' confirmed Grimpow, and though they congratulated each other for solving the riddle, a shadow of worry crossed Salietti's face.

Grimpow woke up with a start. He was soaked in perspiration and his mind still bubbled with the faded images of a strange, incomplete dream. He'd had a terrible nightmare. He'd clearly seen Salietti's bloody body lying on the ground among hundreds of dead. In the dream Grimpow stood beside him, watching the inquisitor Bulvar of Goztell approach him and take the philosopher's stone from his hands while he did nothing to stop him. The Dominican friar laughed loudly and ordered his soldiers to take the boy to the executioners. Then he saw himself tied to a rack, and his own horrified shriek yanked him out of his dream to awaken him, sweating and panting like a dying man.

The wooden heel that levelled Junn's legs pounded down the inn corridor with a rhythmical hammering that woke everyone who was still asleep. Grimpow jumped out of bed and unlocked the door; he could see Salietti also peeking into the corridor from his room.

'Is something wrong, Junn?' Salietti asked the frightened-looking innkeeper.

'You must leave Strasbourg without delay! Bulvar of Goztell has reached the city, escorted by the baron's henchmen, and they are looking for you. They have even detained some of the cathedral's master builders and some sages and alchemists to interrogate them, thinking that they might have given you shelter in their houses.'

'I should have killed that Dominican friar when I had the chance,' muttered Salietti through clenched teeth.

'I'll go down to the courtyard and get the horses ready,' said Grimpow, dressing quickly at the room's door.

'You can't leave the city on horseback. There are soldiers checking everyone entering or leaving the city on the bridges. I'll prepare a cart and you can hide on it in wine barrels – I have empty ones in the cellar.'

'If you succeed in getting us out of the city, we can make

our way to the castles of the Circle,' said Salietti, excited.

'The castles of the Circle? You'll be running away from the stake to go straight into Hell. The attack on the castles has already begun, and I've heard that, though injured, Baron Figueltach of Vokko is leading his army alongside Valdigor of Rostvol. They've already taken three of the western castles, and Duke Gulf's loyal knights have retreated to his central fortress.'

'We'll try to get there through the gorge in the east. If we leave now, we can be there before night falls,' insisted Salietti.

By midday, Junn had prepared a team with his guests' three horses and one of his. He placed a fake wine cargo on the cart's box: several wineskins and six barrels, three normal and three with false bottoms, each concealing a space big enough to hide a person inside. Grimpow, Weienell and Salietti climbed apprehensively into the barrels; it felt as if they were being buried alive. Junn covered the barrels with their respective lids and sealed them with grease to make them appear to be ordinary wine casks, then threw a canvas cover over the whole load. He then jumped into the coachman's seat and drove the horses out of the inn's courtyard.

The cart quickly traversed the craftsmen's quarter and the deserted street of the scribes and bookbinders – bustling at other times, but empty since the Inquisition's persecutions had begun. They passed Strasbourg's graveyard and a long row of high, slender cypress trees.

Further along, he crossed the bridge that rose above the Rhine's delta and headed towards the northeastern gate, where a squad of soldiers armed with lances and swords were on guard. There Junn stopped the cart behind some carriages that were being thoroughly checked by the towers' sentinels. He climbed down from the coachman's seat, supposedly to check the state of his barrels, looking to one side, then the other; the guards were busy inspecting carts full of hay, vegetables, birds and pigs before his. He pretended to tighten the ropes holding his 'goods'.

'Keep quiet and hold your breath as long as you can,' he said softly. 'We are leaving Strasbourg and the soldiers are about to check the cart.'

Just as he finished, he saw the guards' sergeant, a stout man with a reddish face, approach the cart followed by two of his soldiers. Junn walked over to them, exaggerating his limp.

'If it's not Junn the Cripple! Has the baron sent you to quench the soldiers' thirst with your watered-down wines?' said the sergeant with scorn when he recognized the inn-keeper.

'Baron Figueltach of Vokko has better things to do than quench his thirst with my wine, old rascal,' exclaimed Junn, happy about his good fortune, for the sergeant he was talking to was a regular patron of his tavern.

'Go on, show me what's inside and tell me who is the recipient of such valuable goods,' said the sergeant when he reached the back of the cart.

'I'm bringing six barrels of my best wine to a fabric merchant in the neighbouring city of Isbroden, though if you open the barrels I'll lose the goods along the way. They're sealed to prevent the divine liquid from leaking,' said Junn with a laugh. 'But if you'd like to taste the quality of their content, you can keep one of these wineskins I'm bringing as samples, and with which I'm planning to celebrate the deal,' he added as he removed the canvas cover and revealed the six barrels and two wineskins.

The sergeant scratched his head thoughtfully. 'Let's see if what this lame and shrewd swindler of drunks says is true,' he said finally, motioning for his soldiers to grab one of the wineskins.

One of the soldiers handed off his lance, took the wineskin, uncorked it and took a long swig.

'It's good,' said the soldier simply, and offered it to the sergeant.

The sergeant took the wineskin and enjoyed a long taste. Then he rubbed his hand against the corners of his lips to finish the last drop of wine dribbling down on them, and said, 'We'll keep the present. Now get on your cart and get out of here before I decide to keep your barrels as well.'

Junn climbed up to the coachman's seat again and got ready to spur the horses, but paused to ask the sergeant, 'What's happening in Strasbourg that there's such a commotion on the streets?'

'They're looking for three fugitives who ran away from Baron Figueltach of Vokko's fortress after an archer nearly killed him with an arrow. They say that one of them was the knight who won the spring tournament of the Alsatian castles, and that the lady accompanying him is a beautiful witch.'

'And do you believe those stories?' asked Junn.

'I don't believe in anything my own eyes don't see – not even what I see when I'm drunk,' said the sergeant with a loud laugh.

Junn smiled in return and without a reply urged his horses to continue their journey.

Junn soon drove the horses under the last tower on the bridge, leaving behind the city of Strasbourg. They took the road north to Isbroden, and when they were still far from the fortified bridge, he stopped the cart in a clearing surrounded by high brambles and hurried to take off the canvas cover. Then he removed the fake lid on the first barrel – with the help of a pair of arms that pushed from inside. Weienell, somewhat disorientated by the frantic journey, poked her head out into the sunlight, then stood up and jumped out of the barrel with Junn's help.

'I thought I'd never leave that dark hole!' She sucked in a deep breath of air as if for the first time.

'Come on, help me open the other barrels,' said Junn.

Salietti and Grimpow leaped out of their hideouts as happily as a fox's cubs when they discover the way out of their den. They unhitched their horses from the cart and thanked the innkeeper for everything he had done for them. Before leaving, Salietti took out his leather pouch and gave Junn a handful of gold nuggets.

'Perhaps you should spend some time away from Strasbourg,' Salietti told him. 'I hope this will help you live comfortably until you can return safely, without fearing that Bulvar of Goztell will grill you alive like a side of mutton.'

'You know that you don't need to pay me for my help. Your father or you would have done the same for me,' Junn replied. 'But I won't reject the gold you're offering me. I'll go south, to Mulhouse, and visit my brother, whom I haven't seen in years. I might stay there to help his family for a while. He is just a pig farmer, and has eleven children!'

Then they hugged goodbye, and Junn wished them luck in their search.

The Sealed Chamber

From the end of the gorge they could see smoke coming from the castles of the Circle. They watched from afar as thousands of horsemen moved through the valley toward Gulf of Ostemberg's fortress without any opposition.

'It looks like the baron's army has already opened a wide gap in the circle – that's the way they'll be attacking the central castle. If we don't hurry, they'll make it before we can cross its gates,' said Salietti.

Grimpow and Weienell were gazing at the beautiful valley in front of them. A vast meadow was traversed from east to west by the translucent waters of a deep river. Above it stood eight giant rock formations, each crowned at the top by one of the castles of the Circle. In the centre, atop the highest plateau and flanked by smooth rock walls, rose the Duke of Ostemberg's great fortress.

The only possible access to the duke's fortress was through the east, where the land steeply descended until blending with the valley. A wide, deep moat protected this part of the walls, dominated by a small tower at the gate of a drawbridge. Behind it stood two enormous towers, separated by an arch in the wall that housed the portcullis and two thick gates, one after another, through which to enter the small fortress. In the vault and the walls of the tunnel between the first and second gates, traps and ingenious defence mechanisms were set, ready to stop any enemies who had successfully reached that point alive and made it past the first obstacles at the entrance: crossed chains to prevent the entry of horses, loopholes for archers, and a hole in the vault from which to pour boiling oil on the attackers and drop heavy rocks on them. Past this first line of defence was a steep road leading to the entrance of the real fortress – a fortress within a fortress, the towers and walls of which loomed over the cliffs of the immense rock.

The newly arrived trio, however, had no difficulty in entering the duke's castle. As soon as the sentinels stationed in the entrance's towers saw it was a knight, a young squire and a lady fleeing from Baron Figueltach of Vokko's soldiers, they blasted their trumpets and the guards began to open the doors of the small tower and lower the drawbridge.

Once inside the lower fortress, Salietti introduced himself to the guards' captain and asked to be received by the duke immediately. He was still explaining the reasons for his visit when a knight Salietti and Grimpow already knew approached them.

'I didn't expect to see you again after your hasty escape from the baron's jousting field, let alone here in this Templars' sanctuary that is now boiling in the heat of war,' said a grave voice from behind them.

The three of them turned and saw the mysterious knight Rhadoguil of Curnilldonn. He was wearing a coat of mail covered by a large smock, cinched at the waist by a strap with his sword attached. On his chest was embroidered the great red cross of the Templar Order, and a long cloak hung from his shoulders with the same cross embroidered on the left side. Grimpow watched him carefully and remembered the identical garments he'd found in the subterranean cavern in the abbey of Brinkdum.

'May I ask what brings you here?' asked the Knight Templar after extending his hand to greet Salietti and beckoning for the captain to leave them alone.

'We had to run away from Strasbourg – the inquisitor, Bulvar of Goztell, followed us there,' explained Salietti, having recovered from his surprise.

'If you hadn't been in front of my target, I would have finished off that Dominican friar with an arrow between his eyes. What did you do with him after taking him hostage from the jousting field?'

'I threw him in the Rhine's waters, confident that he would be swallowed by the current,' said Salietti, regretting for the second time not having eliminated the evil inquisitor once and for all.

'You should have stabbed him in the heart with your dagger,' said the Templar with a powerful laugh as he put his heavy arm around Salietti's shoulder.

Weienell and Grimpow stayed by the horses, glad to have made it to the fortress before the baron's horsemen reached them. They were both eager to begin their search for the sealed chamber in the Circle's fortress but knew they had to find it before the armies of the baron and the King of France attacked. They had little time.

On their way to the castles of the Circle, Grimpow had told Weienell the legend of the nine Knights Templar and the magical object they had transported two centuries ago from the Temple of Solomon in Jerusalem to France. Now, however, they knew that whatever was hidden between these walls couldn't be the secret of the wise, because according to the riddles in the manuscript, they still had to reach an island, then enter some labyrinth to plant a seed, which would allow them to see a flower grow.

Grimpow hadn't stopped pondering the meaning of that riddle, though he felt sure that if they managed to 'reach immortality' in the 'sealed chamber' they were looking for, they'd finally be able to see the 'Invisible Road' that would lead them to the secret of the wise.

His biggest concern, though, was the nightmare that had woken him in Junn's inn. Salietti's bleeding body had been so real that Grimpow feared that the nightmare could be more than just a bad dream.

A short way away, the two knights were talking of the situation they faced. 'I've seen that the first castles of the Circle have already been destroyed,' said Salietti.

'Alas, you're right,' Rhadoguil answered, sounding tired. 'Little can a thousand men do against more than six thousand armed horsemen and some extraordinary war machines. Luckily, though, all the castles' inhabitants are now safe in this fortress. Now,' Rhadoguil said, changing the subject, 'please come with me. I'll take you to the duke – he's very curious to meet you. He's in the fortress's keep, watching the baron's troops advance through the valley.'

'Does Gulf of Ostemberg know of me?' asked Salietti.

'Of course, and he's told me that he knew your father, Iacopo of Estaglia, for he was a good friend of his,' said the Knight Templar, leaving Salietti speechless again. 'Duke Gulf is very glad to be able to receive you in his castle, even during tragic times such as these. When I reached the fortress after my attempt to kill the baron, I told him about your escape from the jousting field and that you had rescued the young lady now accompanying you. I came down immediately when I saw you from the tower, so that the doors would be opened for you.'

Salietti knew that his father had frequently travelled to Strasbourg, for he himself had accompanied him on many of those trips when he was a young student. But he had no idea that his father and Duke Gulf knew each other. If that was the case, he realized, Weienell was probably right that his father used to meet with other sages in the castles of the Circle of Stone.

Salietti and Rhadoguil collected Grimpow and Weienell, and together they climbed up to the higher fortress along a path so narrow that two horses could hardly walk through it side by side. After the guards raised the portcullis, they walked through the entrance tunnel and entered a large parade ground. A multitude of soldiers and knights patrolled the parapet walks, taking their defensive positions to await the imminent arrival of the enemy army at the bottom of the colossal rock.

From the high battlements of the keep, Duke Gulf of Ostemberg was watching the unstoppable advance of his adversaries. The three eastern castles of the Circle of Stone had been taken rapidly and were now burning like giant torches on the horizon. The duke's knights and vassals had taken refuge in the fortress and were scattered around preparing arrows, sharpening swords, or filling barrels with water to put out fires.

Duke Gulf of Ostemberg was probably only a few years older than Salietti, but his clear blue eyes and trimmed dark beard gave him an air of majestic serenity and wisdom.

'You've arrived in times of barbarism and ignorance that will be stained for ever with blood,' he said sadly in greeting to the travellers.

'If your fortress needs to be defended, I would be

honoured to fight beside you and your knights,' replied Salietti, inclining his body in a bow.

Weienell and Grimpow stayed back, waiting for Salietti to introduce them.

'You are welcome to the castles of the Circle of Stone, as your father Iacopo of Estaglia always was, though he never wielded any sword other than his sharp mind.'

'I didn't know that my father had ever visited your fortress,' said Salietti.

'Your father was a good friend of mine and other sages who gathered in a chamber in this castle several times a year, though that was long ago,' explained the duke with a sigh.

At the mention of the chamber where the sages used to meet, Salietti felt a shiver go down his spine. He, Grimpow and Weienell had assumed they would have to search for the sealed chamber, but it seemed to be right at their fingertips.

'So you must also have known a sage named Gurielf Labox,' said Salietti.

'Yes, he was another whom my father met in the chamber I mentioned,' said the duke.

Salietti motioned for Weienell and Grimpow to step closer and introduced them. Then he told about his father's death in the snow-covered forest of Ullpens and of Weienell's father's death at the hands of the inquisitor Bulvar of Goztell.

The duke gravely expressed his condolences to both.

'I am sure these deaths and such tragic times for the castles of the Circle are not coincidental.' After a pause, he added, 'I'd like to show you the chamber where these sages met. I have a story to tell you that I've never shared with anyone.'

Duke Gulf left Rhadoguil in charge of his troops, and he and his guests descended in silence to the parade ground, from where they could hear the busy comings and goings of the soldiers on the tower's battlements. Normally it would have been unthinkable for the duke, as the master of the castle, to abandon his position in the tower at such a time, but as he told Salietti, Grimpow and Weienell, he believed that the time had come to fulfil an old oath.

As they proceeded to the sages' meeting chamber the duke told them that he hadn't entered this room since the death of his father. Yet he knew these strangers were the ones he had been waiting for.

At the end of the parade ground, Duke Gulf unlocked an iron door embedded in a small arch, lit a torch hanging from a ring on the wall and began to descend a spiral stairway that led to a small round chamber. The room was completely empty and its ceiling was a hemispherical dome that must have been intended to replicate the heavens. Across from the entrance arch, in the centre of the circular wall, letters were carved on the rock:

TEMPUS ET VITA
TEMPUS ET MORTIS

Time and life, time and death — all three of the Duke's companions translated the Latin to themselves. They had no doubt that they were very close to the sealed chamber in the riddle.

Duke Gulf noticed immediately that the text on the rock had powerfully captured the attention of his three companions, especially Grimpow, who was staring at the Latin words as if he could see beyond their apparent meaning.

'This inscription is what I want to tell you about — before it's too late,' said the Duke solemnly. 'During his youth, one of my most distant ancestors, Atberol of Ostemberg, was the disciple of a sage named Aidor Bilbicum, who travelled to the Middle East two centuries ago following his passion for astronomy. When he was there a mysterious sage gave him a miraculous stone legends call the *lapis philosophorum*. The sage also revealed the place in the Temple of Solomon in Jerusalem where a wonderful object was hidden, the power of which was so astonishing that, if they found out about its existence, it would be coveted by all the kings and emperors on earth.

'Atberol accompanied Aidor Bilbicum to those faraway territories before the Crusades to the Holy Land began, but the violence was coming and they knew they must protect this object from evil. Atberol and Aidor formed a secret society called *Ouroboros*, and along with the other sages they decided to move the object back to France. At the time, there was a group of nine knights, who called themselves Templars because they'd settled in the Temple of

Solomon, living as soldier-monks protecting the pilgrims. The group of sages hired the knights to protect the carriage bringing that marvellous object to France. They paid for their service with several pieces of pure gold.

'Once in France, Ouroboros hid the object in an unknown place and the seven Knights Templar founded the powerful Order of the Temple, in honour of the Temple of Solomon in Jerusalem.'

Salietti interrupted the duke. 'Except that your ancestor Atberol of Ostemberg was one of the founders of the Ouroboros, that story is known to us. That's how Aidor Bilbicum himself relates it in *The Cosmic Essence of the Stone*. We're looking for the missing links in the chain of this fantastic legend.'

The duke nodded and continued, 'In fact, the story only became legend because the knights of the Templar Order accumulated so much power and wealth that they provoked the envy of popes, kings and emperors. All these powerful men believed that the nine knights of the Temple in Jerusalem had found an invaluable treasure. But before I go on, you should know that Atberol of Ostemberg was in charge of burying Aidor Bilbicum upon his death in an unknown crypt—'

Salietti interrupted him again. 'Yes – that crypt is located in the church of Cornill, north of the city of Ullpens.'

'I can see I wasn't wrong when I reasoned that you were the holders of the stone. I'm sure you'll find the rest of my story very interesting.

'My ancestor also received the philosopher's stone from Aidor Bilbicum and, after burying the body of his master with the manuscript you know about, he hid the clues that led to the secret of the wise. Atberol didn't tell anyone where he had placed those clues, but once his children were old enough to understand, he made them swear they would never repeat this story to anyone unless a wise man arrived at the fortress with no apparent reason for his visit. Then they should bring him to this chamber and leave him alone as long as was needed – without being surprised if he didn't come out again.'

Grimpow was alarmed by those words. Could he suddenly disappear, as Salietti's father had vanished when he'd found him in the mountains?

'Atberol also made his children avow,' continued the duke, 'that they would share the story he had told them with their own children, demanding the same promise, so that there would always be a Duke of Ostemberg who knew the story and could help the future holders of the stone find the secret of the wise when the time came. I know that my father, like yours, was one of those sages, and that the Ouroboros secret society held its meetings in this chamber. I swore to my father the oath Atberol demanded of his children, and I have now fulfilled it,' concluded Duke Gulf.

'Are you afraid that Baron Figueltach of Vokko might attack the fortress and find the clues your ancestor hid?' asked Salietti.

'The baron and the King of France are only chasing an

illusion, moved by their greed and their fear of death. They think that the treasure of the Templars' legend is here, and that's what they're looking for. I'm sure that a Templar sage under torture spoke about this chamber. I must confess that, tempted by the legend, I myself have searched for the treasure in every corner of the castle and haven't found anything other than this riddle that speaks of time, life and death. Within these empty walls there is nothing more than wisdom, and you, as holders of the stone, should find whatever is left of it.

'Now I must excuse myself. Baron Figueltach's army is already at the fortress's gates, and we should deal with his audacity as he deserves. I trust that we'll see each other again soon,' concluded the duke.

'Please wait,' said Salietti. 'I'll come with you. As I've said before, I will join my sword to yours in defence of the castles of the Circle from those beasts. I'm not a sage, never was, and doubt that I'll ever be. My place as a knight lies in the battle – that's always been my only dream.'

Weienell and Grimpow looked at each other, frightened. If Salietti didn't come with them and they managed to enter the sealed chamber, would they ever see him again?

Time and Life, Time and Death

When they were alone in the chamber, Grimpow grabbed a torch and tried to find any cracks in the walls. But the room's walls were so smooth and polished that they seemed to have been made from only one piece of stone. As they searched, Weienell wondered out loud if her father and the other sages ever knew that they had been gathering in the sealed chamber mentioned in Aidor Bilbicum's manuscript.

'The sealed chamber where time is life and is death must be here. That's the meaning of the Latin words on the rock. I just can't figure out how that chamber can be opened,' said Grimpow, bringing the torch close to the inscription and reading it aloud again.

TEMPUS ET VITA
TEMPUS ET MORTIS

'Time and life, time and death,' repeated Weienell, evidently as curious as Grimpow to understand the real meaning of the mysterious words.

Grimpow handed her the torch and took the stone out from the linen pouch around his neck, then passed the key to the mysteries over the text as he'd done with the inscription in the crypt at Cornill's church, thinking that the opening mechanism of that sealed chamber might be the same as the one for the sarcophagus. He soon realized, however, that the key to the mysteries had no power over the stone walls which enclosed them like an impenetrable circle.

'Atberol of Ostemberg was probably as clever and ingenious as his master, and must have invented a system to protect his secret that's more complex and sophisticated than the cryptogram in the crypt of Cornill's church,' said Grimpow, as if talking to himself. 'But I have a feeling that the words *Tempus et Vita, Tempus et Mortis* don't have a double meaning.'

'I don't think these words contain anagrams either. The solution to this riddle seems to lie in its own meaning,' said Weienell.

As Weienell spoke, she stepped closer to examine the letters on the wall, tracing her fingers over the letter O in the word *mortis*.

'Look!' she called. 'See the O? It's the ouroboros sign.' She brought the torch even closer, so that the shadows of the protruding letter didn't prevent them from seeing it in detail.

Grimpow stood on tiptoe to get a better view of the letters; embossed on the stone was the serpent swallowing its tail. He'd seen the figure so many times since finding Salietti's father, but suddenly he remembered the first time he'd seen the ouroboros symbol – carved on the gold seal – and something clicked.

'The seal! The clue to open this chamber is in the gold seal! That's why the page in Aidor Bilbicum's manuscript talks about the *sealed* chamber,' said Grimpow excitedly.

'What gold seal?' asked Weienell.

'The seal Salietti's father – whose body I found in the mountains – carried in his bag,' he said. He opened the bag hanging from his shoulder and took out the gold seal with the ouroboros sign. 'The chamber was sealed with this seal. This is the only key that can open it again. That's why Salietti's father carried the stone, the message *and the gold seal*. No one who didn't have those three objects would ever be able to find the secret of the wise. The stone, the key to the mysteries,' he explained, 'allowed us to open the crypt where the story of the Ouroboros secret society slept. The coded message contained the clue to find he who doesn't exist and hear the voice from the shadows. And only this seal can open the sealed chamber where time is life and is death. Do you understand now?'

Grimpow brought the gold seal to the small ouroboros sign on the rock, and a massive vibration shook the chamber's floor. In front of them, the block of stone containing the text *Tempus et Vita, Tempus et*

Mortis rotated – and opened the door to a sealed chamber.

Because Weienell carried the torch, she was the first to enter. The light revealed a large octagonal room with different paintings decorating each of the eight walls. On each of the vertices of the octagon was a burner; Weienell lit them with her torch, while she stared at the ceiling in admiration. The room was covered by a representation of the starry heavens that looked as translucent as the infinite night sky.

But before they could fully appreciate the chamber, the stone doors closed and a floodgate opened on one of the walls, releasing a torrent of very thin sand that spread on the floor like a stream of golden water.

'It's a trap! The sealed chamber is a trap!' shouted Grimpow, terrified. The sand flowing like liquid gold would bury them alive if they didn't decipher the riddle quickly!

'The riddle – time is life and is death in the sealed chamber!' yelled Weienell. 'This room is like an hourglass measuring our time to solve the riddle. We must figure it out or we'll be swallowed up by the sand. That's why Duke Gulf said that his ancestor had warned them not to be surprised if the person who entered this room never came out.'

Grimpow understood. He stared at the part of the floor that had already been covered by sand and calculated that they still had some time before the sand would reach their waists. But then Grimpow remembered the hermit. He had spoken of a curse and said, *Damned are those who dare penetrate the essence of the secret, for the doors they manage to open will be closed behind them for ever!* Grimpow feared that the curse had begun to come true.

He stopped and took a deep breath. He needed to think logically. He looked around the chamber for the first time. In the centre stood a large table, also octagonal in shape, on top of which was painted a compass rose. At each of the eight sides of the table was a stone figure sitting on a high-backed stone settee. They were life-size statues of the eight sages dressed in long robes and holding brass letters in their hands, which rested on the table.

Weienell stood gazing at the sculptures as if they were flesh-and-blood beings who only needed a gust of life to begin moving. She told Grimpow she didn't see the face of her father among them, and neither she nor Grimpow recognized anyone else. Among the eight figures, however, was one whose features were strikingly similar to Duke Gulf's, though it was the face of an old man.

'I think these statues represent the eight founders of the Ouroboros secret society,' said Grimpow more calmly, trying to give a reasonable meaning to the scene that seemed frozen in these images of stone. But if time was stilled in the statues, it kept passing for them in the unusual hourglass the chamber had become. 'If we wish to leave this room alive, we must analyse every possible element of the riddle – we have no other option but to solve it.'

'So let's start from the beginning, as my father always advised,' answered Weienell. 'It's clear that these figures at

317

the table are the sages. And each one of them is holding a letter in his hand.'

'That's true,' said Grimpow. 'I thought the letters might be the initials of their names, but I don't see among them any letter A's for Aidor Bilbicum or Atberol of Ostemberg. I'll draw the table and the letters – perhaps that will help us see more clearly through the shadows of this riddle.' Grimpow took the piece of parchment and the charcoal pencil from his bag and sketched the table.

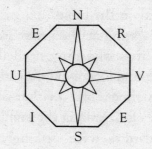

'Now look – a compass rose is painted on the table, and it points to the four cardinal directions,' said Weienell, 'and if you look carefully, you'll be able to see that the sage sitting north is holding the letter N; the sage sitting south is holding the letter S.'

'I hadn't noticed that,' admitted Grimpow. 'It's a sign the sages want to guide us in our search.'

'Look – there are also paintings decorating every side of the octagon formed by the walls of the chamber,' Weienell pointed out while Grimpow sketched. 'If we begin with the one the compass rose indicates as north – just as sailors use the pole star as a guide – and continue in the direction in which the earth rotates on its axis according to the astronomy theories of the Ouroboros society, we can see a progression. In the first painting is a dark and shapeless mass that seems to float in the middle of nowhere; in the second, a group of planets spin; in the third are only a few stars amid blackness; in the fourth, a ball of fire seems to represent the sun; in the fifth, there's a drawing of a beautiful rose; in the sixth, a serpent swallows its tail; in the seventh scene is a garden brimming with life; and in the eighth, a half-naked man sits watching the broken branch of a burning tree,' she finished.

Grimpow thought hard. 'And above us is the dome of the sky,' he added, while he continued with his drawing of the table around which the sages were seated. He showed Weienell the finished sketch.

Their eyes roamed the hasty drawing, which was a good enough rendering to let them analyse it carefully. They remained silent for a while, observing and pondering all the elements of the riddle. Then suddenly Grimpow had an idea.

'I think that the clue might be in the letters the sages are holding,' he said, and walked over to the figure holding the letter *N*, which pointed to the north according to the compass rose. He grabbed the brass letter and realized that it was loose in the statue's cold hands.

'What do you think that could mean?' Weienell asked.

'That these letters must be taken from the sages' hands following a logical order,' reasoned Grimpow. 'Each letter might have something to do with the scene in the painting behind it.'

'Give me an example.'

'Look at my finished sketch of the table,' he said, placing the parchment in front of Weienell's eyes.

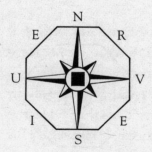

'The compass rose points north,' he continued, 'and the sage sitting on that side of the table is holding the letter *N*, as you pointed out. Let's look in the painting behind it for a word that begins with the letter N. It's just an idea, but maybe we can find something this way. Can you repeat your description of the first scene?'

Weienell raised her eyes from the drawing and looked at the painting located on the north, behind the sage holding the letter *N*.

'It is a dark and shapeless mass that seems to float in the middle of nothing,' she said slowly.

'OK, so only one word begins with the letter *N*, *nothing*.' Grimpow wrote the word on the parchment. 'Now let's look at the next one.'

'A group of planets spin in an imaginary universe,' she said.

'Good, I think this might work. You said planets and universe. None of the sages is holding the letter *P*, but one of them has the letter *U*.' Grimpow jotted down *universe*. The sand was reaching their knees now. 'Now, describe the next scene.'

'On the third painting are only a few stars,' she said thoughtfully. 'So I'd think it was *S*, except that the next one is of the sun, and there's only one *S*.'

'What about the letter *E*? There are two of those,' offered Grimpow. 'What begins with *E*?' He thought for a second, then snapped his fingers. '*Emptiness!* This painting, showing only a few stars in the vastness of space, represents emptiness!' At Weienell's nod, he added the word to his notes.

'So the fourth, with a ball of fire representing the sun, must be *S*,' said Weienell.

'On the fifth painting there's a rose,' Grimpow said, and quickly wrote *rose*, hoping to finish fast, as the sand was beginning to come dangerously close to the top of the octagonal table. If the sand covered the letters held by the sages, all their efforts would have been in vain and they'd have nothing to do but wait until the sand buried them alive.

'The sixth painting is the ouroboros,' she said. Grimpow looked at the letters that were left, *E*, *V* and *I*, but couldn't see how any of them applied to a serpent swallowing its tail. Suddenly he panicked. The sand was so high – what if this was the wrong approach?

Just then Weienell turned to Grimpow calmly and smiled. 'What has the ouroboros been to us this whole journey?' she asked.

'An *enigma*,' replied Grimpow, and as he said it, it clicked in his mind. 'The second E!' He scratched the word onto the parchment.

'The seventh scene represents a beautiful garden full of life,' she went on.

'The G for garden isn't in the sages' letters either, nor is the *L* for life – but the Latin for life is *vita*. The V!' shouted Grimpow, writing down the word *vita*.

'On the eighth, a half-naked man is sitting on the ground looking at a broken branch from a burning tree,' said Weienell.

'Man, face, branch and tree . . . but none of the initials of those words fits the last letter, an *I*. We need to find another interpretation,' said Grimpow anxiously.

Weienell closed her eyes in concentration. Finally she exclaimed: '*Intelligence!* The man watches the branch falling off the tree in flames and discovers fire because he is an intelligent being!'

Grimpow showed Weienell the list:

NOTHING
UNIVERSE
EMPTINESS
SUN
ROSE
ENIGMA
VITA
INTELLIGENCE

'These are all symbols of the mystery of humanity's knowledge, the elements that go into the stone,' exclaimed Grimpow excitedly. 'From *nothing* the *universe* was born, which was filled with *emptiness*. Then came the *sun*, that nourishes the *rose*, a symbol of the *enigma* that is *life*, which we humans are capable of appreciating because of our *intelligence*.' As he spoke, he removed one by one the brass letters held by the sages – NUESREVI – and placed them on the octagonal table, by now almost covered with sand. But instead of stopping, the sand began coming out more rapidly.

'Put them back!' Weienell yelled to Grimpow. 'It must be wrong!'

Grimpow moved as fast as he could to put the letters back in the hand of each sage. As soon as he replaced the last letter, the stream of sand slowed down again.

Buried almost to their waists, they thought desperately; Grimpow feared that these could be the last moments of their lives. Suddenly Weienell, her legs held fast in the sand, leaned toward the sage holding the letter U and began forming the magical word that would allow them to leave the sealed chamber where time was life and was death:

UNIVERSE

The sand stopped and then began to drain out of the room far faster than it had flowed in; in no time they were free of its suffocating weight. Grimpow hugged Weienell, and they both raised their eyes to the dome of the sky above them and looked at the immense beauty of the heavens painted on the ceiling. As they looked up, the centre of the octagonal table opened as if by magic, and from its insides emerged a small golden trunk. Grimpow opened its lid and pulled out the most beautiful map they had ever seen.

Grimpow remembered the text on the missing page of Aidor Bilbicum's manuscript:

> Follow the path of the sign
> And look for the sealed chamber,

Where time is life and is death.
But only if you reach immortality
Will you be able to see the Invisible Road.

The Invisible Road was now before his tearful eyes.

The Fortress Under Attack

The army of Baron Figueltach of Vokko and King Philip of France had positioned itself around the rocky plateau to lay siege to the fortress of the Circle's castles, preventing anyone from entering or leaving it. They had also blocked access to the river that traversed the valley by stationing a group of knights on a stone bridge.

At the bottom of the massive rock, the soldiers set up tents and war machines while the first skirmish took place at the castle's walls and a vanguard of climbers tried to reach some protrusions on the sides of the mountain closer to the lower entrance to the fortress. Duke Gulf of Ostemberg's archers shot at them from the battlements and made the first attackers retreat.

Salietti had joined Duke Gulf and his knights in the battlements of the keep, and they all watched the movements of the baron's troops. Hundreds of men had begun climbing up on the northeast side of the mountain, where the arrows fired from the fortress couldn't reach them.

As the knights surveyed the disheartening scene, Grimpow and Weienell made their way to Salietti's perch, smiling like two cheerful children.

'Have you seen the Invisible Road?' Salietti asked anxiously.

'I don't know if we've reached immortality, but we've managed to escape the hidden trap in the sealed chamber unscathed,' said Weienell. She told Salietti about their surprise when they'd found their way into the sealed chamber. She related how they'd solved the riddle that had allowed them to escape from that lethal hourglass and finally see the Invisible Road.

'Here it is!' said Grimpow excitedly, showing Salietti the unusual map that had been hidden in the trunk.

Salietti examined the map, then raised his head and gestured toward the landscape around the fortress. 'The map shows roads, but look out there. Do you see any roads here that could help you find this Invisible one? There are none!' he yelled.

Instantly Weienell frowned. 'What do you mean, *you*? Why do you say "help *you*" instead of "help *us*"? Aren't you one of us?' she demanded.

Salietti heaved a sigh. 'I've decided to stay here, with Duke Gulf and his knights, until the war is over,' he said, and his sadness was visible in his eyes.

'But this is not your war!' Grimpow interrupted angrily. 'You can't leave us now! We've come all the way here to find this sealed chamber.' He refused to accept that he had to part ways with his best friend once again.

Salietti walked over to him and put his hand on Grimpow's shoulder.

'You have been the best squire any knight could ever want, Grimpow, and Weienell, you are my most wonderful dream come true. But this war is just as much mine as it is Duke Gulf's. Like mine, his father was a great sage, and this is a war of ignorance and superstition against knowledge and wisdom. The army attacking this fortress has no purpose other than to steal the secret our fathers – mine, Duke Gulf's, and yours, Weienell – protected to one day elevate humanity. They only want it to satisfy their own greed and yearning for power. If I left without having fought for the same ideal our fathers died for, I would feel like the most despicable being on earth.'

At that moment, Duke Gulf walked over, a grave expression on his face.

'I'm happy to see that whatever you found in the chamber of the sages has not prevented you from coming back,' said the duke.

Grimpow stepped toward Duke Gulf and offered him the map he held. 'This map belongs to you. Your ancestor Atberol of Ostemberg hid it, and you are its only owner. This is what Baron Figueltach and the King of France are looking for. Perhaps if you offer it to them, you can stop this war?' he said.

Duke Gulf took the map, looked at it curiously for a moment, and then smiled, visibly moved by the young boy's words.

'Dear Grimpow, who can persuade a bunch of men, hungry for death, that their ideas are wrong? If I offered this map to the baron and the king, assuring them that it will lead them to the treasure they're looking for, they would laugh. They wouldn't believe me, as true as my words might be. This map was created by sages who never cared about wealth – for them, there was no bigger treasure than wisdom. You and Weienell have proven to be the only ones who deserve to have this map. It is you who must find the secret of the wise. Search for the light, Grimpow, search for the light amid the shadows. You and Weienell can find it,' he said as a shower of merciless arrows began to fall on the tower.

At dawn, a terrible eruption of rocks and fire awoke everyone at the fortress. During the night the baron's army had made it to the western crest of the hill and set up enormous catapults under the walls. Before midday, the monstrous war machines had begun shooting an avalanche of rocks and balls of fire over the Duke of Ostemberg's castle, making its solid walls and towers tremble as if they were being shaken by an earthquake. The climbers had also managed to reach the ledges on the plateau's walls, and hundreds of soldiers and knights climbed long rope ladders from the valley.

Flaming arrows flew across the sky like deadly streaks of lightning, and the shadow of death hovered over the fortress. The final attack had begun.

In the early morning Salietti went to look for Grimpow and Weienell. They were with the wife and young daughters of Duke Gulf who had taken refuge with their maids and ladies-in-waiting. All the ladies knew what would happen if the soldiers succeeded in storming the fortress – the victors would have no mercy on them – but none of them thought to run away through the castle's secret passages. If their knights were willing to die defending the fortress, they would accept the same fate, preferring to end their own lives if the castle was taken. When they saw Salietti burst in, they feared that the time had come to bid farewell to the world and their loved ones.

'Where is Grimpow?' Salietti asked Weienell. 'You have to get away immediately. The baron's army is about to reach the fortress's walls and they will soon destroy it completely.'

'But I thought this castle was unassailable,' Weienell whispered hoarsely.

'It was. But not against these new powerful machines of war.'

'What will you do?'

'My place is next to Duke Gulf, as our fathers were next to his father in the secret meetings of the wise.'

'But you'll die, you will all die!' gasped Weienell, breaking into tears.

Salietti caressed her cheek. 'That's why you can't stay in

the fortress. If I die in this pointless war, my death will serve at least to honour our fathers' deaths, and their enemies will have only succeeded in killing more people. But your and Grimpow's deaths would be futile – they would prevent the secret of the wise from ever being discovered. You must begin a new era in which wisdom rises from the ashes of this one and leads humanity to a new future. Your father and mine knew it – that's why they believed it was time to find the secret of the wise hidden by the old Ouroboros society. They paid with their lives for their knowledge, and only you and Grimpow can finish what they couldn't. You have the map of the Invisible Road now.'

'And where will Grimpow and I go? We haven't been able to interpret the map yet and don't know where it will take us,' said Weienell, understanding now that she must be separated from Salietti.

'There are secret passages in the fortress's cellars that connect the castles of the Circle of Stone with each other and cross the valley in all directions. Take the one going west and, when you come out to the surface, follow that direction until you find the road to the city of Metz. If you leave now, you'll be able to reach the gates of the city before night falls. Ask in the area about a doctor named Humius Nazs – he is a good friend of Duke Gulf's and you'll only have to mention he sent you to be offered refuge in his house. You can trust him completely.'

'And when will we see you again?' asked Weienell.

'Wait there for me for two days, and if I am not there by

the third sunrise, don't wait any longer. Follow the Invisible Road's map. Take this bag of gold with you; I won't need it here, and it will help you if you have any difficulties. Now tell Grimpow and go down to the parade ground, where your horses are already waiting for you. I will take you to the passages and then return to battle,' said Salietti.

Grimpow couldn't understand why Salietti had decided to stay in the fortress. The nightmare he'd had played itself again and again in Grimpow's mind, and the more he thought about it, the more he feared that it would now come true. The images in his dream had been as clear as spring water, and in them he'd seen Salietti's bloodstained body surrounded by hundreds of corpses. If his friend stayed in the castle with Duke Gulf and his knights, he would probably die with them in the battle. But as much as he begged Salietti to leave with him and Weienell and continue their search for the secret of the wise, Grimpow couldn't make him change his mind.

In the parade ground, Salietti was holding the horses' reins, though he could barely control them given the uproar and flames all around. Archers ran through the galleries emptying out their quivers, and everywhere soldiers threw pails of water on the burning roofs. Duke Gulf's knights were defending the walls and western towers and had begun using their swords against the enemy soldiers who had succeeded in climbing up the battlements with grapples and ladders. Every few minutes a sinister murmur like the growling of a pitiless monster could be heard, and a huge rock enveloped in flames would crash through a wall or roof, shattering it into pieces and setting everything in the vicinity aflame.

From the cellars, Salietti, Weienell and Grimpow descended through a wide, deep tunnel lit by large torches until they reached a great round cave with high ceilings covered with stalactites that glimmered over their heads like stars. On the cave's floor was a compass rose similar to the one they'd found in the sealed chamber, made with stone chips of different colours. It pointed to eight different secret passages hidden beneath the fortress – each one of them leading to one of the eight castles of the Circle, then out to the surface beyond the valley. The long underground roads looked like the dark galleries of a giant burrow.

'Why don't they stop fighting and escape through these holes?' asked Grimpow, trying one more time to convince Salietti to run away with them.

'My dear friend, a knight cannot always choose his fate,' said Salietti, stepping closer and giving Grimpow a long hug.

Then he walked over to Weienell and kissed her as though it would be his last memory of her.

'You should go now,' he said sadly, stepping away from Weienell's arms. 'Go toward the city of Metz, heading always west. And don't forget, if I am not in Humius's house by the third day's sunrise, you should leave without delay and follow your map.'

Having said this, he turned and left so that Grimpow and Weienell wouldn't see the tears in his eyes.

Duke Gulf and his knights were still fighting on the western walls when a large group of mercenaries led by Valdigor of Rostvol conquered the lower barbicans and began attempting to take over the lookout tower protecting the gates. There were thousands of soldiers, armed with battering rams and siege towers, waiting in the moat to get into the higher part of the fortress.

Salietti found the duke's soldiers in the parade ground and joined the several hundred knights, many of them Templars, who were heading toward the lower part of the fortress to regain control of the barbicans and the lookout tower protecting the gates. If Valdigor's mercenaries succeeded in lowering the drawbridge, the lower part of the fortress would be lost for ever.

The archers had retreated to the second line of walls but were still able to slow the advance of the attackers with their arrows. Soldiers were climbing up the stairs to the barbicans by the dozens, though many of them were returned to the abyss shrieking, with an arrow in the chest, in the neck, or between the eyes.

Duke Gulf gave the order to open the back gate and hundreds of his knights lunged at the assailants, raising their swords and holding strongly on to their shields. Salietti swiftly attacked the first mercenaries he encountered. With one blow of his sword, Athena, he broke their helmets, turning their faces into streams of blood. Next to him, the duke's knights were being knocked down by the attackers' arrows and swords. Duke Gulf spun his sword in the air like a windmill, cutting the necks of his enemies around him, while Rhadoguil of Curnilldonn fought tirelessly next to him.

When he recognized the shield of Valdigor of Rostvol – with its image of a tower crossed by a crow's wing – Duke Gulf pushed his way through the fierce crowd around him and attacked him with such force that Valdigor fell to the ground. The duke's sword rose in the air and clashed on the knight's shield like lightning from a cloudy sky. Valdigor, from the ground, took advantage of the failed blow and thrust his sword up into his attacker's unprotected waist with such rage that he buried it up to the handle between the gaps in the armour. Salietti saw Duke Gulf's bulging eyes and watched as he took his last breath, falling dead at the gates of his fortress.

Salietti gave a cry of pain, as if he'd felt his own insides pierced by the steel of Valdigor's sword. Enraged, he ran toward Valdigor, slashing past one after another of the attackers between them.

'You'll pay for the death of the duke with your life!' shouted Salietti when he finally stood in front of his enemy.

Valdigor of Rostvol recognized immediately the sun and moon emblazoned on the shield of the knight challenging him. 'Salietti of Estaglia!' he muttered between clenched teeth.

'Last time I had you at the mercy of my sword I spared your life. Now you can consider yourself dead,' announced Salietti.

'You brag like a naive squire!' yelled Valdigor with a laugh. 'You humiliated me, that's true, but it's time I avenge your affront to my sword.'

He lunged at Salietti with all his might, but Salietti stopped the strike with his own sword. A succession of rapid blows followed, but Salietti's overwhelming rage made his opponent back away until his sword hit the wall behind him. Valdigor managed to avoid Salietti's unforgiving lunges behind his broken shield, but his forehead began to sweat as if he could see the face of death in front of him.

'Do you still think you'll be able to enjoy your victory and take possession of this fortress after killing the master of the castles of the Circle with your own hands?' asked Salietti, disarming Valdigor with a rapid twist of his sword.

Terrified, Valdigor tried to reply, but in a slow succession of seemingly endless images, he saw Salietti hold his sword with both hands at shoulder level and rotate his waist to begin a spinning motion that would sever his head . . .

PART THREE

The Invisible Road

There are Darkness and Light in the Sky

ARTS

THE GATEWAY

SEALED CHAMBER

ISLE OF IPSAR

The Invisible Road

Darkness and Light

Grimpow and Weienell travelled all day without stopping to eat or rest, barely even speaking to each other. They were sad and worried about Salietti's fate and feared that they would never see him again. Not even surviving the sealed chamber and finding the fantastic map of the Invisible Road made them want to talk. Salietti wasn't with them now, and that was all that mattered.

After saying goodbye to their friend in the fortress' cellars, they had entered a long subterranean passage west and lit their way through the darkness with torches. It was a vaulted tunnel with rock walls, on which glistened rivulets of water. Their horses' hoofbeats echoed in that eerie, underground world – the only existing sound other than, once in a while, the fluttering of bats as they abandoned their lairs abruptly, frightened by the flames of the torches. Grimpow couldn't help thinking that this dark and sinister world was probably the kingdom of Hades – the Greek god he'd read about at the abbey.

According to mythology, three gods had divided the world after defeating the Titans. Zeus had the sky, Poseidon the ocean, and Hades the underworld, now called Hell. Grimpow thought fancifully that perhaps this described how the King of France and the baron were going to divide up the spoils after defeating the titanic castles of the Circle of Stone. What Grimpow couldn't know, however, was that Salietti had already sent Valdigor's soul to Hell.

The pale light of dusk blinded them at the tunnel's exit. As Grimpow and Weienell emerged from the passage they found themselves hidden among thick brambles at the bottom of a rocky mountain covered with enormous oak trees. They could see a large river in the distance, gleaming like a silver mirror, and next to it, silhouetted against the western horizon, were the roofs and towers of a small walled city.

They entered Metz through a gate guarded by two round towers that rose over a bridge crossing the river. Some peasants were returning from their work, pulling mules loaded with bundles of wheat. As they passed through the city's gate, they almost immediately saw the towers of a cathedral rising over the rooftops. In a square surrounded by ornate mansions with arcades were a group of ladies on their way to the evening service. The women, clothed in elegant dresses in delicate colours, looked at the young strangers curiously and continued whispering among themselves. Weienell approached them and asked for directions to Dr Humius Nazs' house, saying that her brother suffered from vomiting and dizziness, while Grimpow pretended to be as sick as if he'd caught the plague. The women were alarmed, for they feared that they could catch some incurable disease, but one of them, a beautiful lady with black hair and bright eyes, told them to leave the square through the lane bordering the cathedral and continue down the street on the right. When they'd reached the Templars' chapel they should take the narrow alley opposite the tower and knock on the door of the fourth house on the left.

Grimpow had been thinking of Brother Rinaldo of Metz ever since they'd crossed the bridge and entered the city where he had been raised. But the image of the scholarly old man came alive when they arrived at the closed chapel of the outlawed Templar Order. The walls of the small church were intact, though the bells in its towers hadn't chimed in years. Grimpow touched the chapel's stones and envisioned the old monk Rinaldo of Metz inside, when he was just a boy like him, a young Templar who would one day leave to defend the Holy Land of Jerusalem.

The front of Humius's house consisted of only a few windows located above a door, but its living quarters became richer and wider once you entered an open courtyard full of vines and jasmine. Weienell made her way into the courtyard and knocked on the door while

Grimpow remained outside and held the horses' reins.

An old man with grey hair and a long beard opened the door, obviously surprised to see the two youngsters.

'Duke Gulf of Ostemberg begs that you lodge us in your house for a few days,' said Weienell, inhaling the scent of flowers and medicinal balms emanating from the courtyard.

'If you were sent by the duke, you can consider yourselves at home,' replied the old man without a moment's hesitation. He invited them to bring the horses into the courtyard and guided them to a small stable, then helped them unsaddle the animals before filling one trough with water and another one with forage. 'Your horses will have enough food and water for tonight. Now, come with me to the kitchen, as you look hungry and tired as well. I will let my wife know of your arrival so she can prepare your quarters and add two more plates for dinner. Her name is Mahusle, and I am sure that she'll be delighted with your visit.'

The voice and face of the kind old man seemed familiar to Grimpow. Perhaps it was his own imagination, as he'd been thinking of Brother Rinaldo of Metz, or perhaps it was that the real image of the librarian monk had become blurred in his memory, but the truth was that if Humius's thick beard hadn't been hiding a good part of his face, Grimpow could have sworn they were as similar as two drops of water. So similar that he couldn't stop staring at the doctor.

Finally he spoke to the older man. 'I met a monk in the

abbey of Brinkdum who was born in this city more than eighty years ago.'

'This city has given the world monks, preachers, abbots, noblemen, knights, bandits and a few prophets that wander the roads like lunatics,' said Humius, smiling.

'His name was Rinaldo, Rinaldo of Metz,' added Grimpow.

The old man's expression changed. 'My older brother's name is also Rinaldo, but I haven't heard from him in years.'

'The monk I am talking about joined the Order of the Temple of Solomon when he was a boy a little older than me, following the advice of his uncle, who was a commander of the Temple in this city, and left for the Holy Land before being appointed knight,' added Grimpow, watching to see what effect these details would have on the doctor.

'How do you know these things?' asked Humius, looking surprised.

'He told me himself at the abbey of Brinkdum. He was the librarian monk and, during the few months I lived there, my teacher. I care a great deal about him,' explained Grimpow.

Humius sat thoughtfully on a bench in the centre of the courtyard. Grimpow remained silent, thinking about the capricious twists of fate that tied together lives and destinies that seemed to have no relation to each other, as had happened with him and Humius, and with Weienell and Salietti.

'We always thought that Rinaldo had died in the last Crusade,' the doctor said at last, clearly moved by the news. 'So we were told by the Templars who returned to Metz after the loss of the Holy Land. I find it hard to believe that he is still alive, for we never heard from him again.'

'I can assure you that he is alive and in good health, despite his many years. Your brother Rinaldo told me in the abbey that he had lived in the Holy Land from the age of sixteen, defending the Templar fortresses of Safed, Tripoli, Damascus, Gaza, Galilee, Damietta and Acre. And that he'd joined in the Seventh and Eighth Crusades, led by the King of France. He said that, upon his return to Europe, he was repulsed by the amount of blood shed in the name of God and decided to live a secluded life in the abbey of Brinkdum, to the east of the Alps, and dedicate his life to prayer and study.'

'I would have never thought, when I saw you at the door of my house, that you'd be the carrier of such good news,' said Humius.

'It was a surprise for me as well to see your resemblance to your brother Rinaldo.'

Mahusle, Humius's wife, came out to the courtyard to fetch the small group. She was a small woman with delicate features, despite the wrinkles that creased her elderly face. She had black eyes, deep and mysterious, that reminded Grimpow of his own mother.

'Come to the kitchen. Your rooms are ready, and I have prepared some delicious chicken gruel that will return the cheerfulness to your sad faces,' she said, directing them all into her home and toward its heart.

During dinner, Weienell told Humius and Mahusle about the situation in the castles of the Circle of Stone. She also told them about the death of her father, Gurielf Labox, their persecution by the inquisitor Bulvar of Goztell, her escape from the city of Strasbourg, and Salietti of Estaglia and his decision to join Duke Gulf's loyal knights to defend his fortress. She explained that was why she and Grimpow would wait in the city of Metz – if Salietti didn't come in two days, they would continue their journey without him.

'Are you searching for the secret of the wise?' asked Humius, bluntly, and this time it was Grimpow and Weienell who were surprised.

'How did you guess?' asked Grimpow.

'I didn't guess, I simply know. Iacopo of Estaglia and Gurielf Labox were great friends of mine. We all belonged to the secret society of Ouroboros and used to meet with Duke Gulf's father and other sages in the castles of the Circle of Stone to share our discoveries and knowledge of the mysteries of nature and the cosmos. We stopped when the persecutions began years ago. We dreamed of a peaceful world governed by wise kings and princes, but power always seems to prefer ignorance to wisdom,' said Humius with a sigh. 'I'm afraid that if the King of France and Baron Figueltach of Vokko succeed in taking over the castles of the Circle of Stone, our hopes and everything we longed for will scatter in the air like embers fluttering around the fires of barbarity.'

In spite of their fears about Salietti's fate, Grimpow and Weienell spent the following two days trying to decipher the map of the Invisible Road. They soon realized that this new challenge would require all of their creativity and imagination. Riddles, as Humius pointed out, could only be resolved by those with inquisitive minds interested in wisdom and knowledge.

Humius had left to tend to someone with typhoid fever on the outskirts of the city, and his wife had gone to the market to buy vegetables and meat for dinner. Grimpow and Weienell sat at the kitchen table, alone in the house.

Grimpow dug the map out of his bag and spread it on the table. The unusual piece of parchment was the most fantastic and mysterious map they could have ever imagined, and they had no doubt that the secret of the wise was well protected by a long chain of intertwined riddles. They decided to tackle this new challenge with a method that allowed them to order the ideas brewing in their minds.

'I will draw a sketch of the map so that we can break it into sections,' said Grimpow, grabbing his charcoal pencil and the piece of parchment on which he had done all his previous annotations. When he had finished, he wrote down the text that surrounded the celestial sphere and they both studied it in silence for a while.

After carefully analysing the different elements on the

parchment, Grimpow offered the first conclusion. The groups of stars painted on the map had specially caught his attention, and he was sure that the clue to the enigmas was hidden somewhere among them. He remembered the words of the blind monk, Uberto of Alessandria, who had told him that the answers to the questions about the secret of the wise were beyond the stars. He was sure that the phrase around the celestial sphere was the same as the one written on the sealed message Salietti's father carried: *There are darkness and light in the sky*. Grimpow could only conclude that it meant that the light that would illuminate the Invisible Road was in the sky – covered by the shadows of its own mystery.

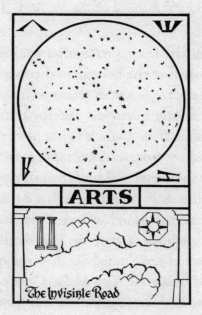

'You might be right, but you've started analysing the map from the top, and I think we should begin at the bottom,' answered Weienell.

'And what does the lower part of the map suggest to you?' asked Grimpow, folding his sketch so that it appeared like this:

'I think that the three phases that lead to the secret of the wise are shown at the bottom of the map. The first one was the sealed chamber where time was life and was death, which we've already overcome. We've seen the Invisible Road – still ahead of us – which will lead us to the island of Ipsar, inhabited by monsters and fantastical beings, where we'll confront the Devil and find the last words at his feet. If you look at the map carefully, you'll see that according to the compass rose the island of Ipsar is located to the west of the sealed chamber, that is to say, to the west of the castles of the Circle of Stone, which is the same direction we've followed since we left Duke Gulf of Ostemberg's fortress. So the first conclusion we can draw is that the island of Ipsar is west, and that must be the direction of our Invisible Road.'

Grimpow accepted her conclusion. 'Your reasoning sounds quite accurate, but then what does the word ARTS mean?' asked Grimpow.

'The secret of the wise, or the place where it is hidden, probably has a lot to do with the arts.'

'And the arts can only be found in churches and cathedrals – sculptures, paintings, stained glass, music,' noted Grimpow.

'I had that thought as well,' replied Weienell.

'So our second conclusion could be that we should find a church or cathedral to the west?'

'No doubt about that,' said Weienell, 'but France is full of churches and cathedrals. There might be hundreds of them. There are chapels and hermitages in every village and town, and rarely does even the smallest city not have a cathedral. There's one in the square here – we walked by it yesterday. The arts are all around us.'

'OK, so maybe we should look at the top of the map among the stars, for a clue instead,' reasoned Grimpow.

He stared at his drawing of the sky and was lost in thought for a while, remembering the nights he'd spent next to the librarian monk Rinaldo of Metz on the abbey of Brinkdum's hill, contemplating the heavens while the old monk created his stellar cards and charts. He remembered that, when the monk showed him the first planisphere, he'd told Grimpow that the drawing represented the night sky above him.

There are darkness and light in the sky

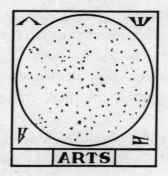

'Those are real constellations on the map! These are paintings of constellations of stars. That's why the road leading to the secret of the wise is invisible!' exclaimed Grimpow, looking at his drawing again.

There are darkness and light in the sky

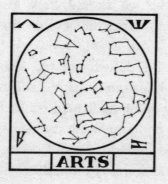

He grabbed the charcoal pencil and began to connect the dots of the stars with fine straight lines until the stars were clustered in perfect and distinct constellations.

'That's wonderful, Grimpow! It's true that there are darkness and light in the sky – by finding the light of the stars, you're making the Invisible Road visible,' said Weienell.

Cassiopeia Perseus Cepheus Auriga Lyra Draco

Ursa Minor Gemini Hercules Boötes Ursa Major

Scorpius Libra Virgo Leo Cancer

Centaurus Hydra

'Now we're facing the most complicated riddle yet. I have no idea which one of these roads will lead us to the secret of the wise,' moaned Grimpow.

'I must admit, I have no idea either – but I know we can't give up,' Weienell told him.

On the evening of the second day they decided to consult Humius, for they couldn't resolve the new riddle hidden among the stars. They had spent countless hours combining the initials of each constellation, looking for anagrams and double meanings in their names, but they hadn't found anything that caught their attention.

Grimpow explained to Humius the clues they had followed since he and Salietti had passed the misty Vale of Scirum and opened the crypt in Cornill's church where the history of the secret of the wise slept. He told him that they had travelled to the city of the message and in Strasbourg's cathedral he had heard the voice of the shadows; that they had followed the path of the sign and found the sealed chamber where time was life and was death; and had seen the Invisible Road painted on the map they'd found there, which he was now showing to the doctor.

Weienell took over at this point, telling Humius about their progress in the solution of the riddle of the Invisible Road. She said that they'd also found out that the island of Ipsar should be located to the west of the castles of the Circle of Stone, and that the secret of the wise had something to do with the arts, almost certainly in churches and cathedrals. She also told him that Grimpow had found the light in the darkness of the sky and had made the Invisible Road visible when he grouped the stars on the map forming the constellations that appeared in his sketch. But as hard as they'd thought about it, they couldn't work out which one of the roads traced by the empty spaces between constellations would help them reveal the secret of the wise.

'I must confess that my knowledge of astronomy is limited. Your father, however,' Humius said, looking at Weienell kindly, 'would have had no trouble deciphering this riddle of stars and constellations. He was a great astronomer.' The doctor paused. 'I do, however, remember hearing him talk, on some occasion, about a theory he was researching at the University of Paris. He said that some of the most important cathedrals in France followed on earth the same pattern as the stars of the constellation of Virgo in the sky.'

'The constellation of Virgo?' repeated Weienell. Grimpow drew that constellation in his parchment of notes.

'Correct. As far as I know, Virgo has always been depicted as a beautiful young woman holding a sheaf of wheat.'

'That's why its brightest star is called Spica, the Latin term for "spike of wheat"! Brother Rinaldo told me about that star in our studies,' explained Grimpow.

'The first sages of the Ouroboros society were closely

involved in the construction of cathedrals. Only they had the necessary knowledge to create such wonders,' continued Humius.

'Perhaps the secret of the wise is hidden in one of them,' thought Grimpow aloud.

'In the old sages' language nothing is what it seems, and the cathedrals are an immense mystery in themselves,' the doctor said. 'Their naves and high vaults, their towers, porticos, rose windows and stained glass are full of paintings and sculptures, symbols and allegories that probably won't be deciphered for centuries. The cathedrals of Rheims, Paris, Chartres and Amiens are the most magnificent in France – and they are all in the west,' concluded Humius.

He got up from the kitchen table, walked over to his study and came back with a map of France, which he unfolded on the table. Taking the charcoal pencil and Grimpow's parchment with his annotations, he began to trace the constellation of Virgo.

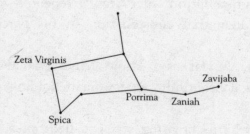

Weienell and Grimpow looked at him curiously, trying to deduce what Humius intended to do with those stars tied

by imaginary lines. And after checking something on the
map of France, he made a new drawing that left the two
youngsters amazed.

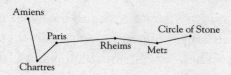

'The Invisible Road!' exclaimed Grimpow after seeing
what the doctor had drawn.

'It's unbelievable!' added Weienell. On the drawing, the
cities of Amiens, Chartres, Paris, Rheims and Metz and the
castles of the Circle of Stone were connected by the same
pattern as the stars in the constellation Virgo.

'Now you know in which direction you should resume
your journey tomorrow, in search of the secret of the wise,'
said Humius humbly.

'Paris!' exclaimed Weienell.

Together Again

Salietti arrived at the city of Metz badly wounded, his arms and face covered with burns. Despite his state, though, he waited outside the city with his horse for night to fall before entering the maze of alleys leading to Dr Humius's house. The roar of rocks falling on the fortress' walls and towers mixed with the cries of agony of the dying still resonated in his ears. He shivered from fever and, in his delirium, even wondered if what had occurred was just a nightmare, a bad dream from which he would never awake. He didn't even know whether anyone else had survived the massacre — everything had happened so quickly and unexpectedly.

He fell, eventually, into a deep slumber. The moon seemed to slide hastily behind a faded and frayed blanket of clouds, and some owls hooted in the trees under which Salietti hid at dusk, like a criminal fleeing the gallows.

After several hours of bad dreams he woke up. The stars flickered timidly in the darkness of the night. A dog barking could be heard in the distance, and the wind swayed the branch of a tree in front of him. Salietti climbed to his feet with difficulty and mounted his horse, setting out along the road into Metz. He crossed the bridge and rode slowly through a labyrinth of narrow cobblestone streets, with no more company than the shadows of the night and the hollow sound of his horse's hoofbeats.

When he finally found Humius's home, he got off his horse and hobbled to the door.

'They've killed them all!' he managed to say weakly when Humius opened the door to his house.

'Who are you?' asked the doctor, disconcerted. 'What's happened to you?'

'Tell – tell Weienell and Grimpow,' stammered Salietti before he fainted.

The strong banging had woken Weienell and Grimpow, and they'd been waiting impatiently in their rooms for news from Humius about the racket. For a moment they feared that Bulvar of Goztell had found their new hideout. But Weienell thought she recognized Salietti's voice, and they both ran down the stairs to see what was happening.

'Someone is asking for you, and he looks badly injured. It must be Salietti,' speculated Humius.

'Yes! It's Salietti!' exclaimed Grimpow when he saw his friend lying on the ground by the door.

Weienell kneeled beside Salietti's inert body and

kissed him on the forehead, sobbing and stroking his hair.

'Let's bring him inside, quickly,' said the doctor. 'Grimpow, you should take his horse to the stable.'

Weienell and Humius lifted the knight's heavy body with difficulty and brought him inside. They managed to get Salietti to a room near the entrance, and laid him on a long table. Around them were shelves filled with thick manuscripts on medicine and an area where several surgical instruments were stored.

The doctor removed Salietti's armour, grabbed a sharp scalpel and sliced open his doublet. His clothes were soaked with dark, dried blood. Humius removed them carefully from the knight's skin, revealing a deep sword cut from his neck to his shoulder.

'I'll take advantage of his unconscious state and sew the wound before he comes to,' said Humius, grabbing from a cupboard the necessary instruments to close Salietti's laceration.

As he spoke, Weienell pulled up her sleeves. 'I'll help you,' she said.

Humius's wife entered the room and gazed at the man on the stretcher. 'I'll warm up water and prepare compresses,' she said, then left the room as discreetly as she had walked in.

Weienell asked anxiously, 'Do you think the injury is serious?'

'I don't think so, though he's lost much blood and is weak from his journey here in such a horrible state. He also seems to have a very high fever,' the doctor said, resting his hand on Salietti's forehead.

Grimpow had just entered the room, and when he heard the doctor's words his face darkened as if some sinister and ghastly shadows had passed over the oil lamps. His worst fears when leaving the city of Strasbourg had come true, and the attack on the castles of the Circle had ended in a ruthless massacre. Still, Salietti was alive!

'If we'd given the stone and the map to the inquisitor, maybe none of this would have happened,' he murmured, angrily staring at the wound.

After Weienell washed Salietti's neck and shoulder, Humius pierced Salietti's skin using a hook-shaped needle as if mending a thick piece of leather.

'They would have killed them all,' the doctor answered, 'even if you had revealed to them the secret of the wise. It's happened before and it will happen again. The last thing murderers such as that Dominican friar care about is the reason why they kill.'

'I'm sad that Duke Gulf and his knights died defending us.'

'Our cause is the cause of humankind, Grimpow – don't forget that. We've never harmed anyone, and all our efforts are aimed toward making a more reasonable and fair world. A world in which wisdom and not ambition reigns. If the King of France and Baron Figueltach ordered the execution of the Circle of Stone's inhabitants, it is they, not you, who should shoulder the responsibility for those crimes. It's enough that we have to hide.'

'I'm afraid that many more people will die before this horror ends,' said Weienell, who was wiping away the blood flowing from Salietti's wound.

'Yes, unfortunately, I think you are right,' confirmed the doctor.

Humius's wife opened the door again and entered the room carrying a few cloth compresses and bandages that smelled strongly of boiled herbs. She passed them to Weienell. 'I'll bring some broth I have on the hearth – it will help him build strength to recover. You need to get some sleep,' Mahusle said, and she left the room silently. She was a woman of few words, and though she was used to helping her husband when he tended to his patients, she rarely interfered unless it was to suggest an ointment or potion that could relieve the ill person's suffering.

After sealing the wound, the old doctor applied some liniment to the burns on Salietti's face and bruised body. He wrapped him in the aromatic bandages Mahusle had prepared, and Weienell and Grimpow helped him carry the patient to an adjoining room, where there was a wide and comfortable bed.

'I'll look after him during what's left of the night,' said Weienell, taking Salietti's hands in hers. And as Humius and Grimpow returned to their quarters, Weienell thought about how different people's desires could be. While some, like Humius, worked hard to save the lives of their fellows, others tried hard to kill them.

* * *

Salietti slept through the day, and the following morning was rainy and cool, even though they were in the midst of spring. Around a well in the house's courtyard, humming-birds quivered their feathers to rid their wings of water. Mahusle bustled about the kitchen attending to the bub-bling cauldrons on the flames of an open fire while Humius, Weienell and Grimpow ate bread with salt fish and a large cup of milk for breakfast. It had been over a day since Salietti arrived, and they were still waiting for him to regain the strength to recount what had happened in Duke Gulf's fortress. They also feared that the baron's soldiers might have followed him to Metz and could be waiting to capture them all. They all remained silent, downcast, and lost in their own thoughts.

Grimpow thought about the city of Paris and what was in store for them there. He knew that he and Weienell had not been wrong to conclude that, according to Aidor Bilbicum's manuscript, the city was the location of the island of Ipsar, inhabited by monsters and fantastical beings, where they should confront the Devil to find the last words at his feet. The map of the Invisible Road Humius had drawn, following the line of stars in the Virgo constellation, coincided perfectly with the line connecting the castles of the Circle of Stone with the cities of Metz, Rheims, Paris, Chartres and Amiens. If his theory was not mistaken, the whole map of the Invisible Road indicated that the secret of the wise should be hidden in a cathedral or church in one of those six cities.

Now their next place to search was the island of Ipsar. When Humius had told them that Paris was one of the cities on the Invisible Road, Grimpow had realized almost immediately that the letters in the word *Ipsar* could be rearranged to form the word *Paris*. Weienell then explained to him that in the middle of the river Seine, which traversed the city, was a large islet on which the cathedral of Notre Dame was built. Grimpow, however, couldn't stop wondering about those monsters and fantastical beings that might inhabit the island – and how they would confront the Devil to find the last words at his feet.

Weienell thought about Paris as well. It was the city where she had been born, and her father had taught astronomy in its university his whole life. A multitude of memories flooded her mind, overwhelming her. Since she had abandoned her house in Paris to accompany her sickly father to the village of Cornill, her life had transformed like the alchemists' lead, going from the darkest and heaviest sorrow to the golden colour of her feelings for Salietti. And now he was by her side again.

'I hope there is something left to satiate a dying man's hunger,' said Salietti, suddenly appearing in the kitchen like a resuscitated corpse.

Weienell's heart leaped. She got up from the table to embrace him.

'You should still rest in bed for a couple of days,' said Humius.

'That will only speed the time of my death, and I think I still have enough life in me to escape its sharp claws,' replied Salietti, clearly happy to be alive. Grimpow too hugged him carefully to avoid aggravating his injuries.

'Salietti, this is Doctor Humius,' Weienell told him. 'He was a friend of our parents' as well – and it was he who treated you and has taken us into his home.' Weienell pointed to the old woman smiling by her side. 'And this is his wife, Mahusle. Your strength proves the power of her ointments and broths.'

'I am indebted to both of you for your generous hospitality,' said Salietti, his gratitude shining in his eyes.

Humius and Mahusle nodded courteously.

'Humius is a great sage and has helped us decipher the riddle of the Invisible Road,' Grimpow interrupted. Weienell could tell he was eager to share the advances they'd made in their search for the treasure of the wise. 'Now we know we must go to Paris.'

'Tell him about that later, Grimpow,' answered Humius with a chuckle. 'Let Salietti sit down with us first and recount what happened at the castles of the Circle of Stone.'

Salietti sat down at the table slowly. He'd rather have talked about anything else than recall the horror he'd lived at Duke Gulf of Ostemberg's fortress. But he knew that Humius was a good friend of Duke Gulf, and out of respect he must relay what had happened.

Weienell and Grimpow were horrified to hear Salietti's account. As Salietti told of the attack and battle, his eyes flashed as if he was living the tragedy over again. Dr Humius shuddered when he heard how Gulf of Ostemberg had died; the doctor had known the duke since he was a child.

'We were surrounded by mercenaries who had managed to pass the walls of the tower,' continued Salietti. 'So when we got a chance, we retreated inside the gate and returned to the upper fortress to reorganize our defences. Rhadoguil of Curnilldonn took over leading the Knights Templar who had taken refuge in the castles of the Circle. They were all willing to die before relinquishing the duke's own castle.

'There was a small lull that night, which we took advantage of to rest and prepare oil burners that we set ablaze on every battlement of the western wall and the castle's towers. The whole fortress looked like it was on fire, and the baron's army thought we had chosen to kill ourselves and go to Hell rather than surrender the treasures they were searching for.

'The following morning, as soon as the sun rose, the enemy started their march – like a colony of ants. We could hear a deafening clamour of trumpets, screams and drums as they approached the eastern rock walls in the thousands, climbing the mountain with hundreds of ladders and ropes, while balls of fire and rock fell on our heads from the catapults under the ramparts. Our archers were able to stop the advance of hundreds of soldiers, but it wasn't enough. They were so many and were so well prepared that they were quickly able to climb the walls and towers, not stopped even by scalding oil.

'The catapults had opened several holes in the walls, and before we knew it we were surrounded by hundreds of soldiers and knights, who had toppled the eastern gates and entered the fortress. We fought bravely for hours until the Templars and the duke's loyal knights started falling one by one, and fewer than a hundred of us were left to defend the keep's chamber, where the children and women were taking refuge.' At this point, Salietti interrupted his tale and sighed, as if he didn't have enough strength to remain sitting straight.

'You don't need to continue if you can't,' said Humius. 'We can imagine what happened next.'

But Salietti recovered and went on, 'No, you can't imagine the horror even if I tell you about it. Bodies covered the floors of the fortress, and those of us who continued fighting – knowing that death was the only other possible choice – fought while stepping on the bodies and slipping in the blood. The last thing I remember is a pain in my neck and a strong blow to my helmet, and the image of one of Baron Figueltach of Vokko's knights standing behind me, guffawing as he saw me fall at his feet. "Kill them all" was the last thing I heard him say.

'When I woke up, it was night and I was surrounded by hundreds of corpses. I was so disorientated and over-whelmed that I thought I had awoken from a terrible nightmare in the middle of the Apocalypse, and then I realized that I was near the door to the secret passageways you escaped through – where I had left my horse. The attackers were entering the keep in hordes, so I sneaked down the stairs. I finally reached the stone tunnel and my horse and escaped as fast as I could. When I came out to the surface, I hid until dark, then made it here. After that my memory is blank – until now.'

The Troubadour's Barge

The trip to Paris was uneventful. They rose before dawn on a cloudy day that cleared when the wind changed direction. The clouds ran through the sky as if they too were fleeing to a remote and unknown place.

When they'd finished packing, they saddled the horses and placed the saddlebags and some rolled blankets on the horses' backs. They bid farewell to Humius and Mahusle, who wished their new friends all the luck the heavens and the stars could bestow upon them on the now-visible road.

They headed southwest and soon left the south gate of the city of Metz behind. All around them stretched vast green plains dotted by red poppies, and toward the horizon rose a sharp-edged chain of mountains.

They rode at a good speed. Even though Salietti's injuries hadn't healed completely, he didn't want to delay their arrival in Paris. The war against the castles of the Circle had ended, and soon the king's army would return to the city of their monarch to celebrate their victory. Salietti suspected, however, that Philip would be celebrating a new massacre, for his hound, the inquisitor Bulvar of Goztell, would return from war without the one treasure the king wanted – the object that could grant him immortality, an object the Dominican friar had promised him could exorcize the curse cast upon him by the Templar Grand Master he'd burned at the stake.

The travellers decided to avoid cities, towns, villages and the roads used by merchants, monks, pilgrims, beggars and bandits who travelled from Alsace to Paris, for they didn't want to risk their lives and their mission again. As they rode by the outskirts of the city of Verdun in mid-afternoon Salietti couldn't help thinking that it had been a futile war for a pointless goal.

On the evening of the second day of travelling, they spotted the small city of Châlons on the horizon. Châlons was located on the banks of the copious river Marne, and it was flanked by a multitude of marshes brimming with waterbirds that squawked and fluttered over the wetlands in large and raucous flocks when the sun went down. The towers of a church and the cathedral loomed over the rooftops of its wood-framed houses, giving the city a noble air of prosperity and elegance. From Châlons a road led north, to Rheims, and another one went west, to Paris.

'I assume you're sure that it's Paris and not Rheims that the map indicates as our next destination. There is also a magnificent cathedral in Rheims, where France's last monarchs were crowned before their courts. It wouldn't be a bad place to hide a valuable treasure,' said Salietti.

Weienell and Grimpow had spent much of the first morning's ride explaining how, with Humius's help, they had deciphered the riddle of the map. Now Weienell began to go back over their reasoning.

'Once you decode it, Aidor Bilbicum's manuscript is very clear – it places the third phase of the search for the secret of the wise on the island of Ipsar. Unscrambled, that spells Paris. So, logically, the Invisible Road would lead us to the island of Ipsar, inhabited by monsters and fantastical beings—'

Salietti interrupted, 'But there aren't monsters or fantastical beings in Paris!'

'We might be surprised,' answered Weienell matter-of-factly.

'I wonder where we'll find the Devil and how we can confront him to find the last words at his feet,' said Grimpow, thinking out loud.

Weienell smiled at Grimpow reassuringly. 'We've succeeded in resolving the riddles up to now – I'm sure we'll know it when the time comes,' she answered.

'But every new riddle is more complicated than the one before, and we don't have Humius now to help us decipher them. Without him, I don't know how we would have worked out that the Invisible Road was hidden among the stars,' pointed out Grimpow.

'If my father's theory is right, the secret of the wise must be hidden in one of these cities' cathedrals, and the clues to find it are contained in Aidor Bilbicum's manuscript. The only thing we have to do is interpret them correctly.'

'I just hope it's not another trap—' said Grimpow.

'At least you have me now to defend you from any perils,' interrupted Salietti. 'I'm afraid that my brains won't be of much help in deciphering the riddles, but I can still take up the sword.'

'We're very happy that you're with us again, despite your slow-wittedness,' Grimpow teased.

'That's true,' said Weienell, offering Salietti her hand with a grin. But her smile quickly turned into a grimace as soon as she saw a group of hooded people not far from them.

Salietti motioned with his hand for them to lower their voices.

'I think they are mendicant friars,' said Grimpow, squinting to get a better view in the darkness of the night.

'I'll get closer to find out who they are,' Salietti said, and spurred his horse over to the crowd.

They turned out to be a small group of lepers roaming aimlessly after the bishop had banished them from their shelter in some caves near the city of Rheims. Salietti gestured to Weienell and Grimpow to approach. 'And why has the bishop expelled you from your colony?' Salietti asked the lepers.

The men remained silent, so a stout woman, her disfigured face hidden underneath her hooded cloak, answered. 'The Bishop of Rheims claims that our disease is a divine punishment for our sins, and has accused us of practising sorcery to spread our incurable illness to all the God-fearing people who attend the cathedral, where we used to beg. They've burned everything we had in the caves and threatened to kill us if we returned.'

'Damn those sons of the Devil!' exclaimed Salietti angrily.

Weienell broke in. 'Have you found any of the king's soldiers in the west?' she asked.

'No, but we heard in a church in Châlons that part of the king's army is returning to Paris. And the soldiers are ravaging the towns and villages on their way,' a man told them.

'If the mercenaries of the king run into you, they'll kill you and eat your horses,' another man warned, convinced that these strangers were escaping from something or someone as well.

'Which is the best way to Paris?' asked Salietti.

'If you fear any dangers, the fastest and safest way is the river. In Châlons harbour you'll be able to find a barge to take you to where the Marne and the Seine connect. Every night several set sail, and they can leave you right at the gates of the city.'

Salietti was about to say goodbye and wish the lepers luck when the first man added, 'Ask for Azkle the

Troubadour at the harbour. He is a little rough in his manners and sings worse than a deaf frog, but nobody knows the river like he does. Tell him you come on my behalf and he'll help you without asking any questions.'

Grimpow and Weienell smiled and glanced at each other, surprised by the stranger's kindness.

'And who are you?' enquired Salietti.

'Just say you are a friend of Prestdal.'

'And where are you going?' asked Weienell.

'We are heading southwest. Some Franciscan monks are building a hospice for lepers outside the city of Toul, and we are hoping to find the shelter there that is denied to us in Rheims.'

Salietti took a few gold nuggets from his bag and offered them to the faceless man in front of him. 'This will help the Franciscan monks of Toul to open the doors of their hospice without delay.'

The lepers stared at Salietti's open hand, mesmerized by the glittering gold.

'Oh, sir,' murmured the man, extending his bony and ulcerated hands, 'how can we ever repay you for such generous alms?'

'You've already done it,' answered the knight kindly. 'Now go in peace, and may God be with you.'

In front of the harbour, the river Marne flowed placidly under the full moon reflected on its waters. Waiting at the harbour's piers for the boats that would take them to Paris were several groups of men, and some women and children. Judging from the hats, bottle gourds and walking sticks they carried, they looked like pilgrims on their way to Compostela to kneel before James the Apostle's relics.

All the travellers dismounted their horses, and Salietti approached a stevedore loading baskets onto a potbellied boat with a mast and two large sails covered with grime.

'Could you tell me which one is Azkle the Troubadour's barge?'

The man glanced at him and kept going about his business. 'Who's asking for him?' he said gruffly.

'A friend of Prestdal's.'

'And why are you looking for him?' enquired the stevedore.

'I will tell him that.'

'He's in front of you.'

'I need you to take me and my family to Paris,' said Salietti. Then, taking Azkle the Troubadour's rough hand, he put three gold nuggets in it. 'Here's your payment in advance – one for each passenger.'

At the sight of the gold the ill-natured man smiled. 'I'll prepare the ramp quickly so you can put your horses in the hold. You and your family can stay on deck,' he said politely.

As they left the harbour, the high towers of Châlon's cathedral, illuminated by the moonlight like two arrows shot at the heavens, stayed behind in the barge's glimmering wake. In their newfound peacefulness Salietti and

Weienell laid their heads on their saddlebags and tried to sleep, while Grimpow leaned on the gunwale and watched the barge's keel slash the water.

And soon after they had set sail, Azkle the Troubadour began singing romances – sounding a lot like a chorus of deranged frogs.

The Last Words

The journey lasted all night and part of the morning, but by midday they had arrived in Paris. The sun shone generously and the cerulean colour of the sky was magically intense, glinting off the murky waters of the Seine. The harbour was located next to the two islands of Paris, which sat between two arms of the Seine forming an untidy figure eight. Grimpow had no doubt that one of those two islands was the island of Ipsar, and he assumed it was the bigger one, where the cathedral of Notre Dame stood. From the Seine, Notre Dame looked a little like a gigantic two-headed crustacean – the two towers its heads, countless legs formed by the flying buttresses attached to the side naves, and a shell full of pointy thorns that covered the domes.

In Paris' river port, dozens of boats of all types and sizes were aligned one behind the other and bustling with frantic activity as stevedores carried goods into the holds and boat-men ran to and fro on the deck preparing the rigging and sails.

Once they'd left the Seine's piers behind, Weienell suggested going to her house. It had been locked since she and her father left for the village of Cornill. There they could take a bath, change their clothing and leave their horses. Salietti, however, didn't think Weienell should be seen entering her house in broad daylight without her father and followed by two strangers.

'I wouldn't be surprised if the inquisitor had a spy among your neighbours to let the king's soldiers know as soon as you return home. If that evil Dominican friar wants to deliver you to the baron's executioners, I'm sure that he'd sell his soul to the Devil if he knew that he could find you – especially now that his hopes to find the Templars' treasure have slipped through his fingers.'

'So what can we do?' asked Grimpow.

'Let's look for an inn and leave our horses there. It will be easier to go unnoticed without them. When it's dark, we'll go to Weienell's house – though spending the night there could be like locking ourselves in a trap. If the king's soldiers look for us there, we won't be able to escape.'

'You're right, but I must return to my house sometime,' said Weienell. 'Everything my father and I owned is there.' Memories flooded her mind, bringing tears to her eyes.

'As hard as it is to admit, you must not forget that you are an outlaw now with a price upon your head,' said Salietti gently. 'We must be very careful in this city. Any shadow could be suspicious, and the enemy could lurk behind any face.'

'We'll leave Paris as soon as we've confronted the Devil on the island of Ipsar and found the last words at his feet. We must continue our search for the secret of the wise. There's no time for regrets now,' Grimpow urged.

Weienell sighed. 'You're right, Grimpow,' she answered, pulling herself together. 'We'll do as Salietti suggested.'

The streets of Paris were swarming with people, which brought Salietti vivid memories of his youth. Brother Brasgdo had told Grimpow the story of the arrogance of the people of Babel, who had decided to build a tower that would reach up to Heaven. God punished them by confusing their languages so that they could no longer understand each other. Grimpow could see the towers of Notre Dame cathedral in the distance, which like the mythical Tower of Babel rose defiantly to the heavens. He wondered if God had not condemned humans again to chaos and upheaval, judging from the bedlam engulfing him now in the merchants' quarter. Hundreds of people bustled back and forth, all surrounded by the racket of peasants in the street markets proclaiming the unequalled deliciousness of their fruits and vegetables, fishermen praising the freshness of their catches, butchers exhibiting their meats like trophies, and spice merchants yelling out the miraculous properties of their herbs, potions and brews, igniting the air with a thousand exhilarating aromas.

Weienell seemed to know the maze of alleys in that quarter like the back of her hand. They passed a small cemetery, then a street of jewellers and another of weavers. Finally they reached the right bank of the Seine.

Weienell indicated the way without hesitating and they soon crossed the bridge leading to the island. To their right were the towers of an eerie fortress, where the heretics captured by the Inquisition were tortured for years. To their left, however, rose the majestic square towers of Notre Dame cathedral. Standing there, Grimpow realized that it was as if a part for Heaven and a part for Hell had been reserved on that very island.

Grimpow was transfixed by the artistic splendour of the cathedral's façade. He had a feeling that the wonderful building hid among its stones more secrets than they hoped to find answers to. Now, too, he remembered the words of the hermit. He'd said that to find the secret of the wise, they needed to learn how to interpret the language of the stones. Grimpow didn't think it would be impossible, but he worried that it wouldn't be easy to solve the final riddles left in Aidor Bilbicum's manuscript. They had to see the monsters and fantastical beings that inhabited the island – and he had no idea where to begin.

As if she could read his mind, Weienell pointed to the cathedral's highest cornices and said: 'Grimpow, look! The monstrous beings the manuscript talks about.'

Grimpow looked up where she was pointing and there, on the cornices, like fabulous creatures contemplating humans' miseries from up high, were dragons, birds, demons and beasts with open and terrifying jaws that seemed to have been suddenly turned to stone and were the guardians of those unreachable heights.

'I understand now,' said Salietti. 'The monsters and fabulous beings are the stone sculptures – the gargoyles. They represent evil – that's why they're *outside* the cathedral.'

'So what are we waiting for?' demanded Grimpow. 'Let's find the Devil that's inside and see what we find at his feet.'

A swarm of blind, crippled and disabled people begged at the cathedral's door, while under the side porticos jugglers were playing with balls of fire. They all reminded Grimpow of a long-ago time in his own life.

Inside the cathedral, the silence was as intense as the multicoloured light that filtered through the stained-glass windows. The main door faced the sunset, and at that time of the afternoon the sun was beginning to illuminate the large rose window on the front of the building. Grimpow could see that a multitude of stories were told in those stained-glass windows and that the interior of the cathedral could hide infinite mysteries that might never be discovered. The coloured windows were like a big open book, written in coded messages that could be read only by those who had the clues to do so.

Grimpow, however, was confident they'd be able to decipher the riddle that had brought them there, and he began looking around, mesmerized by the amazing beauty. As the Invisible Road's cryptogram suggested, each sculpture and painting possessed the brilliance of art as the clearest expression of human beings' creativity. But now he could also appreciate the invisible art of geometry and mathematics he had learned from the librarian monk. Like an explosion of skill and knowledge, it jumped to sight in each side wall, in each gigantic column, and in the immense gothic vaults that floated overhead as if weightless.

Next to him, Salietti stared at the faces of the people praying in the cathedral's main nave and side chapels. Some were plebeians, others merchants, pilgrims, monks or clerics. Salietti was alert for any suspicious gesture or movement.

Weienell interrupted the silence by calling to her companions. 'Come here – I think I know where the Devil might be.' When they'd joined her, she explained, 'When I was a little girl and came to the cathedral with my mother, I was terrified every time I walked by the Devil statue, thinking that it could seize my soul if I looked it in the eye. Almost nobody dares to. Perhaps that's why Aidor Bilbicum's manuscript requires overcoming our fears and confronting it to find the last words at his feet.'

They walked around the choir and the altar, passing under the statue of an innocent-looking man holding a book in his hands. Salietti noticed three words that caught his attention because of the way in which they appeared – one underneath the other, with no apparent connection. He motioned for Grimpow to step closer, and the boy copied the inscription on the piece of parchment.

SUN
AFFABLE
ALTAR

'Do these words mean anything to you?' asked Salietti.

'No idea,' Grimpow answered, shaking his head. 'I have a feeling that there are more mysteries in this cathedral than the ones we're looking for answers to.'

'What if they are the last words mentioned in the manuscript?' suggested Salietti.

Weienell shook her head with certainty. 'The manuscript says that we should confront the Devil to find the last words at his feet. This man in this sculpture is not a devil.'

'But according to the Church, the Devil can disguise itself in a thousand ways to tempt man,' Salietti insisted. 'Perhaps Aidor Bilbicum's manuscript shouldn't be interpreted as literally as we have so far.'

'We haven't been wrong yet, but Salietti could have a point,' Grimpow answered. 'In the chamber the expression *Tempus et Vita, Tempus et Mortis* ended up being a mortal trap.' After a brief silence he added, 'Though they could also be just an inscription from the creator of the sculpture, a simple diversion to distract a curious person contemplating it. In Strasbourg's cathedral the stonemasons carved their signs on the stone – something with special meaning to them that nobody else would understand.'

'At any rate, this is not what I wanted you to see. So let's go find the Devil statue I told you about,' concluded Weienell with her usual good sense. 'If we don't find anything interesting there, we'll come back.'

She guided them to a corner out of view from the cathedral's visitors. Over a stone stood a small figure with bulging eyes, a flattened nose and a grotesquely large mouth. Its face could seem comical, but there was something terrifying when you looked at it directly in the eye.

'There it is. Perhaps this is the Devil we must confront,' said Weienell with a shiver.

'And what should we do now? This Devil doesn't move – how are we going to confront him?' said Salietti. Jokingly he gripped his sword's handle.

'Perhaps the meaning of this confrontation is more symbolic than real,' answered Weienell wisely.

'I was thinking that as well,' Grimpow murmured.

Salietti took a few steps back and turned. 'You'd better find out yourselves. I'll keep watch next to you in case someone comes.'

Ignoring Salietti, the two tried to work out the riddle. 'I believe that confronting the Devil refers to something like defeating it and moving it from its place,' reasoned Grimpow.

'That's not an unlikely hypothesis,' Weienell agreed. 'But we must decide which one of us will confront this devil before we begin.'

'Let me do it,' he answered. 'I think that if I defeat him, I'll overcome fears that haven't stopped haunting me since

Durlib and I found the stone in Salietti's father's hand.'

Weienell nodded, and Grimpow walked slowly toward the image sculpted on the stone, as if it was the real Devil about to unexpectedly come to life. He extended his hand and felt the cold face of the statue to prove that he was confronting only an image of fear. Then he stepped closer and surrounded the Devil with his arms. He squeezed with all his might and shook the body from side to side, as if trying to dislocate the arms and legs of the stone figure.

Suddenly something snapped.

Grimpow let go of the sculpture, and the Devil's image rotated on its axis until its back was facing them. Where before were the Devil's feet, now was a perfect square carved on the stone, full of jumbled letters.

'The last words are a new riddle!' exclaimed Weienell with excitement.

E	S	R	E	V	I	N	U	E	H
T	M	O	R	F	K	R	O	W	D
N	A	E	M	I	T	F	O	R	E
T	T	A	M	A	T	S	U	J	S
T	I	D	O	G	E	M	O	C	E
B	S	G	N	I	E	B	N	A	M
U	H	L	L	I	W	O	S	E	K
I	P	S	A	O	T	N	I	S	N
R	U	T	T	A	E	H	W	F	O
N	I	A	R	G	A	E	K	I	L

'But it won't take us long to solve it,' said Grimpow in anticipation. He fished out the piece of parchment and charcoal pencil in his bag and copied the letters into his notes, exactly as they were written under the Devil's feet.

Salietti turned back to his friends when he heard their excited murmurs. He couldn't believe they'd actually found the last words at the Devil's feet, just as Aidor Bilbicum's manuscript assured. But when he returned to their side he couldn't help but be annoyed too when he saw they had found a new riddle they still had to interpret to continue.

Neither Grimpow nor Weienell knew where the last words would lead them, but they assumed that the place where the secret of the wise was hidden was written within the code they'd just found. Without leaving the cathedral, they sat on a pew before a chapel with a black virgin, and Weienell and Grimpow racked their brains to resolve their newest riddle as Salietti returned to his post, making sure no one came near them.

They spent a long time with their eyes glued to the square of letters. Grimpow was the first one to find a word that made sense in the square. It was located in the top row and had been written backward, from right to left.

'It says *universe* there!' he exclaimed, and added it to his notes.

'That was the word that allowed us to exit the sealed chamber alive,' remembered Weienell.

'Well, it seems to be repeated here, and I'm sure there's a connection.'

'There's also the word *time*, written backwards!' exclaimed Weienell.

'The word that was the clue to enter the sealed chamber,' Grimpow remarked, adding the word to his notes.

'And here's the word *God*,' continued Weienell, while Grimpow jotted it down.

Then he immediately exclaimed, 'And the words *human* and *beings* are here too. It seems we're on the right track,' he said.

They remained silent for some time, as if they'd found all the possibilities offered by the square, but it didn't take Weienell long to find another one.

'*Wheat*. I've found the word *wheat*!'

Grimpow added it to his list. 'That's fantastic! There's also the word *spike* – remember from the doctor? In its Latin form, *spica*, it's the name of the brightest star in the constellation of Virgo – the constellation that hid the map of the Invisible Road,' he nearly shouted, almost unable to believe the connection between the words.

Salietti came closer to see how everything was going and to warn them to be quiet. People were beginning to look in their direction.

'We've found a connection between the words,' whispered Weienell urgently.

Salietti grinned. 'By now I have no doubt that my two friends are sages,' he said, and proudly turned to head back to his surveillance post.

'What could the last words mean?' Grimpow asked himself aloud as he underlined each word they'd found. His mind raced, trying to find a logical meaning in the words, but nothing emerged from the tangle of possibilities that could take days to consider.

E	S	R	E	V	I	N	U	E	H
T	M	O	R	F	K	R	O	W	D
N	A	E	M	I	T	F	O	R	E
T	T	A	M	A	T	S	U	J	S
T	I	D	O	G	E	M	O	C	E
B	S	G	N	I	E	B	N	A	M
U	H	L	L	I	W	O	S	E	K
I	P	S	A	O	T	N	I	S	N
R	U	T	T	A	E	H	W	F	O
N	I	A	R	G	A	E	K	I	L

'I think we need to remind ourselves what exactly it is that we're looking for,' suggested Weienell, trying to find an accurate reasoning method. 'What we must find now is the location of the gateway we'll pass through to enter the labyrinth, plant the seed and see the flower grow.'

'Do you mean a specific place?'

'Exactly. That place must be hidden in these words,' explained Weienell.

'According to the Invisible Road, that place must be either here in Paris, in Chartres, in Amiens or in Rheims.

But we've already left the city of Rheims behind,' noted Grimpow.

'And we're in Paris already, so we should look for Amiens or Chartres,' said Weienell decisively.

Grimpow showed her the seven words again.

UNIVERSE
TIME
GOD
HUMAN BEINGS
SPIKE
WHEAT

For a moment he had the feeling that they had reached an unsolvable point and would only go in circles around the square of letters. Thinking of this, he remembered the drawing the old monk Rinaldo of Metz had made him in the abbey: a drawing of a circle that represented the sky, inside of which was a square that represented the earth. Somehow, thought Grimpow, those seven enigmatic words seemed to suggest the division between the circle and the square, the heavenly and the earthly. For *universe*, *time* and *God* belonged to those nebulas in space, while *wheat*, *spike* and *human beings* are part of the certainties of life on earth.

Perhaps his thoughts could guide them in the darkness that shrouded them?

Weienell listened carefully to Grimpow's explanation

without taking her eyes off the square, which Grimpow now
enclosed in a circle to illustrate his ideas.

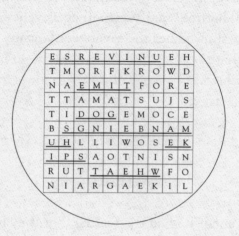

'Brother Rinaldo of Metz told me that fitting a square
peg in a round hole was impossible, for that would be like
blending the earth and the sky and God with men.'
Grimpow was discouraged by the seemingly inescapable
dilemma in which they found themselves.

But Weienell's eyes were sparkling. 'That's exactly the
meaning of this mysterious square of letters! The words in
it are not only the single words *universe*, *time*, *God*, *human
beings*, *spike* and *wheat*.'

Grimpow looked at her questioningly, so she explained.

'I mean that the last words Aidor Bilbicum speaks of in
his manuscript are a complete text. I began to suspect it
when I realized that the seven words we have underlined

were all written from right to left, and what you just said the librarian monk told you confirmed it.'

Taking the piece of parchment and charcoal from Grimpow's hands, Weienell began writing the last words by the sages of the Ouroboros society while she explained to Grimpow that the text in the square was written in reverse, from bottom to top, beginning in the lower right corner, and said exactly this:

> *Like a grain of wheat turns into a spike,*
> *so will human beings become God.*
> *It's just a matter of time*
> *and work from the universe.*

'What the last words mean is that there will be a time in which a square peg will fit in a round hole, when human beings reach divinity and become God. If you think of it carefully, human beings imagined God to explain themselves, the world and the cosmos, and when we reach absolute wisdom, human beings and God will be one and the same. Then the circle will be permanently closed and united to the square for ever. My father spoke to me about this once,' said Weienell.

'And when will that happen?' Grimpow wanted to know.

'When the passing of time and the work of the universe allow it, perhaps in hundreds, thousands or millions of years, but the process of transformation has already begun, and it is our duty to prevent ignorance from stopping it again.'

Grimpow was speechless. Now he understood why the symbol of the secret society of Ouroboros was a serpent swallowing its tail, representing the beginning and the end of wisdom.

When Salietti heard their conclusion, he found it hard to comprehend, even though his friends tried hard to make him understand.

'But then where is the gateway?' he asked. He reminded them that he was eager to leave the cathedral and abandon Paris as soon as possible. With each hour that went by, it was more probable that the first soldiers of the king's army had reached the city, and he wouldn't be surprised if the inquisitor Bulvar of Goztell returned with them to personally inform the king of his failure in bringing back the secret of the wise.

'We haven't found out yet if the gateway is here in Paris or in Rheims, Chartres or Amiens,' said Weienell. 'But it seems clear that the secret of the wise is in a cathedral in one of these cities.'

'And how are you planning to find out where?' enquired Salietti, without taking his eyes off a group of pilgrims who, intoning some hymns of praise, had just entered the cathedral through a side door located across from them.

'If the last words we found at the Devil's feet didn't contain the clue, it might be hidden among the signs surrounding the four corners of the map of the Invisible Road. We haven't analysed those yet,' said Grimpow, showing them his notes again.

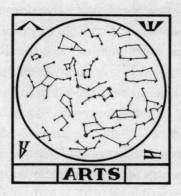

He proceeded to draw each one of the signs, isolating them from the planisphere and grouping them at random.

'We must search for these signs, isolated or together, in any order. The clue to the place where the secret of the wise is hidden must be among them. And it's the last link we need to cross the gateway. That's the last phase of Aidor Bilbicum's manuscript. We'll separate and each of us will walk around a portion of this cathedral until we meet here again,' he said firmly.

'I don't think we should separate,' said Weienell uneasily.

'If we separate, it'll be easier to go unnoticed and it'll be three times as likely we'll find anything in this immense cathedral,' Grimpow said, trying to convince her. 'It's a question of pure mathematics. Brother Rinaldo of Metz showed me in the abbey of Brinkdum that numbers can help find the solution to all the mysteries of the cosmos.'

Weienell finally acceded, and Salietti didn't seem to disagree with Grimpow, who appeared to have taken charge of the search for the secret of the wise the way a captain of archers strategizes his attack. Over the intervening months, and without him realizing it, the work of the universe had turned him into an intrepid and wise young man.

They walked around the cathedral's chapels, the choir and the main altar, and examined every column, sculpture, painting and window, carefully observing the multitude of Biblical stories represented in them. Over by the presbytery, Grimpow thought he saw a shadow slip behind one of the pulpits that flanked it. Had someone been watching him without his realizing it? He mustered his courage, climbed a flight of steps and peered behind the pulpit, but found nobody there. Could it have been his imagination, triggered by his fear of being captured by Bulvar of Goztell's henchmen?

They met at the main door of the central nave again, discouraged by the failure of their investigation. The cathedral was full of signs and symbols, but none of them resembled the ones they were searching for. And if they didn't soon find out in which of the four cities the gateway was located, Bulvar of Goztell's hounds might track them down again.

'Let's go to Amiens,' Salietti suggested. 'Its cathedral is impressive, and it is also the last city on the map of the Invisible Road. If there's only one phase left to enter the labyrinth, the gateway should be there.'

'And if it's not? What if it's here, in Paris, in this cathedral, next to us, and we haven't realized it?' asked Grimpow. His mind couldn't stop turning, considering and reconsidering every possibility.

Weienell tapped the parchment. 'Looking at the map of the Invisible Road, I believe we can draw one conclusion – the gateway is outside the island of Ipsar and to the west. So I don't think that the secret of the wise is hidden in this cathedral. Nor could it be in Rheims, as that city is east of Paris. We only have Amiens and Chartres left – one located northwest of Paris, and the other one southeast. Assuming that Salietti's theory is correct, Amiens is the last city on the map of the Invisible Road and the secret of the wise should be there. But if we pay attention to Grimpow's translation of the map, Chartres corresponds to the star *Spica*, and the word *spike* is one of the words in the letter square.'

At that moment, the rays of the setting sun filtered through the glass of the great rose window at the cathedral's entrance, illuminating it like an alchemist's furnace lights its alembic.

'The clue!' exclaimed Grimpow, staring at the spectacle of light and colour that the sun's rays had created on the rose window. 'It's here!'

Weienell and Salietti looked toward the illuminated glass as if they hadn't noticed it until then. But neither of them saw anything that could help them.

'Do you mean the rose window?' asked Weienell, puzzled.

'No,' said Grimpow, grabbing the charcoal pencil and the piece of parchment with his notes. 'I mean the map of the Invisible Road.'

Grimpow drew the signs around the map again.

ART(S)

'We knew that the secret of the wise had something to do with the word *arts* appearing in the centre of the map of the Invisible Road. And we had also arrived at the conclusion that the arts can be found inside the cathedrals.'

'And where does that reasoning bring us?' Salietti demanded.

'That the arts are to be found inside the cathedral of . . .'

A Flower in the Labyrinth

After leaving Notre Dame through the main portico, they returned to the inn and gathered their horses. They followed the same road back, and crossed over to the left bank of the Seine through a small, narrow bridge heading toward the university quarter, where the Sorbonne was located. Weienell's house was very near its main square.

At that time of the afternoon, the roads were full of students going in and out of taverns, laughing and having fun or conversing in small groups. Most of them spoke Latin and that was why their neighbourhood was known in Paris as the Latin Quarter.

The night closed in on the three travellers as they slowly rode across the Sorbonne's square. Dimly lit by torches, the university where Gurielf Labox had taught geometry, arithmetic and astronomy for years was a modest building.

Weienell shuddered, and Grimpow understood why she was scared – with every step she took, someone might recognize her and wonder why she and her father had disappeared one day and had not been heard from again. But the alleys they traversed were barely lit, so it would be difficult for someone to recognize her amid the thick darkness. A few loaded carts passed them, making a loud noise on the cobblestones and forcing them to stay close to the walls of the houses to avoid being hit by the mules or the rough wood wheels.

Weienell pointed to a door at the end of the street, framed by two columns supporting a stone lintel. 'That's where I live.'

'I didn't know you had such a nice house,' said Grimpow.

'My grandfather was a well-respected scribe in the king's court and was able to make a sizable fortune, enough to allow my father, his only son, to study and have a decent home.'

'I spent two of the best years of my life in that house's attic,' said Salietti, melancholy in his voice.

'Where do you keep the key?' Grimpow asked.

'We brought one with us to the village of Cornill, and that stayed with our belongings in the inn – but my father also left a copy hidden in a hole behind a stone cornice above the door.'

Salietti took charge of the situation immediately. 'Stay here. I'll ride closer and grab the key. Don't come until I've opened the door and made sure there's no danger,' he said in a low voice. But just as he was heading towards the house, a candle was lit behind one of the windows. He stopped as if frozen. 'There's someone in there!' he whispered harshly. 'Did anyone else have a key?'

Weienell shook her head.

Salietti brought his horse close to Weienell's and offered her his hand. 'I think someone may have moved into your house, assuming neither you nor your father would ever return. The inquisitor, or one of his spies or lackeys, maybe? If you'd like, I can knock on the door and find out, but that would be like announcing that you or someone very close to your father is wandering around Paris again.'

'No, it would be stupid to lead that murderer or his henchmen to us,' said Weienell, lifting her chin.

'So let's leave Paris. There's nothing keeping us here now,' said Grimpow.

'And where will we go after Chartres, when our search is over? We can't spend the rest of our lives like outlaws, running from one place to another,' said Weienell sadly.

'We'll go to Italy,' Salietti comforted her. 'I'll sell my grandfather's estate and we'll buy a house in Florence, a free and prosperous republic, far from the influence of popes and emperors. We'll be able to start a new life there without fearing the inquisitor's terror or the French king's greed. We're a family now, and Grimpow is going to need to start a new society of sages – a new secret Ouroboros society.'

Grimpow didn't even look back as they left the city behind. But as they travelled, he mentally joined the lights in the sky as he'd done when he had drawn the constellations of the map of the Invisible Road. To the south was the star Spica, which indicated in the sky the location of Chartres on earth.

The travellers ate and rested for a few hours in a pilgrims' lodge a few miles from Paris, and by dawn's first light they were on the road again. The city of Chartres was still a day away by horse, and they wanted to reach the cathedral before night fell and its doors were closed. The three riders knew that their journey was reaching its end, but neither Grimpow, Weienell nor Salietti knew what they would find in Chartres, or if the secret of the wise was even hidden in that city's cathedral. What was it that the knights of the Temple of Solomon had brought from Jerusalem to France two hundred years ago? What could be so coveted by both the Pope and the king that they had committed merciless massacres to get it? Could the secret of the wise really grant immortality to those who found it? Could it be treasure worth enough to turn its owners into the richest men on earth? Could it be some type of unimaginable weapon, like many legends proclaimed, capable of destroying any enemy regardless of how powerful they might be?

The minds of Grimpow, Weienell and Salietti churned with these questions. Grimpow worried that there was a chance that he still might not be able to cross the gateway or find the labyrinth. He knew that there was a possibility that, in the end, the quest for the secret of the wise could be nothing more than the search for just that – wisdom.

Another thought that didn't escape Grimpow was that two hundred years had passed since Aidor Bilbicum and the first sages of the Ouroboros society hid their secret, and many unexpected events could have occurred since then. Centuries changed the course of history as easily as a devastating storm altered a riverbed, and it was possible that the same sages of the Ouroboros society who'd hidden the secret of the wise could have changed its location or destroyed it. Or even that the whole mystery of the wise was just a new legend, like the ones troubadours evoked in their epic songs and romances.

The towers of Chartres cathedral rose toward an orange sky on the horizon, burning with the flames of twilight, turning the surrounding wheat fields the colour of gold.

Despite the time of the year and the many pilgrims who visited the cathedral, the city that afternoon seemed unusually quiet. As the three riders travelled along a cobbled road they could see the slow-moving river waters, the numerous windmills rotating their blades on the banks, the leather tanneries, the wooden bridges, the washing places, the dwellings, the churches – and the cathedral looming over the city like a stone giant.

They found a stable to leave their horses and entered the cathedral's square. Outside the main portico, the first thing that surprised them was that the doors on the west side were closed. Salietti asked a passing old man why the cathedral's doors were closed and why there was no one on the streets.

The old man told them that this day was a holiday in Chartres; all its inhabitants, noblemen or peasants, participated in a country festival outside the city that lasted until the following morning. But he also told them that they could find the cathedral's north portico – the Portico of the Initiated – open.

These words intrigued Grimpow: 'Why does the portico have such a strange name?' he asked, pretending not to know who the Initiated were.

'That was the door used by the guilds of builders, stone-masons, quarrymen, apprentices, skilled workers and masters. It can never be locked, even if the cathedral is empty,' explained the old man. He bowed and left them to continue on his way to the river.

Grimpow had the strange sensation that this wasn't the first time he'd found himself outside the cathedral. It was as if he'd seen it in his sleep before and already knew all of its secrets, though they were scattered around his brain like a tangle of unfinished dreams.

While Weienell and Salietti talked about their future in Florence, Grimpow walked over to the cathedral's portico to contemplate the sculptures flanking the western doors. To his left were the figures of two men and a woman standing on different pedestals, and to his right, in the same upright position, were the figures of three men and a woman. All but one of the seven held thick books in their hands; the last held a parchment scroll. Grimpow had no doubt that they represented the sages of the Ouroboros society, and that they stood guard over the entrance to the cathedral with wisdom's weapons – books.

'Let's walk around the cathedral and find the north portico,' suggested Salietti. 'The gateway we need to cross must be somewhere.'

They paced around the cathedral in the direction of the south portico, observing the magnificence of the beautiful building. It looked like a work of the gods, where the stone had its own language. Just as the hermit they'd met on the outskirts of Ullpens had said, man's imagination was able to write the most sublime and immortal language – the language of art.

Alert to any sign or signal that could guide them in their search, they walked around the eastern façade, carefully studying every corner, every column and capital, every bas-relief carved on the tympanums and each one of the many sculptures that decorated the cathedral like beings petrified for eternity.

When they reached the north portico – the one the old man had told them was called the Portico of the Initiated – they found an open door that led inside the cathedral.

'Looks like the old man told us the truth – we can go in through this door,' said Salietti.

Weienell noticed that next to the portico were two columns with reliefs engraved on the capitals, and a strange inscription in Latin below.

'Look at this!' she exclaimed. 'In the first scene of the bas-relief it's clear that a coffer is being transported by oxcart; in the second one, a man is covering the coffer with a veil in the middle of a field surrounded by corpses.'

'And one of those corpses seems to belong to a knight wearing a coat of mail,' added Salietti.

'That's the story of the nine knights of the Temple of Solomon,' Grimpow put in.

Salietti was studying the reliefs. 'Below the scenes of the carriage and the coffer is an inscription in Latin.'

'What does it mean?' asked Weienell.

Grimpow grabbed his parchment and the charcoal and copied the inscription.

HIC AMITITUR ARCHA CEDERIS

'In this order it's hard to tell what this means. *Hic* means "here", "in this place". *Amititur* – I don't think that means anything in Latin. It could derive from *amitto*, "to send away", but could also be translated as "to abandon" or "to hide". If we look at the image on the relief, it's clear that *archa* means "ark" or "coffer", but the word *cederis* is more confusing. I can't find a clear meaning for it, unless *cederis* is a way of referring to *cedo*, which means "to cede", or is related to *foederi*, "covenant".'

'So, according to your theory, this inscription seems to be written in an unusual Latin and could mean that the ceded ark, or the Ark of the Covenant, was sent here from far away,' summarized Weienell.

'I'm not sure, but I think that could be very close.

404

Though if we take into consideration what Doctor Humius said – that in the language of the old sages nothing is what it seems – I wouldn't be surprised if that inscription isn't in Latin at all. What if it appears to be in Latin so that only those meant to understand its real meaning are able to interpret it?' reasoned Grimpow. 'What if the inscription said that the secret of the wise was sent from far away and is hidden in this place?'

'Well, the reliefs carved on the capitals of these columns without a doubt reflect the journey of the original Knights Templar,' agreed Weienell. 'This entrance must be the gateway. Let's cross it and enter the labyrinth to plant the seed and see the flower grow.'

When they entered through the Portico of the Initiated, the weak light of dusk still illuminated the countless windows that surrounded the high naves of the cathedral of Chartres, forming a translucent tapestry with delicate shades of red, yellow, blue, white and green. Endless scenes from the Bible and real life were represented in the windows. In front of that never-ending succession of unparalleled lights and images, Grimpow understood why the word *arts* on the map of the Invisible Road was part of the word *Chartres*. And he was amazed to feel the stone hanging from his neck begin to turn warm like an ember within its pouch.

'What if the labyrinth is the labyrinth of images represented in these stained-glass windows?' Weienell exclaimed. 'If we want to find out where the seed needs to be planted, we must hurry – the sun will be setting soon.'

They began by the rose window of the north portico – which represented a seated Virgin surrounded by kings and prophets – and continued on to the side nave facing east, examining the stained-glass windows one by one. In each window were human and divine figures, abstract elements and ornamental motifs framed by innumerable circles, squares, triangles and octagons, aligned in an exuberant exhibition of celestial lights and infinite colours.

Grimpow carried the stone in his hand. He could feel its heat and knew that it was turning a reddish colour in his palm – an undeniable sign that the secret of the wise was very near him, hidden in one of those colossal columns or underneath one of the stones covering the cathedral's floor.

Beneath the gothic arches of those vaults of wisdom and mystery, Weienell and Salietti also sensed the close presence of something magical and powerful. Something capable of illuminating for ever the dark universe of their time and the times to come. After all, the words *universe* and *time* hadn't appeared by coincidence in the riddles.

Weienell was the first one to see the golden light shining on the southern nave's floor. There was a white stone different from all the others in the cathedral's floor, and embedded in it was a metal spike as golden as the alchemists' gold. She squealed in excitement. 'The spike that gives its name to the brightest star in Virgo! Look – it's also here!'

'Perhaps the spike indicates the exact place in which the seed must be planted,' suggested Salietti.

Grimpow didn't say a word; he crouched and brought the stone in his hand close to the golden spike that shone before his eyes in the day's last light.

They waited expectantly for a miracle to happen – hoping that the white stone would open into a secret passage-way, as had happened in the Cornill church's crypt or in the castles of the Circle's sealed chamber. But the spike and the tile remained unchanged, and nothing happened.

'It might not be as simple as we thought,' said Grimpow.

'I'll light some candles before it's too dark in here to see our own shadows,' said Salietti, and he walked over to the presbytery, where a few thick candles burned in front of the altar.

But when he stepped into the central nave, he saw something that immediately caught his attention. Under his feet, the stone floor turned into a succession of concentric circles formed by tiles of a brownish colour that were different from the rest of the flooring.

Startled by his discovery, he ran to the altar and grabbed several candles, lit them with the flame of the candles already blazing, and returned to where Grimpow and Weienell were waiting for him.

'I've found the labyrinth!' he told them. 'Come – it is right next to us, in the central nave, very near the main door.'

Grimpow followed, his thoughts racing as he tried to imagine what would happen. A labyrinth was a place of confusion, a trap you could enter but which was impossible to leave unless you had the thread of Ariadne of Greek mythology. His heart raced, and the light of the stone in his hand – the light of the philosopher's stone, the key to all the mysteries – began to acquire a magical intensity.

They stopped before the first circular line of the labyrinth, on the border of which were innumerable semi-circles that gave it a scalloped look.

'Yes, there's no doubt that this is a labyrinth, though it's not exactly the way I imagined it. I was expecting a maze we could walk through,' admitted Weienell, looking around the cathedral's floor.

'And I thought we needed to find the entrance to some underground tunnel – but clearly this is much different,' said Grimpow.

'Look,' Salietti interrupted, 'the centre of the labyrinth.'

'The flower!' shouted Grimpow. 'The flower is in the centre of the labyrinth.' He grabbed his notes and traced out the path in front of him. And the three of them contemplated, astonished, the petals of the flower located in the centre of that unusual and intricate trail.

'Let's look for the entrance to the labyrinth,' suggested Weienell. She began to walk around the border of the circle until she found a point of access to the road painted on the cathedral's floor.

They were so excited, it was as if all their senses could perceive the presence of something miraculous, in spite of its still being hidden. Finally before them was the path to the flower mentioned in Aidor Bilbicum's manuscript; now, they only had to follow it and plant the seed, which couldn't be anything other than the stone Grimpow had.

'Let's walk through the labyrinth to its centre. We'll think about how to plant the seed when we get there,' said Grimpow.

Weienell and Salietti gazed at the boy, and their shining eyes expressed all the affection and respect they felt for him. Neither of them had ever imagined they would meet a boy as clever and wise as he, and they were proud that he was their friend.

'Grimpow, you should enter by yourself,' said Weienell, taking his hand with tenderness. 'I think the lines on the floor are narrow to indicate that the road to the flower can only be travelled by one person.'

'Weienell is right,' Salietti echoed. 'You found the stone and it chose *you*, remember? You are the only one who can reveal its secret.'

'But we've all come here together! This mysterious stone belongs to both of you as much as it belongs to me,' protested Grimpow, unwilling to assume the responsibility of entering the labyrinth and finding the secret of the wise by himself.

'We've only accompanied you so that you could finish the mission began by our parents,' Weienell told him. 'We owe it to them and their dream. But neither Salietti nor I can feel the stone's influence as you can. In our hands, the stone is just that, a mere stone. But in your hands, the stone turns into something miraculous – just look at the reddish light burning inside it.'

'Go on, Grimpow, enter the labyrinth. We'll be waiting here and won't take our eyes off you for a moment,' urged Salietti.

Grimpow took a deep breath and stood at the entrance to the labyrinth. He hesitated for an instant and then began walking slowly between the lines that indicated the way. After a few steps, the path traced on the floor of Chartres cathedral turned left. As Grimpow slowly relaxed, he began to feel a strange and intense sensation coming from the light of the stone in his hands. It seemed to illuminate his mind and soul in a way it had never done before. And as he moved forward in the labyrinth drawn on the floor, turning one way and then another, he remembered the text of the note Gurielf Labox had left for Salietti in Cornill's church, and the text on Aidor Bilbicum's manuscript. He began to recite it in his mind like a beautiful poem written by a troubadour.

If you pass the misty Vale of Scirum in Sciripto
The crypt without a corpse will open
In which History sleeps.
Go to the city in the message
And there ask for he who doesn't exist,
And you will hear the voice of the shadows.
Follow the path of the sign
And look for the sealed chamber,
Where time is life and is death.
But only if you reach immortality
Will you be able to see the Invisible Road.
It will lead you to the island of Ipsar,
Inhabited by monsters and fantastical beings;
Confront the Devil,
And at his feet you will find the last words.
Then cross the gateway
And enter the labyrinth.
Plant the seed there
And you'll see the flower grow.

In a quick succession of images, Grimpow's life flashed before him from the time he was a mere boy and left the village where he had been born. He remembered his friend Durlib, the dead knight in the mountains of Ullpens, the monks in the abbey of Brinkdum and everything he had learned with them. And he felt fortunate to have met Salietti and have set out with him in search of the secret of the wise. Together they had found the manuscript that told

the story of the stone. And together they had rescued
Weienell from Baron Figueltach and, with her, had
travelled to Strasbourg, fleeing afterward from the
inquisitor to the castles of the Circle of Stone. He and
Weienell had survived the trap in the sealed chamber,
and they had followed the Invisible Road, which led them
to the city of Paris, and found the last words of the wise,
which talked about fitting a square peg in a round hole and
the union of human beings with God.

And now he had just crossed the gateway and entered
the labyrinth. The only thing left was to plant the seed and
see the flower grow.

When he got to the centre, Grimpow admired the petals
of the flower before him. The stone felt as warm as a tender
caress in his hand, and its light was so intense that it looked
like pure fire.

He didn't know where to plant the magical seed he
carried in his hand. Weienell and Salietti were very close,
but he saw them as if they were separated from him by a
chasm, as if the reality within that labyrinth was different
from everything beyond its limits. Then he grabbed his
parchment and drew the flower.

When he finished drawing, he realized that on the floor of the cathedral, in the centre of the flower, was a small hole just barely larger than his stone. Without hesitation, he placed the stone in this hole.

Then the miracle happened.

The stone's reddish light turned into a blue glow so intense that it nearly blinded him. And like an incandescent spark that spreads as fast as a shooting star slashing the sky, the intense glow suddenly extended to the outline of the flower and continued moving, illuminating every line on the stone floor, zigzagging in every corner of the labyrinth until everything seemed to blaze with blue fire. And all the windows on the walls surrounding the labyrinth lit up as if the sun had been ignited in the middle of the night. The cathedral's black dome filled with tiny stars and planets in motion, as if the very universe had been created in that moment.

Astonished, Grimpow noticed that over the labyrinth's flower floated a beautiful celestial sphere surrounded by thin veils of fog. Inside it were a multitude of numbers and mathematical formulas, images of past and future times, unimaginable and incomprehensible signs and symbols. He only had to think of something, even if he didn't understand it, to find the answer. Soon he realized that all the mysteries of nature and the cosmos were there before his eyes, and that everything could be explained and understood if one had the clues to reveal its mysterious essence.

The philosopher's stone was the *key* to the secret of the

wise. It was what the Templars had brought back with them to France, but it could only unlock the mysteries to those who were wise enough to complete the journey set before them, and pure enough to seek the wisdom only for the good of humanity. The stone had chosen Grimpow so that he could serve humanity, passing on the knowledge – and, when it was time, the stone – to the next sage until humankind was able to embrace the absolute wisdom contained in that prodigious sphere and the dark firmament around it.

He sat on the cold floor and for long hours stared engrossed at the perfect harmony of the small universe that had magically appeared when the light of the stone touched the labyrinth's flower. And he clearly saw again the images he'd glimpsed in confusing dreams at the abbey of Brinkdum.

He saw blue explosions that multiplied by millions the stars in the skies, planetary cataclysms that turned continents and oceans into beautiful timeless landscapes, eternal glaciers that covered the world under skies darkened by ashes, epidemics that devastated the earth, monstrous and merciless machines that threw tongues of fire, and wars that exterminated millions of men, women and children.

But, inside that fascinating sphere, Grimpow also saw unparalleled works of art, objects beautiful beyond description, and unbelievable instruments of a thousand shapes and uses, fantastic cities with crystal palaces full of lights that flickered in the darkness of night and reached the sky, people in strange clothing who walked among thousands of fast and shiny metallic vehicles in permanent motion, enormous machines the colour of silver that flew like gigantic and unusual birds, and gigantic arrows of fire that crossed the heavens and reached faraway galaxies, lost in the hazy infinity of the universe.

Grimpow knew that he'd found the secret of the wise in that extraordinary universe of light, and that it was the stone that allowed him to understand it – to reach absolute wisdom and perhaps immortality. But he also knew that the secret of the wise was a continual, marvellous mystery, only the beginnings of which had been revealed, and thousands of years would pass before humanity could decipher that riddle completely. He didn't discover what kind of magical mechanism was capable of creating the wonders before his eyes, but he didn't care.

The sages of the Ouroboros society probably never knew it either, for as the blind monk Uberto of Alessandria had assured him, the answer to that question was beyond the stars. And that was a new Invisible Road no one person could ever travel alone. Like the last words of the sages he and Weienell had found at the Devil's feet had assured them, it was a question of time and work from the universe, in which the whole of humankind would be involved. But the map of that Invisible Road was there and in his stone. They would begin to interpret it and, from now on, would look in nature and the cosmos for the magical essence of the stone and the human soul, which one day would merge with God.

He was woken up by rays of sunlight that filtered through the glass of the rose window above the door of Chartres cathedral. Grimpow was lying on the floor in the centre of the labyrinth. He had the stone of the wise in his hand; it was lit with an intense blue colour like a precious jewel.

'Everything has disappeared again,' he said, gazing at the cathedral's dome, where only a few hours ago he'd seen a strange sphere hovering in an infinite firmament of stars.

'The universe of wisdom is now in your hand,' said Salietti.

'And a new era will begin that will enlighten the universe of humankind for ever. That was always our fathers' dream and that of all the sages of the Ouroboros secret society. And you are the only heir now,' Weienell stated.

Salietti was about to say that they should leave for Florence at once, but a murmur of chants and people approaching the cathedral startled them to attention. The night festival had ended, and the inhabitants of Chartres were heading toward the cathedral for the early morning service.

The great doors of the main portico opened wide to the new day, and a cheerful and festive procession stepped into the central nave as Grimpow, Weienell and Salietti abandoned it stealthily through the same Portico of the

Initiated through which they had entered. As the travellers crept back to the stable where they'd left their horses, they were intrigued by the voice of an old man shouting among the crowd. They listened carefully to what he was saying and Grimpow realized that he'd heard that voice before.

Listen to my words,
Incredulous inhabitants of the Earth,
People who distrust
Any prodigy,
Unbelievers and sceptics,
Whom magic never
Unsettles or disturbs.
Listen carefully and believe me,
For the story herein told,
Besides beautiful is true.
Heighten your senses,
Open them to greatness,
And let your imagination guide you,
Without vileness or deceit,
To a castle in the stars . . .

Glossary

ALCHEMY: a medieval science and philosophy concerned with ultimate knowledge

ALSACE: a region in northeastern France

ALTDORF: an area in central Switzerland

ARK OF THE COVENANT: described in the Old Testament as a sacred container built at the command of Moses, wherein rested the stone tablets containing the Ten Commandments

ATHENA: the Greek goddess of wisdom and a superb warrior

AVIGNON: a city in southeastern France, home of the papacy from 1309 to 1377 for political reasons

BARBICAN: a tower at a gate or bridge, used for defence

BESTIARY: medieval illustrated volumes that described various real or imaginary animals and birds, usually phrased in terms of a moral lesson

BLACK VIRGIN: an image, originating in Eastern Europe, of the Virgin Mary with darkened skin; the interpretation of the colouration is unclear

BOOK OF HOURS: a book widely popular in the Middle Ages, containing prayers to be said at various times of the day

CAPARISON: an ornamental covering for a horse

CATAFALQUE: a platform to hold a body lying in state

CENTENARIAN: a person who has reached the age of 100

CERBERUS: in Greek mythology, a monstrous three-headed dog that guarded the gate to Hades, the Underworld

CHAIN MAIL: armour consisting of small metal rings linked to form a mesh

CHASUBLE: a sleeveless outer vestment worn by a priest at mass

CLEMENT V: Pope from 1305 to 1314; moved the seat of the papacy from Rome to Avignon, France, under pressure from King Philip IV of France

COFFER: a chest or strongbox

COMMANDERY: the smallest division of the European landed estate or manor under the control of a commendator, or commander, of an order of knights

COMPASS ROSE: a circle showing the cardinal directions

COWL: a hood or a long hooded cloak, especially one worn by a monk

CROTONE: a city in southern Italy

CRUSADER: a knight who participated in the Crusades

CRUSADES: a series of military expeditions begun in the eleventh century by Western Christians in response to Muslim wars of expansion

CRYPT: an underground chamber, generally under the main floor of a church, often used to hold the remains of the deceased

DOMINICAN: a member of a Catholic religious order founded by Saint Dominic of Guzman in the early thirteenth century

DOUBLET: a man's snug-fitting buttoned jacket

FOUR HORSEMEN OF THE APOCALYPSE: mentioned in the book of Revelation in the Bible, which predicts that they will ride during the Apocalypse; traditionally named War, Famine, Pestilence and Death

GRANARY: a storehouse for threshed grain

HERESY: a religious opinion contrary to church dogma
HERETIC: one who believes a heresy
HOLY COMPANY: a deep-rooted mythical belief referring to the presence of the dead in the world of the living and involving a procession of the dead or souls in torment wandering a parish at midnight
HOLY GRAIL: in Christian mythology, the vessel used by Jesus at the Last Supper, said to possess miraculous powers
HOLY LAND: the name for the area of Palestine around Jerusalem
HOLY OFFICE: a major department of the Catholic church that oversees doctrine
HOLY SEE: the headquarters in Avignon of the Pope
HOLY SEPULCHRE: a tomb in Jerusalem where it is believed Christ was buried and arose from the dead; the destination of Christian pilgrims
HOSE: medieval leg covering

INFIDELS: a pejorative name used by Western Christians for Muslims
INQUISITION: in the Middle Ages, a judicial procedure used to combat heresy
INQUISITOR: an official appointed by the church to root out heresy

KABBALAH: a Jewish doctrine of esoteric knowledge concerning God and the universe. Kabbalah stresses the reasons for and understanding of the commandments, and the causes of events described in the Torah
KNIGHT TEMPLAR: a member of the Templar Order

LEGATE: an official emissary
LUTE: a stringed instrument popular in the Middle Ages
LYON: a city in central France

MACHICOLATIONS: openings in a castle's walls or roof through which missiles could be discharged at enemies

NAVE: the main part of the interior of a church
NECROMANCER: someone who conjures spirits of the dead in order to reveal the future or influence the course of events

OBERNAI: a town and region in Alsace, France, southwest of Strasbourg
OSSUARY: a depository for the bones of the dead
OUROBOROS: an ancient symbol depicting a serpent or dragon swallowing its own tail, its body forming a circle; used to represent many things over the years, but most generally symbolizes ideas of cyclicity and primordial unity

PAPAL BULL: a letter from the Pope, usually a decree of some kind, named for its bulla, or seal
PARCHMENT: writing material made from the skin of sheep or goats
PHILIP IV: King of France from 1285 to 1314; also known as Philip the Fair
PLANISPHERE: a map of the night sky
PORTCULLIS: an iron grating hung over a gateway in a castle to prevent entry
PORTICO: a covered area or walkway, often with the roof supported by columns

POSTERN: a back door or gate

PRECEPTOR: the head of a subordinate house of the Knights Templar

PRIME: a fixed time of prayer, usually six o'clock in the morning, in most traditional Christian liturgies

PYTHAGORAS: Greek mathematician and philosopher (ca. 580–500 BC) known as the father of numbers; made influential contributions to philosophy

RACK: an instrument of torture on which the victim's body was stretched

ROSE WINDOW: a circular stained-glass window

SAINT VITUS' DANCE: a movement disorder caused by overactivity of the neurotransmitter dopamine in the areas of the brain that control movement; also known as epilepsy

SCAPULARY: a sleeveless overlayer for a monk's robe

SIREN: a mythical sea creature with the body of a woman and the tail of a fish

STRASBOURG: a city in northeastern France, sometimes called Little Venice for its network of canals feeding into the Rhine River, which traverses the city

SUIT OF ARMOUR: armour formed of steel plates

TEMPLAR ORDER: officially, the Poor Knights of Christ and of the Order of Solomon, a religious military order originally founded in the early twelfth century to protect Christians on their pilgrimage to Jerusalem

TEMPLE OF SOLOMON: ruins of one of the earliest Jewish temples in Jerusalem; a sacred site for both Jews and Christians